VICTOR HUGO

THE TOILERS OF THE SEA

E.G. Reilly

28·8·1990

ALAN SUTTON

GUERNSEY PRESS

First published in 1866 as *Les Travailleurs de la mer*.

First published in this edition in the United Kingdom in 1990 by
Alan Sutton Publishing Ltd · Phoenix Mill · Far Thrupp ·
Stroud · Gloucestershire

The Guernsey Press Company Limited · Vale · Guernsey

British Library Cataloguing in Publication Data

Hugo, Victor *1802–1885*
    The toilers of the sea.
    I. Title   II. Les travailleurs de la mer. *English*
843.7

ISBN 0-86299-823-9

Cover picture: The Shipwreck *by Phillippe de Louthebourg. (Photograph: The Bridgeman Art Library.)*

Typeset in 9/10 Bembo.
Typesetting and origination by
Alan Sutton Publishing Limited.
Printed in Great Britain by
The Guernsey Press Company Limited,
Guernsey, Channel Islands.

CONTENTS

CONTENTS

THIRD PART

BIOGRAPHICAL NOTE

VICTOR-MARIE HUGO (1802–85) was born at Besançon in eastern France during the night of 26 February 1802. As he characteristically put it, 'I was born in time for my glory . . . I was born astride two centuries.' Indeed, as the century gathered pace, Hugo, as both writer and political thinker, was to develop with it and bring his own influence to bear upon it.

Hugo's early life was spent in several different European locations, the military responsibilities of his father, Joseph-Léopold-Sigisbert Hugo (1774–1828), a general in Napoleon's army, taking the family to Corsica, Italy and Spain. In February 1818, however, General Hugo and his wife, Sophie (née Trébuchet), the daughter of a Breton sea-captain, were legally separated after twenty years of marriage, and Victor, along with his two brothers, Abel and Eugène, left the Paris boarding school of Cordier and Decotte, where they had been placed by their father in September 1814, to stay with their mother at Les Feuillantines in rue des Petits-Augustine (now rue Bonaparte). Madame Hugo encouraged the literary ambitions of her children, and was rewarded when, in December 1819, the three brothers brought out a magazine of literature and criticism, heavily indebted to their mentor Chateaubriand, entitled *Le Conservateur Littéraire* (later absorbed into *Annales de la Littérature et des Arts*), and in 1822 Hugo published his first book, a collection of poems entitled *Odes et Poésies diverses*. This set a significant precedent for Hugo's later work by announcing his belief in the prophetic role of the poet in both religious and political terms, alongside his conviction that poetry must concern itself with all aspects of life. Hugo thus made clear from the very start of his literary career his denial of traditional tastes and restraints and his endeavour to replace them with an ethic of individualistic value – the Romanticism which had already taken root in Germany and England had now found its champion in France.

The year 1822 was significant in other ways too for Hugo, for on 12 October, after an engagement of eight months, he married Adèle Foucher, a childhood friend with whom he had fallen in love some three years earlier. The event was, however, marred by the damaging effect it had on the mental health of Victor's brother Eugène, who had also loved Adèle. Eugène's condition grew steadily worse thereafter and in June 1823 he was confined to the Hospice Saint-Maurice, where Victor was dissuaded from visiting him, and where he died, deemed insane, fifteen years later.

Recovering from the shock of the onset of this was made doubly difficult by the death in infancy of Victor and Adèle's first child, Léopold Hugo III, in July 1823. To their great joy, however, another child, Léopoldine, was born the following year, in August 1824; of the three further children who were born in their first eight years of marriage, Léopoldine remained their favourite.

At the beginning of 1823 Hugo's first novel, *Han d'Islande*, a tale of horror and romance, had been published, and later the same year Émile Deschamps invited him to join with like-minded young writers in the founding of *La Muse française*, a conservative review which has with hindsight come to be regarded as a herald of French Romanticism; at the same time Hugo regularly attended the Romantic *salon* (the first *cénacle*) of Charles Nodier at the Arsenal Library. Hugo's output, meanwhile, increased at a rapid rate, and his *Nouvelles Odes*, which were published in March 1824, attracted for the first time serious critical attention to his work.

Hugo remained at this time politically conservative and a committed royalist. His first two books earned him royal pensions from Louis XVIII, and in 1825, at the age of twenty-three, he was created Chevalier de la Légion d'honneur. His Romantic inclinations continued to inform his poetry, however, and his third collection, *Odes et Ballades* (1826), received an enthusiastic and influential review in the *Globe* from the young critic Charles-Augustin Saint-Beuve. Hugo, with his drama *Cromwell*, now avowedly opposing the Classicists, began a *salon* of his own for the young Romantics at his new home of 11 rue Notre-Dame-des-Champs, and Saint-Beuve, a regular member, soon became a close friend.

The battle with the Classicists continued through the poems of *Les Orientales* (1829) and came to the fore in the melodrama *Hernani*, which refuted the Classical unities of time, place and action and sought a relaxation of the conventions determining dramatic language. The *bataille d'Hernani* which followed the first night performance of 25 February 1830, between the young Romantics, led by Théophile Gautier and Gérard de Nerval, and the supporters of Classicism, resulted in what Émile Zola described as the demolition of the crumbling Classical edifice.

In the wake of this victory and of the fall of Charles X and the Bourbon Restoration in the summer of 1830 Hugo conceded that his own royalist sympathies had likewise collapsed, and he declared his support for the new regime under Louis-Philippe in the poems of *Les Feuilles d'automne* (1831) and *Les Chants du crépuscule* (1835). Meanwhile, in 1831, Hugo had completed his novel of medieval Paris, *Notre-Dame de Paris*, which circuitously told the story of the tragic love of the hunchback bellringer Quasimodo for the ill-fated gipsy Esmerelda. The novel's contemporary impact lay to a large extent in the appreciation it encouraged of pre-Renaissance architecture; in terms of Hugo's own development it marked a consolidation of his wayward and imaginative prose style as a vehicle for the endorsement of his growing moral and social concerns.

The family background to Hugo's growing literary success was less harmonious; Adèle had become romantically involved with their friend, Saint-Beuve, while Hugo had by 1832 taken as his mistress the actress Juliette Drouet. Though this was the first of many such affairs, it was Juliette who was to remain with him as a friend, companion and copyist of his writings until her death fifty-one years later. The greatest blow to the family occurred, however, in 1843, when news reached them of the death of their daughter Léopoldine in a boating accident at Villequier while on holiday with her newly married husband, Charles Vacquerie. The same year also saw the failure of Hugo's play *Les Burgraves*. Undeterred, Hugo turned his back on the theatre and assuaged his grief by addressing his dead daughter through his poetry, while at the same time working on a new novel, *Les Misères*. His collections of poems entitled *Les Voix intérieures* (1837) and *Les*

Rayons et les Ombres (1840) had confirmed his status as France's leading Romantic poet, and his literary and social success was recognized by his entrance to the Académie française in 1841 and to the peerage, as Vicomte Hugo, in 1845.

After the 1848 revolution Hugo became an elected member of the *Assemblée législative*. Now a strong republican, his speeches in the *Assemblée* and articles in the newspaper he had founded, *L'Événement*, angered many by their vehement demands for social justice and reform. When, in December 1851, Louis-Napoleon dissolved the *Assemblée* and inaugurated the Second Empire ('an odious, repulsive, infamous crime', wrote Hugo in *Napoleon le petit*, published in Brussels the following year) the republican reformer could no longer stay in Paris. With Juliette Drouet's help he fled the country disguised as a workman. After a short period in Brussels he travelled to Jersey, where he was re-united with his wife and children. The initial impulse for his writing at this time was anger, and he voiced his frustration in the collection *Les Châtiments* (1853) in poems such as 'A Recollection of the Night of 4 December 1851' ('The boy had been shot – / two bullets in the head. . . .'). Subsequently, however, exile provided the opportunity for inward reflection, and in 1856 perhaps his finest work appeared – the six-volume collection of poems entitled *Les Contemplations*, which brought together a vast range of work, from love poems and nature poems to poems of memory and of expectation – of mystery and eternity. The collection brought literary acclaim and financial success, and in October 1856 he bought Hauteville House on the island of Guernsey (he had been living at 20 Hauteville Street since his arrival from Jersey the previous year) and it was here that he and his family were to remain for the succeeding fourteen years of exile. At the top of the house, in a room overlooking the sea, Hugo found the ideal location for his writing. He felt confident enough to embark upon the grand scale of *La Légende des siècles*, which sought to dramatize in verse nothing less than the whole history of mankind. The three series of this work were to be his major poetic undertaking for the rest of his life.

In June 1861 Hugo finally completed his great novel of social realism and Romantic intent, *Les Misérables* (originally conceived, as *Les Misères*, in 1840), the story of the ex-convict Jean Valjean and his heroic struggle on behalf of fundamental human values. The book was published in 1862 in Brussels and proved a triumphant success. His creative strength and energy at this time were at a peak. It had been his dream to live within sight of the sea, and now the sea, which had informed many of the poems of *Les Contemplations*, became a consolation and a challenge which he incorporated into his dramatic novel *Toilers of the Sea* (*Les Traivailleurs de la mer*) (1866). Once again Hugo's novel proved immensely popular. His son, François-Victor, wrote from Paris: 'Your success is enormous, universal. . . .' Included in the earliest editions were Hugo's own illustrations; as Gautier had written in his preface to *Dessins de Victor Hugo* (1860), 'If Victor Hugo were not a poet, he would be an artist of the first order.'

In August 1868 Hugo's creative surge was abruptly checked by the death of his wife Adèle. His diary entries of the time were later reproduced in *Choses vues* (1887–1900) – within a week of the passing of 'that great, gentle soul' and the transport of her body to Villequier to lie alongside that of her daughter, he countenanced: 'Come now! I must get back to work and return to life. Duty.' His next novel, *L'homme qui rit*, an historical romance set in seventeenth-century England, was not successful, however, and in August 1870, soon after the outbreak of the Franco–Prussian War, Hugo left Guernsey for Brussels and from there, two days after the proclamation of the Third Republic, he returned to Paris on 5 September 1870, to be welcomed by an enormous crowd. He vigorously supported the city's defence against the besieging Prussians, but after the death of his elder son, Charles, he retreated from the chaos inflicted on Paris by the Commune to the safety of Brussels with Juliette, his daughter-in-law, Alice, and his grandchildren, Georges and Jeanne.

Hugo returned to Paris in October 1871. Though defeated in the elections the following year on account of his sympathy for the Communards, he once again achieved success with a new production of *Ruy Blas* (1838), starring the young Sarah Bernhardt. He continued writing, spending another year at Hauteville House while working on further sections of *La Légende des siècles* and a new novel, *Quatrevingt-treize*. He returned to France in July 1873 and was thus able to be near his surviving son, François-Victor, who was very ill and who died on 26 December. The next year he moved to 21 rue de Clichy, providing rooms for Alice and her children and for Juliette Drouet. In 1876 he was elected a Senator of the Third Republic; his position as an elder statesman and national symbol was endorsed by the national holiday by which his eightieth year was celebrated in 1881. Two years later, however, Juliette Drouet died, and Hugo, whose health had been failing for several years followed her on 22 May 1885. In his will he declared, 'God. The Soul. Responsibility. This threefold idea is sufficient for mankind. It has been sufficient for me.' National mourning was declared, and a procession of two million followed the corpse, which had lain in state beneath the Arc de Triomphe, to the Panthéon, where Victor Hugo was ceremoniously laid to rest on 1 June 1885.

R.J. THORP

FIRST PART

BOOK I

HOW TO GAIN A BAD REPUTATION

CHAPTER 1

WRITTEN IN THE SNOW

Christmas in Guernsey, in 182 . . . , was remarkable, for that day snow fell. In the Channel Islands a severe winter is so rare that a fall of snow is quite an event. On that Christmas morning the road above the beach, from Saint Pierre Port to Valle, was white with the snow, which commenced to fall at midnight, and did not cease until daybreak. About nine in the morning, too early for the church-goers to be on their way to the parish church of Saint Sampson, or for the Wesleyans to be proceeding to Eldad Chapel, the road was almost deserted. In that portion of it, between the first and second towns, there were only a man, a woman, and a child. They were all three at some distance apart, and there was no connection between them. The child, about eight years old, was looking at the snow. The man was walking some distance behind the woman, and both had come from the direction of Saint Sampson. The man was young. He wore his everyday clothes, a jersey, and waterproof gaiters – which showed that, in spite of the day, he had not come out to attend any place of worship. His clumsy shoes of untanned leather, the soles studded with nails, left on the snow an impression more like the lock of a dungeon than the print of a human foot.

1

The woman was dressed in her best. She wore a silk mantle, and had on a tastefully made dress of Irish poplin, with pink and white stripes, and, but for her red stockings, might have been taken for a Parisian. She moved with a light step, and you might easily guess that she was a young girl who had not experienced any of the troubles of life. Her every movement betrayed that half-concealed pace which marks the most delicate of all transitions – the budding of the girl into womanhood, like two twilights melting into one – the commencement of the woman, the end of the child.

The man did not appear to notice her. All of a sudden she stopped at the corner of a field, and seemed to reflect; then she stooped, and wrote with her finger upon the snow.

This movement attracted the man's attention. She raised herself and went on her way at a quicker pace, looking round with a smile, and turning to the left, disappeared down a lane with a hedge on each side. As she turned, the man recognized her: she was Déruchette, the prettiest girl in the neighbourhood. He felt no inclination to hasten, but in time he found himself at the corner of the field. The girl had already been forgotten, and if a porpoise had risen in the sea, or a redbreast flitted from the hedge, he would have continued on his way, his eyes fixed on the redbreast or the porpoise; but, by chance, his eyes were fixed upon the ground, and his looks fell upon the spot where the girl had stopped.

There were the prints of two little feet, and in front of him he read the word that she had written in the snow:

'Gilliatt.'

It was his own name.

For a time he remained motionless, looking at the name, the tiny footprints, and the snow, and then, half sadly, he proceeded on his way.

CHAPTER II

LE BÛ DE LA RUE

Gilliatt lived in Saint Sampson, where he was far from popular.
For this there was a reason. In the first place, he lived in a
'haunted house'. In the country parts of Jersey and Guernsey –
sometimes in the towns – you find a house the entrance to which
is quite blocked up. Holly-bushes choke the door, whilst ugly
planks are nailed across the windows. The glass in the
window-frames of the upper storeys has been broken, and the
frames look gaunt and hideous. In the back yard, the grass has
sprouted up between the stones, and the wall is broken down in
many places. If there be a garden, it is overgrown with nettles,
and thornbushes; whilst insects of strange appearance abound in
it. The chimneys are ready to fall, and in places the roof has
given way. The rooms through the shattered casements show a
scene of ruin and desolation; the woodwork is worm-eaten, and
the stone decayed. The paper hangs from the wall in strips, one
overlapping the other, and disclosing the various periods at
which they have been affixed. Long cobwebs, choked with
innumerable flies, show the undisturbed empire of generations
of spiders. Fragments of broken crockery can be noticed on the
shelves. It is not unreasonable to suppose such houses to be
haunted; and, it is believed that the Prince of Darkness pays
them nocturnal visits.

Houses resemble those who dwell in them, and can, as it
were, die. The breath of superstition is the destruction of a
dwelling; then it has a terrible aspect. These weird-looking
abodes are not rare in the Channel Islands; all agricultural and
seafaring classes have strong faith in the active agency of Satan.

The former inhabitants of these parts relate that in bygone
times, the Roman Catholics of the Norman Archipelago were,
in spite of themselves, in closer connection with Satanic
influences than the Huguenots. Why this should have been the
case we cannot say; but there can be no doubt that much
annoyance was experienced by the minority from this source.
Satan had a weakness for the Catholics, which has given rise to
the opinion that the Devil is more Catholic than Protestant.

One of his most unbearable tricks consisted in paying nightly visits to married Catholics, at the moment when the husband was asleep, and the wife dozing off, which gave rise to much unpleasantness. Patouillet, indeed, asserted that Voltaire owes his existence to one of these Satanic visits. However this may have been, it is certain that this possibility of a visit from the demon at night, when it is impossible to see distinctly, or even in slumber, caused much embarrassment among orthodox dames. The idea of giving to the world a Voltaire was by no means pleasant. One of these consulted her confessor on this difficult subject, and the best mode for the discovery of the cheat. The confessor replied, 'To be sure that it is your husband by your side, and not a demon, put your hand upon his head. If you find no horns, you may be sure that all is right.' But this test was far from satisfactory.

Gilliatt's house had been haunted, but was no longer in that condition; it was on that account, however, regarded with more suspicion. No one can be ignorant of the fact, that when a sorcerer has installed himself in a haunted dwelling, the devil considers the house sufficiently occupied, and abstains from visiting it, unless called in, like a doctor might be.

This house was named Le Bû de la Rue. It was situated at the extremity of a little promontory of rock, rather than of land, forming a little harbourage in the creek of Houmet Paradis. The water at this spot is deep. The house stood alone, almost separated from the island, and had sufficient ground about it for a small garden, which was at times inundated by the tide. Between the port of Saint Sampson and Houmet Paradis, is a steep hill surmounted by the block of towers covered with ivy, and known as the Château de l'Archange; so that, at Saint Sampson, the Bû de la Rue could not be seen.

Sorcerers are common in Guernsey. They exercise their profession in profound indifference to the enlightenment of this century. Some of their practices are shocking. They set gold boiling, gather herbs at midnight, and cast the evil eye upon cattle. When the people consult them they send for bottles containing 'water of the sick', and mutter mysteriously, 'the water has a sad look.' In 1857, one of them discovered, in water of this kind, seven demons. They are feared by all. Another had the wickedness to seal up envelopes containing nothing. Another went so far as to have on a shelf four bottles labelled 'B'. These facts are well authenticated. Some sorcerers are obliging, and for two or three guineas will take on themselves the complaint from which you suffer. Then they roll upon their beds, and groan with pain; and while they are in agonies, you exclaim, 'There! I am well again.' Others cure diseases by merely tying a handkerchief round the patient's loins, a remedy so simple that it is astonishing that no one had yet thought of it. In the last century the Cour Royale of Guernsey bound such folks and burnt them alive. Now it condemns them to eight weeks' imprisonment; four on bread and water, and the remainder in solitary confinement.

The last burning of sorcerers in Guernsey took place in 1747. The authorities devoted the Carrefour du Bordage to that ceremony. Between 1565 and 1700, eleven sorcerers suffered at this spot. As a rule the criminals admitted their guilt. The Carrefour du Bordage has rendered other services to society and religion, for it was here that heretics were brought to the stake. In the reign of Queen Mary, among the Huguenots burnt here, were a mother and two daughters. The mother was named Perrotine Massy. One of the daughters was *enceinte*, and was delivered of a child in the midst of the flames. The newly-born infant rolled beyond the flames, and a man took it in his arms; but Helier Gosselin, the Bailiff, like a good Catholic, sternly commanded the child to be thrown again into the fire.

CHAPTER III

FOR YOUR BRIDE WHEN YOU MARRY

Let us now return to Gilliatt.

Towards the end of the great Revolution, a woman, with a little child, came to live in Guernsey. She was English, unless, indeed, she was French. Her name, through Guernsey pro- nunciation or country orthography, was finally converted into Gilliatt. She and the child lived alone; some said it was her son, others her nephew; whilst a third report was that it was a child that she had adopted. She had just sufficient means to live on. She bought a piece of ground at La Sergentée, and another at La Roque Crespel, near Roquanis. At this time the house of Bû de la Rue was haunted. For thirty years no one had lived in it, and it was falling to ruin. The garden, continually inundated by the tide, was useless. But, in addition, strange noises were heard, and lights seen in the house after dark. There was another peculiarity in the house: if anyone would in the evening place upon the mantelshelf a ball of worsted, a few needles, and a bowl of soup, in the morning they would find the soup eaten and a pair of mittens ready for wear. The house, with its spirit, was offered for a few pounds. The woman became the purchaser, and took up her abode there with the child. All supernatural noises ceased. 'The tenant suits the house,' said the neighbours. No lights were now to be seen, save the candle of the owner. 'A witch's candle is as good as the Devil's torch,' and this saying satisfied the public. The woman cultivated the few acres that she possessed, and bought a cow. She gathered white beans, and potatoes, and like other people, sold her parsnips by the barrel, onions by the hundred, and beans by the *dénerel*.* She did not go to market, but entrusted her crops to Guilbert Falliot, at the sign of the 'Drinking Pond', at Saint Sampson, to sell for her. Falliot's books show that at one time he sold for her as much as twelve bushels of early potatoes.

She had some repairs done to the house, to render it weathertight, and the rooms only leaked when the rain was exceptional. The house consisted of two bed-rooms and a parlour, with a loft, reached by a ladder. The woman looked after the house, and taught the child to read. She attended no place of worship, and people therefore declared that she must be French. It is very likely that she was French. Revolutions disperse mankind. Families are removed to great distances; and scattered here and there. People fall, as if from the clouds, and the inhabitants of the country are astonished at them. Whence come all these unknown people? These individuals, driven out and expelled from their native land, are called refugees, emigrants, adventurers. If they remain they are tolerated; if they go away, every one is pleased. Sometimes

* A measure peculiar to the Channel Islands.

these poor pilgrims – the women especially – are absolute strangers to the events which have led to their exile, and are astonished at the persecution to which they have been subjected. They settle down as they can. They have never done anyone an injury, and cannot comprehend why so cruel a fate has befallen them. I have seen a little tuft of grass hurled into space by the explosion of a mine. That mighty upheaval, the French Revolution, scattered many far and wide.

The woman, whom the Guernsey people called Gilliatt, was, perhaps, one of these.

The woman increased in years, and the boy became a young man. They lived a solitary life, shunned by all, but happy in each other's society. 'The she-wolf will lick her cub' – this was another of the kindly sayings of the neighbourhood; but as the youth grew to manhood, the mother – as the bark falls from the ancient tree – died. She left him the field at Tuguitée, the house at Bû de la Rue, and, in addition, 'one hundred guineas in an old stocking-foot'. The house was furnished with two oak chests, six chairs, two beds, a table, crockery, and kitchen utensils. There were some books upon a shelf, and a leather trunk. It was ornamented with nails in patterns, and small tin stars. This contained a complete wedding outfit, perfectly new – all made of the finest linen – chemises, petticoats, and a few pieces of silk for dresses. Upon a scrap of paper was written, 'For your bride when you marry.' The young man suffered terribly from the loss of his mother. He had never attempted to mix with his neighbours, and he now avoided them. He lived as though in a desert; it was no longer isolation, it was perfect solitude. When two live together life is possible; but when left entirely alone, it seems as if existence can be no longer continued. We cease to care for anything, and abandon every effort – it is the first sign of despair. As years pass by, however, we find that duty is but a series of abnegations. We gaze on our life, we think of our death, and we bend to fate; but in yielding we feel that the very blood is drawn from our heart.

But Gilliatt was young, and with time his wound healed. Sorrow does not remain long with youth. Little by little his grief wore away, and melted in the scenes around him. Nature drew him from mankind and to herself; and his soul grew more and more accustomed to the solitude in which he passed his days.

CHAPTER IV

A MAN NOT AT ALL POPULAR

Gilliatt, we now know, was very unpopular, and nothing could be more natural than the dislike of his neighbours. Their reasons were many. There was the house he lived; there was the mystery of his origin. Who was that woman? and what was the meaning of this child? Then his dress was the dress of a workman, while he had, though not rich, means to live without working. There was his garden, which he cultivated, and which produced crops of potatoes; and there were the books which he read from time to time.

Why did he live his solitary life? The Bû de la Rue was a lazaretto, in which Gilliatt was kept in a moral quarantine. This, in the judgment of all, rendered it natural that people should wonder at his isolation, and blame him for a solitude made by others around him.

He did not go to chapel. He often went out at night. He conversed with sorcerers, and he had been seen on one occasion, sitting on the grass with a look of astonishment on his features. He haunted the druidical stones of the Ancresse, and the fairy caverns scattered here and there. It was said that he had been seen to salute the Roque qui Chante, or Singing Rock. He bought birds which people brought to him, and set them at liberty. He was civil to the people of Saint Sampson, but always avoided them if possible. He often went fishing, and always caught fish. He did his gardening on Sundays. He had a bagpipe, bought from a Highland soldier in Guernsey, and on it he played in the twilight, on the seashore. He had been seen to make gestures, like a man sowing seeds. What treatment could be expected by a man like this?

The neighbours were very suspicious respecting the books left by the dead woman. The rector of Saint Sampson, when at the house on the occasion of the funeral, had read on the backs of these the titles *Rosier's Dictionary*, *Candide*, by Voltaire, *Advice on Health* by Tissot. A French noble, an émigré, living at Saint Sampson, said that Tissot 'must have been the Tissot who carried the head of the Princess de Lamballe upon a pike'.

The Reverend gentleman had also seen upon one book, the terribly significant title, *De Rhubarbaro*. But this volume was in Latin – a language which it is probable he did not understand – so Gilliatt had probably never read it.

But it is those books which a man possesses, but does not read, which are the most suspicious evidence. The Spanish Inquisition on that point has come to a conclusion which makes that matter certain.

The book, however, was only the Treatise of Tilinguis upon the Rhubarb plant, published in Germany.

It was believed, however, that Gilliatt prepared philters and unholy decoctions. He was known to possess certain phials.

Why did he walk at evening, and at times at midnight, on the cliffs? Of course it was to converse with evil spirits who, at night, frequent the seashore, enveloped in mist.

Once he had helped a witch at Torteval to clean her cart: she was an old woman called Moutonne Gahy.

When a census was taken, describing his calling, he replied, 'Fisherman; when there are any fish.' Put yourself in the place of Gilliatt's neighbours, and you will own that there was something uncanny in such an answer.

Poverty and wealth are comparative terms. Gilliatt had some fields and a house; compared with others who owned nothing, he was rich. One day, to test this, and perhaps also with a view to ultimate results – for there are women who would marry an evil spirit for the sake of money – a girl said to Gilliatt, 'When are you going to take a wife?' He replied, 'I shall wed a wife when the Roque qui Chante takes a husband.'

This Roque qui Chante is a huge stone, and stands in a field. It is a stone of a highly evil repute. No one knows what is done around it. At times you may hear a cock crow, when no cock is near – an extremely disagreeable circumstance. Then it is said that this stone was originally placed in the field by the elfin people known as *Sarregousets*, who are the same as *Sins*.

At night, in a storm of thunder, if you should see men flying in the lurid light of the clouds, these are the Sarregousets. One evening, when some Sarregousets happened to be together at a cross-road, a woman said to a man with a cart, who did not know the road, 'Ask them your way. They are always ready to direct a stranger.' This woman was a sorceress.

The learned King James I boiled women of this kind, and then tasting the water, could say from its taste, 'This was a sorceress;' or 'This was not.'

It is a pity that kings in these days do not possess a talent which places in so strong a light the use of monarchical institutions.

Not without good grounds did Gilliatt live in this odour of sorcery. One midnight, during a storm, Gilliatt being at sea alone on the coast by La Sommeilleuse, was heard to ask:

'Is there a passage sufficient for me?'

And a voice replied from the heights above:

'Yes: steer boldly.'

Now to whom could he have spoken, if it were not to him who answered? This is most conclusive.

On another occasion, when it was so dark that nothing could be seen, Gilliatt was near the Catiau Roque – a double row of rocks where witches, goats, and other devilish creatures meet and dance every Friday – and here, it was said the voice of Gilliatt was heard in this terrible conversation:

'How is Brovard?' (He was a mason who had fallen from a roof.)

'He is much better.'

'He fell from a greater height than that of yonder peak. I am glad he was not dashed to pieces.'

'Our folks had a fine time for gathering seaweed last week.'

'Yes, finer than to-day.'

'True! There will be no fish at market to-day.'

'There is too much wind.'

'Yes, they cannot use the nets.'

'How is Catherine?'

'She is charming.'

Catherine was no doubt the name of a Sarregouset.

According to report, Gilliatt had work at night: none doubted it.

Sometimes he was seen with a pitcher, watering the ground. Water, poured upon the ground, makes a shape like that of a devil.

On the road to Saint Sampson are three stones, arranged in the form of steps. Upon the platform of these, stood in old times a cross, or it may be a gallows. These stones are full of evil influences.

Steady honest people testified to having here seen Gilliatt conversing with a toad. Now there are no toads in Guernsey. Jersey has all the toads. This toad swam from Jersey to converse with Gilliatt, and their talk was of a friendly nature.

These things were proved; and the proof is that the three stones are there to this day. If you doubt, then go and see them; and near at hand, is a house on which the passer-by may read this inscription:

'DEALER IN CATTLE, ALIVE AND DEAD, OLD CORDAGE, IRON, BONES, AND TOBACCO FOR CHEWING, CASH PAID FOR ALL GOODS, AND EVERY ATTENTION GIVEN TO ORDERS.'

The most unbelieving could not deny the existence of the stones, and the house. And these facts damage the reputation of Gilliatt.

All know that the greatest danger of the coasts of the Channel Islands is the King of the Auxcriniers. Whoever has seen him is certain to be wrecked. He is small, in fact a dwarf. The names of all who have been drowned and the spots where they lie are well known to him. He has a deep knowledge of that great grave-yard which stretches far and wide beneath the waters of the deep. His head is massive in the lower part and narrow in the forehead; his squat and corpulent figure; his skull, covered with warty excrescences; long legs, long arms, fins for feet, claws for hands, and a sea-green countenance; these are the characteristics of this king of the waves. Imagine a spectral fish with the face of a man. Nothing is more terrible than an interview with this monster: amid the rolling waves, or in the thick of the mist, the sailor sees sometimes, a strange creature with wide nostrils, flattened ears, an enormous mouth, gap-toothed jaws, and large glaring eyes. In the livid lightning he appears red; when it is purple, he looks wan. He has a stiff spreading beard, running with water, and over-lapping a sort of pelerine, ornamented with fourteen shells, seven before and seven behind. These shells are curious to those who are learned in conchology. The King of the Auxcriniers is seen in stormy seas. He is the terrible forerunner of the tempest. His form traces itself in the fog, in the squall, in the tempest of rain. Scales cover his sides like a vest. He rises above the waves which fly before the wind, twisting and curling like thin shavings beneath the carpenter's plane.

Then his hateful form issues from the foam, and if there should be on the horizon a vessel in distress, his face lights up with an evil smile, and he dances a terrible and uncouth dance. It is an omen full of evil to meet him on a voyage.

At the period when the people of Saint Sampson were excited on the subject of Gilliatt, the last persons who had seen the King of the Auxcriniers declared that his pelerine was now ornamented with only thirteen shells. But what had become of the fourteenth? Had he given it to some one? No one would say positively; and folks could only conjecture. But it was a fact that M. Lupin Mabier, a man of property, was ready to make oath, that he had seen in the possession of Gilliatt a very remarkable shell.

It was not uncommon to hear dialogues like this among the country people:

'I have a fine bull here, neighbour, don't you think so?'

'Very fine!'

'It is a fact, though I say it.'

'He is better for tallow than meat.'

'Do you think that Gilliatt has cast the evil eye upon it?'

Gilliatt would stop occasionally beside a field where some labourers were working, or near gardens in which gardeners were engaged, and would utter these strange words:

'When the *mors du diable* thrives, reap the winter rye.'

(The *mors du diable* is the scabwort plant.)

'The ash tree is putting out its leaves. The frost is over.'

'Summer solstice, thistle in flower.'

'If it rain not in June, the wheat will become white. Beware of mildew.'

'When the wild cherry appears, beware of the full moon.'

'When the weather on the sixth day of the new moon resembles that of the fourth, or of the fifth day, it will be the same nine times out of twelve in the first case, and eleven times out of twelve in the second, during the whole month.'

'Shun neighbours who go to law with you. Beware of evil influences. A pig which has had warm milk given to it will die. A cow whose teeth have been rubbed with leeks will eat no more.'

'Spawning time with the smelts; beware of fevers.'

'When frogs begin to appear, sow your melons.'

And, it is shocking to say, these precepts were not without truth. Those who believed in them could vouch for it.

One night, when Gilliatt was playing upon his bagpipe, upon the sand-hills on the shore, it happened that the mackerel fishing failed.

One evening, at low tide, a cart filled with sea-weed was overturned on the beach, near Gilliatt's house. He took much trouble in helping to raise the cart, and filled it again himself. Most likely he feared that he would be brought before the magistrate.

Gilliatt was said to look into wells – a dangerous practice with those who have the evil eye. At Arculons, near Saint Peter's Port, the water of a well became bad. The woman to whom the well belonged said to Gilliatt: 'Look at this water!'

'The water is muddy,' he said.

The woman, who feared him, said, 'Make it good again.'

Gilliatt asked her a few questions: had she a stable? had the stable a drain? did the drain flow near the well? The woman said, 'Yes.' Gilliatt set to work upon the drain, and turned it in another direction; and the water at once became pure. Now a well does not become foul to-day and sweet to-morrow without a cause; it is difficult to escape the opinion that Gilliatt had betwitched the water.

When he went to Jersey, he took a lodging in the Rue des Alleurs, and *alleurs* means spirits from the other world.

He was once seen with his nose bleeding. The master of a ship, who had sailed round the world, said that among the Tongusians all sorcerers would bleed at the nose. In fact, when you see a man in those parts bleeding at the nose, you know what is going on.

He had been seen to stop in a field, skirting the highway from the Videclins. He whistled and soon a crow alighted; and, a moment later, a magpie. The fact was attested to by a worthy man.

At Hamel, there lived two old women who heard one morning a number of swallows calling 'Gilliatt'.

And besides he was of a most evil temper.

One day, a man was thrashing a donkey and the animal was stubborn. The poor man kicked him once or twice in the belly, and the donkey fell. Upon this, Gilliatt ran to aid the poor creature, but he was dead. Upon this, Gilliatt gave the man a thrashing.

And again, Gilliatt once saw a boy descending a tree with a nest of little birds, newly hatched. He took them from the boy, and was so malicious that he took them back and replaced them in the tree.

Some people passing took the boy's part; but Gilliatt pointed to the old birds, who were crying plaintively, as they looked for the nest. He was fond of birds – another sign of a wizard.

Children rob the nests of birds along the cliffs. They bring home yellow, blue, and green eggs, with which they make mantlepiece ornaments. Gilliatt would climb, at the peril of his life, into the steep places of the rocks, and hang up all kinds of scarecrows, to frighten the birds from building there, and, as a result, to prevent the children from visiting those spots; for in climbing, they often slip and are killed.

Now you know why Gilliatt was unpopular. It was to be expected.

CHAPTER V

OTHER FACTS ABOUT GILLIATT

But public opinion was not settled with regard to Gilliatt.

He was considered to be a *Marcou*: some even believed him a *Cambion*. A cambion is a child whose father is a devil.

When a woman bears seven male children consecutively, the seventh is a marcou.

The marcou has a natural fleur-de-lys upon some part of his body; and can cure scrofula, the same as the kings of France. The sick are cured by the marcou breathing upon their wounds, or they touch his fleur-de-lys.

Some people, who were near one day when Gilliatt was bathing, said they could see upon him a fleur-de-lys. Questioned, he made no answer, but burst into laughter. From that time, no one ever saw him bathe: be bathed only in lonely places; and by moonlight: a suspicious thing to do.

Gilliatt, for the reason that he caused disquietude, was consulted by the people. The peasants came to talk of their diseases. Gilliatt had certain remedies, which he had received from the dead woman. He imparted them to all who asked, and never took money for doing so. Some of those who criticised him owned that he was not so evil in his affairs with the sick, so far as ordinary remedies went. But as a marcou, he did nothing. If scrofulous persons asked to touch the fleur-de-lys on his skin, he made no reply, but shut the door in their faces. He persistently refused to perform miracles – a silly thing for a sorcerer to do. When a man is a sorcerer, he ought not to shirk his duties.

But a few exceptions might be found to his antipathy. Sieur Landoys was clerk and registrar of Saint Peter's Port, and keeper of the register of births, marriages, and deaths. Landoys was proud of his descent from Peter Landoys, treasurer of the province of Brittany, hanged in 1485. One day, when Landoys was bathing, he was on the point of drowning: Gilliatt, narrowly escaping drowning himself, saved him. And Landoys never again spoke evil of Gilliatt. To those who were surprised at this, he said, 'Why should I hate one who has rendered me such a service?' The registrar came at last to feel a friendship for Gilliatt, for he was a man without prejudices, and had no belief in sorcerers. He laughed at people who were afraid of ghosts. He had a boat in which he amused himself by fishing in his spare time; but he had never seen anything out of the common, unless it was on one occasion – a woman in white, who rose about the waters in the moonlight – and even of this he would not be positive. Moutonne Gahy, the witch of Torteval, had given him a little bag to be worn under his cravat, as a protection against evil spirits: he laughed at the bag, and did not know its contents, though he always wore it, feeling more safe with this charm hanging round his neck.

Some bold spirits, made brave by the example of Landoys, mentioned, in Gilliatt's favour, certain circumstances; a few good qualities, his sobriety, his abstinence from spirits; and sometimes they would even praise him thus: 'He does not smoke, drink, chew tobacco, or take snuff.'

Sobriety, however, can only be esteemed a virtue when other virtues support it, and thus the ban of public opionion lay heavily upon Gilliatt.

But, as a marcou, Gilliatt could if he chose, render great services. On a certain Good Friday, at midnight, the day and hour propitious, all the scrofulous people of the island, by agreement, came in a crowd to the Bû de la Rue, and showing dreadful sores, with piteous gestures, begged Gilliatt to cure them. But he would not; and herein was seen another proof of his evil disposition.

CHAPTER VI

HOW GILLIATT WON THE SLOOP

We now know the character of Gilliatt.

The young women called him ugly, but he was not. He might have been called handsome. There was something in his profile of rude but antique grace. In repose it resembled a sculptured Dacian on the Trajan column. His ears were small and delicate. Between his eyes he had the proud vertical line, which denotes boldness and perseverance. The corners of his mouth were depressed, giving an expression of bitterness. His forehead had a calm and noble roundness. His laugh was pleasing. His teeth were more white than ivory; but exposure had made him as dark as a Moor. The ocean, the tempest, and the darkness are not to be braved with impunity. At thirty, he looked a man of forty-five. He wore the sombre mask of the wind and the sea.

The people had nicknamed him 'Malicious Gilliatt'.

An Indian fable tells us that one day Brahma asked the Spirit of Power, 'What is stronger than thou?' and the Spirit replied 'Cunning.' The Chinese say, 'What could not the lion do, if he were the monkey also?' Now Gilliatt was not the lion or the monkey, yet the accuracy of the Chinese saying and of the Hindoo fable was proved by his actions; for, so strong and ingenious was his dexterity, that he was capable of raising weights which would have taxed a Hercules, and of accomplishing feats of which an athlete might be proud, yet his height and strength were not beyond the ordinary. He was by nature a gymnast, and used his left hand and his right with equal skill.

A gun was never in his hand, for he was merciful to the birds; but he made frequent use of his net, and did not spare the fish, being in fact a very skilful fisherman. He was an expert swimmer too.

The powers of the mind are often developed by solitude, which sometimes, on the contrary, makes men cheerless and depraved. Gilliatt might sometimes be seen under both these varying aspects. You might take him for a man with a mind but little above that of a savage, when occasionally his face assumed the look of odd surprise we have spoken of; but at times his features shone with a wonderful look of discernment. In old times Chaldea produced men of his cast: the dull mind of the shepherd rendered transparent, revealed the inspired sage.

Yet he was poor and uneducated, except that he could write and read. His state of mind was at that boundary which divides the dreamer and the thinker. The latter exercises will, the former is but an unresisting instrument. Pure natures are affected to a certain extent by solitude which sinks deeply into them, they being unconsciously penetrated with a solemn awe. Gilliatt's mind always dwelt in a shadow equally consisting of two obscure and different elements. All within him was weak and ignorant; without, was infinity and incomprehensible power.

Constantly climbing the rugged cliffs, he became a sailor of rare skill through sailing among the islands, regardless of weather, in any sort of vessel which might be at hand, and in threading by day or night the most difficult channels, in pursuit of his liking and amusement.

And he was by nature a pilot. The ocean's bed is studied by a true pilot more than its surface, for the sea's waves are a problem for ever varied by the submarine state of the waters through which a vessel sails. Gilliatt, when navigating his vessel among the rocks and shoals of the Norman Archipelago, appeared to possess a chart of the bottom of the sea; and indeed he was afraid of nothing for his knowledge was perfect.

The buoys marking the channels were more familiar to him than to the sea-birds which pitch upon them; and even when enveloped in mist the slight differences between the upright buoys of the Creux, Alligande, the Trémies, and the Sardrette, were easily distinguished by him. He knew at once the oval buoy of Anfré, the white ball of the Corbette, the triple point of the Rousse, and Longue Pierre with its black ball; and he would have laughed at the idea of confusing the sword planted in the earth at La Platte with the cross of Goubeau, the hammer-shaped buoy of the Barbécs with the curled-tail buoy of the Moulinet.

At Guernsey, in one of those marine contests termed regattas, he on one occasion gave a striking proof of his skill as a seaman. The feat to be carried out was to sail, unaided, a four-sailed boat from Saint Sampson to Herm, a distance of three miles, and back again. Any fisherman can without help work a boat with four sails, and the task seemed simple, but in reality was not so; for the boat was large and clumsy, a sloop of the sort styled by sailors in the last century a 'Dutch Belly Boat'. These antique pot-bellied old tubs, without keel, in place of which, on the port and starboard sides, were two wings which were, one or the other, lowered according to the wind, are still occasionally met with. Besides, the return journey from Herm was more difficult, as it was a condition that the boat should go thither empty, but return with a load of stones. The sloop itself was the prize; it had been used as a pilot-boat, and the man who had sailed it for twenty years was one of the best sailors in those waters. At his death there was none who could work it, and it was therefore selected as the prize in the regatta. In the hands of a skilful sailor it was of value, and though without a deck was a good sea-boat. The draw of the sails was increased by the mast being stepped well forward, which was thus not in the way of the pilot. Well-built, strong, roomy, and serviceable, there was great competition to win the prize, and many fishermen competed. Each in turn made the attempt but none could reach Herm. The last man to try was one well-known for having rowed across the terribly dangerous sea between Brecq-Hou and

Sark. But, overcome with fatigue, he gave up, saying, 'It cannot be done.' Then came Gilliatt's turn: he went on board, took an oar and set sail. He reached Herm in forty-five minutes, and three hours after, he steered the sloop into Saint Sampson loaded with stones, and this although a gale had in the meantime arisen. As additional proof of what he could do, he had also brought with him the little cannon which the people of Herm fire off every fifth of November in commemoration of Guy Fawkes's Conspiracy.

On seeing Gilliatt thus loaded and encumbered bring back the clumsy bark to Saint Sampson, the cannon in the boat and the south wind swelling his sails, Mess Lethierry cried out, 'This man is a brave sailor!' at the same time shaking Gilliatt by the hand. We shall know more of Mess Lethierry as we proceed.

Gilliatt's evil reputation was not lessened by this feat; and many asserted that there was nothing in it, for he had a branch of wild medlar concealed with him at the time. No proof of this was however advanced.

Henceforth Gilliatt always used the old boat. It was moored in a safe spot close to his house in the Bû de la Rue, and as night fell he would take his nets, cross his garden, and clambering over the rough stone wall, he would, after jumping from one rock to another, enter the boat and put out to sea. He always caught fish, but, though nobody had seen it, everybody said and believed that the wild medlar branch was always in the boat.

He never sold his fish, and gave them to the poor when he had more than enough. But no one thanked him – they thought of the wild medlar; and said one should not use magic with the sea.

Not only was he a fisherman, he was a smith, a wheel-wright, a cabinet-maker, a boat-caulker, and something of an engineer, all of which trades he had taught himself in his leisure time. He made his own fishing gear; he could repair a wheel with the most skilful. In one of his rooms he had arranged a small forge and anvil, and wanting a second anchor for his boat, he had, unaided, made an excellent one. The ring was sufficiently strong, and, though uninstructed, he had made the stock of the right measurement to prevent the flukes from turning. He altered his vessel and much improved her, and having done so he made frequent journeys to remote little islets such as the Caskets or Chousey. And folks would say, 'There goes Gilliatt again!' But nobody felt any grief on that account.

CHAPTER VII

THE TENANT OF A HAUNTED HOUSE

Gilliatt was only a dreamer; this might account for his courage and timidity. His disposition united the characteristics of the hallucinationist, and visionary halucination may inspire a peasant as well as a king. Sometimes the unknown reveals itself suddenly to the mind of man. A momentary rent allows what has been invisible to be seen for an instant, and then closes over it again. These visions sometimes change the destinies of those to whom they are revealed, and convert a camel-driver into a Mahomet, and a tender of goats into a Jeanne d'Arc. Divine inspiration is frequently engendered by solitude. It is the smoke that rises from the burning bush. A strange mixture of ideas is the result, converting the seeker after knowledge into an all-seeing sage, and giving the gift of prophecy to the poet. By this we arrive at the mysteries of Horeb, Cedron, Ombos, the intoxication derived from chewing the laurels of Castalia, and the revelation of the month of Busion. Often visionary exaltation stupifies the man. Sacred stupefaction does exist. The Indian Fakir carries about with him the burden of hallucination; Luther holding converse with the devils, Pascal concealing the mouth of hell with his screen; the negro Obeah man conversing with the god Bossum of the white face, all display the same characteristics, only varying by the different intellects through which they pass. Luther and Pascal were giants: the Obeah man is an idiot.

Gilliatt did not rise so high nor sink so low; he was but a dreamer. He took a strange view of nature. Many times when the sea was calm, he had seen forms of various creatures of the genus Medusa, which, when taken from the water, resemble a soft mass of crystal, and when restored to it again, seem to mingle themselves with the sea, and to disappear from view. He drew the conclusion that, since living diaphanous substances inhabit the water, there is reason to suppose that others similar dwell in the air. Birds belong to earth and sky. Gilliatt did not believe the air uninhabited. He reasoned, if the sea is filled with its creatures, why should the atmosphere be empty? May there not be living things in it, which disappear in the light, and so cannot be seen? Reasoning by analogy, we arrive at the conclusion that the air should have fish as well as the sea.

The fish of the air would be transparent, for their sakes as well as for ours, the light passing through their bodies, and casting no shadows; they remain unknown, and we can learn nothing regarding them.

Gilliatt had a strange idea that, if you could divest the earth of its atmosphere, and drag it, as you would a piece of water, numbers of strange and unknown creatures would reward the fisherman's efforts; and, as such thoughts flowed through his brain, he wondered at the strange revelations which would be made.

Reverie borders on the realms of slumber, and is divided from it by an imperceptible barrier. The atmosphere, filled by these living transparencies, would be the ante-room to the unknown; but beyond open wide fields of conjecture. We should find beings with different modes of life. Nothing supernatural, but the wonderful continuation of the infinity of nature.

Gilliatt, in his hard-working idleness, which was the chief feature in his existence, was singularly observant; he now sought to investigate the realm of sleep.

Sleep is meeting with the Possible, which we name also the Unlikely. Night is a universe of itself. The body subjected to the pressure of an atmospheric column fifteen leagues in height, becomes wearied by nightfall, and seeks repose. It rests; the eyes close, and in that sleeping head, less helpless and inert than is supposed, other ages open. The Unknown; the darker side of human life is more fully revealed. Is it that there is a real communication, or that the visionary has power given to pierce those unknown abysses till now hidden in gloom? It seems as though the shadowy denizens of space come to look curiously upon the inhabitants of the earthly sphere.

A creation of spectres rises around us; another life than ours, composed of ourselves and something else, comes and goes; and the sleeper, not seeing clearly, and yet not unconscious, gazes on those strange phantasms, spectres, faces, and those confused visions, the moonlight, with no moon, fragments, without form or name – all these, floating in the troubled atmosphere of the night, are the mystery we term a dream, and are but the approach of an invisible reality. The dream is the aquarium of the night. At least Gilliatt thought so.

CHAPTER VIII

THE SEAT OF GILD-HOLM-'UR

To-day it would be fruitless to look for Gilliatt's house, or garden, or the little anchorage where he moored his boat. The rocks of the little peninsula on which stood his home have been demolished by the quarry-man, and carted away by the dealers in granite. You must seek them now in portions of the buildings of London, for the whole of that reef of rocks has long ago been carried to the great capital. These rocks stretch far away out to sea, and with their shattered crests and deep crevices form small chains of mountains. The inhabitants call them 'Banques'. Varying in form and shape some look like a back-bone with the rocks as vertebrae, some resemble the back-bone of a fish, and some have a strange resemblance to a crocodile which is drinking.

A high rock formed the termination of the banque of the Bû de la Rue, and this was named the 'Horn of the Beast'. In shape like a pyramid, it somewhat resembled the 'Pinnacle' of Jersey, but was not so lofty. Cut off from the land by the sea, at high tide the Horn became an island, but when the tide was low it could be easily reached by walking across the rocks. On the side of the Horn nearest the sea the tireless waves had hollowed out a natural seat and this the rain had polished. But it was a dangerous seat. The loveliness of the view would detain you, for what is more entrancing than an unimpeded view of the ocean? A welcome place of rest, it was easily reached, for the waves, when shaping it, had also formed a series of steps by which to approach it. Beware of it! Tempted to rest, you climb up and seat yourself comfortably. The waves of hundreds of years have fashioned the seat from the worn granite, and two pieces of rock appear to have been purposely placed there as elbow rests. The whole vertical height of the rock serves as a support for the back, and on this you look wonderingly, thinking how impossible of success would be the effort to reach its summit. And in this pleasant seat it is so easy to forget everything. Before you is the ocean, in the distance the white sails of the ships, which can be followed by the eye until they disappear below the horizon. Entranced and admiring you revel in the scene, lulled by the soft murmur of the waves and the gentle caresses of the summer air. The dreaded Vampire Bat of Cayenne lulls you to slumber by the measured beating of its shadow-like wings. The breath of the sea is like this unseen bat; when it is not active in destruction it gently invites you to repose. A sensation of delightful ease comes upon you as you listen to the whispering of the breeze and look out over the sea. Wearied by the bright light and the beauty of the scene, it is a pleasure to close the eyes. You sleep. Suddenly with a start you wake. Too late! Escape is cut off, for the tide has risen rapidly and in silence. You are lost. The water rises higher, inch by inch, then in fury it bursts in from just below you. Thus many a man has perished at the Horn of the Beast, for the strongest swimmer could not pass through its breakers.

The sea at certain times and in certain places may not be gazed upon with impunity; at times the ocean is as fatal as a woman's eyes. The former natives of Guernsey, named this seat, hollowed from the rock by the waves 'The seat of Gild-Holm-'Ur', or Kidormur. If you understand the Celt language you do now know the meaning of the name; if you speak French its meaning is clear.

Qui dort meurt (he who sleeps, dies). It is thus that the

peasants translate the name; though according to another translation, it means 'the resting place of the birds'.

At high tide the seat of Gild-Holm-'Ur is not visible from the sea, being completely submerged. Gilliatt was well acquainted with this spot, and there he often sat. He did not come to think, for he never thought, he only dreamed. Be that as it may, the sea had never caught him there unawares.

BOOK II

MESS LETHIERRY

CHAPTER I

A LIFE OF LABOUR AND A CONSCIENCE AT PEACE

Mess Lethierry, well-known in Saint Sampson, was a thorough sailor. He had worked his way from a cabin-boy, and was now a shipowner. There was no other man with so much knowledge of the sea. He was always saving lives. In heavy weather he would wander on the shore, fixing his eyes on the horizon. What is that – a boat in distress? A smack from Weymouth, a nobleman's yacht; a rich man's pleasure boat or a poor man's craft, it did not signify. He would jump into a boat, call on a few brave fellows, or start by himself: up with the anchor, and make for the sea; rise on the waves, brave storm and tempest, incur every risk. Far away in the squall, he might be seen in his boat, drenched with rain, whilst the lightning flashed around him. He would pass the day in danger, exposed to waves and rain, saving men and cargoes, aiding ships in distress, and disputing its prey with the sea. In the evening he would return home and knit stockings.

For fifty years he lived in this way. At sixty, finding that he could no longer lift the anvil in the forge at Varclin, which weighed three hundred pounds, and as at that time rheumatism seized him, he gave up the sea. Then from the heroic he reached the patriarchal age, and became a respected neighbour. Rheumatism and independence came upon him at the same time. These two results of toil often keep company. With riches, frequently comes paralysis, the melancholy ending of a life of labour!

The population of Guernsey is composed of two sorts of

25

workers – workers on the land, and workers on the sea. Mess Lethierry belonged to the latter class. He had worked hard. He had had his fingers in many businesses, but had always maintained a reputation for honesty. From the bottom of his heart he was a sailor. Water was his element. 'I am at home with the fish,' he was accustomed to say. With the exception of two or three years, all his life had been devoted to the sea. 'I was pitched into the water,' said he. He had sailed the Atlantic and Pacific, but preferred the Channel. He would exclaim with delight, 'Give me a rough sea!' And having been round the world twice, he came home to Guernsey, and settled there. His sea-voyages were now limited to Granville and Saint Malo.

Mess Lethierry was a Guernseyman – that is a Norman, an Englishman, a Frenchman. These four lands, united in him, were ruled by his native element, the Ocean. He always preserved the simple habits of a Norman fisherman. This in no way prevented him from finding pleasure in some old book, and having more or less knowledge of many tongues.

CHAPTER II

A FASTIDIOUS TASTE

Gilliatt was one kind of savage, Mess Lethierry another; but the latter had a certain amount of taste. He had his opinions regarding a woman's hands. In his youth, he had heard Admiral Suffren say, 'There goes a pretty girl, but what red hands she has!' The admiral's remarks had made Lethierry fastidious regarding white hands. His own hand was a huge fist the colour of mahogany; and when clenched could break a paving-stone. He had never married. Perhaps this rough sea-dog wanted a girl with the hands of a duchess.

You do not meet with hands of this description amongst the fisher-girls of Portbail. It was said, however, that at Rochefort, he had met a *grisette*, whose hands came up to his standard. She was pretty, with pretty hands, but she had a tongue, and a nasty habit of scratching. It was not safe to quarrel with her. Though her nails were pink, and always in perfect order, they could turn into claws. Lethierry, at first delighted, soon became alarmed with these beautiful nails, and, fearing he might not be the master, determined not to carry the matter so far as to marry.

Another girl from Aurigny took his fancy, and he was really thinking of marrying, when a neighbour said to him, 'I compliment you; she can prepare fuel better than any girl in the place.'

A certain custom is prevalent in Aurigny. They take fresh cow-dung and fling it against the wall. When dry it falls off, and they use it for lighting fires. A girl from Aurigny has a difficulty to get a husband unless she is clever at making this fuel. Lethierry's matrimonial ideas at once took flight.

Besides, in all his love affairs, he possessed a strong element of provincial philosophy, mingled with the cunning of the old sailor – always in love, but never captured, and he boasted that in his youth he had always been easily conquered by a petticoat, or, as he termed it, a *cotillon*. What we call a *crinoline* was then called a *cotillon*, and more or less meant a woman.

These hardy sailors of the Norman Archipelago possess much shrewdness. All can read and write. From time immemorial Norman sailors have been celebrated for satire, and a talent for repartee. The remark that the pilot, Queripel, made to Montgomery, when he sought refuge in Jersey, after his disastrous lance thrust, which resulted in the death of Henry II, was '*Tête folle a cassé tête vide.*' Then there was Touzeau, the master mariner of Saint Brelade, who made the joke: '*Après la mort, les papes deviennent papillons, et les sires deviennent cirons.*'

CHAPTER III

A WEAK PLACE IN THE ARMOUR

Mess Lethierry always carried his heart in his hand. His great weakness was excusable: he believed too much in his fellow-men. He had only one method of entering into any engagement, to say solemnly, 'I give my word of honour.' That said, he would carry out the matter to the end. He believed in God, and in nothing else. He did not frequent churches often, and, when he went, did so out of politeness. He was full of superstition, but no storm could frighten him. He would no more submit to the violence of the sea than to that of man. He expected obedience, and all the worse for the sea if it opposed him; it might do what it liked, but Mess Lethierry would not budge an inch. A wave that thundered against him had no more effect than the abuse of an angry man. What he said he meant, and what he ordered had to be done. He yielded no more to opposition than before a hurricane. There was for him no such word as 'No', either in the mouth of a man or in the howling of the storm. He would take no refusal on any point. Hence his obstinacy through life, and his courage at sea. To complete Lethierry's portrait the reader must picture a man who would have been spoiled in the dress of a landsman, and who, with his hair streaming in the wind, looked like an old portrait of Jean Bart, but who, in a tall hat, would have appeared imbecile. Uncomfortable in towns, but at ease on deck; shoulders as broad as a porter's; seldom uttering an oath, and hardly ever giving way to passion; a gentle voice, which swelled to tones of thunder through a speaking-trumpet. A peasant who had read the Encyclopaedia; a Guernseyman who had witnessed the Revolution; an ignorant man, with much learning, and without religious prejudice, but filled with dreams and ideas; having more faith in the White Lady than in the Holy Virgin; possessing the strength of Polyphemus and no more logical power than a weather-cock. To these qualities may be added a flat nose, rosy cheeks, a mouth with a perfect set of teeth, and a wrinkled face, upon which the storms that he had gone through were written – a man resembling a rock in the open sea. And finally a frank and open smile, and you have a living portrait of Mess Lethierry. And Déruchette and Durande were his two loves.

BOOK III

DÉRUCHETTE AND DURANDE

CHAPTER I

PRATTLE AND VAPOUR

Our human bodies are but envelopes which hide our reality; and by them either our darkness is increased or our light is thrown into shadow. Our reality is the soul. In short, the features of every man are only a mark. Far beneath the surface of the man we see lies hidden the real man. Could we but make a study of the inner man, veiled and hidden behind that illusion which we term the flesh, what mysteries would be disclosed! Take that young girl as an example: might she not seem a bird, could we but see her as she truly is?

A bird in the form of a maiden – what conception more beautiful? Think that in your own home there is such a being: then you realise Déruchette. Exquisite being! 'Good morning, Miss Linnet!' You are tempted to greet her thus, when you meet her. Her wings are invisible, but her musical notes may be heard. At times she sings. In childhood's lisping accents, it may be above common humanity. A mystery is concealed in this sweet song; an angel is hidden in the inmost recesses of the virgin's soul. On the approach of womanhood, the angel takes its flight, but later it re-appears, carrying with it a sweet blossom of love to the mother. But, for a long time, the future mother remains a child; the child becomes a maiden, bright and merry as a linnet. You marvel at her being so kind, in not taking wing. The sweet being to whom you have become accustomed flits from one branch to another, or rather from room to room, enters and goes out, approaches you, flies from you, plumes her feathers, or rather combs her hair, murmuring all those sweet, cooing sounds which are so sweet – who can say why? – to the listener.

She asks a question and is answered; in her turn she is interrogated, and in reply bursts into a flood of song. How sweet, when tired of serious conversation, to sit and talk with her! She casts a radiance upon your most gloomy thoughts. Seeing how airy and impalpable she is, you feel grateful to her for not rendering herself invisible; for in this life the beautiful becomes a necessity. There is no duty more important than that of being charming. Without the gemmed plumage of the humming-bird, how gloomy would be the depths of the forest! Is it not one of the most delightful duties of life to shed joy around you; to scatter happiness with every word and movement; to cast light into the dark corners of life; to be the golden cord that leads our destiny; to be the living spirit of beauty and harmony?

The beautiful deserves our gratitude, simply because it is the beautiful. How often do we meet someone who, unconsciously, has the magic power of casting a spell upon those around her? Her mere presence lights up everything; her coming sheds a warmth; she passes by, you are happy; she stops, and your joy is at its height. To see her is like taking a fresh draught of life. She is the sunrise in human form. You only want her presence. She turns your house into a Paradise. And to do all this – to shed around her this joy and happiness – all she has to do is to breathe the same air with yourself. Her smile lessens the weight of life's heavy chain, which poor mortals painfully drag after them. What more can I say? It was heaven itself. Déruchette possessed that smile. I will go further, and say that that smile was Déruchette!

The inhabitants of Jersey and Guernsey are of a very attractive type. The women – especially the young girls – have a peculiar beauty, in which is combined the fresh colour of the Norman and the fairness of the Saxon race. They have delicately pink complexions and blue eyes, but these latter want fire. English education dulls them. Those limpid eyes would be irresistable were they lighted up with the arch expression to be found in the glance of a French woman. Unfortunately, English girls have not yet arrived at this pitch of perfection. Déruchette was not a Parisian, but, then, she was not entirely a Guernsey girl. She was born at Saint Peter's Port, but Mess Lethierry had brought her up, and taught her to be neat and pretty. Déruchette possessed an air of languor – sometimes mingled with an arch expression of mischief, which she appeared quite ignorant of possessing. Very likely she did not know the meaning of love, and yet she inspired all those about her with the tender passion. But this was in innocence, and without a thought of marriage. An old French gentleman, who was living in Guernsey, used to say, 'The child is flirting with a blank-cartridge.'

No other hands in the world were so pretty as hers, and her feet matched her hands. Mess Lethierry called them 'a fairy's feet'. She was kindness and purity personified. All she had to depend on in the world was her uncle Lethierry; her only occupation was to exist; her only accomplishment a few simple songs; in place of intellect she possessed innocence; in place of learning, beauty; whilst simplicity served her instead of worldly wisdom. In her the soft indolence of the Creole race was mingled with vivacity, and the harmless provocations of a spoiled child; and through all ran an occasional vein of sadness. Her countrified dress became her well, for all the year round she wore flowers in her hat. Her brow was frank and open; her neck slender and beautifully moulded; her luxuriant tresses were of a light brown hue; her skin was snowy white, slightly bronzed by the sun; her mouth was beautifully shaped, and on her lips was a smile which was dangerous to gaze upon. Such was Déruchette.

At times, after sunset, when evening drew on and dark night fell upon the darker sea – a time when every object is invested by twilight with a terror not its own, a huge mis-shapen mass, which appeared to have risen from the ocean's depths, might be seen entering the harbour of Saint Sampson – a something which, shrieking, spat out sparks, a thing of terror which roared like a wild beast, and belched forth clouds of smoke like a volcano – a kind of dragon, churning the sea into foam, and leaving in its wake a long line of smoke, hurrying on towards the town, ceaselessly striking the water with fin-like paddles, and opening a mouth which sent forth flames of fire. And this was Durande.

CHAPTER II

THE OLD STORY OF UTOPIA

In 182 . . a steamboat was quite a novelty in the Channel, and excited the utmost astonishment throughout the whole coast of Normandy. To-day no one looks at the steamers which cross these seas. At the most, some may claim to decide, from the colour of the smoke from their funnels, whether the coals they burn are from Wales or Newcastle. No further attention is paid them. In the first part of the present century people did not take matters so calmly, and these vessels, with their long clouds of smoke behind them, were looked upon with great disfavour by the Channel Islanders. The first steamer in these waters was christened the *Devil Boat*. In the eyes of these simple fishermen, who relinquishing Catholicism for Calvinism, had yet remained bigots, the steamer seemed a fragment of hell floating on the waves. One of the local preachers selected for his text the first chapter of the Book of Genesis and the fourth verse, and asked this question: '*Have we a right to make fire and water unite, when God separated these elements? Does not this monster of fire and iron, resemble the Leviathan? Would not the use of it reduce the earth again to chaos?*' This is not the first time that the progress of science has been scoffed at as a return to chaos.

An insane idea, a gross blunder, an absurdity; – such was the opinion of the Academy of Science at the beginning of this century, when questioned as to the practicability of the steamboat by Napoleon. The fishermen of Saint Sampson may be forgiven for not possessing a higher intellect than the scientists of Paris; and when a religious point is in question a little island like Guernsey may be forgiven for not being more enlightened than the United States. When Fulton's steamship was sent from England, its first trip was commenced on the 17th of August. The Dissenting community seized upon this, and in their chapels the preachers cursed the vessel, asserting that number 17 formed the total of the ten horns and seven heads of the Beast of the Revelations. In Europe to the Serpent of Genesis. That was the only difference.

Scientific men declared the steamboat to be an impossibility. The clergy denounced it as impious. Science set its face
against it. Religion dismissed it to the lower regions. The
primitive inhabitants of the coast adhered to their prejudices
from the discomfort they had felt at looking at this novelty.
Religious persons promulgated this opinion on steamboats: 'In
the beginning, fire and water were separated by the Creator,
and man has no right to join what He has put asunder.' The
peasants' argument was simpler – '*It frightened us!*'

At this period, to run a steamer from Guernsey to Saint
Malo required the daring of a Mess Lethierry. As a free-
thinker, he alone dared to conceive the idea, and, as a seaman,
to execute it. The French side of his character conceived it.
The English side carried it out. Let us now relate how it came
about.

CHAPTER III

RANTAINE

About forty years before the period of our narrative, there
stood in the suburbs of Paris, near the city wall, a house of
doubtful reputation. It was a lonely, ruinous building, evidently a place for dark deeds. Here lived, with his wife and
child, a species of town bandit; a man who had been clerk to
an attorney practising at the Châtelet; the name of this family
was Rantaine. On a chest of drawers in the house were two
china cups, ornamented with flowers, on one of which
appeared the words, 'A souvenir of friendship'; on the other,
'A token of esteem'. The child lived in an atmosphere of vice
in this miserable home. The father and mother having
belonged to the lower middle class, the boy had learnt to read,
and they brought it up in a fashion. The mother, almost in
rags, gave 'instruction' as she called it, mechanically, to the
little one, heard it spell a few words, and interrupted the lesson
to accompany her husband on some criminal expedition.

Meanwhile, the book remained on the table as she had left it, and the boy sat beside it meditating.

The father and mother, detected in some criminal enterprise, suddenly vanished into that obscurity in which the law envelop convicted malefactors. The child, too, disappeared.

Lethierry, in his wanderings, stumbled, one day, on an adventurer like himself; rendered him a service, and was apparently repaid with gratitude. He took a fancy to the stranger, and brought him to Guernsey, where, finding him useful aboard a coasting vessel, he made him a companion. This was the little Rantaine, now grown to manhood.

Rantaine, like Lethierry, had a bull neck, a large breadth of shoulders for carrying burdens, and loins like those of the Farnese Hercules. Lethierry and he were remarkably similar in appearance, but Rantaine was taller. People who saw their forms behind as they were walking side by side, exclaimed, 'There are two brothers.' On looking them in the face the effect was different: all that was open in the countenance of Lethierry was reserved in that of Rantaine. Rantaine was an expert swordsman, could snuff a candle at twenty paces with a pistol-ball, strike a tremendous blow with the fist, recite verses from Voltaire's *Henriade*, and interpret dreams. He talked sometimes of having relations with the Sultan of Calicut, 'whom the Portuguese call Zamorin.' If any one had seen the memorandum-book which he carried, he would have found notes of this kind: 'At Lyons in the wall of one of the cells in the prison of St Joseph, a file.' He spoke always with deliberation; and called himself the son of a Chevalier de Saint Louis. His linen was marked with different initials. Nobody was more tender than he on the point of honour; he fought and killed his man. The mother of a pretty actress could not have an eye more watchful for an insult.

It was the power of his fist, applied one day at a fair, upon a *cabeza de more*, which had taken the fancy of Lethierry. No one in Guernsey knew of his adventures. They were chequered. If the great theatre of destiny had a special wardrobe, Rantaine ought to have taken the dress of a harlequin. He had lived, and seen the world. He had run through the gamut of possible trades; had been a cook at Madagascar, trainer of birds at Honolulu, a religious journalist at the Galapagos Islands, a poet at Oomrawuttee. He declared himself a white of pure caste, and hated the negroes; though, for all that, he would certainly have been an admirer of the Emperor Soulouque. In 1815, at Bordeaux, his royalist enthusiasm broke forth in the shape of a huge white feather in his cap. His life had been a series of eclipses – of appearances and disappearances. He was a sort of revolving light upon the coast of scampdom. He knew a little Turkish. He had been a slave in Tripoli, and had learnt Turkish by dint of blows. His employment had been to stand at the doors of the mosque, there to read aloud to the faithful the Koran inscribed upon wood, or pieces of leather. Probably he was a renegade, for he was capable of that and worse.

He had a trick of laughing loudly and knitting his brows at the same time. His manner was cheerful and cordial. The expression of his mouth contradicted his words. His nostrils had a way of distending themselves. In the corners of his eyes he had a little network of wrinkles, in which many dark thoughts seemed to meet. It was only here that the secret of his physiognomy could be studied. His flat foot was a vulture's claw. His skull was too low at the top and large about the temples. His ugly ears bristled with hair, and seemed to say, 'Beware of speaking to the animal in this cave.'

One day Rantaine was missing.

Lethierry's partner had absconded, leaving the treasury of their partnership empty.

In this treasury there was money of Rantaine's, but there were also fifty thousand francs belonging to Lethierry.

By forty years of industry Lethierry had saved one hundred thousand francs. Rantaine robbed him of half the sum.

Lethierry did not lose heart, but began to think how to repair his misfortune. A stout heart may be ruined in fortune, but not in spirit. It was at that time that people began to talk of the new kind of boat to be moved by steam. Lethierry conceived the idea of connecting, by one of these fire-boats, the Channel Islands with the French coast. He staked his all upon this plan; he devoted to it the wreck of his savings. Accordingly, six months after Rantaine's flight, the astonished people of Saint Sampson saw, issuing from the port, a vessel sending out huge volumes of smoke, and looking like a ship on fire. This was the first steam-vessel in the Channel.

This vessel, to which the people immediately gave the nickname of 'Lethierry's Galley', was intended to maintain a constant communication between Guernsey and Saint Malo.

CHAPTER IV

THE STORY OF UTOPIA CONTINUED

At first Lethierry's venture was not a success. The owners of the cutters sailing between France and Guernsey were loud in complaint; they denounced his attack upon Holy Writ and their monopoly. One preacher called the steamer 'a Freethinking idea', and sailing vessels only were considered orthodox. Everyone saw the horns of Satan on the heads of the cattle carried by the steamer. This prejudice lasted a time; the people began to see that the cattle were less fatigued on arrival, and consequently fetched better prices; that the passage-money was lower, the time consumed shorter, and the hours of arrival and departure more regular. That the fish, delivered at fixed times, were fresh, and therefore a market was found in France for the surplus of the large catches common in Guernsey. Then the butter made a more rapid passage in 'the Devil's Boat' than in the sailing ships, and lost none of its excellent qualities, so that it was in demand at Dinan, at Saint Brieuc, and at Rennes; and at last, thanks to 'Lethierry's Galley', there was prompt communication with the opposite coast, easy transport, a better market, and general extension of commerce, and, in fine, it was admitted that 'the Devil's Boat', if it went against the Bible, was bringing much money into the island.

Some advanced minds approved of it openly. Landoys, the clerk, gave the vessel cordial approval, an act of great impartiality; for he did not like Lethierry, because Lethierry was called *Mess*, and Landoys simply *Sieur*. Besides, Landoys was a parishioner of Saint Sampson, and there were only two great men in the parish, Lethierry and himself; therefore there was every reason for their not believing in one another.

However, Sieur Landoys had the fairness to approve of the steamboat, and others followed. Opinions swell like the tide, and people began to change their views, and, with the exception of a few, who maintained their prejudices, all began to speak well of 'Lethierry's Galley'.

At the present day his vessel would not be much admired. Modern builders would laugh at such a craft, for it was very clumsy. The difference between our ocean-liners of the present day and the boats with steam-paddles, which Papin placed on the Fulda in 1707, is not greater than between a three-decker, and the old Danish canoe of the second century, discovered in the mud salt-marshes of Wester Satrup, and placed in the Hotel de Ville at Flensbourg.

One hundred years separate Papin's first attempt from Fulton's invention. 'Lethierry's Galley' was a step in advance of both; but, it was susceptible of great improvement; yet, it was a great success. Every scientific discovery has a double appearance – a monster in its beginning, a marvel in its origin.

CHAPTER V

'THE DEVIL'S BOAT'

'Lethierry's Galley' was not masted with a view to fast sailing. This was no defect, but only following the rules of naval architecture. Steam being used for propulsion, canvas was merely an auxiliary. The steamer was too bluff for a good sailing vessel; she had too much beam, for builders as yet did not construct their vessels light. The galley had some of the faults of Gilliatt's boat; she rolled terribly. Her paddle-boxes were too high, her beam was not in proportion to her length. Her engines encumbered her, and, to enable her to carry a large freight, her builders had raised the bulwarks to an inordinate height. She was steered by the tiller, and not by a wheel. Two boats hung at her davits. Her speed was about six knots an hour. On the whole, she was a fair sea-boat, but there was a feeling that she would not be a manageable vessel. She was built entirely for a cargo boat, and everything had been sacrificed to stowage room. She had but little accommodation for passengers. The paddle-boxes were white, the hull red, and the rest of the vessel black, according to the fashion of the day. Empty, she drew seven feet of water; laden, fourteen. The engine was powerful – one horse-power to every three tons of cargo.

Considering the period at which it was made, the engine was an excellent one. Mess Lethierry partially designed it, and the engineer who had constructed it was dead, so that it was unique, and almost impossible to replace. The man who planned it lived, but the constructor was no more. It cost forty thousand francs. Lethierry had himself built the galley in the large covered yard by the side of the first Martello Tower, between Saint Peter's Port and Saint Sampson. He had exerted in her construction all the knowledge acquired during the years that he had worked as a ship-carpenter. The vessel proved a success, as we have already said. By chance, she was launched on the 14th of July. On that day Lethierry stood upon the paddle-box, and, looking upon the ocean, exclaimed, 'Now it is your turn. To-day the Parisians took the Bastile, to-day we capture you.' The steamer plied between Guernsey and Saint Malo, weekly. She was a larger vessel than any of the coasting sloops, and one trip brought in a profit equal to four of an ordinary boat. Hence, Lethierry's profits were considerable. The success of a vessel greatly depends upon the way in which the cargo is stowed, and Lethierry was a clever stevedore. After two years the steamer brought in a yearly revenue of seven hundred and fifty pounds.

CHAPTER VI

THE TRIUMPH OF LETHIERRY

The 'Galley' was making money, and Mess Lethierry began to anticipate the time for him to be termed Monsieur. In Guernsey it takes time for you to arrive at the dignity of 'Monsieur'. Between Mess and Monsieur there are many steps of the social ladder. The first rung is the plain name, without prefix – say Pierre; then comes the second, Neighbour Pierre; then the third, Father Pierre; the fourth, Sieur Pierre; fifth, Mess Pierre; then, we can ascend no higher, Monsieur Pierre. Thanks to the idea which he had carried out, thanks to steam, and to 'the Devil's Boat' Mess Lethierry had become a person of importance. To build the 'Galley', he had borrowed money; but each year he reduced the amount of what he owed.

He had purchased, on credit, a pretty house, newly built, with the sea in front and a garden behind. On one of the corners its name was painted – 'Les Bravées'. The front of the house had two rows of windows, the north side looking upon the flower-garden, the south upon the sea. The house thus had two aspects – one on the ocean, the other upon nature, perfumed by roses.

Each inhabitant of the house, therefore, enjoyed a congenial view – the south for Mess Lethierry, the north for Déruchette.

Les Bravées had become a popular place amongst the inhabitants, for Lethierry rose rapidly in public estimation. This change in popular feeling was due, chiefly, to the success of his enterprise, and to his having made Saint Sampson the port of arrival and departure of his steamboat. When the inhabitants of Saint Peter's Port saw what a success 'the Devil's Boat' was becoming, they were anxious to make their port its starting point; but Lethierry insisted that his native town should retain that advantage.

'I was first cast upon the sea here,' said he. And this saying obtained for him great popularity. His standing as a landed proprietor made him what in Guernsey, is called a *habitant*, and he was elected to certain parochial offices.

The old salt had ascended six of the rungs of the ladder of Guernsey social precedence. He was close to the title of *Monsieur*. Who could say that one day the proud title of 'Lethierry, Esq.' might not be written in the book containing the list of the nobility and gentry of the island?

But Lethierry despised such distinctions as empty vanities. He liked best the useful; and to be indispensable pleased him more than to be popular. He had only two weaknesses: Durande and Déruchette.

His chance in the lottery of life had drawn a prize, and the prize was the Durande churning the waves of the Channel.

CHAPTER VII

PATRON SAINT AND GODFATHER

Having built his steamer, Lethierry christened her, and called her Durande. The Durande, we shall in future term her so, and refrain from printing her name in italics, in accordance with the opinion of Mess Lethierry, in whose sight the Durande was a living creature.

Durande and Déruchette are the same; the latter is the diminutive, and is used in the western parts of France.

Saint Durande is much respected in the Angoumois and La Charente. Lethierry, when a young sailor at Rochefort, had made this saint's acquaintance – probably in the shape of some pretty girl of Charente; perhaps the grisette with pink nails. At any rate, some pleasant memory induced him to give her name to the two things he loved best. He was the father of one and the uncle of the other. Déruchette, the daughter of his brother, was an orphan. She was not only his niece, she was his godchild. He had held her in his arms at the baptismal font; he had chosen her patron saint, and found for her the name of Déruchette. As long as the uncle and niece were poor, no one cared what she was called; but when the girl became a miss, and the sailor a gentleman, the name of Déruchette shocked and astonished them. They asked Lethierry, 'Henceforth I shall call your niece Nancy.'

'Why not Lons le Saunier, if we call her after a city?' asked he. The lady did not, however, abandon her idea, and next day said to him, 'We cannot really have Déruchette any more; I have found a name for your niece, *Marianne*.' 'A very pretty name,' answered Lethierry, 'but composed of the abominable words, husband [*mari*] and donkey [*âne*];' and he firmly adhered to Déruchette. You must not suppose, from Lethierry's joke, that he did not wish his niece to marry. On the contrary, but he wanted to select her husband himself. He desired a man of his own stamp, a hard worker, who would keep his wife like a lady. He liked a man's hands to show that he worked, much as he appreciated white hands in a woman. To prevent Déruchette from spoiling her pretty fingers he had always brought her up as a lady. He had engaged a music-master for her, given her a piano, a small library, and a work-basket fitted up with needles and thread. But she read more than she sewed, she played more than she read. This pleased Mess Lethierry. All he desired was that she should be pretty. He had brought her up more like a flower than a young girl. Anyone who has studied a sailor's character will understand this. Rough and uncultured as he may be, he loves refinement in others. To the end that the niece should become what the uncle wished it was necessary that she should be rich. His steamer was working for this purpose. It was for La Durande to earn a marriage portion for Déruchette.

CHAPTER VIII

'BONNIE DUNDEE'

Déruchette's room, the prettiest in the house, was furnished with well-polished mahogany. The windows looked on the garden and the lofty hill on which stands the Château de Valle. The Bû de la Rue is on the other side of the hill. Déruchette's piano was in her room; she often played on it, singing the song she loved best – 'Bonnie Dundee'. The mists of evening were rising, but her voice recalled the bright sunrise, and made a pleasant contrast. Passers-by said, 'Miss Déruchette is at the piano', and often stopped to listen to so sweet a voice.

Déruchette was the life of the house, as she flitted to and fro. She was like eternal spring; she was beautiful, but more pretty than beautiful, and more graceful than pretty.

As a child, she was charming; some people objected to her

nose, but, as the child, determined to be pretty, grew up, even this feature satisfied her critics. Her beauty increased; her nose was neither too long nor too short, and every day she became more charming.

Mess Lethierry's room was a cupboard, with a window overlooking the harbour, and communciating with the hall on the ground floor. The furniture consisted of his hammock, a chronometer, and a pipe. There was a table and some chairs; the beams, the ceiling, and walls were whitewashed. On the right side of the door, was a chart; on the left, stretched upon the wall, was a large handkerchief, on which were depicted the signal-code, the flags of France, Russia, Spain, and America in the corners, and the Union Jack in the centre.

There were two servants: Douce, good-natured, and Grace, good-looking. Douce was unmarried, and had a young man. Grace, coquettish, was always looking out to sea, with anxiety. Report said that this arose from the fact, that not only had she, like Douce, a young man, but that she was married to a sailor, whose returns she feared. But that does not concern us. In a home conducted with this simplicity, Douce would have remained the servant, and Grace become the confidential maid, but the possible talents of Grace were lost on an innocent mind like that of her youthful mistress. Grace and Douce carefully kept their love affairs in the background. Mess Lethierry had no suspicion, and Déruchette never thought of such things. The ground-floor room, which was a large one, with a deep fire-place, surrounded by benches, and a table in front, had been used as a meeting-house for refugees. At the end of the rom, near Lethierry's door, was a wooden erection, formerly the Hugenot pulpit, which now with the addition of iron railings and a pigeon-hole, had become the steamboat office – that is, the office of the Durande, at which Mess Lethierry himself presided. The Bible in the old oak pulpit had been replaced by another book, the pages of which were marked 'Dr' and 'Cr'.

CHAPTER IX

THE MAN WHO SUSPECTED RANTAINE

As long as health permitted, Lethierry commanded the Durande, and employed no other captain; but the time had at last arrived when he was compelled to employ a substitute. He chose for this post Sieur Clubin, of Torteval, a taciturn man, considered by all to be of the strictest probity.

Clubin was a bold and skilful seaman. He had all the knowledge necessary to his profession. He was a good stevedore, and an intrepid captain. He was prudent, yet his natural fear of danger was toned down by a knowledge of what to do when danger arose. He was one of those who have no hesitation in facing danger up to a point in which they have experience, and generally manage to escape from the peril somehow. He possessed all the knowledge which a man can attain to who has to deal with the ocean. In addition, Clubin was a magnificent swimmer. He came from Torteval, and it was said that he had swam the passage between the Honois rocks and Plainmont. He had inspired Mess Lethierry with the greatest confidence, by estimating Rantaine's character correctly at a glance. 'That man will rob you,' he said. And the event justified the assertion. More than once – in trifling matters – Lethierry had tested Clubin's honesty, and he treated him with perfect confidence.

'An honest man should be treated with full confidence,' was a saying of Mess Lethierry.

CHAPTER X

A LONG STORY

Lethierry always wore his sea-going clothes, and preferred a sailor's jersey to a pilot's jacket. This made Déruchette turn up her little nose. Nothing is more charming than to see a pretty girl about. She would scold him, and, smiling archly, would say, 'How you smell of tar, dear father!' (she always called him father) and then she would tap him gently on his broad shoulders.

The old seaman had many tales to tell of adventures in his voyages. In Madagascar he had seen birds, three of the feathers of which would roof a house. In New Holland he had seen flocks of geese, guarded by a bird, who acted the same as a shepherd's dog. In California he had examined the hollow trunk of a tree, through which a man on horseback could ride a distance of one hundred and fifty paces. In Morocco he had witnessed the Mozabites and Biskris, fighting with *matraks* and bars of iron. The Biskris fought because they had been called 'kelb', which means dog, and the Mozabites because they had been treated as *khamsi*, which means men of the fifth caste. In China he had been a spectator of the execution of the pirate Chanhuthong-quan-larh-Quoi, cut into pieces for having murdered the head man of a village. At Thu-dan-mot he was present when a lion carried off a woman. He had assisted at the arrival of the Great Serpent, brought from Canton to Saigon, to celebrate the festival of Quan-nam, the godess of sailors in the Pagoda of Cho-len. In Brazil he had seen the ladies put little muslin caps in their hair, each containing a fire-fly, making a luminous head-dress. In Uruguay he had fought with ants, and in Paraguay with gigantic spiders, as large as a child's head, with legs a foot long, who attack human beings by darting their bristles into them like arrows. He had seen, in the primaeval forests of the Diamantina, a race of bat-shaped men, with white hair and red eyes, who dwell in the recesses of the wood, sleeping by day, hunting and fishing by night, and seeing best when there is no moon. Once, near Beirut, a pluviameter was stolen from an expeditionary camp which he had joined. A sorcerer, wearing only two or three strips of leather, like a man with nothing on but his braces, who had been called, rang a bell so violently that at last a hyena ran up with the rain-guage in his mouth.

The beast had stolen it.

These stories, which had the air of romance, were what he would amuse Déruchette with.

The figure-head of the Durande, the connecting link

between the ship and his niece, was an object of great affection to Mess Lethierry. He had had it made in likeness of Déruchette. It was but roughly executed, and resembled a block of wood trying to look like a girl.

This block, however, had great influence upon Mess Lethierry. He had a superstitious feeling regarding it, and believed it a perfect portrait of Déruchette. Thus the article of faith resembles the truth, and the idol of deity.

Mess Lethierry had two festivals a week – Tuesday and Friday. His first pleasure was to see the Durande leave the harbour; his next to watch her returning. He would lean his elbows on the window-sill and gaze with admiration on his work, and feel completely happy. It was something like the verse in Genesis, which says, 'And He saw that it was good.' On Friday the appearance of Mess Lethierry at his window was a signal, and when the neighbours saw him light his pipe, they cried out, 'Ah! the steamer is in sight.' In fact, one smoke announced the coming of the other.

When the Durande entered the harbour she was moored to a large ring in the wall of the house under Lethierry's window. Then Lethierry slept peacefully, feeling that Durande and Déruchette were at hand.

The moorings of the Durande were near the harbour bell, and there was between it and Les Bravées a narrow piece of pavement. The quay, the house, the garden, the lanes bordered with hedges, and nearly all the neighbouring houses have disappeared. The demand for Guernsey stone has brought about the destruction of all. Their sites are now occupied by the yards of the workers in stone.

CHAPTER XI

A FUTURE HUSBAND

Déruchette grew up, but remained single. Mess Lethierry, bringing up his daughter without allowing her to soil her hands, had rendered her fastidious. Lethierry too had prejudice; he wanted to find in one man a husband for Déruchette and a master for Durande. His wish was to provide for both daughters at once; and find a guide for one and a pilot for the other.

Sieur Clubin was only fifteen years younger than Lethierry, so that he could not expect him to retain command for many years. A younger man must be sought for, a permanent commander, a successor to the builder and inventor. The permanent captain of the Durande would be half a son-in-law, in Lethierry's opinion: why not combine the two? The idea pleased him, and he pictured to himself the husband for his niece – a powerful seaman, bronzed by exposure to the elements. Déruchette had not quite the same idea of a husband; in her dreams on that subject, there was a tinge of romance.

But on one point both uncle and niece were of the same opinion – that there was no necessity for hurry.   When the fact was known that Déruchette was an heiress, suitors presented themselves quickly enough. But, eagerness does not prove that the wooer would make a desirable husband, and Lethierry knew this. He had a habit of grumbling out the old French proverb, 'A maiden of gold, a lover of brass', and he sent away the suitors, politely, determining to wait, as also did Déruchette.

CHAPTER XII

AN UNCHARITABLE TRAIT IN THE CHARACTER OF LETHIERRY

Mess Lethierry had one fault, by many considered a serious one: he detested a priest. There was nothing personal in this; it was not the man that he hated, but the profession. One day, when reading in Voltaire – for he read Voltaire – these words, 'Priests are cats', he threw down the book and muttered,

'Then I wish I were a dog.' We must remember that, at the time of the building of the boat, the whole array of priests – Catholics, Protestants, and Dissenters – had opposed its construction, and subjected its builder to persecution. We have told the reader that, in the eyes of these reverend gentlemen, the attempt to revolutionize navigation, and to try new inventions in the island of Guernsey, was an act of shocking rashness, almost as bad as heresy; and, therefore, they had not hesitated to condemn it.

In a hundred ways they had cast stumbling-blocks in Lethierry's path, and even employed the pulpit as an engine of opposition. Disliked by the clerical party, he, in his turn, hated them, and their treatment was some excuse for him.

Small as the island of Guernsey is there are two religions in it – Catholic and Protestant. Nowadays they do not use the same building for the two religions. Each has its own church. At Heidelberg, they are not so particular, and have divided a church – half for Saint Peter and half for Calvin. A partition prevents the rival sects from coming to blows; the Catholics have three altars as well as the Protestants, the services are at the same times, and the same bell calls the different congregations to worship. This is one way of simplifying matters.

German calmness tolerates such close quarters; but in Guernsey each religion has its own home. There is the orthodox church and the heretic church. You can belong to which you like, or to neither, and this was the choice made by Mess Lethierry.

This seaman, this philosopher, though simple in manner, was shrewd in reasoning; he had his prejudices and opinions. On the matter of priests he was immovable. He would, at times, make ill-placed jokes, and use expressions which sounded rather strange. He called confession 'combing the hair of one's conscience'. He had a smattering of learning, picked up during the intervals between storms and calms; and he made errors in pronunciation which sometimes appeared intentional. As when, after Waterloo, peace was signed between Louis XVIII, and Wellington, Mess Lethierry said, '*Bourmont a été le traitre d'union entre les deux camps.*'

But his hatred of Papal doctrines did not conciliate the Protestants. The Rector liked him as little as did the Priest. His contempt for religion broke out in the very face of the most essential canons of the Church. Once, chance had led him into church where the Reverend Jacquemin Hérode was preaching on the terrors of hell, crammed with texts from Holy Writ, proving eternal punishment, fire without ceasing, the wrath of the Almighty, and Divine vengeance, to be matters concerning which not a doubt remained. Lethierry, after listening to the sermon with great attention, was heard to murmur, 'What a mistake I have made! I though that God was merciful.'

This leaven of atheism he had become imbued with during his residence in France.

Although a Guernseyman, he was nicknamed the 'Frenchman', because of his *improper* notions. He was full of ideas for upsetting existing things. His obstinacy in building the Devil's Boat proved this. There were many other things against him, for it is difficult to remain neutral in a country place. To live a peaceful life you have, in France, *to keep up appearances*; in England, *to be respectable*. To be respectable implies many observances: from keeping the Sabbath holy, to wearing a clean necktie. 'Never have a finger pointed at you' is another stern law. To be pointed at is a sort of interdict. Gossip is rampant in small towns, where malignity punishes its victims by isolation, and resembles the thunders of the Church seen through the small end of a telescope.

The bravest dread this; they will face any other danger, but fly ignominiously before the tongue of scandal. Mess Lethierry was more obstinate than logical, but, under his compulsion, even his firmness gave way. He mixed, to use one of his odd phrases, 'a little water in his wine'; that is to say he kept aloof from the clergy, yet received them in his house. At the seasons upon which pastoral visits were made, he received, in an equally courteous manner, either the Lutheran minister or the Popish priest, and at times would escort Déruchette to the Protestant Church, to which she went on the four great festivals of the year. But these compromises cost him many pangs, and, far from making him more friendly with the priesthood, widened the breach, and he recompensed himself by a little more scoffing.

This was the only uncharitable trait in his nature; in all other points he was generous.

The ministers of every form of religion were distasteful to him. He considered there was no distinction between one sect and another. His blindness in religious matters prevented his seeing any diference between a minister and a priest. If he saw a clergyman walking with his wife, he would mutter, 'A married priest!' in that satirical voice which conveys so much.

He was fond of telling how on a visit to England, he had seen the '*Bishopess of London!*' His anger at this kind of marriage was great. 'Gown should not marry gown!' he would say. The priesthood was, in his opinion, a kind of sex, and his expression would certainly be, 'Not a man or a woman, but a priest!' With decided bad taste, he applied the same epithets to the Protestant clergy, he took no pains to alter the rough phrases which he applied to them; and his constant injunction of Déruchette was, '*Marry whom you please, so long as it is not a parson!*'

CHAPTER XIII

CARELESSNESS ADDS TO BEAUTY'S CHARMS

What Lethierry once said he remembered; Déruchette forgot everything the moment it was uttered. Thus the uncle and niece differed.

Brought up as we have described, Déruchette had no sense of responsibility. There is hidden danger in a system of education not based on sufficiently strict principles. It is not wise to make children happy too early. Déruchette had an idea that as long as she was pleased all would go well, and she knew her uncle was glad to see her happy. She had imbibed many of Lethierry's opinions, and considered four visits a year to the Parish Church were sufficient. She was ignorant of the realities of life, but was of the temperament to love passionately some day. Meanwhile she was happy. She sang as fancy seized her, talked in the same manner; fulfilled some little duty, throwing a word to the passers-by, came and went at her own will, and enjoyed all the English freedom. In England the very infants go alone; maidens are their own mistresses, and womanhood had the reins given to it. Such are the habits of the country. Later on, the girls become slaves. We speak figuratively. Free in belief, but slaves to duty.

Every morning Déruchette awoke without a thought of what had passed the day previous. She would have been puzzled to see what had happened during the last week. This, however, did not prevent her from having in hours of depression, a feeling of melancholy, and experiencing a dark shadow in her otherwise happy life.

But such clouds pass quickly. She would shake off these feelings with a laugh, never knowing why she had been sad or the reason she had regained her happiness. She was always joking, teasing the passers-by and playing tricks. If Satan himself had been at hand she would have played some prank with him. She was pretty and innocent, and was as ready with her smile as a cat is with its talons. So much the worse for those who were scratched, for she thought nothing of them. Yesterday had no existence for her; she lived only for to-day.

This is the result of being too happy. Recollection vanished from Déruchette's heart like snow in the sunshine.

BOOK IV

THE PIPES

CHAPTER I

GLEAMS OF SUNRISE IN THE HORIZON

Gilliatt had never spoken to Déruchette; he only knew her from having seen her at a distance.

At the period when Déruchette had met Gilliatt on the road and had traced his name in the snow she was just sixteen. Only the evening before Mess Lethierry had said, 'Come, no more childish tricks; you are a young woman now.'

That word 'Gilliatt', written by the maiden, had sunk into an unfathomed depth.

What were women to Gilliatt? He could not have answered. When he met one he generally inspired her with the timidity he felt himself. He never spoke to a woman except from necessity. When he perceived a woman coming towards him, he would climb a fence, or plunge into some copse: he even avoided old women. Once he had seen a Parisian lady. A *Parisienne* was a strange event in Guernsey at that epoch; and Gilliatt had heard this lady relate her troubles thus: 'I am annoyed. I have got some drops of rain upon my bonnet. Pale buff is a sad colour for rain.' Having found, some time afterwards, an old picture, representing 'a lady of the Chaussée d'Antin' in full dress, he had fastened it to the wall at home in memory of this apparition.

On that Christmas morning when he met Déruchette, and she had written his name and gone away laughing, he reached home, scarcely knowing why he had gone out. That night he slept little; he was dreaming of many things: that it would be well to grow black radishes in his garden: that he had not seen

51

the boat from Sark pass by. Had an accident happened? Then he remembered having seen the white stonecrop in flower, a rare thing at that season. He had never known who was the woman who had reared him, and he thought that she must have been his mother, and remembered her with redoubled tenderness. He called to mind the lady's clothing in the old trunk. Then, he remembered that the morrow of Christmas would be the twenty-seventh day of the moon, and that high water would be at twenty-one minutes past three. He recalled the details of the costume of the Highlander who had sold him the bagpipe; his bonnet with a thistle ornament; his claymore; his black-sheathed knife, with its handle ornamented with cairngorms; and the bare knees of the soldier. This figure became a spectre in his imagination, which pursued him with a sense of feverishness as he sunk into slumber. When he awoke it was daylight, and his first thought was of Déruchette.

The next night he slept more soundly, but dreamed again of the Scottish soldier. He thought of Déruchette, and seemed in a violent anger with her. He wished himself a child again to throw stones at her windows. Then he thought that were he young he should have his mother near him, and he began to sob.

Gilliatt had an idea at this time of going to pass three months at Chousey; but he did not go. He walked no more along the road to Saint Peter's Port, for he fancied that his name had remained there traced upon the snow, and that people stopped to look at it.

CHAPTER II

THE UNKNOWN IS REVEALED

This being so, Gilliatt saw the Bravées every day. By some chance he was always that way. His business always led him by the path under the wall of Déruchette's garden. One morning, while walking along this path, he heard a market-woman who was coming from the Bravées, say to another: 'Mess Lethierry likes sea-kale.' So he dug in his garden of the Bû de la Rue a trench for sea-kale.

The wall of the garden of the Bravées was low, and easy to climb. The idea of doing so would have appeared terrible. But there was nothing to prevent his hearing the voices of persons talking in the rooms, or in the garden. Once he heard the two servants, Grace and Douce, disputing. It was a sound belonging to the house, and their quarrel remained in his memory like a strain of music. On another occasion, he distinguished a voice which seemed to him to be that of Déruchette. He quickened his pace, and was soon out of hearing. The words uttered remained fixed in his memory. He continually repeated them. They were, 'Will you please give me the little broom?'

Soon he became bolder. He ventured to stay. One day Déruchette was singing at her piano, invisible from without, but the window was open. She was singing 'Bonnie Dundee'. He grew pale, but he screwed up his courage, and remained to listen. Spring came. One day Gilliatt enjoyed a beatific vision. There, before his eyes, appeared Déruchette, watering lettuces in her garden. Soon he took to doing more than listening. He watched her habits, observed her for hours, and waited to catch a glimpse of her. But he was very careful not to be seen.

The year advanced; and in time the trellises were laden with roses, and haunted by the butterflies. By degrees, he had come to hide himself for hours behind her wall, seen by no one, and holding his breath as Déruchette passed in and out of her garden.

From his hiding-place he could hear Déruchette talking with Mess Lethierry, in a spot where there was a garden-seat. Her words were distinctly audible.

From the flowers he observed her gathering, he guessed her taste in perfumes. The scent of the bindweed was her favourite; then the pink; then the honeysuckle; then the jasmine. The rose came only fifth. She looked at the lilies, but never smelt them.

Gilliatt pictured her in his imagination from this choice of perfumes. With each he associated some perfection.

The idea of speaking to Déruchette would have frightened him. A poor rag-picker, whose wanderings brought her there from time to time, had occasionally remarked Gilliatt beside the wall, and his fondness for this spot. Did she connect the presence of a man before this wall with the possibility of a woman behind it? Was she, in her decrepit old-age, still youthful enough to remember old happier days? And could she, in the black night and winter of her dismal life, still recognize the dawn? Who can say! but, on one occasion, passing near Gilliatt, she brought to bear upon him something as like a smile as she was capable of, and murmured between her teeth, 'It is getting warmer.'

Gilliatt heard her, and was struck by the words. 'It is getting warmer', he muttered, wonderingly. 'What does the old woman mean?'

CHAPTER III

'BONNIE DUNDEE' IS ECHOED ON THE HILL

It was in a spot behind the garden of the Bravées, at an angle of the wall, partly concealed with holly and ivy, and covered with nettles, growing between the stones, that he passed a great part of that summer. The lizards grew accustomed to him, and sunned themselves upon the same stones. The summer was bright: overhead, the light clouds came and passed. Gilliatt sat upon the grass. The air was full of the songs of birds. He held his hands to his forehead, trying to think: 'Why did she write my name in the snow?' The sea breeze came in gentle breaths, at times the horn of the quarrymen sounded, warning passers-by to take shelter, as they shattered some rock with gunpowder. Saint Sampson was not visible, but he could see the tops of masts over the trees. The sea-gulls flew around. Gilliatt had heard his mother say that women could love men; that such things happened. He remembered it, and thought to himself, 'Who knows, may not Déruchette love me?' Then sadness would come upon him. He remembered that Déruchette was rich, and that he was poor. He would stare listlessly at the great bees, with their yellow bodies and their short wings, buzzing as they entered the holes in the wall.

One evening when Déruchette was going to bed, she approached the window to close it. The night was dark. Suddenly, a sound reached her ear, and she listened. Out in the darkness there was music. Déruchette recognized her favourite melody, 'Bonnie Dundee', being played upon the bagpipe. She did not think highly of it.

From that night the music could be heard from time to time, particularly when the nights were dark.

Déruchette was not at all pleased.

CHAPTER IV

'By night, a serenade may please a lady fair,
But of uncle and of guardian let the troubadour take care.'
Old Comedy

Four years had passed. Déruchette was approaching her twenty-first year, and was still unmarried. Some writer says that a fixed idea is like a gimlet; every year gives it a turn. To pull it out the first year is like pulling out the hair by the roots; in the second year like tearing off the skin; in the third, like breaking the bones; and in the fourth, like removing the brain itself. Gilliatt had arrived at the fourth stage.

He had never yet spoken to Déruchette. He lived and dreamed near that vision of delight.

One day, finding himself at Saint Sampson, he had seen Déruchette talking with Mess Lethierry at the door of the Bravées. Gilliatt ventured to draw near. He fancied that at the moment he passed she smiled. It was not unlikely.

Déruchette still heard, every now and then, the sound of the bagpipe.

Mess Lethierry had also heard it. By degrees he had remarked this persevering musician under Déruchette's window. It was suspicious. A nocturnal gallant was not to his liking. He wished to marry Déruchette without romance, or music, or anything of the kind. Irritated at it, he kept watch, and he fancied that it was Gilliatt. He passed his fingers through his beard – a sign of anger – and grumbled, 'What has that fellow got to pipe about? He is in love with Déruchette, evidently. You make a mistake, young man. Any one who wants Déruchette must ask me, and not waste time in playing music.'

An event of importance occurred soon afterwards. It was announced that the Reverend Jaquemin Hérode would leave Saint Sampson for Saint Peter's, immediately after a successor should be installed. It would not be long before the new rector arrived. He was of Norman extraction, Monsieur Ebenezer Caudray.

Some facts were known about him, which the benevolent and malevolent interpreted differently. He was young and poor, but his youth was tempered with learning, and his poverty by expectations. He was the nephew and heir of the aged and wealthy dean of Saint Asaph, at whose death he would be rich. As regarded his doctrine, people varied in opinion. He was an Anglican, but, according to the expression of Bishop Tillotson, a 'libertine' – that is, one who was severe. He repudiated pharisaism. He was a friend rather of the Presbytery than the Episcopacy. He dreamed of the Primitive Church of the days when even Adam had the right to choose his Eve, and when the Bishop of Hierapolis carried off a young maiden to make her his wife, saying to her parents, 'Her will is such, and such is mine. You are no longer her mother and father. I am the Bishop of Hierapolis, and she is my wife. Her father is in heaven.' If common belief could be trusted, M. Caudray subordinated the text, 'Honour thy father and thy mother', to another text of greater significance in his eyes, 'The woman is the flesh of the man. She shall leave her father and mother to follow her husband.' This tendency, however, to limit parental authority, and to favour every method of forming the conjugal tie, is peculiar to Protestantism, particularly in England and America.

CHAPTER V

HATRED IS THE REWARD OF WELL-DESERVED SUCCESS

This is how Mess Lethierry stood. The Durande had fulfilled all the hopes entertained concerning her. He had paid his debts; repaired the breaches made in his fortune by Rantaine; discharged the claims against him at Brême, and met his bills at Saint Malo. He had paid off the mortgages on Les Bravées, and was the proprietor of the Durande, a vessel which brought in an annual income of over one thousand pounds, and there was a probability of his making a larger income than that. Strictly speaking, the Durande was his sole source of income; she was also of great benefit to the island. As the cattle trade produced the largest profits, he had, in order to facilitate the entrance and exit of the animals, to do away with the places for storing luggage on the decks, and with the two gigs. This was imprudent, for the only boat left to the Durande was the long boat, but this was a good one. Ten years had passed since Rantaine had robbed him and absconded.

The weak point in the Durande's successful career was that it inspired no confidence. People thought it only a lucky hit, and Lethierry's fortune was looked upon as chance. An attempt had been made in the Isle of Wight to imitate him, and the venture had ruined the shareholders. Lethierry said that the boat was badly built. But at this they shook their heads. New undertakings are never popular, and the slightest accident ruins them. One of the commercial oracles of the Island – Jauge, the banker – on being consulted as to an investment in steamers, turned his back, remarking, 'It is a conversion that you propose; a conversion of money into smoke.' On the other hand, sailing vessels could always obtain cargo. The capitalists were firmly in favour of sails against steam. In Guernsey the Durande was a fact, but steam was not yet fairly established – so strong is prejudice against progress. People said of Lethierry, 'True! he has been lucky, but these things are not to be done a second time.'

His success, in fact, alarmed them, and no one would have dared to start another Durande.

CHAPTER VI

A SHIPWRECKED CREW IS RESCUED

The equinoctial gales blow early in the Channel. The winds soon lash the narrow sea into fury. In the beginning of February the westerly winds commence, and the seas are high. Navigation becomes dangerous. The fishermen watch the signals, and look out for ships in distress. The sea is like an ambush – a trumpet announcing an invisible warfare. Furious storms of winds sweep the horizon, and a tempest soon arises, whistling and howling through the dark night. In the depths of the clouds the wild hurricane prepares to blow. Fog is another danger, and from time immemorial, fogs have been dreaded by sailors. In certain fogs microscopic prisms of ice are suspended, to which Marriott attributes halos, parphelions, and par-aselenes. Storm-fogs are composites, formed of various gases of unequal specific gravity, combined with vapour from the water, in layers, which divides the fog into zones, and makes it a solid formation. Below is iodide, above the iodide is sulphur, above that brome and phosphorus. This, making allowance for electric and magnetic tension, explains certain phenomena, such as the fires of Saint Elmo; Seneca's flaming stars moving about the vessel, and the twin lights of Castor and Pollux, which Plutarch speaks of; the Roman Legion, whose spears Caesar thought were tipped with flame; the ornamental ironwork on the Château of Duino, which the sentinel, by a touch of his lance, caused to send out flashes of fire; and, perhaps, for those lights which emanate from the earth, and called by the ancients, 'Saturn's terrestrial lightnings'. At the equator there is a permanent band of mist round the globe, called the 'cloud ring'. The cloud ring lessens the heat of the tropics, as the gulf stream warms the waters at the Poles. Under the cloud ring the fog is very dangerous. These are the 'horse latitudes'. Navigators in ancient times threw horses overboard in storms, to lighten their ships, and in times of calm to economize the water. The Etruscans, who bore the palm for meteorology, had their chief priests – one for thunder and one for the clouds; the 'fulgurators' watched the lightnings, the 'aquileges' the fogs. The College of Priest Augurs, founded by the Tarquins, was consulted by the Syrians, the Phoenicians, the Pelasgians, and all the early mariners of the inland seas. The origin of storms was well understood. It is closely connected with the formation of fogs, and is, properly speaking, derived from the same source. On the ocean there are three foggy zones – one equatorial, and two polar. Sailors have only one name for all this, 'The Pitch Pot'.

In all latitudes, and especially in the Channel, the equinoctial fogs are particularly dangerous. One of the chief perils of fog is that it hinders sailors from recognizing the changes in the bed of the ocean by the altered colour of the water, preventing them from perceiving when they are approaching shallows or breakers; and a vessel thus often grounds without warning. Often ships, enveloped in fog, have no recourse but to anchor. There are as many casualties in a fog as in a storm.

After a heavy gale which followed one of these foggy days, the mail boat arrived from England in the early morning, just as the gun from Castle Cornet announced the sunrise. Every-one had been anxiously expecting her arrival, as she was to bring the new Rector of Saint Sampson. Shortly after her arrival a report spread through the town that she had picked up a boat in which were some shipwrecked sailors.

CHAPTER VII

A FORTUNATE ESCAPE FROM DROWNING

That night, the wind having gone down, Gilliatt went out to fish, keeping tolerably close in shore. About two in the afternoon the tide was coming in rapidly, and he was returning, when, passing before the Horn of the Beast, he fancied that he perceived a shadow, not thrown by any projection of the rock. He steered towards it, and saw a man sitting in the seat of Gild-Holm-'Ur. The tide was already high, and the rock surrounded by the sea, so that escape was impossible. Gilliatt shouted to the man, but he took no notice. He drew nearer and saw that he was sleeping.

The man was dressed in black. 'He looks like a priest,' said Gilliatt, and as he came near he saw that he was a young man; but a complete stranger to him.

Fortunately, the rock being perpendicular, there was deep water close to it, so that Gilliatt was able to sail his boat alongside. The rising tide lifted the boat, and Gilliatt, standing on the gunwale, could touch the man's feet. He raised himself to his full height and stretched out his hands. If he had slipped there would have been small chance of his coming to the surface again. The waves were rushing in, and the position was full of danger.

He pulled the sleeping man's foot. 'What can you be doing?' he cried.

The man woke. 'I have been enjoying the view,' answered he.

He was now wide awake, and continued: 'I have only just landed, and passed this rock. I had been at sea all night, and, being tired, I sat down and went to sleep.'

'In ten minutes you would have been drowned,' said Gilliatt.

'Indeed!'

'Get into the boat.'

Gilliatt kept the boat in its position with one foot, and, clinging to the rock with one hand, he offered the other to the stranger, who at once sprang into the vessel. He was a handsome young man.

Gilliatt took the oars, and soon the boat was at anchor beside the Bû de la Rue. The stranger wore a tall hat and a white tie; his long frock coat was buttoned up to his throat; his fair hair brushed back from his forehead; his face was of almost feminine beauty, his eye clear, and his manner grave.

Gilliatt moored his boat, and, turning, saw the young man extend his white hand in which was a gold coin.

He put the hand aside. There was a silence which the stranger broke. 'But you saved my life,' said he.

'Perhaps I did,' replied Gilliatt.

The mooring was completed, and they landed. The young man continued, 'I owe my life to you, sir.'

'Say nothing of it,' replied Gilliatt.

Gilliatt's answer was again followed by a pause.

'Are you of this parish?' asked the stranger.

'No,' answered Gilliatt.

Gilliatt pointed towards the heavens, and simply replied, 'There!'

The stranger bowed, and left him. After taking a few steps, he stopped, and taking a book from his pocket, offered it to Gilliatt.

'Will you accept this from me?'

Gilliatt took it; it was a Bible! Resting his elbow on the parapet of his garden wall, he watched the stranger disappear round the corner of the road leading to Saint Sampson.

In a few minutes all recollection of the event passed from his mind – the stranger, the chair of Gild–Holm–'Ur and all beside; for there was only one continued line of thought for him, and that was Déruchette.

A voice calling him, aroused him from his dream.

'Gilliatt!'

He raised his eyes, for he recognized the voice.

'What do you want?' he asked.

It was Sieur Landoys, driving along the road in his little trap. He had stopped for a moment to speak to Gilliatt, but he seemed anxious and in a hurry.

'There is news, Gilliatt.'

'Where?'

'At Les Bravées.'

'What news is it?'

'I am too far off to tell you.'

Gilliatt shuddered.

'Is Miss Déruchette going to be married?'

'No, but she should be.'

'What can it be, then?'

'Go to Les Bravées, and you will learn.'

And Sieur Landoys drove off.

BOOK V

THE REVOLVER

CHAPTER I

THE CONVERSATION AT THE JEAN AUBERGE

Sieur Clubin was one who knew how to wait for an opportunity. A short man, with a sallow complexion, he had the strength of a bull. The sea air had never tanned him; he was the colour of a wax-candle, and some of its steady light shone in his eyes. His was a wonderfully retentive memory. Only let him see a man once, and he would know him again anywhere. His keen gaze caught all the salient points at once. He took stock of a face at a glance, and it was impossible to throw him of the scent. Sieur Clubin was reserved; his manner was cold, but he was quick in action; his demeanour was quiet. Everyone was attracted by his frank and open manner, and thought him simplicity itself. No one was quicker than he at taking in a reef, or making the best of a breeze. No one possessed a higher character for religion and integrity. To have suspected him would have caused you to be looked upon with suspicion. He was most intimate with Rebuchet, the money-changer, who lived at Saint Malo, in the Rue Saint Vincent, next door to the gun-maker. Rebuchet would say, 'I could trust Clubin with my shop.' Sieur Clubin was a widower; his wife had borne as high a character as himself. She had left behind her a most honourable reputation. Sieur Clubin and his wife had, in Torteval, the reputation of being thoroughly respectable. Swans' down was no whiter than Madame Clubin's character, nor ermine than that of her husband – a single spot would have been fatal to either. He would not keep a pin which he chanced to find, and he would have sent the town-crier round if he had picked up a box of matches. One day he went into a carabet at Saint Servan, and said to the proprietor, 'Three years ago I had breakfast here, and you did not charge me enough,' and he handed over sixty-five centimes, the amount of the error in the bill. He was honesty itself, whilst his tightly-shut lips showed that he was never off his guard.

He seemed always to be watching. What for? Perhaps for rogues.

Every Tuesday he sailed the Durande from Guernsey to Saint Malo. He arrived on the evening of the same day, took two days to discharge his cargo and take in another, and left for Guernsey on Friday morning.

At that period there was, close to the harbour of Saint Malo, a small tavern, called the Jean Auberge. The building of the new quays has demolished this house, and no traces of it remain. At this time the sea used to reach the gates of Saint Vincent and Dinan; the communication between Saint Malo and Saint Servan was maintained at low tide by carts which piled between the vessels lying high and dry. Between high and low tides the drivers drove over sands which, six hours afterwards, were covered by foaming waves. On these same sands formerly wandered the twenty-four porter dogs of Saint Malo, until, owing to their having, in mistaken zeal, eaten a naval officer in 1770, they were done away with, and their nocturnal barking is now no longer heard. Sieur Clubin always stopped at the Jean Auberge.

The Custom-house officers and coastguardsmen used to take their meals at the tavern, where a table was reserved for them; and the officers of the Customs from Binic made it a meeting-place with their brethren from Saint Malo. The captains of vessels also frequented the place; but they, also, had a table of their own. Sieur Clubin sat sometimes at one table and sometimes at another, but he preferred that of the Custom-house officers, though he was welcome wherever he might sit. The tables were well appointed, and there were all kinds of strange liquors at hand, in the event of their being called for by foreign sailors. A Spaniard from Bilbao would not have been without his *helada*. You could get stout equal to that of Greenwich, and it was very common to see the brown beer of Antwerp on the table. Captains returned from long voyages and shipowners sat at the chief table and news of all kinds were interchanged: – 'How are sugars?' – 'How goes indigo?' – 'Only seven surons of Guatemala having changed hands.' 'The *Nanine Julie*, from Brittany, is coming in.' – 'They are fighting again in La Plata.' – 'They have had to discharge the cargo of the *Regina Caeli*, she has been condemned at Callao.' – 'Cocoas are brisk; bags of Caracas are quoted at two hundred and thirty-four, and Trinidads at seventy-three.' – 'Green Saladero hides are selling – ox hides at sixty, and cow-hides at forty-eight.' – 'Olive oil is quiet.' – etc., etc.

These topics were loudly discussed; but, at the coastguard table, they spoke in lower tones. The doings of the revenue require more privacy. The captains' table was presided over by an old skipper – Mons Gertrais Gaboureau.

Now Gaboureau was not a man; he was a barometer. His experience had given him almost prophetic powers, and he could always tell what the weather would be to-morrow. He listened to the winds, and felt the pulse of the sea. He would say to the clouds, 'Put out your tongue,' – that is to say, the lightning. He was the physician of the wave and the breeze; the wide ocean was his patient. He had made a kind of medical tour of the world, examining every climate, and making a note on it, either favourable or the opposite. He knew all about the diseases of the seasons. He was a sailor, because he loved the sea, and he hated England in the same degree as he adored the ocean. He had carefully studied English shipping, and believed that he had discovered all its weak points. In explaining the differences between the *Sovereign* of 1637, the *Royal William* of 1670, and the *Victory* of 1755, he compared their upper works. He regretted the towers on deck, and the funnel-shaped tops of the *Great Harry* in 1514, considering that they would be marks for the French gunners. In his opinion, nations were only great by their strength at sea. When he spoke of England, he used the words 'Trinity House', considering that quite sufficient. 'Northern Commisioners' was well enough for Scotland, whilst 'Ballast Board' meant Ireland. Well posted in marine matters, he was a perfect naval almanac; he was a tariff of freights and an authority on tides, all wrapped up in one. He knew all the lighthouse dues, especially those upon the English coast – one penny per ton for passing here, one farthing per ton for passing there. One day, in one of his voyages, he was taken ill, and his life was despaired of. When the crew surrounded his hammock, he ceased his groans to order the carpenter to put mortices in each side of the maincaps, and fix in an iron ring to run the top ropes through. His habit of command had given him an expression of authority.

There was generally no similarity in the conversation at the captains' table and that of the Custom-house officers. The reverse, however, happened in the early days of February, to which date we have now come. The three-master *Tamaulipas*, commanded by Captain Zuela, trading between Chili and Saint Malo, attracted the attention of both tables. At the captains' they spoke of its cargo, at the Custom-house officers' of its appearance.

Captain Zuela de Copiapo was partly Chilian and partly Columbian. He had served in the wars of independence, sometimes under Bolivar, and sometimes under Morillo, according to which side paid best. He had made money by serving all the world. No one could have been, at one and the same time more Bourbonists, more Bonapartist, more Absolutist, more Liberal, more Atheist, or more Catholic. He belonged to that great faction, the Lucrative party. Every now and then he made his appearance in France – on commercial voyages; and if rumour spoke truly, he gave passage to fugitives of any kind – bankrupts or political refugees, it was all one to him, provided they paid. His mode of taking them aboard was simple. The fugitive waited at a lonely part of the coast, and at the moment of sailing, Zuela would send a boat to fetch him. On his last voyage he had assisted a fugitive from justice, named Berton; and on this occasion he was also suspected. The police, in fact, had their eye upon him.

This was an epoch of flights. The Restoration in France was reactionary. Revolutions are fruitful of voluntary exile; restorations of wholesale banishment. During the first eight years following the return of the Bourbons, panic was universal – men felt the ground tremble beneath them. Bankruptcies were many in the commerical world; in the political, there was a general rush to escape. Lavalette, Lefebvre Desnouettes, and Delon had taken flight. The special tribunals were very harsh.

People shunned the Pont de Saumur, the esplanade de la Réole, the wall of the Observatoire in Paris, the tower of Taurias d'Avignon – dismal landmarks in history where the epoch of reaction has left its sign-spots, on which the marks of that blood-stained hand are still to be seen. In London the Thistle-wood affair, with its ramifications in Belgium, Switzerland, and Italy, had increased the motives for flight, and given an impetus to that mysterious rout which left so many gaps in society. To find a place of security, was the general care. To be implicated was ruin. Martial law had its way and sentences were pre-arranged. People fled to Texas, to the Rocky Mountains, to Peru. The men of the Loire, considered traitors then, but now regarded as patriots, had founded the Camp of Refuge. Béranger in one of his songs says:

> Barbarians! we are Frenchmen born;
> Pity us, glorious, though forlorn.

Self-banishment was the only resource left to many. Nothing seems simpler than flight, but every obstacle is in the way of the man who flees. Flight necessitates disguise. Persons of importance – illustrious characters – were reduced to this expedient, fit only for criminals. Their independent habits rendered it difficult for them to escape. A rogue who violates his ticket-of-leave comports himself before the police innocently; but imagine innocence forced to act a part; virtue disguising its voice; a great reputation hiding under a mask. Yonder passer-by is a man of celebrity; he is trying to obtain a false passport. Under cover of these flights and concealments of honest men, genuine rogues, less watched, managed often to get clear off. A scoundrel, finding it convenient to disappear, would tack himself on to the political refugees, and, thanks to his skill in the art, contrive to appear more honest even than his honest neighbours. Nothing looks more awkward and confused sometimes than honesty unjustly condemned. It is out of its element, and nearly certain to commit itself.

It is curious that this voluntary expatriation appears to lead to every strange turn of fortune. There is nothing impossible in a man's escaping thus from the law, to re-appear elsewhere as a dignitary among the priesthood. There was something phantasmagorial in these sudden disappearances; and more than one has led to events like the wonders of a dream. An escapade of this kind, indeed, seems to find a natural end in the wild and wonderful; as when some broken bankrupt suddenly decamps to re-appear many years later as Grand Vizier to the Mogul, or as a monarch in Tasmania.

To help these fugitives was a regular trade, and there was much business which paid well. This occupation was generally grafted on to some illegal mode of trade. Anyone, for instance, wishing to escape to England applied to the smuggling fraternity, whilst those, who wanted to get to America, had recourse to captains such as Zuela.

CHAPTER II

CLUBIN ON THE LOOK-OUT

Sometimes Captain Zuela took his meals at the Auberge. Sieur Clubin knew him by sight.

Clubin was not proud; he did not mind being acquainted, by sight, with rogues. Sometimes he was friendly with them, and shook their hands in the open street, wishing them good-day! He could converse in English with the smugglers, and knew enough Spanish to talk with a contrabandista. He had various aphorisms, which he quoted as an apology for the bad company that he sometimes kept. 'Good,' said he, 'can be got from evil. The gamekeeper should be on good terms with the poacher. A pilot should take soundings of a pirate, who, after all, is a sunken rock. I analyse a villain as a doctor analyses poison.' This was unanswerable, and all agreed that Clubin was right. They liked his not being fettered with any feeling of absurd delicacy. Who could blame him, when all he did was for the best? He always acted in a straightforward manner, and would not, on any account, tarnish his reputation. The universal confidence placed in him was the result of a life of honourable integrity and a good reputation. Whatever Clubin did was for the best, and people had the opinion that it was impossible for him to do wrong. Everyone knew how careful he was of his reputation and acquaintanceships; that which would in others have caused suspicion made his honesty and skill to stand out more boldly than ever. Sieur Clubin was one of those whom you might meet in company with a swindler, but this would in no way affect your opinion of him, and you would discreetly close your eyes as to the character of his associates. The *Tamaulipas* had completed loading; she was ready for sea, and would sail soon.

On Tuesday the Durande arrived at Saint Malo while it was daylight. Clubin was on the bridge, piloting the vessel into harbour, when he perceived on the sands of Petit Bay two figures between some rocks, in a solitary part. Using his telescope he recognized in the one, Captain Zuela and also seemed to know his companion, a tall man, with grey hair. He wore the broad-brimmed hat and the sober dress of a Quaker. He cast down his eyes with an air of modesty. Upon arriving at the Auberge, Sieur Clubin learned that the *Tamaulipas* would probably sail in ten days.

Later it was found that he obtained information on other matters.

That evening he called in at the gunmaker's, in the Rue Saint Vincent, and said:

'Do you know what a revolver is?'

'Yes,' answered the gunsmith, 'an American weapon.'

'It is a pistol that re-commences the conversation.'

'Quite right; it is good for questioning and answering.'

'Yes, and has more replies than one.'

'And, a revolving chamber.'

'With many bullets in it.'

The gunsmith winked and nodded vigorously in token of his admiration.

'The style of weapon is good, Mons Clubin, and will do excellent service.'

'I want a six-chambered revolver.'

'I have not got one.'

'What! Do you call yourself a gun-maker?'

'I have not kept them yet. You see it is an entirely new invention. It is only just coming into use, and French makers still keep to the ordinary pistol.'

'Nonsense!'

'It is quite new in the market.'

'Rubbish!'

'I have first-rate pistols.'

'But I want a revolver.'

'I quite agree with you that it by far the most useful; but wait a moment, Mons. Clubin.'

'Well, what now?'

'I think I know of one in Saint Malo that can be bought for a bargain.'

'A revolver?'

'Yes.'

'To be sold?'

'Certainly!'

'Where?'

'I believe I know, and will enquire.'

'When can you give me an answer?'

'It is second-hand, but of good quality.'

'When shall I come in again?'

'If I offer you a revolver, remember that it will be one of the best.'

'When will you give me a reply?'

'When you return from your next trip.'

'Do not mention that it is for me,' remarked Sieur Clubin.

CHAPTER III

CLUBIN CARRIES SOMETHING AWAY BUT FAILS TO BRING BACK ANYTHING

Clubin superintended his loading, got on board his cattle, and passengers, and left Saint Malo for Guernsey, as usual, on Friday. As soon as the vessel was out at sea, and he could quit the bridge, he went to his cabin, and, taking a travelling bag, put into it some clothes, biscuits, and other food, a chronometer, and a telescope, and, locking the bag, passed a cord through the handles to carry it. Then he went to the hold, and from thence to a place where the cables are kept, from which he brought a rope, with knots at regular intervals and a hook at the end, such as is used by ships' caulkers at sea, and by robbers on shore. Cords of this kind are useful in climbing. On his arrival in Guernsey, Clubin went to Torteval, where he remained thirty-six hours. He took his bag and the rope with him, and did not bring them back.

In those days, smuggling was carried on to a very large extent. Smuggling vessels abounded, especially upon the west coast of Guernsey. Persons who know everything, and are acquainted with what happened fifty years ago, quote the names of many of these vessels, which were chiefly Asturian and Guiposcoan. What is certain, however, is that hardly a day passed without some running into the Bay of Saints or Pleinmont. They acted with great regularity, as though they formed part of a legitimate service. A cavern on the sea-coast of Sark is still known as the 'Shops', because people came there to buy goods of the smugglers. To carry on this traffic there was a smugglers' language spoken in the channel, now fallen into disuse. Upon many points of the coast of both France and England the smugglers were on the best of terms with legitimate traders. They had access to the houses of more than one pillar of commerce, by the back door, it is true – and they had a mysterious connection with the mercantile world and the many varied lines of industrial manufacturers. Merchant on one side and smuggler on the other, such was the way in which many great fortunes were made.

All this required much connivance and management, and its mysteries were shrouded in impenetrable secrecy. A smuggler had many secrets, which he knew how to keep. Inviolable secrecy was the first duty. No loyalty, no smuggling! Fraud has its secrets as well as the confessional. Its mysteries were jealously guarded. No one was more worthy of confidence than a smuggler. The Alcade of Oyarzun once captured a smuggler, and had him tortured to reveal the name of the capitalist who supplied him with money. In fact, the Alcade was the capitalist, but the smuggler divulged nothing. These two men each performed their duty – the Alcade, in applying the torture; the smuggler, in keeping his oath. The most renowned smugglers who, at this period, frequented Pleinmont were Blasco and Blasquito. They were *Tocayos*. This is a species of Spanish and Catholic connection, which consists in men having the same patron-saint in Paradise – a matter not less worthy of consideration than having the same father on earth. When you wished to do a little business with the smugglers nothing was easier, or, from a certain point of view, more troublesome. If you had no fear on a dark night you had only to go to Pleinmont and consult the oracle located there.

CHAPTER IV

PLEINMONT

Pleinmont, near Torteval, is one of the three corners of Guernsey. At the extremity of the Cape is a high turfy hill, which commands a wide sea view. It is a very lonely spot, all the more so, for on it is a solitary house. This house adds a sense of terror to that of solitude.

It is believed to be haunted.

Haunted or not, its appearance is strange. It is a one-storeyed house, built of granite, and stands in the midst of the grassy solitude. It is in good repair; the walls are sound, and the roof watertight. Not a stone is wanting in the walls; not a tile missing from the roof; a brick chimney-stack stands up at an angle to the roof. The house stands with its back to the sea. On examining this wall you will see a bricked-up window. The gables have three windows – one to the east and two to the west – all three are walled up. The front that looks inland has a door and two windows; the door is bricked-up, as are also the two windows on the ground floor. On the first floor – and this is what strikes you as you approach the house – are two open windows, but the walled-up windows have a less weird appearance than these. They look black and dismal even in the light of day; there is not an atom of sash in them. They simply open on the darkness within. They resemble the sockets of the eyes from which the balls have been torn. The house is empty, and through the yawning casements you can perceive that within all is ruin and desolation. No wainscoting, no woodwork; naught but bare stone walls. You might fancy it a tomb, with two open windows, to permit its ghostly tenants to gaze out upon the world. On the side next to the sea the rain has washed away the earth from the foundations. Nettles, quivering with every breath of wind, grow thickly round the house. Far around the horizon there is no other human habitation. It is empty, and in it dwells Silence; but if you stand and put your ear against the wall you will distinguish a strange, confused sound, like the flutter of wings. Above the bricked-up door on the keep-stone are engraved these letters, 'E L M – P B I L G', and this date, '1780'. During the night the pale moon shines through the gaping windows, and the glowing night folds the deserted house in its embrace. The sea is seen on all sides of the house. Its situation is magnificent; but for that very reason it has the more terrible aspect, and its very beauty becomes a species of enigma. Why is there no human tenant? The situation is beautiful, the house is a good one. Why has it been deserted? Added to these questions, are others. The land around is capable of cultivation. Why is it not cultivated? Is there no owner? Why is the doorway bricked up? What is the matter with the place? Why do men shun it? What has happened here? If nothing has happened, why are there no occupants? Is it only when the rest of the world is asleep that some one in this spot is awake? Dark squalls, wild winds, birds of prey, unknown forms, connect themselves somehow with this deserted house. For what wayfarers can this be the hostelry? You imagine to yourself whirlwinds of rain and hail beating in at the open casements. Tempests have left their vague traces upon the interior walls. The chambers, though covered in, are visited by the hurricanes. Has the house been the scene of some crime? You may almost fancy that this spectral dwelling, given up to solitude and darkness, might be heard calling for succour. Do voices indeed issue from it? The mystery of the dark hours rests securely here. If its aspect is so disquieting at mid-day, what must it be at dead of night? The dreamer asks himself what this house may be between the dusk of evening and the twilight of approaching dawn. Has the supernatural world some relation with this deserted spot, which sometimes compels it to arrest its movements here, and to descend and become visible? Do the scattered elements of the spirit world whirl around it? Insoluble riddles! A dread terror is in the very stones; that dim twilight has surely relations with the infinite Unknown. When the sun has set, the song of the birds will be hushed, the goatherd will go homeward with his goats; reptiles taking courage from the growing darkness, will creep through the fissures of rocks; the stars will appear, night will come, but yonder two blank casements will stare at the sky. They open to welcome spirits and apparitions; for it is by the names of apparitions, ghosts, phantom faces vaguely distinct, masks in the lurid light, and shadows, that the popular faith translates the sombre relations of this dwelling with the world of darkness.

The house is 'haunted'. The phrase comprises everything.

Credulous minds have their explanation; common-sense thinkers have theirs also. 'Nothing is more simple,' say the latter, 'than the history of this house. It is an old observatory of the time of the revolutionary wars and the days of smuggling. It was built for such objects. The wars being ended, the house was abandoned; but it was not demolished, as it might one day again be useful. The door and windows have been walled to prevent people entering. The walls of the windows, on the three sides facing the sea, have been bricked up to keep out the wind. That is all.'

The credulous, however, are not satisfied. The house was not built at the period of the wars of the Revolution. It bears the date '1780', which was anterior to the Revolution. In the next place it was not an observatory. It bears the letters, 'E L M – P B I L G', which are the double monogram of two families, and which show that the house was built for a newly-married couple. Then as it has been inhabited, why should it be deserted? If the door and windows were bricked up to prevent people entering the house, why were two windows left open? Why are there no shutters, no window-frames, no glass? The wind is prevented from entering from the south; but why may it enter from the north?

The credulous are no doubt wrong; but it is clear that the common-sense thinkers have not solved the mystery.

It is certain that the house is believed to have been useful to the smugglers.

Without doubt, many of the nocturnal phenomena which have secured to the building the reputation of being haunted, might be explained by obscure and furtive visits, by brief sojourns of sailors near the spot, and sometimes by the precaution of men engaged in suspicious occupations, concealing themselves, or allowing themselves to be seen in order to inspire dread.

Add to this, that if the house was really a resort of the smugglers, their meetings there must have been safe from interruption, because the house was dreaded by the superstitious people. Its reputation prevented its being visited. People do not apply to the officers of customs, on the subject of spectres. The superstitious rely on the sign of the cross; not on magistrates. There is always a tacit connivance, involuntary, but not the less real, between the objects which inspire fear and their victims. The terror-stricken feel a culpability in having encountered their terrors; they imagine themselves to have unveiled a secret; and they have an inward fear, of exciting the anger of the apparitions. And over and above this, the very instinct of the credulous is silence; fear is akin to dumbness; the terrified speak but little; horror seems ever to whisper, 'Hush!'

Remember this was a period when the Guernsey peasants believed that the Mystery of the Holy Manger is repeated by oxen and asses every year on a certain day; a period when no one would dare to enter a stable at night, fearing to come upon the animals on their knees.

If local legends and stories can be credited, suspicion went so far as to fasten to the walls of the house at Pleinmont, things of which the traces are still visible – rats without feet, bats without wings, and dead bodies of other animals. Here were toads crushed between the pages of a Bible, and other offerings, placed there by passers-by at night, who, fancying

that they had seen something, hoped by such sacrifices to
appease the ill-humours of evil spirits.

But, if the house at Pleinmont had its secrets, it kept them to
itself; for but seldom did anyone go there. It was left alone.
Few people like to risk an encounter with the other world.

Owing to the terror which kept at a distance all who could
bear testimony on the subject, it had always been easy to
obtain entrance at night by a rope ladder, or by any ladder,
from a neighbouring field. Goods or provisions left there,
might await in safety the time and opportunity for stealthy
embarkation. Tradition says that forty years ago a fugitive
remained for some time concealed in the haunted house at
Pleinmont; whence he succeeded in embarking in a fishing-
boat for England.

Tradition also avers that provisions deposited in this house
remain there untouched, Satan and the smugglers having an
interest in inducing whoever places them there to return.

CHAPTER V

LOOKING FOR BIRDS' NESTS

It was on the Saturday that Sieur Clubin passed at Torteval,
that we must refer to a strange occurrence that took place, and
which was for a time kept quiet; owing to the dread caused to
those who witnessed it.

On that Saturday night, three boys climbed up the hill at
Pleinmont.

These boys were on their way to the village, from the
sea-shore. They were birds'-nesters, and we have before
mentioned that Gilliatt used to try to prevent the children
from robbing the nests, out of consideration for both birds
and children.

It was very dark, and a mass of clouds obscured the vault of
heaven. Three o'clock had just struck from the belfry of
Torteval, which is circular, and pointed like the hat of a

wizard. Why should these children return so late? The reason was simple: they had been in search of seagulls' nests; the season having been mild, the birds had paired early. The children, watching the birds flying around their nests, and, carried away by the excitement of the sport, had forgotten the time. The tide had caught them, and, unable to gain the creek in which they had moored their boat, they had to seek refuge on one of the higher portions of the rock until the tide receded. This was the reason for their late return home.

These delays in returning to the domestic hearth cause expectant mothers the deepest anxiety, and, when their minds are eased, by boxing the ears of the truants. And so, trembling for their reception, the boys hastened home; but with that kind of haste which takes every opportunity of delaying; for they were sure of a reception in which a kiss would be certainly followed by many blows. One amongst them had nothing to fear, for he was an orphan – a French boy. Just then he felt proud of having no parents; for no one had sufficient interest in him to beat him. The other two boys were Guernsey lads, from the parish of Torteval. When they had climbed the hill they came upon the platform on which was the haunted house. They began by being frightened, which is the right thing for anyone, when in such a situation at such a time.

Divided between the wish to run away as fast as they could, and to stop and look about, they stopped.

They looked at the house, black and terrifying.

The boys' first idea had been to flee; the second, to draw nearer. They had never visited the house at this hour. Fear sometimes will induce curiosity. With them was a French boy, which fact encouraged them to approach the building.

It is a well known fact that Frenchmen and boys believe in nothing. Besides, companionship in danger is reassuring, and to have three companions all equally alarmed gives one courage. And, then, they were boys, not thirty years among the three; they were accustomed to search out things that were hidden. They were in the habit of peeping into holes. Why not into this hole? There is excitement in tracing things. Looking into birds' nests gives one a desire to look into a ghost's nest.

Going from one kind of game to another, one comes at last to the Devil after hunting birds; we look for hobgoblins. Now they will know how much truth there is in those stories their parents have told them. All these ideas filled the minds of the Guernsey birds'-nesters, and raising their courage to a pitch of rashness, they once more drew nearer to the house.

The boy who gave them so much courage was worthy of their confidence. He was a bold lad, a caulker's apprentice, one of those children who have already become men: sleeping in the yard upon straw, earning his own living, having a loud voice, and red hair, and never hesitating to climb walls and trees, and caring nothing to whom belonged the apples that he saw in the orchards – one who had worked in a yard for the repairing of ships-of-war – a child of chance, a merry orphan, born in France, no one knew where, which were reasons for his being courageous, free in giving a penny to a beggar – mischievous, but good at heart, and one who had spoken to people from Paris. He was earning a shilling a day by caulking the fishermens' boats which were being repaired at Pêqueries. When he thought he should like a holiday he took one, and went birds'-nesting. Such was the little French boy.

There was something funereal in the dead silence that surrounded them. It was wild and weird. The desolate plateau terminated abruptly in a steep precipice. The sea beneath was calm, and not a blade of grass quivered in the breeze. The young birds'-nesters approached slowly, the French boy leading, and drew near the house. One of them afterwards telling the story, or as much of it as he could remember said, '*It did not speak.*' They still advanced, holding their breath, as one does when approaching a savage animal. They had ascended the hill on the seaward side of the house, where the ground ran down to a little rocky isthmus, almost inaccessible, and had now got close to the building; but they only had a view of the south side, all the apertures in which were bricked up, for they had not dared to turn to the left, which would have brought them in front of the terrible open windows. But, plucking up courage, the caulker's apprentice murmured, 'Steer to port, that is the good-looking side; let us have a peep at the two back windows.'

They steered to port, and came to the other side of the house.

The two windows were lighted up.

The boys took to their heels immediately.

When they had run some distance, the French boy stopped, and looked back.

'Hulloa!' said he; 'the light is gone.'

'It was true; the windows were as dark as ever, and the outline of the house could be seen sharply defined against the livid sky as though cut out by a punch. Terror was not entirely gone, but curiosity resumed her sway, and the boys returned to the house.

All at once, both windows were again lit up.

The two boys from Torteval scampered off, but the French urchin, though he did not advance, kept his ground.

He remained motionless, facing the house and looking intently upon it.

The light vanished, then re-appeared. Nothing could be more horrible.

The reflection made a faint streak of light upon the grass, wet with the night-dew. Suddenly, through the light, he saw upon one of the inner walls, black shadowy profiles, with gigantic heads. Seeing the French boy stand firm, the two other lads crept back, shaking with fright, but still curious.

'There are ghosts in the house,' whispered the caulker's apprentice; 'I saw the nose of one.' His two companions shrunk behind him, and, standing on tiptoe, peeped over his shoulder, using him as a shield, and, emboldened by having some one between them and the ghost, looked at the house, with their mouths open.

The building, on its part, seemed to watch them. There it stod in the vast darkness, with two glaring eyes. These were the windows on the upper floor.

These unearthly lights, caused, perhaps, by the opening and shutting of the entrance to the internal regions, showed themselves for a time, and then disappeared again.

Suddenly a thick, black shadow, having some resemblance to a human being, showed itself at one of the windows, as if from without, and disappeared into the interior of the house. Spirits enter houses by the windows. For a moment the light grew more vivid, and then vanished entirely. The house was again in darkness. Then sounds were heard issuing from it; these resembled human voices. It is invariably the case; when there is anything to be seen, there is silence; when there is nothing, we hear sounds. There is something awe-inspiring in the silence of night at sea. The silence of darkness is deeper there than on land. When there is neither wind and wave on that wide-stretching expanse of water, over which, at other times, the eagle's flight makes no sound, we can hear the movement of a fly. This sepulchral silence gave a dismal relief to the sounds that issued from the building.

'Let us go and look,' said the French boy, and he made a few steps towards the house. The two others were so terrified that they followed him; they were afraid to run away alone. As they passed a heap of faggots, which, strange to say, served to encourage them, a white owl flew out of a bush. Owls have a weird kind of flight, a sidelong movement, suggestive of mischief near. The bird passed near the boys, gazing at them with its large eyes which shone in the darkness.

The two boys behind shuddered, but their leader addressed the owl. 'You come too late, my bird: I *will* look.'

And he advanced boldly.

The crackling sound made by his heavy-nailed boots among the bushes did not prevent him from hearing the sounds from the house, which rose and fell with the continuousness and calm accent of a dialogue. A moment after the boy added, 'Besides, it is only fools who believe in ghosts!'

Contempt for danger gives courage to the most timid, and the two Torteval boys continued to approach the house, following the caulker's apprentice.

The haunted house seemed to grow larger. In this there was some reality, for the house grew larger because they were nearing it.

Meanwhile, the voices sounded more distinct. The children listened. The sense of hearing has a power of exaggeration. The sound was not a murmur, more than a whisper, and not an uproar. Now and then a word could be distinguished; but it was impossible to understand, for the conversation seemed to be in a foreign tongue. The boys stopped and listened, and then began to advance once more.

'The ghosts are talking,' said the French boy; 'but I have no belief in ghosts.'

The Torteval lads were tempted to hide themselves behind

the faggots, but these were now far behind, and their friend
continued to advance towards the house. They trembled at
remaining with him, but dared not quit him.

Step by step they went on in the greatest perplexity, the
French boy turning to them every now and then, and saying,
'You know there are no such things as ghosts.'

The house grew larger and larger, and the sounds more
distinct.

They drew nearer.

They now saw that there was a shaded light in the house. It
was very faint, like the light of a dark lantern, but the faint
glimmer that it gave reminded one of the illumination at a
meeting of witches.

When they were close under the walls they stood still. One
of the boys from Torteval hazarded a remark. 'They are not
ghosts, they are women dressed in white.'

'What is hanging out of the window?' asked the other.

'It looks like a rope.'

'It's a snake.'

'It is only a hangman's halter,' said the French boy, with an
air of superiority. 'They always use one; but still I don't
believe in them.'

And in three bounds, he was at the foot of the wall. The
others imitated him in fear and trembling, keeping close to
him, one on his right and one on his left. They placed their
ears against the wall of the house, and could hear the ghosts
talking thus:

'So that is understood?'

'Quite.'

'And all is settled?'

'Everything!'

'A man will wait here, and Blasquito will convey him to
England?'

'He will pay Blasquito?'

'Yes, he will do so; and Blasquito will take the man on
board without asking whence he comes?'

'That does not concern him.'

'Without asking his name?'

'We want no names; purses are our business.'

'Good! The man will wait in this house.'

'He will want food.'

'He will be supplied.'

'Where will we find it?'

'From the bag I have with me.'

'Very good!'

'Can I leave the bag here?'

'We smuggle, but we do not steal!'

'When do you sail?'

'To-morrow morning. If your man was ready he could have sailed with us.'

'But he is not ready yet.'

'That is his affair.'

'How many days will he have to wait here?'

'Two, three, or four days, perhaps, more.'

'Blasquito will not fail to come.'

'Oh! that is certain.'

'Here to Pleinmont?'

'To Pleinmont.'

'How soon?'

'Next week.'

'What day?'

'Friday, Saturday, or Sunday.'

'Perhaps he will fail?'

'He is my *Tocayo*.'

'Weather will not delay him?'

'All weathers are alike to him: he fears nothing. I am Blasco, he is Blasquito.'

'Then he will not fail to come to Guernsey?'

'I come here one month, he the following one.'

'I understand.'

'Counting from Saturday last, one week from to-day, five days will not pass before Blasquito arrives.'

'But if there is much sea?'

'Rough weather, do you mean?'

'Yes.'

'Blasquito will come all the same, but he will be later.'

'Where is he coming from now?'

'Bilbao.'

'Where is he going to?'

'To Portland.'

'Good!'

'Or to Torbay.'

'That would be better still.'

'Your friend may rest easy.'

'Blasquito will not betray him.'

'It is only cowards who are traitors; we are brave men!'

'Can anyone hear us?'

'It is impossible either to see or hear us. Terror makes this place deserted!'

'Yes, I know.'

'Who would dare to come and listen here?'

'True!'

'Besides, if any one listened, how much would he understand? We speak a language which few can follow here. Since you can speak it, you are one of us.'

'I only came to arrange with you.'

'That is true.'

'And now I must go.'

'Very well!'

'Tell me, if the passenger should wish Blasquito to land him somewhere else than at Portland or Torbay?'

'Let him offer some more money.'

'Then Blasquito will obey his wishes?'

'Blasquito will do anything, if he's paid.'

'How long will it take to make Torbay?'

'All depends on the wind and weather.'

'Eight hours?'

'About that.'

'Will Blasquito consult the passenger's desires?'

'If the sea will obey Blasquito.'

'He shall be handsomely paid.'

'Gold is gold, but the sea is the sea.'

'That is true.'

'A man with gold, does what he likes. God does with the wind, what He wills.'

'Well, the man who will sail with Blasquito will be here on Friday.'

'Good!'

'What time will Blasquito be here?'

'During the night. We always arrive and leave at night. We

have a wife who is called the Sea, and a sister named Night; the wife sometimes deceives us, the sister never.'

'Then all is settled. Good-night, lads!'

'Good-night. A drop of brandy before you go?'

'Thank you.'

'It is better than syrup.'

'I have your promise?'

'My name is "Word of Honour".'

'Good-night, then!'

'You are a gentleman, I am a caballero.'

Only devils would talk like this. The boys listened for no more, but now took to their heels in earnest, the French lad – convinced at last – running faster than the others.

The Tuesday following this Saturday, Sieur Clubin returned in the Durande to Saint Malo.

The *Tamaulipas* was still in the roads.

Sieur Clubin, between the puffs of his pipe, asked the landlord of the Auberge, 'When will the *Tamaulipas* sail?'

'Thursday – the day after to-morrow,' was the reply.

That evening Clubin supped at the coastguard-men's table, and, contrary to his habit, went out after supper. He was, therefore, absent from the office, and the Durande missed some freight. This was remarkable in a man generally so exact and business-like. He had a short conversation with his friend the money-changer. He returned to his lodgings two hours after Noguette had sounded the curfew; it was midnight.

CHAPTER VI

A NOTORIOUS LODGING HOUSE

In Saint Malo, many years ago, existed an alley known by the name of the 'Ruelle Coutanchez'. This alley no longer exists, having been removed for the improvement of the town.

It consisted of a double row of houses, leaning one towards the other, and leaving between them just room enough for a very narrow street. Indeed, by stretching the legs, it was possible to walk on both sides, touching with hand or elbows, as you went, the houses either on the right or on the left. Old relics of mediaeval Normandy have almost a human interest. Dilapidated houses and witchcraft always go together. In fact, villainy and the like are closely connected with an architecture of this kind.

One of these houses in the alley was known by the name of the Jacressade. It was a lodging-house for people who do not come to stay for any length of time. In all towns, and particularly in sea-ports, there is always to be found the dregs of all grades of life. It is the refuse of the social state, heaped up in an obscure corner.

These lurking-places are open to all. To fall in the social scale, places such men on the same footing. Sometimes honesty in tatters was there. Virtue and probity have been known before now to be brought to strange passes. We must not judge by appearances, even in the palace or in the slums. Public respect, as well as universal reprobation, requires testing. Surprising results sometimes spring from this principle.

The Jacressade had no windows looking on to the so-called street. Its facade was simply a high wall, with a low gateway, which led into the courtyard.

In the midst of the yard might be perceived a round hole, encircled with a margin of stones, and even with the ground. This was the well. A pavement of broken stones surrounded it.

This courtyard was square, and built on three sides only. On the side of the street was only the wall; and facing the gateway stood the house, the two wings of which formed the sides to right and left.

Anyone entering there late at night, would have heard a confused murmur of voices; and, if there had been moonlight or starlight enough to give shape to the obscure forms before his eyes, that is what he would have seen.

In the centre, the well; around which, upon a litter of straw, a kind of circle, formed the soles of boots and shoes; some showing the toes of the wearers, some the naked heels.

Beyond this, the eye might have distinguished, a strange and revolting mass of life. The sleeping accommodation was for the use of all, for the small sum of two sous a week. On stormy nights, the rain fell upon the feet and bodies of those wretched beings.

Who are these creatures? The unknown. They came there at night, and departed in the morning. People of this kind form part of the social fabric. Some stole in during the darkness, without paying, and most of them had scarcely eaten during the day. All kinds of vice, and every species of distress were there. The same sleep settled down upon this bed of filth. The dreams of all these companions in misery were similar. Truly, dismal meeting-place. Such was this heap of blighted humanity, fermenting in this wretched place. Every day brought some new accumulation of misery. Let him enter who would, sleep who could, speak who dared; for it was a place of whispers. The new comers hastened to bury themselves in the mass, or tried to seek oblivion in sleep, since there was none in the darkness of the place. They could not all obtain a share of the straw, and more than one figure was stretched out naked. The well, which was 30 feet in depth, was without lid or protection of any kind, and gaped open day and night. Rain fell around it, filth accumulated in the gutters of the yard ran down and filtered through its sides. A pail was used for drawing the water, and those who were thirsty drank from it. In the year 1819, the body of a boy was taken out of this well.

To be safe in this house, it was necessary to be one of 'them'. The uninitiated were regarded with suspicion. It was by instinct that they knew each other, and so they scented out the genuine guest of the Jacressade.

The mistress of the house was quite a young woman, and wore a cap trimmed with ribons. She washed herself now and then, with water from the well. She was lame, and had an artificial limb.

At early morn, the courtyard became empty. Its inmates had all vanished.

A rooster and some hens were kept in the courtyard, where they raked among the débris of the place all day. A long beam, supported by posts, traversed the yard. Sometimes, a silk dress, mudded and wet, would be seen hanging out to dry upon this beam. It belonged to the lame woman.

Above the shed, surrounding the yard, was a storey, and above this storey a loft. A decayed wooden ladder passing through a hole in the roof of the shed, was the means of access to this storey; and up this ladder the woman would climb, sometimes staggering while its crazy rounds creaked beneath her weight.

Occasional lodgers, whether by the week or by the night, slept in the courtyard; but the regular ones lived in the house.

The windows were without glass, door-frames with no hinges, fireplaces without fire; such was the state of things here. You might pass from one room to the other, by a long square aperture which had been the door, or by a triangular hole between the joists of the partitions. Plaster from the ceiling lay about the floor. It was a marvel how the old house still stood. The very wind shook it. The lodgers ascended as best they could by the worn and slippery steps of the ladder. Everything was open to the air. The wintry atmosphere was absorbed into the house, like water into a sponge. The multitude of spiders seemed alone to guarantee the place against falling to pieces immediately. There was no sign of furniture. Two or three paillasses were in the corner, their ticking torn in parts, and showing more dust than straw within. Here and there were a water-pot and an earthern jar. A close disagreeable odour haunted the rooms.

The windows looked out upon the yard. The scene was like the inside of a scavenger's cart. The things, not to speak of the human beings, which lay rusting, mouldering, and putrifying there, were indescribable. The fragments seemed to fraternize together. Some fell from the walls, others from the living tenants of the place. The débris were sown with their tatters.

Besides the population which congregated nightly in the square yard, the Jacressade had three permanent lodgers – a charcoal man, a rag-picker, and a 'gold-maker'. The charcoal-man and the rag-picker occupied two of the paillasses of the first storey; the 'gold-maker', a chemist, lodged in the loft. Where the woman slept was a mystery. The 'gold-maker' was of a poetical turn of mind. He inhabited a room in the roof – a chamber with a narrow window, and a large stone fireplace like a gulf, in which the wind howled at will. The garret window having no frame, he had nailed across it a piece of iron plating. This left little room for the entrance of light and much for the entrance of cold. The charcoal-man paid rent from time to time in the shape of a sack of charcoal; the rag-picker paid with a bowl of grain for the fowls every week; the 'gold-maker' paid nothing. Meanwhile the latter consumed the very house itself for fuel. He had pulled down the little wood-work which remained; and every now and then he took from the wall or the roof some of the timber, to heat his crucible. Upon the partition, above the rag-picker's mattress, were two columns of figures, marked in chalk by the rag-picker himself from week to week – a column of threes, and a column of fives – according to whether the bowl of grain had cost him three liards or five centimes. The gold-pot of the 'chemist' was a piece of an old bomb-shell, used by him as a crucible, in which he mixed his ingredients. The manipulation of metals absorbed all his thoughts. He was determined before he died, to revenge himself by breaking the windows of orthodox science with the real philosopher's stone. His furnace consumed a good deal of wood. The hand-rail of the stairs had disappeared. The house was slowly burning away. The landlady said to him, 'You will leave us nothing but the shell.' He pacified her by addressing her in verses.

Such was the building known as the Jacressade.

A lad of twelve, perhaps, older – for he was like a dwarf, with a large lump upon his neck, and generally carrying a broom in his hand – was the domestic of the place.

The habitués entered by the gateway of the courtyard; the public entered by the shop.

In the high wall, facing the street, and to the right of the entrance to the courtyard, was a square opening, which served as a door and a window. This was the shop. The square opening had a shuter and a frame – the only shutter in all the house which was undamaged. Behind the square aperture, which was open to the street, was a little room, a compartment obtained by curtailing the sleeping-shed in the courtyard. Over the door, passers-by read the inscription in charcoal, 'Curios sold here'. On three boards, forming the shop front, were several china pots without ears, a Chinese parasol made of gold-beater's skin, and ornamented with figures, torn here and there, and impossible to open or shut; fragments of iron, and shapeless pieces of old pottery, and dilapidated hats and bonnets: three or four shells, some packets of old bone and metal buttons, a tobacco-box with a portrait of Marie-Antoinette, and a dog's-eared volume of Boisbertrand's *Algebra*. Such was the stock of the shop; this assortment completed the 'curiosities'. The communication to the shop was by means of a back door, which opened into the yard in which was the well. In the said shop was a table and stool. The lame woman served at the counter.

CHAPTER VII

A MYSTERIOUS TRANSACTION

Clubin was not at the Auberge on Tuesday, nor again on Wednesday evening.

On that night, just about dusk, two men entered Coutanchez Alley and stopped before the Jacressade. One of them tapped at the window. The shop door being open, they entered. The woman with the wooden leg gave them the smile which she used for her best customers. There was a lighted candle upon the table. The men looked like two respectable towns-people.

The one who had rapped at the window said, 'Good evening; I have come about that little matter.' The woman smiled again, and, opening the back door which led to the courtyard, went out. In a few moments a man presented himself on the threshold. He wore a cap and blouse, underneath which he had something hidden. There were bits of straw in his hair, and it seemed as if he had just been aroused from sleep. He made a step forward. All three looked at each other. The man in the blouse had an expression in which there was a mixture of embarrassment and cunning. At last he spoke.

'You are the gunmaker?'

He who had tapped at the window replied by asking another question.

'Are you the man called the "Parisian"?'

'Yes, and sometimes "Redskin".'

'Let me see it!'

'Here is it,' and from under his blouse he drew something very rare at that time – a revolver.

It was quite new and shining. The two men examined it carefully. The man who seemed to know the locality, and whom the man in the blouse had spoken of as the gunsmith, tested the lock. He handed the weapon, at length, to the other, who had not the same appearance of a landsman, and who kept his back turned to the light.

The gunsmith again spoke and asked: 'What is its price?'

The man in the blouse resumed. 'I brought it from America. There are people who bring over monkeys, parrots, and all sorts of beasts, as if Frenchmen were savages. As for me, I brought this. It is a useful thing.'

'What is the price?' repeated the gunsmith.

'It is a pistol that repeats.'

'Its price?'

'Crack! the first shot. Crack! the second. Crack! – one after another. It will serve you well.'

'Its price?'

'It has six chambers.'

'Six chambers, that is six louis.'

'Will you take five?'

'Impossible; a louis for each bullet is the price.'

'Come, if you want to buy, you must be moderate.'

'I have put a fair price upon it; just look at it, Master Gunsmith.'

'I have done so.'

'The chambers twist and turn like Talleyrand himself. A pistol like this ought to be put in the Dictionary of Weathercocks. It is a veritable treasure.'

'So I see.'

'The barrel is of Spanish make.'

'I see it is.'

'And a twisted barrel, too. This is the way they make the twists. They empty into the furnace the contents of a basket full of old iron. They fill it up with scraps of steel, broken horse-shoes, old nails, and ——'

'And old scythe-blades.'

'The very remark I was just going to make, Master Gunsmith. Then they bring it all to a white heat, and this produces the grandest stuff for gun-barrels.'

'Yes, but there may be flaws in it.'

'So there may; but they remedy these by welding it well together, and give it two or three more turns in the furnace. Then they bring the big hammer to work. If it has been too much heated, they re-temper it with dull heats and light hammers; then they take it out and roll it well, and with it they manufacture a barrel like this.'

'You must have been in the trade, I should think.'

'I have been in many trades.'

'The barrel is rather pale.'

'That is one of its beauties; you get it that colour by using antimony.'

'I am to give you five louis, then?'

'Allow me to say, sir, that I had the honour to ask six.'

The gunsmith drew him aside and whispered to him, 'Listen to me, Parisian; take advantage of the opportunity, and get rid of it. A weapon like this can be of no use to you, it will only draw attention to you.'

'Yes,' answered the Parisian; 'it is somewhat conspicuous, and more suited for a gentleman than for myself.'

'Will you accept five louis?'

'No, six – one for each chamber.'

'Well, six napoleons, then?'

'My price is six louis.'

'You are not a Bonapartist, then – you prefer a Louis to a Napoleon?'

The Parisian called 'Redskin' smiled. 'Napoleon is the best,' answered he, 'but Louis is worth more.'

'Six napoleons.'

'Six louis; there is a difference of twenty-four francs.'

'Then we cannot deal.'

'Very well, then; I will keep the toy.'

'Keep it.'

'To bargain with me like that! It shall never be said that I got rid of such a work of art for so low a price.'

'Will you take five louis, and I'll throw you back five francs?'

'Sir, my price is six.'

The man who had kept all this time his back to the light, and taken no part in this conversation, had been examining and testing the movements of the weapon, and now whispered to the gunsmith, 'Is the weapon a good one?'

'Excellent.'

'Then I will pay the price he asks.'

Five minutes afterwards, whilst 'Redskin' was hiding in a secret pocket under his armpit the six louis which he had been paid, the gunsmith and the purchaser, the latter carrying the revolver in his trouser-pocket, left Coutanchez Alley.

CHAPTER VIII

A 'CANNON' OFF THE BLACK AND RED BALLS

It was on the following day, at the point called Décollé, a little way out of Saint Malo, where the cliff is lofty and the sea deep, that a tragical occurrence took place. A line of rocks, in the shape of the head of a lance, and joined to the land by a narrow isthmus, stretch out to sea, and end abruptly in a perpendicular descent. To arrive at this spot you must ascend an inclined plane – rather steep in places. On the platform of this peak stood a man, wearing a cloak. It was easy to see that he carried arms, from the straight and curved lines which showed under his cloak. The summit of the rock upon which he was standing was covered with huge blocks of stone, scattered about, and having narrow passages between. The platform, carpeted with a short, thick grass, ended on the side next to the sea in a perpendicular precipice. Its left angle, however, was broken away, and formed one of those natural staircases common in granite cliffs, but whose steps, out of all proportion, require sometimes the strides of a giant, and sometimes the leaps of an acrobat, to ascend or descend. It was a regular break-neck path, yet from it you might reach a boat, which it was easy to bring right under the cliff. The man enveloped in his cloak, and standing firmly on his feet, was using a telescope, and seemed absorbed in watching something. He moved to the edge of the precipice, and stood motionless, his eyes fixed on the horizon. It was high tide, and the waves broke gently against the foot of the cliff on which he was standing.

The object attracting the man's attention was a ship in the offing, which was being handled in a strange manner. She had not got clear of Saint Malo more than an hour when she had brought-to-behind the Banquetiers. She was a large vessel, and did not anchor, but contented herself with lying-to.

It was still broad daylight on the clifs, but over the sea below, darkness was spreading.

The man watching was a coastguardsman, as could be seen from his cloak – was carefully watching the movements of the ship, and appeared to take a mental note of them. She was lying-to a little off the wind, with her topsails aback. Her captain had spread his mizen, so as to make as little way as possible in either direction. He evidently had no wish to expose his vessel to the wind, for he had brailed up the small mizen-topsail, so that she would scarcely drift half a league in an hour.

The coastguardsman, engaged in performing his duty, took no heed to scrutinize the rocks beside him and below him. He had turned his back to the kind of staircase, from which access could be gained to the sea from the cliff. He did not, therefore, remark that behind a large rock a man was hidden, who, to all appearances, had been there before the arrival of the coastguardsman. From time to time his head peeped out from the side of the rock, watching the watcher. This head was covered by a broad-brimmed American hat – like that worn by the Quaker who, ten days ago, was talking with Captain Zuela on the sands of Petit Bay.

All of a sudden the attention of the man seemed to be aroused. Hastily wiping the glass of his telescope with the cuff of his coat, he pointed it again in the direction of the ship.

A small black spot appeared to detach itself from her side.

This spot, which seemed no bigger than an ant, was a boat.

The boat was evidently bound for the shore. The sailors in it pulled vigorously.

They pulled in the direction of Décollé Point.

The interest of the coastguardsman had reached its height.

He lost not a movement of the boat, and, in his eagerness, approached close to the edge of the cliff.

Then a tall man dressed like a Quaker stood up behind him, but the coastguard did not see him.

The man stood still for a moment, his arms hanging down by his side; he clenched his fists, and, with the expression of a hunter waiting for his prey, watched the back of the coastguardsman. Four paces separated the two men. He took one step, then stopped, then he took a second, and again halted. His feet fell on the turf and made no sound. He took the third step, and paused again. He could have put out his hand and touched the coastguardsman, who still had his telescope fixed on the boat. The man raised his two clenched hands to the height of his shoulders, then struck out fiercely with his fists, and smote the coastguardsman between the shoulders.

The blow was fatal.

The unfortunate man had not the time to utter a cry; he fell headforemost from the cliff into the sea, and disappeared like a flash of lightning. He sank like a stone.

A few circles formed on the dark sea, widened, and by degrees, disappeared.

The telescope, which had fallen from his hands upon the grass, alone remained.

The Quaker looked over the precipice and watched the circles till they vanished, paused for a few moments, and then rose to his feet, humming between his teeth:

> The captain of police is dead –
> The man has lost his life, 'tis said.

He bent over once more. Nothing came to the surface. Only, at the place where the man had disappeared, a dark spot formed on the surface, and gradually mingled with the waves. No doubt, the unhappy man had fractured his skull on some rock beneath the water, and his blood formed the dark spot which discoloured the sea.

The Quaker, whilst considering the meaning of this dark spot, began to hum once more:

A little while before his death,
The luckless man still drew his breath –

But he was not allowed to finish his song, for he heard a quiet voice, which said:

'Ah, Rantaine! Good-day. Why, you have killed the man!'

He turned hurriedly round, and about fifteen paces away, was a man standing in one of the passages of the rocks, and holding a revolver.

'Ah! you saw it, did you?' he said. 'How do you do, Clubin?'

The man, who was short, started.

'You know me, do you?'

'You know me well enough,' replied Rantaine.

And now the sound of oars was heard. The boat, which the coastguardsman had been watching, was approaching the shore.

Sieur Clubin said, in a half-whisper, as though conversing with himself:

'It was finished very quickly.'

'In what way can I aid you?' asked Rantaine.

'A mere trifle. Why, it must be ten years since I last saw you. I hope you have prospered.'

'Pretty well,' answered Rantaine; 'and yourself?'

'Very fairly indeed,' responded Clubin.

Rantaine made a step in the direction of Clubin, but stopped suddenly, for a sharp click struck upon his ear. It was Clubin, cocking his revolver.

'Rantaine, we are about fifteen paces from each other; it is a convenient distance. Stay where you are, please.'

'As you like,' answered Rantaine. 'What is it you want?'

'Why, to talk with you, of course.'

Rantaine made no further effort to move, and Clubin added:

'You have just murdered a coastguardsman.'

Rantaine raised his hat, and replied, 'You have already mentioned that.'

'So I did, but not so precisely. Now I am more precise, and say a coastguardsman. His number was 619; he was married, and leaves a wife and five children.'

'That may be true,' said Rantaine.

There was a pause.

'These coastguards are picked men,' continued Clubin – 'most of them old sailors.'

'I have remarked,' observed Rantaine, 'that that class of people always leave a wife and five children.'

Clubin resumed the conversation.

'Do you know how much I paid for this revolver?'

'It seems a handy weapon,' answered Rantaine.

'What sum do you say?'

'Rather a large one, I should think.'

'It cost me one hundred and forty-four francs.'

'Then you bought it,' said Rantaine, 'at the shop in the Jacressade?'

Clubin resumed. 'He had not time to make a sound; the fall choked his voice.'

'Sieur Clubin, there will be a breeze this evening.'

'I alone witnessed it.'

'Do you still stop at the Auberge Jean?'

'Yes; it is a comfortable house.'

'I remember getting some excellent sauerkraut there.'

'You must be powerful, Rantaine. What shoulders you have! I should be sorry to get a blow from you. When I was born, I seemed so delicate that they never thought they would be able to rear me.'

'Happily, they succeeded.'

'Yes; I still stay at the Auberge Jean.'

'Do you know, Sieur Clubin, how I recognized you? It was because you recognized me. I said to myself there is no man like Clubin for that kind of thing'; and as he spoke he advanced a step.

'Stay where you are, Rantaine.'

Rantaine obeyed, muttering to himself, 'Before a thing like that man is as helpless as a child.'

Sieur Clubin continued. 'Now, this is the situation: we have on our right, in the direction of Saint Enogat, at about three hundred paces from here, another coastguard, No. 618, who is alive, and, on our left, towards Saint Lunaire, a coastguard-station; so that seven armed men could be here in five minutes. This rock could be surrounded – the passage of escape barred. It would be impossible to get away, and at the foot of the precipice is a dead man.'

Rantaine cast a sidelong glance at the revolver. 'As you said, Rantaine, it is a handy weapon. Perhaps it is only loaded with blank cartridges: but what does that matter. One shot would bring a body of armed men here, and I can fire six times.'

The sound of oars grew more distinct; the boat was very near now.

The big man looked at the little man enquiringly.

Sieur Clubin continued, in the same gentle voice, 'Rantaine, the men in the boat that is approaching, if they knew what you have done, would aid in capturing you. You are paying for your passage ten thousand francs to Captain Zuela. You would have a better bargain with the smugglers of Pleinmont; but they would only have taken you to England, and it would hardly have done for you to risk going to Guernsey, where so many people know you. Well, I return to your position. If I discharge this pistol, your arrest follows. You are to pay Zuela ten thousand francs for your passage, and you have given him five thousand in advance. Zuela, in the event of your arrest, would keep the five thousand, and sail off. Rantaine, your disguise is good; that hat, that coat, and those gaiters, make a most decided change; but you forget your spectacles, though you were right to let your whiskers grow.'

Rantaine tried to force a smile, as Clubin continued, 'Rantaine, you are wearing a pair of American trousers, with double fobs; in one of them there is your watch; you can keep that.'

'Thank you, Sieur Clubin.'

'In the other, however, there is a little box, which opens and shuts with a spring; it is a sailor's tobacco box. Take it out of your pocket, and throw it to me.'

'But this is robbery.'

'You are free to call for assistance.'

'Look here, Mess Clubin ——' said Rantaine, taking a step forward, and extending his open hand.

'Stay where you are, Rantaine!'

'Mess Clubin, let us come to some arrangement. I offer you one-half.'

Clubin folded his arms, letting the barrel of his revolver peep out.

'What do you take me for, Rantaine? I am an honest man.'

Then after a moment's pause, he added, 'I must have all.'

Rantaine muttered between his teeth, 'This fellow is like flint.'

Suddenly a gleam flashed from Clubin's eyes, and his voice became clear and cold. 'I see that you are in error,' he said. 'Robbery is your aim, mine is restitution. Listen to me, Rantaine: it is ten years since you left Guernsey, taking with you a cash-box, containing fifty thousand francs, which belonged to you, but omitting to leave behind another fifty thousand, the property of your partner. These fifty thousand frances stolen by you from Mess Lethierry, at present form, with compound interest for ten years, eighty thousand six hundred and sixty-six francs, sixty-six centimes. Yesterday you went to a money-changer's office – his name is Rébuchet, in the Rue Saint Vincent – you gave him seventy-six thousand francs in French notes, in exchange for which he gave you three Bank of England notes for a thousand pounds each, in addition to the exchange. These bank-notes you put into the tobacco-box, and the tobacco-box you put into the right-hand pocket of your trousers. These three-thousand pound sterling amount to seventy-five thousand francs, and this I will accept on behalf of Mess Lethierry. To-morrow I leave for Guernsey, and will hand over the money to him. Rantaine, the ship lying-to out yonder is the *Tamaulipas*; you had your baggage sent on board last night with that of the crew. You are leaving France, and have good reasons for doing so. You are going to Arequipa. The boat is on its way to take you off to the vessel. You are waiting for it here. It is close at hand; you can hear the sound of oars. It depends upon me to let you go or to keep you here. Not another word; throw me the tobacco-box.'

Rantaine put his hand in his pocket, drew out the box, and threw it at Clubin, to whose feet it rolled.

Clubin stooped to pick it up, never moving his eyes from Rantaine, lifted the tobacco-box from the ground with his left hand, pointing the barrel of his revolver at Rantaine with his right. Then he cried out, 'Turn your back.' Rantaine obeyed the order.

Sieur Clubin tucked the pistol under his arm, and touched the spring of the box; which opened. There were four bank-notes in it, three for one thousand pounds each, and one for ten pounds. He refolded the three one thousand pound notes, replaced them in the box, shut it, and placed it in his pocket.

Then stooping for a stone, he wrapped the bank-note for ten pounds around it, and said:

'Now turn round.'

Rantaine obeyed, and Sieur Clubin added: 'I told you that I should be satisfied with three thousand pounds; so I return this note for ten pounds,' and as he spoke he threw Rantaine the note wrapped round the stone.

Rantaine gave it a kick, and stone and note fell into the sea.

'Please yourself,' said Clubin. 'You must be in funds. My conscience is clear.'

The plash of oars, which had continued during the whole of this conversation, now ceased, for the boat had reached the foot of the cliff.

'Your carriage is ready; you may leave, Rantaine.'

Rantaine moved towards the staircase and began to descend and Clubin moved to the edge of the precipice, and, bending over, watched him.

The boat was waiting off the last step, close to the place where the coastguard had sunk. Whilst he watched Rantaine stumbling from rock to rock, Clubin muttered between his teeth, 'Good! No. 619 thought that he was alone. Rantaine thought there were only two; I only knew that we were three.' Then perceiving on the grass at his feet the telescope, dropped by the dead man, he picked it up.

The sound of oars began again; Rantaine had reached the boat, which had shoved off. When Rantaine was safely in the boat, and the cliff began to recede, he jumped to his feet, and, with a face distorted with rage, shook his fist in the direction of the land, crying, 'Ha! the devil is a child compared to him!'

Clubin, from his position on the summit of the cliff, still keeping the telescope fixed on the boat, distinctly heard these words, shouted in loud tones that rose above the murmur of the sea:

'Sieur Clubin, you are an honest man, but you must not be surprised if I send a letter to Lethierry telling him of this. In this boat is a sailor, a Guernsey man, belonging to the crew of the *Tamaulipas*, who will be at Saint Malo soon. He will bear witness that I placed in your hands the sum of three thousand pounds for Mess Lethierry.'

It was Rantaine who spoke.

Motionless as the coastguardsman had been, and almost in the same spot, Clubin stood with his eyes to the glass, never allowing the boat to escape his sight for an instant. It grew less and less amongst the waves; he watched it appear and disappear, run alongside the vessel that was lying-to, and presently he saw the tall figure of Rantaine on the deck of the *Tamaulipas*.

When the boat was hauled on board and secured, the *Tamaulipas* set sail. Clubin still kept the telescope pointed towards her, as her outline grew fainter and more indistinct, and in the course of half-an-hour the *Tamaulipas* was but a black spot, rapidly vanishing from sight against the pale sky of fading day.

CHAPTER IX

WHICH IS OF USE TO THOSE EXPECTING LETTERS FROM ABROAD

On that evening, for the second time, Sieur Clubin returned home late.

One cause of his delay was that, before returning, he had gone to the Dinan Gate, where are many spirit ships, and had purchased in one, where he was not known, a bottle of brandy, which he stowed in one of his large pockets; then as the Durande was to sail next day, he looked over her to see that everything was in readiness.

When Clubin returned to the Auberge Jean, there was no one in the lower room except the old captain, Gaboureau, sitting over his pipe and ale. He nodded to Clubin in the interval of taking a sip and a whiff.

'Good evening, captain.'

'Well, the *Tamaulipas* is off at last.'

'Is she?' replied Clubin; 'I paid no attention to her.'

Captain Gaboureau used his spittoon, and said, 'Zeula is off too.'

'When did he go?'

'This evening.'

'Where has he gone to?'

'To the devil!'

'No doubt, but by which route?'

'By Arequipa.'

'I know nothing of it,' returned Clubin; then he added, 'I shall turn in.'

He lifted his candle, took a few steps towards the door, and returned.

'Have you ever been to Arequipa, captain?'

'Yes, some years ago.'

'Where do they touch on the outward voyage?'

'Here and there; but the *Tamaulipas* will not touch at all.'

Gaboureau knocked the ashes out of his pipe, and continued:

'You know the sloop *Trojan Horse*, and that fine vessel, the *Trentemaisons*, which sailed for Cardiff? I advised them not to put out, on account of the weather. Well, they have come back in a sad condition; the sloop had a cargo of turpentine; she sprang a leak, and when they used the pumps they pumped up the cargo with the water. As for the ship; her cut-water, her headrail, and the stock of her port anchor are broken. The mizen-mast I expect is badly strained. This all comes from not taking advice.'

Clubin had placed his candle on the table, and was engaged in arranging some pins in the collar of his overcoat, when he suddenly said:

'Did you not say, Captain, that the *Tamaulipas* would not touch anywhere?'

'Yes, she goes straight to Chili.'

'In that case we can hear nothing of her until she reaches her destination?'

'I beg your pardon, Captain Clubin. She can send letters by any vessels she may meet who are on their way to Europe.'

'True.'

'Then there is the Sea Post-Office.'

'What do you mean by the Sea Post-Office?'

'Do you not know what that is?'

'No.'

'When you pass the Straits of Magellan.'

'Well?'

'Snow everywhere, heavy weather, contrary winds, and chopping seas.'

'Well, go on.'

'When you have doubled Cape Monmouth.'

'Yes, go on.'

'Then you double Cape Valentine.'

'And then?'

'Why, then you double Cape Isidore.'

'And after that?'

'You double Point Anne.'

'Good! but what do you call the Sea Post-Office?'

'We are coming to that. Mountains to the right, mountains to the left; penguins and stormy petrels all about you. An awful place. Ah! thousand saints, and thousand monkeys, what a hammering one gets there! There, one has to cling to the belaying-pins, and to shorten sail. That's where you have to take in the mainsail and set the storm jib. A series of capfuls of wind and then, days of scudding under bare poles. Every rag of canvas blown out of the bolt ropes. Squalls, heavy enough to make a three-master hop like a flea. I have often had all my sails blown to ribons. Fifty-gun frigates leak as though they were wicker baskets; and then the infernal coast – jagged rocks, and reefs of all kinds. At last you get to Port Famine. Then things grow worse. The biggest waves that I ever saw in my life; the devil's own latitude. All at once you see, in big red letters, "Post-Office".'

'What do you mean, Captain Gertrais?'

'What I mean, Captain Clubin, is that, immediately after doubling Point Anne, you see on a rock, more than a hundred feet high, a big post, with a big barrel hung from it. This barrel is the letter-box. The English, of course, have the impudence to write up "Post-Office". What have they got to do with it? It belongs to the ocean – it doesn't belong to the King of England, but is common to all the world. "Post-office", indeed! Why, it sounds like Chinese. It makes me feel as if the Devil had offered me a cup of tea. But now I will tell you how they arrange matters: Every vessel which passes sends a boat with letters to the rock. A vessel which comes from the Atlantic, deposits its letters for Europe there, whilst a vessel from the Pacific its letters for New Zealand or California. The officer in charge of the boat puts in his lot, and takes away any that he may find there. You take charge of these letters, and the next ship that follows takes yours. As ships are always sailing in contrary directions, the port which I am leaving may be the one to which you are going. I carry your letters, you carry mine. The *Tamaulipas* will pass by there. The barrel has a good lid, with hinges, but no padlock. You see, a man can communicate with home easily, and that letters reach here safely.'

'It is very curious,' murmured Clubin, thoughtfully. Captain Gertrais Gaboureau took a fresh draught of ale. 'Let us suppose that Zuela should write to me. If he shoves his scrawl into the barrel in the Straits of Magellan, in about four months I should get the scoundrel's scrawl . . . Well, Captain Clubin, do you start to-morrow?'

Clubin, absorbed in dreams, did not reply, and Captain Gertrais repeated the question.

Clubin woke up. 'Certainly, Captain Gertrais, it is my day. I am off in the morning.'

'If I were you, Captain Clubin, I should do nothing of the kind. The hair on dogs' coats felt damp the last two nights; the sea birds have been flying round the lighthouse lantern – a bad sign. I have a storm glass, too, which gives good advice now and then. The moon is in her second quarter, and the bulb of the thermometer is damp. There will be a heavy fog to-morrow, and I advise you to keep in port. I dread fog more than a storm – fog is such a dangerous customer.'

BOOK VI

THE CAPTAIN IS SOBER, BUT

THE MAN AT THE HELM IS TIPSY

CHAPTER I

THE DOUVRES

At about five leagues out, in the open sea, to the south of Guernsey, opposite Pleinmont Point, and between the Channel Islands and Saint Malo, is a group of rocks, called the Douvres. The spot is highly dangerous.

This term Douvres, applied to rocks and cliffs, is very common. There is near the *Côtes du Nord,* a Douvre, on which is a lighthouse, a dangerous reef; but one not to be confounded with the rock referred to above.

The nearest point on the French coast to the Douvres is Cape Bréhat. The Douvres are a little further from the coast of France than from the nearest of the Channel Islands. The distance from Jersey may be pretty nearly measured by the extreme length of Jersey. If the Island of Jersey could be turned round upon Corbière, as upon a hinge, Saint Catherine's Point would almost touch the Douvres, at a distance of more than four leagues.

In these civilized regions the wildest rocks are rarely deserted. Smugglers are found at Hagot, custom-house men at Binic, Celts at Bréhat, oyster-dredgers at Cancale, rabbit-shooters at Césambre or Caesar's Island, crab-gatherers at Brecqhou, trawlers at the Minquiers, dredgers at Ecréhou, but upon the Douvres no one is ever seen.

The sea birds alone make their home there.

No spot in the ocean is more dreaded. The Casquets, where legend says the Blanche Nef was lost; the Bank of Calvados; the Ronesse, which makes the coast of Beaulieu so dangerous; the sunken reefs at Préel, which block the entrance to Merquel, and which necessitate the red-painted beacon in twenty fathoms of water, the treacherous approaches to Etables and Plouha; the two granite Druids to the south of Guernsey, the Old Anderlo and the Little Anderlo, the Corbière, the Hanways, the Isle of Ras, associated with terror in the proverb:

> Si jamais tu passes le Ras,
> Si tu ne meurs, tu trembleras,

the Mortes-Femmes, the Déroute between Guernsey and Jersey, the Hardent between the Minquiers and Chousey, the Mauvais Cheval between Bouley Bay and Barneville, have not so evil a reputation. It would be preferable to have to encounter all these dangers, one after the other, than the Douvres once.

In all that perilous sea of the Channel, which is the Egean of the West, the Douvres have no equal in their terrors, except the Paternoster between Guernsey and Sark.

From the Paternoster, however, it is possible to give a signal – a ship in distress there may obtain succour. To the north rises Dicard or D'Icare Point, and to the south Grosnez. From the Douvres nothing can be seen.

Its associations are storm, wild sea, desolate waste, and uninhabited coast. The blocks of granite are hideous and enormous – everywhere perpendicular wall – the cruel inhospitality of the abyss.

It is in the open sea; the water around is very deep. A rock completely isolated like the Douvres shelters creatures which shun the haunts of men. It is a sort of huge submarine cave of fossil coral branches – a drowned labyrinth. There, at a depth to which divers would find it difficult to desend, are caverns, and dusky mazes, where monstrous creatures multiply and destroy one another. Huge crabs devour fish and are in their turn devoured. Hideous shapes of living things, not created to be seen by human eyes, wander in this twilight. Vague forms of antennae, tentacles, fins, open jaws, scales, and claws float there, quivering, growing larger, or decomposing or disappearing in the gloom, while fearful swarms of swimming things prowl about seeking their prey.

To gaze into the depths of the sea is, in the imagination, like viewing the vast unknown, and from its most terrible side. The submarine gulf is analogous to the realm of night and dreams. There is also sleep, unconsciousness, or at least apparently so, of creation. There, in the awful silence and darkness, the rude first forms of life, phantomlike, demoniacal, pursue their dread instincts.

Forty years ago, two rocks of strange form denoted the Douvres from afar to passers on the ocean. They were vertical points, sharp and curved – their summits almost touching one another. They looked like the tusks of an elephant rising out of the sea; but they were tusks, high as tall towers, of an elephant huge as a mountain. These two natural towers, rising out of the hidden home of marine monsters, left only a narrow passage between them, where the waves poured through. This passage, tortuous and full of angles, resembled a straggling street between high walls. The two twin rocks were the Great Douvre and the Little Douvre; one sixty feet high, the other forty. The constant beating of the waves had at last worn away part of the base of the towers, and a violent gale on the 26th of October, 1859, overthrew one of them. The smaller one still remains, but it is worn and must soon fall in its turn.

One of the most singular points of the Douvres is a rock known as 'The Man'. Some fisherman at the end of the last century visiting this spot discovered on the height of the rock a human body. By its side were many empty sea-shells. A shipwrecked sailor had found a refuge there; had lived for a time upon limpets, and had died. Hence its name.

The solitudes of the ocean are dismal. The things which happen there seem to have no relation to the human race; their objects are unknown. Such is the solitude of the Douvres. All around, as far as the eye can reach, spreads the vast and never resting sea.

CHAPTER II

AN UNLOOKED FOR BOTTLE OF BRANDY

On Friday morning, the day after the departure of the *Tamaulipas*, the Durande started for Guernsey.

She left Saint Malo at nine. The weather was fine; no haze. Old Captain Gertrais-Gaboureau was evidently in his dotage to suggest such a thing as a fog.

Sieur Clubin's numerous occupations had certainly been unfavourable to the collection of cargo for the Durande. He had only taken aboard some packages for the fancy shops of Saint Peter's Port; three cases for the Guernsey hospital, one containing soap and candles, and the other shoe leather. He had embarked very few cattle; some bullocks only. These bullocks were in the hold loosely tethered.

There were six passengers on board – a Guernseyman, two cattle merchants from Saint Malo, 'a tourist' (a phrase already in use), a denizen of Paris, most likely on a commercial mission, and an American missionary, travelling to distribute Bibles. The Durande had a crew of seven (not including Clubin), a helmsman, a stoker, a carpenter, a cook (who could lend a hand as a seaman in an emergency), two engineers, and a cabin-boy. One of the two engineers was a good working mechanic; he was a Dutch negro, escaped from one of the sugar-factories at Surinam, and was called Imbrancam. Imbrancam understood the engine, and worked it admirably. In those days, when the steamer first began to run, his black face, appearing from the engine-room, enhanced the evil reputation of the Durande.

The helmsman was, by birth, a Jerseyman, but of a Cotentin family, and was named Tangrouille, which was originally the name of a family of high distinction.

This is a fact. In the Channel Islands, as in England and all other aristocratic countries, there is a great division of classes. Nobility is won by the sword and lost by toil, and is only preserved by refraining from labour of any kind. To have no occupation is to live honourably. He who works is not thought much of. Business is fatal to rank and position. In

former times, in France, there was one exception to this rule –
the trade of glass manufacturers. French gentlemen took a
pride in emptying bottles, and considered it not derogatory to
make them. In the Channel Islands, as well as in Great Britain,
he who wishes to remain noble must remain rich. No artisan
can be a gentleman. If he ever has been one he loses his
privleges. A sailor may be descended from a knight or a
baronet, but is none the less a simple sailor. Thirty years ago
there was in Aurigny a lineal descendant of the Gorges, who
might have laid claim to the manor of Gorges, confiscated by
Philip Augustus. This man used to crawl along the beach with
bare feet, picking up seaweed. A draper in Jersey, and a
shoemaker in Guernsey, called Gruchy, say that their real
names are Grouchy, and that they are cousins of the Marshal
of Waterloo. The old chronicles of the Bishopric of Coutance
mention a lordship of Tangroville, evidently from Tancarville
in the Lower Seine, which is, in point of fact, Montmorency.
In Normandy, if poverty overtakes a man, he is soon removed
from the ranks of nobility. A change in the pronunciation is
sufficient – Tangroille becomes Tangrouille, and all is
finished.

This is what happened to the helmsman of the Durande.

Tangrouille, probably Tancarville, and possibly Montmorency had a very gentlemanly failing, but which, however,
was against his getting on in his profession – he was a
drunkard.

Clubin persisted on retaining his services on the ship's
books, and had passed his word for him with Mess Lethierry.
Tangrouille never left the boat, and slept on board. On the day
before the departure of the Durande, when Clubin came on
board, late in the night, Tangrouille was in his hammock
asleep. During the night Tangrouille woke, according to his
habit. Every drunkard, who is not his own master, has some
secret place in which to conceal drink. This place Tangrouille
called his 'store-room'. It was in the hold. He had settled it
there as the most unlikely place to be discovered that he could
think of, and imagined that he alone knew of its existence.
Clubin was a sober man, and very strict, and the small amount
of rum and gin that the helmsman could conceal from his
superior he secreted in this mysterious corner of the hold

behind a coil of rope, and every night went to visit his treasure. The watch that was kept upon him was strict, and the debauch was not much to boast of, and, as a rule, Tangrouille's orgies were confined to one or two timid mouthfuls, taken in fear and trembling. But on this occasion, to his surprise, he found a bottle of brandy in his store-room. His joy was only equalled by his astonishment. What good angel had sent him this bottle? He drank it at once. Partly from prudence, and partly from fear of being discovered, he threw the bottle into the sea. Next morning, when he went to the helm, he was a little unsteady, but his steering did not vary much from his usual performance.

As to Clubin, he had, as we know returned to the Auberge, and gone to bed.

Clubin always carried, under his shirt, a leather travelling-belt, which he only took off at night, and in which he kept in reserve, in case of need, some twenty guineas. On the inside of this belt was his name. Next morning, when he got up, before leaving his room, he put into his belt the box containing the seventy-five thousand francs in bank-notes, and then, as usual, fastened it round his waist.

CHAPTER III

CONVERSATION SUDDENLY INTERRUPTED

The Durande made a good start. The passengers, as soon as they had stowed away their belongings, began to criticize the vessel in the manner now habitual with travellers. The tourist and the Parisian had never seen a steamer before, and the first turn of the paddles caused them to wonder and admire the foam. Then they looked at the smoke, and then, bit by bit, they examined every part of the vessel – the upper and lower decks, and all the marine fixtures, such as rising-bolts, grap-nels, and bolts, which form a sort of gigantic jewellery – a species of iron trinkets, gilded by rust caused by exposure.

They examined the signal-gun fastened on the upper deck. 'Chained like a watch-dog', said the tourist.

'And with a waterproof on, to prevent it taking cold,' returned the Parisian; and, changing the subject, they made the usual remarks on the view of Saint Malo. One argued that the approach to a place by sea was always deceptive, and that, at a league's distance, Ostend was as like Dunkirk as could be.

As they steamed on, Saint Malo grew smaller, and finally disappeared. The sea was quite smooth. The long line, fringed with foam, which formed in the wake of the vessel, was lost in the distance. Guernsey is in the midst of a straight line, drawn from Saint Malo to Exeter. But the most direct line is not always the one that can be taken at sea, though in this, steamers have an advantage over sailing-ships. The sea, in conjunction with the wind, forms an allied force. A ship is a combination of man's skill. Elemental force is boundless, whilst art has bounds. Navigation is a struggle between these two forces – the one possesses unlimited resources, and the other is bounded by man's genius.

Intellect brought to bear upon machinery counterbalances the power of the elements. The infinite has a machinery of its own. The elements know what they are doing and where they are going to. Force is never blind, and human intellect has to keep watch upon force, and study its natural laws. Whilst any portion of these laws are buried in obscurity the struggle continues, and steam navigation forms one of a series of victories which human skill has gained over the brute strength of the ocean. The chief feature in steam is that it disciplines the ship itself; it gives her power against the wind, and renders her obedient to the guidance of man.

By eleven o'clock, the Durande was off the Minquiers, under half-steam, hugging the wind, and steering due west. The day was clear and fine; but for all this, the fishing-boats were making for the shore.

As if every one was anxious to get into port, the sea by degrees became clear of vessels. It must be allowed that the Durande was a little out of her course, but the crew paid no attention to it, for their trust in the captain was unlimited; but, at the same time, there was a decided deviation – no doubt through an error on the part of the helmsman. The Durande seemed to be heading more in the direction of Jersey than Guernsey. Shortly after eleven the captain rectified the ship's course, and put her head for Guernsey. There had not been much time lost; but when the days are short you must not lose time.

In the state in which Tangrouille was, he had neither a steady hand nor a firm footing; the result was that he lurched about a good deal, and stopped the way of the vessel considerably.

The wind had almost entirely died away.

The passenger from Guernsey, who had a telescope, directed it from time to time on a small grey cloud which was lightly floating before the wind on the western horizon. It resembled a piece of wool, sprinkled with dust.

Captain Clubin wore his usual austere expression of countenance, and appeared to redouble his attention. All was tranquil on board the Durande; and the passengers talked together. It is easy to judge of the state of the sea during a passage by closing your eyes and listening to the conversation on board. Perfect freedom of conversation amongst passengers shows that the sea is calm. It would be impossible for a conversation like this to take place if the sea were rough:

'Sir, do you see that pretty green and red fly?'

'It has flown out to sea, and has come on board to rest.'

'A fly does not get tired soon.'

'No; they are light, and the wind carries them along.'

'Once, sir, they weighed an ounce of flies, and then counted them, and there were six thousand two hundred and sixty-eight.'

The Guernseyman with the telescope had come up to the two cattle merchants from Saint Malo, who were talking in this manner:

'A bull from Aubrac has a thick round back and a yellow hide. He is rather slow, because his legs are short.'

'A Saler is better in that point.'

'Sir, in my life I have seen two perfect bulls. The first had short legs, thick breast, broad haunches, a proper length from neck to tail, good withers, and a skin easy to take off; the other was one that would fatten well – a powerful black, strong neck and shoulders, brown and white hide, and sloping hind-quarters.'

'He must have come from Cotentin.'

'I do not know if you will believe me, sir, but in the south they have donkey-shows.'

'Donkey-shows!'

'Yes, and the ugliest are most admired.'

'Indeed! Why, that is the same as in the mule-shows; the prize is given to the ugliest.'

'Just so! Why, look at a Poitevin mare – large belly and thick legs.'

'The finest mule is only a barrel on four posts.'

'Men and beasts differ in good looks.'

'And women too.'

'That is true.'

'I like a woman to be pretty.'

'And I like her to be well dressed.'

'Yes, as neat as a new pin.'

'Everything fresh about her. A pretty girl ought to look as if she had come out of a bandbox.'

'But to come back to my bulls; I saw those two at Thouars.'

'Thouars – I know it well.'

The tourist and the Parisian were talking with the American missionary.

'Sir,' said the tourist, 'I will tell you the floating tonnage of the civilized world. France, seven hundred and sixteen thousand tons; Germany, a million; United States, five millions; England, five millions five hundred thousand. Add to these the tonnage of the smaller countries, twelve millions nine hundred and four thousand tons, distributed amongst the one hundred and forty-five thousand vessels in different parts of the globe.'

The American interrupted him. 'The United States, sir, has five millions five hundred thousand tons.'

'I bow to your superior knowledge,' said the tourist. 'You are an American.'

'Yes, sir.'

'The more reason for your being right.'

There was a pause, the missionary wondering if this would be the right moment to begin a distribution of Bibles.

'Sir,' began the tourist; 'is it true that you have a passion for nicknames in America, and that you give one to all your leading men? For instance, your famous Missouri banker, Thomas Burton, is called "Old Ingots".'

'Certainly, as we call Zachariah Taylor "Old Zach", and General Harrison, "Old Tip", and General Jackson, "Old Hickory"?'

''Tis because Jackson is as hard as hickory wood, and Harrison beat the red-skins at Tippecanoe.'

'It is a strange fashion.'

The little white cloud had now increased in size. It hung low upon the water, for there was hardly a breath of wind. The sea was as smooth as glass. Although it was not yet noon, the sun was growing very pale.

'I think', remarked the tourist, 'that the weather is going to change.'

'We shall have rain,' said the Parisian.

'Or fog,' suggested the American.

At twelve o'clock, according to custom, the dinner-bell rang. Those who wished to dine went below. Others, who had brought provisions in their bags, ate them upon deck. All went merrily. Clubin ate nothing.

Whilst they were eating the conversation went on.

The Guernseyman, having perhaps a liking for Bibles, approached the American, when the latter asked:

'Do you know these seas?'

'Yes, I belong to these parts.'

'And so do I,' broke in one of the Saint Malo men.

The Guernseyman bowed, and continued. 'At present we are in the open sea, but I should not like to have been overtaken by a fog when off the Minquiers.'

'What are the Minquiers?' asked the American.

'Very dangerous rocks,' answered the Saint Malo man.

'There are also the Grelets,' said the Guernseyman.

'Quite true,' said the other.

'And the Chouas.'

The man from Saint Malo smiled. 'For the matter of that there are the Savages also.'

The tourist interrupted with a question: 'Have we to pass through all these rocks?'

'No, we have left them behind us.'

The Guernseyman continued: 'Counting them altogether the Grelets have fifty-seven peaks.'

'And the Minquiers forty-eight', replied the other.

Here the conversation was continued on between the man from Saint Malo and the Guernseyman. 'It seems to me, that you have not included three rocks.'

'I thought that I had mentioned all.'

'From the Dérée to Maître-Ile?'

'Yes.'

'And the Maisons?'

'Yes, I know them – seven rocks in the midst of the Minquiers.'

'Ah! you know every stone, I see.'

If I did not know them I should not be fit to live at Saint Malo.'

'The Savages are three rocks.'

'Yes; and the Monks, two.'

'The Duck, one.'

'It is not nice to pass between the Chouas and the Duck.'

'Only a bird can do it.'

'How about the fish?'

'Not so easy for them in rough weather; they would drive themselves against the walls.'

'There are sandbanks at the Minquiers.'

'Yes; and round the Maisons.'

'When the tide is out you can walk all over the Minquiers.'

'Of course, the sands would be bare.'

'And the Dirouilles?'

'The Dirouilles are not like the Minquiers.'

'No; I only mean that they, also, are dangerous.'

'They are not far from Granville.'

'I see that you Saint Malo people are like us, fond of sailing.'

'Yes,' replied the man from Saint Malo – with this difference. We say, "we are accustomed"; you say, "we are fond of it".'

'You are good sailors.'

'I am a cattle merchant.'

'Who was that celebrated naval officer born at Saint Malo?'

'Surcouf.'

'There was some one beside.'

'Dugay Trouin.'

Here the commercial man from Paris joined the conversation. 'Dugay Trouin! He was captured by the English. He was handsome and brave, and an English lady fell in love with him, and helped him to escape.'

At this moment a voice loudly exclaimed:

'*You are tipsy!*'

CHAPTER IV

'OUR CAPTAIN IS A MAN OF STRONG RELIGIOUS PRINCIPLES'

Everybody turned round at once.

It was the captain addressing the man at the helm. Clubin, from the manner in which he spoke to Tangrouille, was either very angry or wished to appear so.

An outburst of anger at a judicious moment often shifts responsibility from the shoulders of one to those of another. The captain, on the bridge, between the two paddle boxes, looked sternly at the man at the helm, and repeated between his teeth the word '*Drunkard!*'

The unhappy Tangrouille hung his head.

The fog was coming on rapidly. It had now spread over nearly half the horizon. It seemed to close in on all sides at once, moving on mutely before the faint breeze. It was like a vast moving cliff, and stood up like a wall across the sea. You could see the exact spot where the fog came down upon the water. The entrance to the fog was still half a league distant. If the wind changed they might avoid it, but to do so, it must change at once. The half league of interval was rapidly decreasing, for the Durande was approaching the fog, and the fog was coming nearer to her.

Clubin ordered them to put on more steam, and to take a half turn to starboard. By this means they, for a time, skirted the edge of the fog. It, however, still made way; but the ship was, as yet, in the light of day. The time, however, that was lost in these manoeuvres was hard to regain. Night falls quickly in February.

The Guernseyman watched the fog; he said to the passenger from Saint Malo:

'It is coming on thicker.'

'It will be a dirty night at sea,' observed one of the men from Saint Malo.

'We shall not have so fine a passage, after all,' observed the other.

The Guernseyman approached Clubin.

'Captain,' said he, 'I am afraid that we shall be caught in a fog.'

'I would rather not have left Saint Malo to-day,' replied Clubin, 'but they advised me to do so.'

'Who did!'

'Some old sailors.'

'Well,' replied the Guernseyman; 'perhaps you were right in leaving. Who knows but there may be a storm to-morrow? At this time of year we must always expect the worst.'

A few minutes later, and the Durande steamed into the fog. In an instant, those aft lost sight of those who were forward. A moist grey partition divided the vessel into two parts. Then the whole steamer glided into the fog. The sun grew pale, like a clear moon. Everyone shivered; the passengers put on their over-coats, and the sailors their oilskins.

The sea, without even a ripple on it, seemed to threaten more from its tranquillity. It appeared as if there was a menacing meaning hidden beneath this unusual calm. The colouring of the atmosphere was pale and wan. The dark funnel and the black smoke stood boldly out against the faint light with which the ship was surrounded. It was no use keeping to the east any longer; so the captain put her head towards Guernsey, and ordered full speed.

The Guernseyman, who was standing near the skylight above the engines, heard the negro speaking to the stoker. The passengers listened.

The negro said: 'This morning when we had plenty of light, we slowed down; and now that we are in the fog we have full steam on.'

The Guernseyman came back to Clubin.

'Captain,' said he, 'have we not too much steam on?'

'What can I do, sir? I must pick up the time I have lost through that drunken fellow.'

'That is true, Captain.'

'Besides,' added Clubin, 'it is foggy now; it will be worse when night falls, and therefore I am in a hurry to get into port.'

The Guernseyman rejoined the passengers from Saint Malo, remarking, 'We have a most careful captain.' At intervals, great masses of mist floated heavily by, and obscured the sun, which, after a time, emerged, looking pale and sickly. The small portion of the sky that could be seen resembled those painted strips of canvas, stained and dirty, which do duty for it amongst theatrical scenery.

The Durande passed close to a cutter, which had prudently anchored. She was the *Shealtiel*, of Guernsey. Her skipper noticed the speed at which the Durande was steaming, and, in his opinion, she was out of her right course. At two o'clock the weather had become so thick that the captain had to leave the bridge and take his stand close to the man at the helm. The sun had totally disappeared, and the fog was all round them, the Durande being wrapped in a white mist. Both sea and sky had become quite invisible.

The wind had entirely died away.

The can of turpentine that hung under the bridge between the paddle-boxes never even quivered.

The Parisian every now and then hummed just above his breath one of Béranger's songs '*Un jour le bon Dieu s'eveillant.*'

One of the men from Saint Malo interrupted him.

'You are from Paris, sir?'

'I am, sir. *Il mit la tête à la fenêtre.*'

'What is doing in Paris just now?'

'*Leur planète a peri peut-être.* Everything is going wrong there, sir.'

'Then it is the same on land as at sea.'

'Quite true; we are having a horrible fog.'

'And one which might cause an accident.'

The Parisian exclaimed – 'Accident! yes, but why all these accidents? What good is done by accidents? It is like the burning of the Odéon Theatre, when people were thrown out of work. Is that right? I do not know what your belief is, but I am far from satisfied with the way in which religious matters are arranged.'

'I agree with you,' answered the man from Saint Malo.

'Everything down here', continued the Parisian, 'seems out of order; and I have an idea that the hand of Providence is absent.'

The man from Saint Malo scratched his head, as though puzzled. The Parisian went on:

'Yes, Providence is certainly not to the fore. There should be a decree passed to compel our Ruler to remain at His post. He is most likely taking a holiday, and so everything goes amiss. It is evident, that He has gone for a holiday, and has during His absence entrusted affairs to some substitute – to some inferior class of angel – some poor creature with the wings of a sparrow, who has charge of earthly matters.'

Captain Clubin, who, during this conversation had drawn near to the speakers, laid his hand upon the Parisian's shoulder. 'Silence, sir!' said he. 'We do not talk like that at sea.'

No one replied.

Then the Guernseyman, who had heard all, whispered to the man from Saint Malo, 'Our Captain is a man of strong religious principles.'

There was no rain, and yet all were damp. It seemed as if a feeling of melancholy had fallen upon all. Fog creates silence on the ocean; it calms the wave and stills the wind. In this deep silence, the noise made by the Durande as she passed through the sea had something sad and melancholy in it.

They met no more ships. If there were any vessels outside the fog, the Durande would have been invisible to them; and her long line of smoke, appearing to issue from nowhere, looked like a black comet in a white sky.

Suddenly Clubin shouted, 'You rascal! you are steering wild again! You will do some mischief before you have finished. Get below, you scoundrel!' and he snatched the tiller from him.

Tangrouille, overwhelmed with shame, slunk away forward amongst the men.

The Guernseyman exclaimed, 'Now we shall be safe!'

But the vessel still went at full speed, and about three o'clock the lower part of the fog began to lift, and the sea was once more visible.

'I do not like this,' said the Guernseyman.

Fog can only be dispersed by the sun or the wind. When the sun does it, it is good, but it is not so advantageous when the wind performs the operation. It was too late in the day for the sun to do it. It happens often that if the wind rises at this hour it may blow a hurricane before morning.

But to-day, if there was any wind, it could hardly be felt.

Clubin, his eyes on the binnacle, and holding the tiller, uttered to himself some words which reached the passengers. 'No time to be lost; that tipsy fellow has made us lose time.'

But there was no shadow of doubt or alarm upon his face.

Under the mist the sea was less clam, and a slight swell could be at times detected. Small patches of light appeared on the surface of the water, showing the rents made by the wind in the ceiling of fog. The mist lifted again, and then settled down more dense than ever.

At times the darkness was profound, and the ship seemed involved in a misty field of ice. Now and then this terrible circle opened, giving a momentary view of the horizon, and then closed again.

The Guernseyman, telescope in hand, had posted himself like a watchman in the bows.

The mist lifted for an instant, then closed again.

The Guernseyman turned, his face white with terror.

'Captain Clubin!' he cried.

'What is it?'

'We are running right upon the Hanois.'

'You make a mistake,' answered Clubin, coolly.

The Guernseyman persisted, 'I'm positive of it.'

'Absurd!'

'I just this moment saw the rock.'

'Where?'

'There!'

'That is the open sea. You are mistaken.'

And Clubin still kept the head of the vessel towards the point denoted by the passenger.

Again the Guernseyman made use of his telescope. and in another instant came rushing aft. 'Captain!'

'Well?'

'Go about.'

'Why?'

'I am positive that I saw a tall rock right ahead; it must be the Great Hanois.'

'You have only seen a fog-bank.'

'It *is* the Great Hanois; for God's sake go about!'

Clubin moved the tiller.

CHAPTER V

CLUBIN'S ACT OF SELF-SACRIFICE

At once there was a loud crash. The rending of a ship's timbers on a sunken rock in the open sea is a more melancholy sound than the saddest dreams have ever pictured. The Durande was brought up in an instant.

The Guernseyman raised his hands in despair.

'We are on the Hanois!' cried he; 'I said we would be.'

One wild cry of terror burst from the group gathered on the deck, 'We are lost!' But Clubin's voice, sharp and decided, was at once raised also. 'Silence! No one is lost.'

The dusky figure of Imbrancam, naked to the waist, appeared at the hatchway of the engine-room.

Quite calm and self possessed, he uttered these terrible words, 'Captain, the water is pouring in, and will soon extinguish the fires.'

It was an awful moment. The affair seemed suicidal. Had it been done intentionally it could not have been more terrible. The Durande had rushed upon the rock as if it had been an enemy, and a sharp point had penetrated her timbers like a nail. The stern was crushed; and, through a huge rent in her hull, the waves rushed in with a horrible sound. The shock had been so great that it had shattered the hooks by which the rudder was suspended, and the rudder itself was unshipped, and hung grinding against the stern. The ship lay pierced through and through by the sunken rock, while all around nothing could be seen but the thick and impenetrable fog. Night was falling.

The Durande lurched heavily forward, like the horse which feels the horns of a bull buried in its vitals. There was no hope of saving her. It was low water.

Tangrouille's intoxication had left him; no one is tipsy when there is a wreck to sober him. He went between decks, and came up again in a moment. 'Captain,' he said, 'she is making water fast; in a few minutes it will be up to the scupper-holes.'

The passengers ran about the deck, wringing their hands and bending over the bulwarks, and making all sorts of useless movements in their fright.

Clubin raised his hand, and all were silent. Then he asked Imbrancam, 'How long can you keep the engines going?'

'Five or six minutes.'

Then Clubin turned to the Guernseyman and said, 'Take the helm. You know the rock. Upon which part of the Hanois are we?'

'On the Mauve; as the fog lifted, I recognized it.'

'If we are on the Mauve,' returned Clubin, 'we have the Great Hanois to port, and the Little Hanois to starboard and are only a mile from land.'

The crew and passengers listened with deep anxiety, fixing their eyes intently upon their captain.

It would have availed nothing to have lightened the ship; nor, indeed, would it have been possible. In order to throw the cargo overboard it would have been necessary to open the ports, and the water would have at once rushed in. The engines were not damaged, and could be worked as long as the fires were not extinguished – that is to say, for a few minutes. She might, therefore, have been backed off the rocks, but would most likely have foundered at once. The rock acted as a plug, and prevented water entering through the leak; or at any rate, was an obstacle to its so doing. But if the hole was once thoroughly opened, it would have been impossible to have stopped the leak. To back off the rock would result in sinking at once.

The oxen, feeling the water rising, commenced to bellow piteously.

Clubin gave the command.

'Lower the long-boat.'

Imbrancam and Tangrouille hastened to obey the order, and let go the tackle. The rest of the crew looked on and seemed half-dazed.

'All hands lower the boats!' said Clubin, and this time all obeyed his order.

Clubin, with the utmost coolness, issued his orders, and the long boat was lowered at last.

The passengers went down the ladder, clutching at every rope on their way, and huddled into the long-boat. Then the crew made a rush, knocking down the cabin-boy, and trampling on him, but Imbrancam interposed. 'The boy first!' cried he, and, with his black, muscular arms, he hurled the sailors right and left, and picking up the boy, lowered him to the Guernseyman, who, standing up in the boat, received the lad in his arms. When he saw the boy safe, Imbrancam drew aside, and said to the crew, 'You may pass now.'

Meanwhile, Clubin had been to his cabin, and got together the ship's papers and instruments. He took the compass from the binnacle, handed the papers and the instruments to Imbrancam, and the compass to Tangrouille, saying, 'Get on board at once.'

When they had obeyed him, the long-boat was almost full, and her gunwale nearly level with the water.

'Now,' said Clubin, 'push off!'

A shout was raised.

'But you, captain?'

'I must remain.'

Men leaving a wreck have but short time in which to deliberate, and still less for indulging feelings of sentiment. However, those in the boat experienced a sensation not entirely selfish. All with one voice raised the same cry, 'Come with us, captain.'

'I must remain with my ship.'

The Guernseyman, who knew something of the sea, now spoke, 'Listen to me, captain. We are on the Hanois. It is not more than a mile to Pleinmont, but in a boat we can only land at Rocquaine, which is twice the distance. There is a swell rising up and a nasty fog. We shall not be at Rocquaine before two hours, and it will be a dirty night. The sea and the wind are rising; we shall have a storm. If you remain here you will perish. Come with us.'

As he finished the Parisian added, 'The boat is full – too full, and one man more is a man too many; but we are thirteen, and thirteen is an unlucky number. It is wiser to overload the boat with a man and so avoid an unlucky number. Come along, captain.'

Tangrouille said, 'It is all my fault. It is not fair that you should remain.'

'I *shall* remain,' said Clubin. 'The vessel will probably go to pieces to-night; but I will not leave her. When his ship is lost, the captain should die. They shall say of me, "He did his duty." I forgive you, Tangrouille.'

Then he folded his arms, and exclaimed, 'Cast off!'

The long-boat rose and fell with the heave of the sea; Imbrancam took the tiller; every hand that did not pull an oar was waved to the captain, and every voice shouted, 'God bless you, Captain Clubin!'

'There is a brave man!' exclaimed the American.

'Sir!' answered the Guernseyman, 'he is the bravest man that ever trod a ship's deck.'

Tangrouille was weeping.

'Had I had the courage,' he murmured, 'I would have died with him.'

The boat pushed off into the fog, and Clubin lost sight of it immediately.

The sound of oars grew fainter and fainter, and soon died away.

Clubin was alone on the wreck.

CHAPTER VI

CLUBIN'S TRUE CHARACTER REVEALED

When this man realized that he was alone, in the depth of the fog and the waste of waters – far from any human being, counted as dead – alone between the rising sea and the gathering storm – he experienced a feeling of intense pleasure. All his wishes were fulfilled.

His dream was about to be realized; the bill which he had drawn upon the future at so long a date was now about to be met.

In his eyes, to be deserted was to be saved. He was only a mile from shore, and in possession of seventy-five thousand francs. There was no hitch, for had he not arranged every step with care? Clubin's idea had been to pose as an honest man, and to wait for his opportunity, to await his chance, guess the right moment, to play one card only, and thus carry off everything before him, leaving his dupes to bewail their losses. He intended to realize at one stroke what lesser rogues try for many times; and, whilst they fail, he determined to finish his career a rich man. His meeting with Rantaine had been like a lucky hit, and he had immediately formed his plan to make Rantaine disgorge his plunder – parry his threatened revelations by disappearing, and pass for dead. And as a means to this end he decided to wreck the Durande. This last was necessary, and his reputation would remain intact; indeed, if anything enhanced. Anyone seeing Clubin rejoicing over the wreck might have thought him a fiend, happy in the commission of a deadly sin.

He had lived all his life for that which had now happened. The whole of his character was summed up in the words 'At last!' An awful calmness illumined his gloomy brow; his dull eye – the depth of expression of which seemed fathomless – shone clear and terrible. The inward fire of his soul was therein reflected.

The inner conscience, like exterior nature, has its electric spark. An idea is a meteor. At the moment of success the pent-up designs which preceded it burst asunder, and a spark gleams out. To have your prey grasped in your cruel hand is a happiness which lights up the face; an evil thought illumines every feature. The success of certain combinations, of certain cruel desires, causes sinister flashes of satisfaction to show themselves in men's eyes. It is the pleasure found in a threatening storm, from a conscience enveloped in clouds and obscurity. This evil light shone in the eyes of Clubin.

The long-repressed evil of his heart burst forth at once. His eyes pierced the darkness around him, and he could not restrain a burst of fiendish laughter.

At last he was free – rich and free. The unknown was opening before him; he had solved the problem. Clubin had plenty of time. The ship was firmly fixed upon the rock, with no fear of her sinking. Besides, time must be given to the boat to get away – to founder, perhaps. Clubin hoped she would sink. Standing on the deck, he folded his arms, enjoying his lonely situation. For thirty years the man had been weighed down beneath his burden of hypocrisy. He loathed virtue like one who hates an unsuitable helpmate. He was always premeditating some dishonest act; and, ever since he had come to man's estate, he had worn the armour of appearance. Underneath it he was a fiend. He lived under the guise of an honest man, with the soul of a devil. Enclosed in the garb of innocence, he carried on his back those angels' pinions so inexpressibly galling to a villain. He was overwhelmed with public esteem. It was hard for him to pass for a man of honour. Always to walk in the same track, to think evil, yet act and speak well – this had been indeed a labour. He had posed as the shadow of honesty, whilst in reality he was the spectre of crime. Always compelled to appear what he was not, virtue for him was something that suffocated him. He passed his life longing to bite the hand that fed him, and, instead of biting, he had been compelled to kiss it.

The serpent and the worm crawl along the ground in the same manner, and have the same way of raising their heads. A traitor is a fettered despot, unable to bring himself to play a secondary part. Littleness is equal to any enormity. A true hypocrite is a giant and a dwarf at one and the same moment. Clubin really believed himself ill-treated.

Why was he not born rich? He would have asked nothing better than to have had parents with a fortune. Why had he not had them? Why not all the pleasures of life his? He had been compelled to work. Why had he to submit to the torture of stooping, and flattering, in order to make himself respected, and to wear, night and day, a face different from his own? To dissimulate was a hardship. Men hate those they injure. But at last his turn came and Clubin was avenged.

Upon whom? Upon all, and everything.

He had received nothing but kindness from Lethierry – another grievance – and he had avenged himself on him. He was revenged upon all in whose presence he had been obliged to constrain himself. Whoever had had a good opinion of him, he had, to a certain extent, been that man's slave. Clubin had regained his liberty. What others looked upon as death, was, to him, the commencement of a new life. He had cast aside the false Clubin, and put on the true. He had crushed Rantaine, ruined Lethierry, thrust human justice into darkness, and compelled public opinion to err. He had humanity cast from him, and blotted out the world.

As for God, those three letters troubled him not at all. He had always been considered a pious man. What was he in reality?

There are depths in hypocrisy, or, to speak correctly, hypocrisy is a depth in itself. When Clubin found himself at last alone, his conscience opened, and he had a moment of exquisite pleasure. *He aired his soul*. With all the force of his lungs he inhaled a deep breath of crime.

The depth of evil in him showed in his every feature. At that instant, had Rantaine stood beside him, his features, compared with Clubin's, would have looked like the innocent face of a babe. What a relief it was to throw off that mask!

A protracted life of restraint had forced him at last to long for vice. He felt a certain lascivious enjoyment in wickedness. In these frightful moral abysses, which are but seldom fathomed, there exists a strange and atrocious pleasure, the obscenity of vice. The insipidity of a false reputation gives you a longing for shame. You begin to look upon disgrace with desire, if that disgrace is living at its ease. Eyes that are cast down often glance shyly at sin. The distinction between a Messalina and a Marié Alacoque is not great. Remember La Cadière, and the nun of Louviers. Clubin had for years lived behind the veil, and open audacity had been his ambition. He envied the bedizened harlot and the brazen brow of the undisguised ruffian; he experienced a feeling at having passed for a good man, and a hideous pride in outdoing them both. After long years, alone on that rock, he could be frank and open; and he was so. The long-outstanding debt of dissimulation was paid at last. Clubin gave way to the intoxication of being alone with himself and heaven. He cried aloud, 'I am a villain!' and was thoroughly satisfied. No mind had ever expressed such a strange flood of feeling.

Solitude made him certain of his victory, but took away some of its pleasure, for he alone was the spectator of his own triumph. To be linked to the galley-slave's chain has its charm; everyone then knows that you are infamous. To compel the crowd to gaze upon you is an act of pain in itself. A galley-slave, standing on a platform in an open square, with his neck fixed in an iron-collar, is the tyrant who compels all looks to be riveted on himself. To be the centre of a circle of admiring eyes, what a triumph! To direct the glances of the eyes of the populace, does not that show unbridled supremacy? To those whose ideal is evil, disgrace is a crown of glory. It is a height to look down from. You tower above others in something – a proud position from which you can show yourself – a pillory which all the world can see is not widely different from a throne.

All these thoughts passed through Clubin's mind, and he enjoyed them a good deal. A cloud of fiery sparks whirled from the mouth of the pit of hell are emblems of the wild whirl of thoughts that filled his soul.

He remained for some time buried in reverie, gazing upon his discarded honesty as a snake looks at its cast-off skin.

All the world had had such trust in this honesty that even he had come to believe in it a little. He again burst into a shout of laughter.

People would believe him drowned, and yet he would be alive and rich. What a trick to play upon the world's imbecility! And in this imbecility Rantaine, too, had played a part. Clubin considered him beneath contempt – the scorn of the fox for the tiger. Rantaine had failed, he had succeeded. Rantaine had slunk off abashed, whilst he, Clubin, triumphed. He had stepped in between Rantaine and his spoils, and had carried them off. He had no definite plan for the future. He had the bank-notes in the iron box carried in the belt round his waist, and that was sufficent for him. He would assume a new game. There were countries where sixty thousand francs would soon gain six hundred thousand. He could solve the riddle by living in one of those places, upon the money that he

had forced that robber Rantaine to give up. He could specu-
late, increase his capital, and become a millionaire; there were
tons of gold to be made. Besides, these matters were but of
secondary importance; there was plenty of time to think about
them. The chief difficulty had been overcome. To spoil the
spoiler and to vanish with the Durande, had been the chief
point, and it had been effected. The rest was all simple. There
was nothing more to be feared. He could swim to shore, and
reach Pleinmont in the night, climb the cliff, and go to the
haunted house; he could enter it by means of the cord that he
had hidden among the rocks. In the house was his bag, with
dry clothes and provisions in it. He could hide there, and in
eight days the Spanish smuggler would arrive. Blasquito
would come to Pleinmont, and for a few guineas would
convey him, not to Tor Bay, as he had mentioned, to divert
suspicion, but to Passage, or Bilbao. From there he would get
to Vera Cruz, or New Orleans. And now it was time to take
to the water; the boat would be now far off. An hour's swim
was nothing to Clubin, and there was but one mile between
him and the shore; for he was on the Hanois. At this instant
the fog suddenly lifted, and Clubin saw before him the terrible
peaks of the Douvres in all their hideous lonesomeness.

CHAPTER VII

THE UNEXPECTED HAPPENS

Clubin, overwhelmed by the shock, stared round him. It was
but too true; he was on that lonely and isolated rock. The two
peaks of the Douvres arose before him in all their hideousness.
The narrow passage between them, which resembled a trap
for the wayfarers of the sea, was clearly visible. It looked like
some dangerous ambuscade which the inhabitants of the sea
had prepared for the denizens of the land.

He was close to them. Up to now the fog had concealed
them. It had misled Clubin, and had made him take a wrong

course. In spite of all his care, the same accident had befallen him that many navigators have experienced: for instance, Gonzalez – who discovered Cape Blanco, and Fernandez – who discovered Cape Verd. The fog, which had been so useful for the execution of his plan, but which had also its perils, was clearing off. Clubin's error arose from keeping too much to the west. When the Guernseyman had said that he recognized the Hanois, Clubin had given a decisive turn to the helm, thinking that the bow of the vessel was straight for those rocks. The Durande – whose timbers had been pierced by one of the sunken reefs which extend some distance from the main rocks – was not separated from the peaks of the Douvres by more than two cable lengths. About two hundred yards further on was a gigantic mass of granite; upon its steep sides were some small indentations, at irregular intervals, which might afford aid in climbing it. The square corners on the summit showed that some sort of platform existed there.

It was the Man-Rock.

The Man-Rock rises to even a greater height than the Douvres, and the platform on its summit overlooks the two inaccessible peaks of the latter. The crumbling edges of the platform had a certain rough kind of regularity. No spot more solitary or melancholy could be imagined. The waves rolled calmly in against the square sides of this gigantic and sombre fragment, which seemed as though placed in that spot to serve as a refuge for the mighty phantoms of sea and land. All round was calm and still, not a ripple on the sea, not a breath in the air.

Clubin had often seen these from a distance, and soon satisfied himself as to his true position.

It was a strange and awful dilemma. The Douvres, not the Hanois. Five leagues of water instead of one mile between himself and safety. The unhappy sailor cast upon these rocks has death ever before him. From them there is no hope of reaching the land. Clubin shuddered. He had, by his own act, ventured in the jaws of death. No other refuge was left but the Man-Rock. It was probable that there would be a storm, and that the boat, overcrowded as she was, would founder, so that no tidings of the wreck would come to land. It would not even be known that Clubin was on the Douvres. There was nothing before him but the prospect of lingering death from exposure and starvation. His seventy-five thousand francs could not procure even a mouthful of bread. The course which he had pursued with so much care had ended but in this. He had flung away his life. No chance of help, no possible escape – his triumph ending in a precipice, his deliverance in imprisonment; instead of a prosperous career, a lingering death. In a lightning's flash, his plans had crumbled away. The paradise that the fiend had hoped to enjoy had taken its true aspect – it was a tomb.

And now a slight breeze sprung up, and the fog, divided by it, floated away in huge masses, and permitted the surface of the ocean to be visible.

The cattle in the hold, finding the water rising, bellowed piteously.

The rising tide began to fill the Durande slowly, and she commenced to swing, turning on the rock upon which she was fixed like a pivot. The moment was near when a wave would sweep her from her position, and throw her on her side. It was not so dark as it had been when she struck. Though it was later in the day there was more light, for the fog clearing away, much of the gloom had disappeared. The Durande was lying in a slanting position, with her bow higher than her stern. Clubin climbed on to the taffrail, which was high out of the water, and swept the horizon with eager glance. One of the characteristics of the true hypocrite is to be very sanguine. A hypocrite is always ready to seize a chance. Hypocrisy is nothing more than a terrible species of hopefulness, and the foundation of its falsehood, mingled with that divine feeling, forms a vice.

Clubin still gazed seawards with great anxiety. He said to himself that, now the fog was lifting, vessels that had been lying-to or at anchor could resume their course, and he thought it possible that some might come within sight of the rock.

His hope proved correct, for a sail appeared on the horizon, and gradually drew near. As she approached he could make out her rig. She was a cutter.

In half an hour she would pass the Douvres.

'I am saved!' thought Clubin. In the awful position in which he found himself, his first thought was for life. The cutter looked like a foreign ship – very likely it was a smuggler, bound for Pleinmont. It might be Blasquito himself. In that case not only was his life saved, but his fortune too, and the wreck on the Douvres would bring about the end more speedily, and do away with the necessity of concealment in the haunted house. It was very fortunate. Again his evil soul rejoiced over the prospect of success.

There was but one course to pursue.

The Durande was so far on the rocks that their peaks and projections were mingled with her outline, so that from a distance she was hardly distinguishable, and in the fading light would most likely be unseen. But a human being, standing out against the pale sky, and making signals of distress from the Man-Rock, would attract attention, and a boat would be lowered to rescue the castaway. The Man-Rock was but two hundred yards off. Nothing was more simple than to swim to it and climb it; but not a moment must be lost. The forepart of the Durande being high on the rocks, it was from the very part upon which Clubin was standing that it was necessary to plunge. He commenced by taking soundings, and found that there was plenty of water under the stern. The minute shells which adhered to the line showed that large caverns existed below, in which the water was always calm, however rough the surface of the sea might be.

He undressed, and threw his clothes upon the deck. He knew that he should get others on the cutter, but he took care to keep his belt. When he had stripped he examined it, and readjusted the buckle; then he cast a hurried glance at the course that he must take through the breakers to reach the Man-Rock, and plunged headforemost into the sea.

Diving from a great height, he descended deep beneath the surface. Deeper and deeper he went, reached the bottom, touched it, and then, with a spring, prepared to return to the surface.

At that moment, he felt his foot seized by something which drew him backwards.

BOOK VII

THE RISK OF OPENING A BOOK

BY CHANCE

CHAPTER I

A PEARL AT THE BOTTOM OF A PRECIPICE

A few minutes after his conversation with Sieur Landoys, Gilliatt arrived at Saint Sampson.

He felt troubled and anxious. What could have happened.

There was excitement in Saint Sampson as in a startled hive. All were at their doors. The women were talking loudly. People were relating some occurrence and gesticulating. A group surrounded them. The words could be heard, 'What a misfortune!' Some faces were smiling.

Gilliatt questioned no one. It was not his habit to ask questions. He was, besides, too anxious to speak to strangers. He had no belief in rumours. He preferred to go direct to the Bravées.

His anxiety was so great that he was not even deterred from entering the house. The door of the lower room opening upon the Quay, stood quite open. There was a crowd of men and women on the threshold. Everybody was going in, and Gilliatt entered with the rest. Sieur Landoys was standing near the door.

'You have heard, no doubt, of it?'

'No.'

'I did not like to tell it to you on the road. It makes one seem like a bird of bad omen.'

'What has happened?'

131

'The Durande is lost.'

There was a crowd in the large room, and the groups spoke low, like people in a sick room. The assemblage, consisting of neighbours, curious to learn the news, huddled together near the door with a kind of timidity, leaving clear the end of the room, where Déruchette was sitting and in tears. Mess Lethierry stood close to her.

His back was against the wall. His sailor's cap came down over his eyebrows. A lock of grey hair hung upon his cheek. He was silent. His arms were without movement; he did not seem to breathe. He had the look of something lifeless leaning against the wall.

His aspect was that of a man whose life has been crushed within him. The Durande being lost, Lethierry had no longer any object in his existence. He had had a being on the sea; that being had suddenly foundered. What was left him to do? Rise every morning; go to sleep every night. Never again to wait the arrival of the Durande; to see her get under way, or steam again into port. He had crowned the work of his life by a master-piece: won by his zeal a new step in civilization. The step was lost: the masterpiece destroyed. To live a few empty years more! of what avail? At his age men do not begin life over again. Besides, ruin was before him. Poor old man!

Déruchette, sitting near him on a chair and crying, held one of Mess Lethierry's hands. Her hands were joined: his hand was clenched fast. It was the sign of the difference in their sorrows. In joined hands there is a token of hope, in the clenched fist none.

Mess Lethierry abandoned his arm to her, and she did with it what she pleased. He was passive. Struck down by a thunderbolt, he had scarcely any life left.

The various groups were whispering together. They exchanged the information they had gathered. This was the substance of their story.

The Durande had been wrecked the day previous in the fog on the Douvres, about an hour before sunset. With the exception of Captain Clubin, who would not leave his ship, the crew and passengers had all escaped in the boat. A squall springing up as the fog cleared, wrecked them for the second time, and had carried them out to sea beyond Guernsey. In the night they had fortunately met with the Cashmere, which had taken them aboard and brought them to Saint Peter's Port. The accident was due to the drunkenness of the helmsman Tangrouille, who was in prison. Clubin had behaved like a hero.

The pilots, who mustered in force, uttered the name, 'The Douvres', with a sad emphasis. 'A dreary house to stop at,' said one.

A compass and a bundle of registers and books lay on the table; they were the compass and the ship's papers, handed by Clubin to Imbrancam and Tangrouille on the departure of the boat. They were the evidences of the heroic self-denial of that man who had thought of saving these documents in the presence of death itself – an incident full of moral grandeur; an instance of sublime self-abnegation which could never be forgotten.

They were of one mind in their admiration of Clubin; unanimous also in believing him to be saved after all. The Shealtiel cutter had arrived some hours after the Cashmere. It was this vessel which brought the last intelligence. She had spent four-and-twenty hours in the same water as the Durande. She had lain-to in the fog, and tacked about during the squall. The captain of the Shealtiel was present among the company.

He had just finished his narrative to Lethierry as Gilliatt entered. It was a true one. Towards morning, the storm having abated, and the wind moderating, the captain of the Shealtiel heard the lowing of oxen. This sound in the midst of the ocean had startled him. He steered in its direction, and saw the Durande among the Douvres. The sea had sufficiently subsided for him to approach. He hailed the wreck; the bellowing of the cattle was the only reply. He was confident that there was no one on board the Durande. The wreck held together well, and in spite of the squall, Clubin could have spent the night on board. He was not there, however; so he must have been taken off. It was certain that several vessels, from Granville and Saint Malo, must, after lying-to in the fog on the preceding evening, have passed near the rocks. One of these must have taken Clubin aboard. The boat of the Durande was full when it left the unlucky vessel; and was certain to encounter great risks; another man aboard would have overloaded it, and perhaps caused it to sink; these circumstances no doubt weighed with Clubin in deciding to stay on the wreck. His duty, however, once fulfilled, and a vessel at hand, Clubin surely would not have hesitated to avail himself of its aid. A hero is not necessarily a fool. The idea of suicide was absurd in connection with a man of Clubin's spotless character. The culprit was Tangrouille, not Clubin. The captain of the *Shealtiel* was evidently right, and everybody expected Clubin to reappear shortly. There was a project on foot to give him a triumphant reception.

Two things appeared clear from the narrative of the captain: Clubin was saved, the Durande was lost.

As regarded the Durande, there was nothing but to accept the fact; the catastrophe was without remedy. The captain of the *Shealtiel* had witnessed the end of the wreck. The sharp rock on which the vessel had been, as it were, impaled, had held her fast during the night, and resisted the violence of the tempest as if reluctant to part with its prey: but in the morning, at the moment when the captain of the *Shealtiel* had convinced himself that there was no life to be saved, and was about to depart, one of the last angry blows of the tempest had struck her. A wave lifted her violently from her place and with the speed and directness of an arrow from a bow had hurled her against the two Douvres Rocks. 'A frightful crash was heard,' said the captain. The vessel, lifted by the wave, had plunged between the two rocks to her midship frame. She had stuck fast again; but more firmly fixed than on the submarine rocks. She would remain there suspended, and exposed to the violence of the wind and waves.

The Durande, according to the statements of the crew of the Shealtiel, was already in part broken up. She would have foundered during the night, if not kept up by the rocks. The captain of the Shealtiel had watched her a long time with his telescope. He gave, with nautical precision, the details of her disaster. She had broken her back; the sea now must destroy her piecemeal. In a few days no part of her would remain.

It appeared that the engine was scarcely injured by all these ravages – a remarkable fact, and one which proved its excellence. The captain of the *Shealtiel* thought he could say that the crank had received no serious injury. The masts had given way, but the funnel had resisted everything. Only the iron guards of the captain's gangway were twisted; the paddle boxes were damaged, the frames were bruised, but the paddles had not a single float missing. The machinery was perfect. Such was the conviction of the captain of the *Shealtiel*. Imbrancam, the engineer, who was among the crowd, said the same. The negro, was proud of his engine. He lifted his arms, opened the ten fingers of his swarthy hands, and said to Lethierry, as he stood there silent, 'Master, the machinery is still alive!'

Clubin's safety seeming certain, and the hull of the Durande being already lost, the engine became the topic of interest among the crowd. They took an interest in it. They felt delight in praising it. 'That's what I call well-built,' said a French sailor. 'Something like a good one,' cried a Guernsey fisherman. 'It must have some good stuff in it,' said the captain of the *Shealtiel*, 'to come out of that affair like that.'

Thus the machinery of the Durande became the sole object of their thoughts. Opinions waxed warm for and against. It had enemies and it had friends. More than one who owned a cutter, and who wished to get a part of the business of the Durande, was glad to hear that the Douvres had disposed of her. The discussion grew noisy, though the conversation was a little restrained; and now and then there was a lowering of voices out of respect to Lethierry's death-like silence.

The result of the colloquy was as follows:

Her engines were the vital part of the vessel. To save the Durande was impossible; but the machinery might still be rescued. The engines were unique. To build others similar, would require money; but to find the engineer would have been still more difficult. It was remembered that the constructor of the machinery was dead. It had cost forty thousand francs. No one would again risk such a sum of money upon such a chance: besides, it was now seen that steamboats could be lost like any other vessel. The loss of the Durande destroyed the renown of all her previous success. Still, it was sad to think that at that very moment this valuable machinery was entire and in sound condition, and that in five or six days it would probably be destroyed, like the ship itself. As long as it existed, it might almost be said that there was no shipwreck. The loss of the engines was alone irreparable. To save the machinery would almost counterbalance the disaster.

Save the machinery! It was easy to talk of it; but who would do it? Was it possible? To propose and to execute are two different things. Now if ever a dream had appeared impracticable, it was that of saving the engines then wedged between the Douvres. To think of sending a ship and a crew to work at those rocks was ridiculous. It could not be thought of. It was the season of heavy seas. In the first gale the chains of the anchors would snap upon the submarine rocks, and the vessel would go to pieces. That would only add a second shipwreck to the first. On the dreary narrow summit where legend spoke of the shipwrecked mariner as having died of hunger, there was hardly room for one man. To save the engines, therefore, it would be necessary for a man to go to the Douvres, to be alone in that sea, alone in that wild spot, alone at five leagues from the land, alone for weeks, alone in the face of dangers foreseen and unforeseen – without supplies, in the face of hunger and nakedness, without aid in time of distress, without sign of human life around him save the whitened bones of the unhappy wretch who had perished there in his misery, with no companion but death. And how would it be possible to extricate the machinery? It would require not only a sailor, but an engineer; and for what labours must he not be ready. The man who would attempt such a task must be more than a hero. He must be mad; for in certain enterprises, where superhuman power appears necessary, there is a sort of madness far more potent than courage. And besides, would it not be a folly to sacrifice oneself for a mass of rusty iron. No: nobody would go to the Douvres on such business. The engine must be left like the ship. The engineer for such a task would not be forthcoming. Where, indeed, should such a man be looked for?

The captain of the *Shealtiel*, who had been a pilot, expressed the view of all by saying aloud:

'No; it is all over. The man does not live who could go and save the engines of the Durande.'

'My reason for not going,' said Imbrancam, 'is because nobody can do it.'

The captain of the *Shealtiel* shook his head with that movement which expresses a conviction of impossibility.

'If one did exist ——' continued the captain.

Déruchette turned her head hastily, and interrupted him.

'I would marry him,' she said, innocently.

There was a silence.

A man came forward out of the crowd, and standing in front of her, white and anxious, asked:

'You would be willing to marry him, Miss Déruchette?'

It was Gilliatt.

All eyes were turned upon him. Mess Lethierry had at that moment stood upright, and looked around him. His eyes shone with a wild light.

He took off his cap, and flung it on the ground: then looked solemnly before him, and without paying attention to any of those present, he said:

'Déruchette should be his wife. I swear it by God's name.'

CHAPTER II

GREAT ASTONISHMENT ON THE WESTERN COAST

The full moon rose at ten on the next night; but however fine the night, however favourable the wind and sea, no fisherman thought of going out that evening from any port or harbour in Guernsey; and the reason for it was simple. A cock had crowed at mid-day.

When the cock crows at that hour, fishing is at an end.

But at dusk that evening, a fisherman returning to Omptolle, met with a strange adventure. On the height above Houmet Paradis, stands to the left the beacon of the Plattes Tougères, representing a tub reversed; and to the right, the beacon of Saint Sampson, representing a man's face. Between these, the fisherman thought he perceived a third beacon. What could be the meaning of this? When had a third beacon been erected there? What did it indicate? The beacon replied immediately to these interrogations. It moved. It was a mast. The wonder of the fisherman did not grow less. A beacon would have been strange; a mast was more so; it could be no fishing-boat. When everybody was returning, a boat was going out. Who was it? and what was his business?

After ten minutes the vessel came within a short distance of the fisherman. He could not recognize it. He heard the sound of oars: there were evidently only two. Therefore, there was probably only one man on board. The wind was northerly, and the man was evidently paddling along in order to catch the breeze of Point Fontenelle. There he would no doubt use his sails. If so, he intended to double the Ancresse and Mount Crevel. What could the explanation of this be?

The vessel passed on, the fisherman reached home. On that same night, at different hours, and in different parts, various persons scattered and isolated on the western coast of Guernsey, noticed certain things.

As the fisherman was mooring his bark, a carter of seaweed about half-a-mile off, driving his horses along the solitary road from the Clôtures near the Druid stones, saw out at sea, in a part, but little frequented, because it requires much knowledge of the waters, a sail. He paid no attention to this, not being a seaman.

About half-an-hour after the carter had seen this, a plasterer returning from the town, and passing round Pelée Pool, found himself suddenly opposite a vessel sailing among the rocks of the Quenon, the Rousse de Mer, and the Gripe de Rousse. It was a dark night, but the sky was light over the sea, and he could see a great distance in all directions. Except this vessel, no sail was visible.

A little lower, a gatherer of cray-fish, on the beach which separates Port Soif from the Port Enfer, was puzzled by the movement of a vessel between the Boue Corneille and the Moubrette. The man on board must have been a skilful sailor, and in haste to arrive somewhere, to risk his boat in such a spot.

Eight o'clock was striking at the Catel, when the tavern-keeper at Cobo Bay saw with surprise a sail out beyond the Boue du Jardin and the Grunettes, and near the Susanne and the Western Grunes.

Not far from Cobo Bay, and upon the solitary point of the Houmet of Vason Bay, two lovers were lingering, hesitating before saying good-night. The young woman addressed the young man saying, 'I am not going because I don't care to stop with you: I've a great deal to do.' Their parting kiss was interrupted by a boat which sailed near them, in the direction of the Messellettes.

Monsieur le Peyre des Norgiots, an inhabitant of Cotillon Pipet, was busied about nine in the evening in examining a hole made by some boys in the hedge of his property. Even while lamenting the amount of damage done, he could not help observing a fishing-boat rashly making its way round the Crocq Point at that late hour.

On the morrow of a tempest, when there is always a disturbed sea, that route was very unsafe. It was rash to choose it, unless the steersman had a sound knowledge of all the channels.

At half-past nine, a trawler carrying home his net stopped to observe between Colombelle and the Soufleresse something which appeared to be a boat. It was in a dangerous position. Sudden and dangerous gusts of wind are very common in that spot. The *Soufleresse*, or Blower, derives it name from the sudden gusts of wind which it seems to direct upon any vessels, which by chance come there.

At the moment when the moon was rising, the tide then being high and the sea quiet, in the little strait of Li-Hou, the solitary keeper of the island of Li-Hou was much alarmed. A long dark object slowly passed between the moon and himself. This sombre form, high and narrow, resembled a winding-sheet spread out and in motion. It glided along the line of the top of the wall formed by the ridges of rock. The keeper believed that he saw the Black Lady.

The White Lady haunts the Tau de Pez d'Amont; the Grey Lady, the Tau de Pez d'Aval; the Red Lady, the Silleuse, to the north of the Marquis Bank; and the Black Lady, the Grand Etacré, to the west of Li-Houmet. At night, in the moonlight, these ladies walk abroad, and sometimes meet.

That dark form might perhaps be a sail. The long masses of rocks on which she seemed to be walking, might conceal the hull of a boat sailing behind them, and allow her sail only to be visible. But as the keeper said, 'What boat would dare, at that hour, to venture herself between Li-Hou and the Pécheresses, and the Anguillières and Lérée Point? And for what object?' So it seemed to him quite certain that it was the Black Lady.

As the moon was passing the clock-tower of St Peter in the Wood, the serjeant at Castle Rocquaine, while in the act of raising the drawbridge of the castle, saw at the end of the bay beyond the Haute Canée, but nearer than the Sambule, a sailing-vessel which seemed to be dropping down from north to south.

On the southern coast of Guernsey behind Pleinmont, in the curve of a bay composed of precipices and rocky walls rising in peaks from the sea, there is a landing place called 'The Port on the Fourth Floor.' This landing-place, then called the Moie, is a rocky plateau formed partly by nature, partly by art, raised about forty feet above the waves and communicating with the water by two beams laid parallel and in the form of an inclined plane. The fishing vessels are hoisted up from the sea by chains and pulleys, and are lowered again in the same way along these beams, which resemble two rails. For the fishermen there is a ladder. The port was at that time much frequented by smugglers. Being difficult of access, it was well adapted for their business.

Towards eleven o'clock, some smugglers – perhaps those upon whose aid Clubin had reckoned – stood with their bales on the summit of this platform of the Moie. A smuggler is necessarily always on the look-out, it is a part of his business to watch. They wondered to perceive a sail make its appearance beyond the outline of Cape Pleinmont. It was moonlight. The smugglers watched the sail narrowly, fearing that it might be some revenue cutter about to lie in ambush behind the Great Hanway. But the sail passed the Hanways, sailed on to the north-west of the Boue Blondel, and disappeared in the white mists of the horizon far out on the sea.

'Where the devil can that boat be bound to?' asked the smuggler.

That evening, just after sunset, some one had knocked at the door of the house of the Bû de la Rue. It was a boy who wore brown clothes and yellow stockings, which indicated that he was a little parish clerk. An old fisherwoman, prowling about the shore with a lantern, called to the boy, and this conversation took place between the fisherwoman and the boy, before the entrance:

'What d'ye want, my boy?'

'The man who lives here.'

'He's not at home.'

'Do you know where he is?'

'No, I don't.'

'Has he gone away?'

'I don't know.'

'I've come from the new rector, the Reverend Ebenezer Caudray, who has sent me.'

'I can't say where he is.'

'The rector told me to ask if the man who lives here would be home in the morning.'

'I can't tell.'

CHAPTER III

A PASSAGE FROM THE BIBLE

For the next twenty-four hours, Mess Lethierry neither slept, ate, nor drank. He kissed Déruchette, asked after Clubin, of whom there was no news, signed a document certifying that he had no intention of prosecuting any one, and thus set Tangrouille free.

All the morning of the next day he remained half supporting himself on the table of the office of the Durande, neither standing nor sitting: answering softly when any one spoke to him. Curiosity being satisfied, the Bravées had become deserted. There is much curiosity as a rule mixed with the hurry of condolence. The door was closed, and the old man was again alone with Déruchette. The strange light that had shone in Lethierry's eyes had vanished. The sad look which filled them on the first news of the wreck had reappeared.

Déruchette, anxious on his account, had, advised by Grace

and Douce, quietly laid beside him a pair of stockings, which he had been knitting when the evil news had been brought.

He smiled sadly, and said:

'They must think me childish.'

After a silence of a quarter of an hour, he added:

'These things are all very well when you are not in trouble.'

Déruchette carried off the stockings, and at the same time removed also the compass and ship's papers which Lethierry had been brooding over.

In the afternoon, a little before tea-time, the door opened and there entered two strangers, attired in black. One was old, the other young. The latter has already been spoken of in our story.

The two men had each a grave air; but their gravity varied. The old man possessed what might be called state gravity; the gravity of the young man was in his nature. Habit causes the one; thought the other. They were, as their dress indicated, two clergymen, belonging to the Established Church.

The first thing in the appearance of the younger man which might have struck the observer was that his gravity, though conspicuous in the expression of his features, and evidently springing from the mind, was not indicated by his person. Gravity is not inconsistent with passion, which it exalts by purifying it; but the idea of gravity could with difficulty be associated with an exterior remarkable above all for personal beauty. He must have been at least four-and-twenty, but he seemed scarcely more than eighteen. He possessed those gifts at once in harmony with, and in opposition to, each other. A soul which seemed created for exalted passion, and a body created for love. He was fair, slim, and elegant in his severe attire, and he had the cheeks of a young girl, and delicate hands. His movements were natural and lively, though subdued. Everything about him was elegant, almost voluptuous. The beauty of his expression served to correct this excess of personal attraction. His open smile, which showed his teeth, white as those of a child, had something in it pensive, even devotional. He had the gracefulness of a page, combined with the dignity of a bishop. His hair, fair and golden as to be almost effeminate, clustered over his white forehead, which was high and well-shaped. A slight double line between the eyebrows awakened associations with studious thought. Those who saw him felt themselves in the presence of one of those natures, benevolent, and pure, whose progress is in inverse sense with that of vulgar minds; natures whom illusion renders wise, and whom experience makes enthusiasts.

His older companion was Doctor Jacquemin Hérode. Doctor Jacquemin Hérode belonged to the High Church; a party whose system is a sort of popery without a pope. The Church of England was at that epoch labouring with the tendencies which have since become strengthened and condensed in the form of Puseyism. Doctor Jacquemin Hérode belonged to that shade of Anglicanism which is almost a variety of the Church of Rome. He was haughty, precise, stiff, and commanding. His inner sight scarcely penetrated outwardly. He possessed the letter in the place of the spirit. His manner was arrogant; his presence imposing. He had less the appearance of a 'Reverend', than of a *Monsignore*. His frock-coat was cut somewhat in the fashion of a cassock. His true centre would have been Rome. He was a born Prelate of the Antechamber. He seemed to have been created expressly to fill a part in the Papal Court, to walk behind the Pontifical litter, with all the Court of Rome in *abitto paonazzo*. The accident of his English birth and his theological education, directed more towards the Old than the New Testament, had deprived him of that destiny. All his splendours were comprised in his preferments as Rector of Saint Peter's Port, Dean of the Island of Guernsey, and Surrogate of the Bishop of Winchester. These were, undoubtedly, not without their glories. These glories did not prevent M. Jacquemin Hérode being, on the whole, a worthy man.

He had the true air of erudition; a learned contraction of the eyes; bristling nostrils; teeth which showed themselves at all times; a thin upper lip and a thick lower one. He was the possessor of several learned degrees, a valuable prebend, titled friends, the confidence of the bishop, and a Bible which he carried always in his pocket.

Mess Lethierry was so absorbed that the entrance of the two clergymen produced no effect upon him, other than a slight movement of the eyebrows.

M. Jacquemin Hérode advanced, bowed, alluded in a few dignified words to his recent promotion, and mentioned that he came according to custom to introduce among the inhabitants, and to Mess Lethierry in particular, his successor in the parish, the new Rector of Saint Sampson, the Revd Ebenezer Caudray, henceforth the pastor of Mess Lethierry.

Déruchette rose.

The young clergyman, who was the Revd Ebenezer, saluted her.

Mess Lethierry looked at Monsieur Ebenezer Caudray, and muttered, 'A poor sailor.'

Grace placed chairs, and the visitors seated themselves.

Doctor Hérode commenced a discourse. It had reached his ears that a great misfortune had befallen his host. He came as Lethierry's pastor to condole and advise. This shipwreck was unfortunate, but not without compensations. Let us examine our own hearts. Are we not puffed up with prosperity? Troubles must be submitted to cheerfully. The ways of Providence are mysterious. Mess Lethierry was ruined. But riches were a danger. You may have false friends; poverty will reveal them, and leave you alone. The Durande brought in a revenue of one thousand pounds per annum. Let us not put our faith in gold, but bow the head to losses and neglect. Isolation is full of good. Let us not rebel against the decrees of Providence. The holy man Job, after his misery, had put faith in riches. Who can say that the loss of the Durande may not have advantages of a temporal kind. He, for instance, Doctor Jacquemin Hérode had invested some money in an excellent enterprise at Sheffield. If Mess Lethierry, with such wealth as might still remain to him, should choose to embark in the same affair, he might transfer his capital to that town. It was a large manufactory of arms for the supply of the Czar, now engaged in subduing insurrection in Poland. There was a fair prospect of gaining three hundred per cent profit.

The word "Czar" appeared to awaken Lethierry. He interrupted Dr Hérode.

'I have nothing to do with the Czar.'

The Reverend Jacquemin Hérode replied:

'Mess Lethierry, princes are recognized by God. It is written, "Render unto Caesar the things which are Caesar's." The Czar is Caesar.'

Lethierry relapsed into his reverie and muttered:

'Caesar? Who is Caesar? I don't know.'

The Revd Jacquemin Hérode continued his exhortations. He did not urge the question of Sheffield.

To contemn a Caesar was republicanism. He could understand a man being a republican. In that case he could turn his thoughts towards a republic. Mess Lethierry might repair his fortune in the United States, better even than in England. Should he desire to invest what remained to him at great profit he could take shares in the great company for developing the resources of Texas, which owned more than twenty thousand slaves.

'I have nothing to do with slavery,' said Lethierry.

'Slavery,' replied the Reverend Hérode, 'is an institution recognized by Holy Writ. It is written, "If a man smite his slave, he shall not be punished, for he is his money."'

Grace and Douce at the door of the room listened in a sort of awe to the words of the Reverend Doctor.

The Doctor continued. He was, all things considered, as we have said, a worthy man; and whatever his differences, personal or connected with caste, with Mess Lethierry, he had come in all sincerity to offer him that spiritual and even temporal aid which he, Doctor Jacquemin Hérode, dispensed.

If Mess Lethierry's fortune had shrunk to that point that he was unable to take a part in any speculation, Russian or American, why should he not obtain some government appointment? There were many respectable places open to him, and the reverend gentleman was ready to recommend him. The office of Deputy-Vicomte was vacant. Mess Lethierry was popular and respected, and the Reverend Jacquemin Hérode would secure this post for Mess Lethierry. The Deputy-Vicomte is an important officer. He is present as the representative of the Sovereign at the Sessions, at the debates of the *Cohue*, and at executions of justice.

Lethierry fixed his gaze upon the Doctor.

'I detest hanging,' said he.

Doctor Hérode, who up to now had uttered his words with the same intonation, had now a fit of severity; his tone became slightly changed.

'Mess Lethierry, the punishment of death is a divine ordinance. God has placed the sword in the hands of rulers. It is written, "An eye for an eye, a tooth for a tooth."'

The Reverend Ebenezer drew his chair nearer to the Reverend Doctor and said, so as only to be heard by him:

'What this man says, is dictated to him.'

'By whom? By what?' asked the Reverend Jacquemin Hérode, in the same tone.

The young man replied in a whisper, 'By his conscience.'

The Reverend Jacquemin Hérode felt in his pocket, pulled out a thick little bound volume and said aloud:

'Conscience is here.'

The book was a Bible.

Then Doctor Hérode's tone became gentler. 'His wish was to aid Mess Lethierry, whom he respected. As his pastor, it was his duty to offer counsel. Mess Lethierry, however, was free.'

Mess Lethierry, plunged once more in his overwhelming absorption, listened no longer. Déruchette, seated near him, and pensive, also did not lift her eyes, and by her silent presence added to the embarrassment of a conversation far from animated. A witness who utters no word is an indefinable weight. Doctor Hérode, however, did not appear to notice it.

Lethierry no longer replying, Doctor Hérode expatiated freely. Counsel is from man; inspiration is from God. In the counsels of the priests there is inspiration. It is good to accept, dangerous to refuse them. Sochoh was seized by eleven devils for scorning the exhortations of Nathaniel. Tiburianus was afflicted with a leprosy for having driven from his house the Apostle Andrew. Aholibamah, who is also called Judith, obeyed the Councils, Reuben and Peniel listened to the counsels from on high, as their names indeed indicate. Reuben signifes son of the vision; and Peniel, the face of God.

Mess Lethierry smote the table with his clenched hand.

'Parbleu!' he cried; 'I was to blame.'

'What do you mean?' asked M. Jacquemin Hérode.

'I say that I was to blame.'

'To blame! Why?'

'Because I let the Durande return on a Friday.'

M Jacquemin Hérode whispered in Caudray's ear:

'This man is superstitious.'

He continued, raising his voice, and in a tone of command.

'Mess Lethierry, it is childish to fear Fridays. You ought not to credit fables. Friday is a day like any other. It is very often propitious. It was on a Friday that Henry the Seventh gave his commission to John Cabot; the Pilgrims of the *Mayflower* landed on a Friday. Christopher Columbus discovered America on Friday, the 12th of October, 1492.'

Having delivered himself thus, he rose.

Caudray, whom he had brought with him, rose at the same moment.

Grace and Douce, seeing that the clergymen were about to leave, opened the folding-doors.

Mess Lethierry saw and heard nothing.

M Jacquemin Hérode said, aside to M. Caudray:

'He does not even recognize us. This is not grief; it is vacancy. He must have lost his senses.'

He took his Bible, however, from the table, and held it between his hands outstretched, as one holds a bird fearing that it may fly away. This attitude awakened among the persons present a certain degree of attention. Grace and Douce listened eagerly.

His voice assumed all the solemnity of which it was capable.

'Mess Lethierry,' he began, 'let us not part without reading a page of the Sacred Book. It is from books that wise men derive consolation in trouble. The profane have their oracles; but believers have their ready resource in the Bible. The first book which comes to hand, opened by chance, may afford counsel; but the Bible, opened at any page, yields a revelation. It is, above all, a boon to the afflicted. Yes, Holy Scripture is a never-failing balm for their wounds. In affliction it is good to consult its sacred pages – to open without even choosing the place, and to read with faith the passage we find. What man does not choose is chosen by God. He knoweth best what suiteth us. Whatever the page, it will infallibly enlighten. Let us seek, then, no other light; but hold fast to His. It is a message from on high. In the text which is evoked with confidence and reverence, often do we find a mysterious significance in our present troubles. Let us listen, then, and obey. Mess Lethierry, you are in affliction, but I hold here the book of comfort. You are sick at heart, but I have here the book of spiritual health.'

The Reverend Jacquemin Hérode touched the spring of the clasp, and let his finger slip between the leaves. Then he placed his hand a moment upon the open volume, collected his thoughts, and, raising his eyes impressively, read with a loud voice.

The passage which he had lighted on was as follows:

'And Isaac went out to meditate in the field at the eventide, and he lifted up his eyes and saw and beheld the camels were coming.

'And Rebekah lifted up her eyes, and when she saw Isaac she lighted off the camel.

'For she had said unto the servant, What man is this that walketh in the field to meet us?

'And Isaac brought her into his mother Sarah's tent, and took Rebekah, and she became his wife, and he loved her; and Isaac was comforted after his mother's death.'

Caudray and Déruchette looked at one another.

SECOND PART

BOOK I

EVIL-MINDED GILLIATT

CHAPTER I

A PLACE WHICH ONE FINDS DIFFICULT TO REACH, AND STILL MORE DIFFICULT TO LEAVE

That which had been seen at so many points on the Guernsey coast on the previous evening, was the old Dutch sloop. Gilliatt had chosen the channel along the coast among the rocks. It was the most dangerous way, but the most direct. To take the shortest route was his only thought. Shipwrecks will not wait; the sea is a pressing creditor; an hour's delay may be irreparable. His anxiety was to go at once to save the endangered machinery.

One of his objects in leaving Guernsey was to avoid notice. He set out like one escaping from justice, and appeared anxious to hide from human eyes. He shunned the eastern coast, as if he did not wish to pass in sight of Saint Sampson and Saint Peter's Port, and glided silently along the opposite coast, which is almost uninhabited. Among the breakers, it was necessary to use the oars; but Gilliatt managed them on scientific principles; taking the water quietly, and dropping it with exact regularity, he was able to proceed in the darkness with but little noise and as rapidly as possible. So quiet were his movements, that he might have seemed to be occupied upon some evil errand.

In fact, though embarking desperately in an enterprise which might well be deemed impossible, and hazarding his life with nearly every chance against him, he dreaded nothing but the appearance of some rival in the work which he had undertaken.

When day broke, those invisible eyes which look down upon the world from boundless space might have beheld, at one of the most dangerous and solitary spots at sea, two objects, the distance between which was gradually decreasing, as the one approached the other. One, almost imperceptible in the wide movement of the waters, was a sailing boat. In it was a man. It was the sloop. The other, black, immovable, colossal, rose above the waves, a singular form. Two tall pillars rising from the sea bore aloft a sort of cross-beam which resembled a bridge between them. This bridge, of so strange a shape that it was impossible to imagine what it was from a distance, touched both the pillars. It resembled a vast portal. Of what use could such an erection be in that open plain, the sea, which stretched around it far and wide? It might have been imagined to be a Titanic Cromlech, planted in mid-ocean, and built by hands accustomed to proportion their labours to the great deep. Its wild outline stood out well-defined against the clear sky.

The morning light grew stronger in the east; the whiteness in the horizon deepened the shadow on the sea. In the opposite sky the moon was sinking.

The two perpendicular forms were the Douvres. The huge mass suspended between them, was the wreck of the Durande.

The rock, thus holding fast its prey, was terrible to behold. Inanimate things look at times as if endowed with a sombre and hostile spirit towards man. There was menace in the attitude of the rocks. They seemed to be waiting their time.

Nothing could be more suggestive of haughtiness and arrogance than their appearance: the conquered vessel; the triumphant abyss. The two rocks, still streaming with the tempest of the previous day, were like two wrestlers sweating from a recent struggle. The wind had fallen; the sea rippled gently; here and there the presence of breakers might be detected in the graceful streaks of foam upon the surface of the waters. All round was level except the Douvres, rising erect, like two ebon pillars. Up to a certain height they were bearded with seaweed; above this their steep sides glittered like shining armour. They seemed ready to commence the strife again. The spectator felt that they were implanted deep in mountains whose summits were beneath the waves.

Ordinarily the sea conceals her crimes in privacy. Her unfathomable deeps keep silence. She wraps herself in a mystery which rarely consents to reveal its secrets. We know her fierce nature, but who can tell the extent of her dark deeds? She is both open and secret; she hides carefully, and does not divulge her actions; destroys a vessel, and, covering it with her waves, engulfs it as if conscious of her guilt. Among her sins is hypocrisy. She steals and slays, hides her booty, puts on an air of unconsciousness, and smiles.

Here, however, was nothing of the kind. The Douvres, lifting above the level of the waters the shattered hull of the Durande, had an air of boasting. The imagination might have pictured them as two gigantic arms, stretched upwards from the gulf, and revealing to the tempest the dead body of the ship. Their aspect was like that of a murderer boasting of his crimes.

The solemnity of the hour added something to the impression of the scene. There is a solemn grandeur in the dawn, as of the border-land between the region of consciousness and the world of dreams. There is something spectral in that confused transition time. The immense form of the two Douvres, like a capital H, the Durande being its cross-stroke, stood up against the horizon in all their majesty.

Gilliatt was dressed in his seaman's clothes: a Guernsey shirt, woollen stockings, thick shoes, a homespun jacket, thick trousers, with pockets, and a cap of red worsted, of a kind then much in vogue among sailors.

He recognized the Douvres, and steered towards them.

The situation of the Durande was the very contrary of that of a vessel sunk to the bottom: she was a vessel suspended in mid-air.

No problem more strange ever came before a salvor.

It was broad daylight when Gilliatt arrived at the rock.

As we have already said, there was but little sea. The slight agitation of the water was almost entirely due to its confinement among the rocks. Every passage, small or large, is subject to this chopping movement. The inside of a channel is always more or less white with foam. Gilliatt did not approach the Douvres without using every precaution. He cast the sounding-lead many times.

He had a cargo to disembark. Accustomed to long absences, he had at home a number of necessaries always ready. He had brought a sack of biscuits, another of rye-meal, a basket of salt fish and smoked beef, a large can of fresh-water; a Norwegian chest painted with flowers, containing several coarse woollen shirts, his tarpaulin and his waterproof overalls, and a sheep-skin which he threw at night over his clothes. On leaving home he had put all these things into the barge, with the addition of a large loaf. In his haste he had brought no other tools but his huge forge-hammer, his chopper and hatchet, and a knotted rope. Furnished with a grappling-iron and with a ladder of that sort, the steepest rocks became accessible, and a good sailor will find it possible to scale the rudest escarpment. In the island of Sark the visitor may see what the fishermen of the Havre Gosselin can do with the aid of a knotted cord.

His nets and fishing apparatus were in the barge. He had placed them there by habit; for he intended, if his enterprise continued, to remain for some time in an archipelago of rocks and breakers, where fishing nets and tackle are of little use.

At the time when Gilliatt was skirting the great rock the sea was ebbing; a circumstance favourable to his purpose. The departing tide laid bare, at the foot of the smaller Douvre, one or two table-rocks, horizontal, or only slightly inclined, and bearing a resemblance to boards supported by crows. These table-rocks, sometimes narrow, sometimes broad, standing at unequal distances along the side of the great perpendicular column, were continued in the form of a thin cornice up to a spot just beneath the Durande, the hull of which stood protruding between the two rocks. The wreck was held firm as in a vice.

This series of platforms was convenient for surveying the position of affairs. It was convenient also for disembarking the contents of the sloop provisionally; but it was necessary to make haste, for it was only bare for a short time. When the tide should rise the table-rock would be again submerged.

It was to these table-rocks, some level, some slanting, that Gilliatt pushed in and brought the barge. A tangled mass of wet and slimy sea-weed covered them, rendered more slippery here and there by their slanting surfaces.

Gilliatt pulled off his shoes and sprang bare-footed on to the slippery weeds, and moored the sloop to a projecting rock.

Then he advanced as far as he could along the granite cornice, reached the rock immediately under the wreck, looked up, and examined it.

The Durande was suspended, and as it were fixed in between the two rocks, at about twenty feet above the water. It must have been a very heavy sea which had hurled her there.

But the Douvres held only a portion of the Durande. The vessel snatched from the waves had been, as it were, torn from the waters by the hurricane. A whirlwind had wrenched it against the counteracting force of the rolling waves, and the vessel thus turned in contrary directions by the two claws of the tempest had broken in twain. The after-part, with the engine and the paddles, lifted out of the foam and driven by the violence of the cyclone into the defile of the Douvres, had plunged in up to her midship beam and there remained. The blow had been well given. To force it in this manner between the two rocks, the storm had struck it as with a gigantic sledge hammer. The forecastle carried away and rolled down by the sea, had gone to pieces among the breakers.

The hold had broken in, and the carcasses of the drowned cattle had been carried away by the sea.

A large portion of the forward side and bulwarks still hung to the riders by the larboard paddle-box, and by some shattered braces easy to strike off with the blow of a hatchet.

Here and there, among beams, planks, rags of canvas, fragments of chains, and other wreckage were seen lying about among the rugged fragments of shattered rock. Gilliatt surveyed the Durande attentively. The keel formed a roof over his head.

A calm sky stretched far and wide over the waters scarcely crisped with a breath of air. The sun rose in his glory in the midst of the vast azure circle.

From time to time a drop of water dripped from the hull and fell into the sea.

CHAPTER II

GILLIATT SURVEYS THE WRECK

Differing in height the Douvres differed also in shape.

Upon the Little Douvre, which was curved and pointed, long veins of reddish-coloured rock, of a comparatively soft kind, branched out and divided the interior of the granite. At the edges of these red dykes were fractures, which aided favourably to climbing. One of these fractures, situated a little above the wreck, had been so worn and scooped out by the action of the waves, that it had become a sort of niche, in which it would have been quite possible to fix a statue. The granite of the Little Douvre was rounded at the surface, and, to the feel was soft like touchstone; but this detracted nothing from its durability. The Little Douvre ended in a point like a horn. The Great Douvre, polished, glossy, perpendicular, and looking as if shaped by the builder's square, was in one piece, and appeared as if made of black ivory. Not a flaw, not a break in its smooth surface. The escarpment looked inhospitable. A convict could not have used it for escape, nor would a bird have found on it a place for a nest. On its summit was a horizontal surface as upon the Man-Rock; but that summit was quite inaccessible.

It was feasible to scale the Little Douvre, but not to remain on its summit; it would have been possible to remain on the summit of the Great Douvre, but it could not possibly be scaled.

Gilliatt, having hurriedly surveyed the situation, returned to the sloop, landed its cargo upon the largest of the horizontal cornice rocks, made of the whole a kind of bale, which he rolled up in a tarpaulin, fitted a sling rope to it with a hoisting block, pushed the package into a corner of the rocks where the waves could not reach it, and then clutching the Little Douvre with his hands, and holding on with his bare feet, he clambered from projection to projection, until he was high up in the air and on a level with the wreck. Then having reached the height of the paddles, he sprang upon the poop.

The interior of the wreck presented a sad sight.

Traces of a great struggle were visible on all sides. There were plainly to be seen the frightful ravages of the sea and wind.

Nothing is more like the victim of a cruel outrage than a wrecked ship outraged and stripped bare by those terrible accomplices, storm, thunder, rain, waves, and breakers.

Standing upon the dismantled deck, it was natural to dream of the presence of something like a mad stamping of the spirits of the storm. Everywhere were marks of their rage. The strange contortions of certain parts of the iron-work bore witness to the wild force of the winds. The between-decks were like the cell of a madman, in which everything has been destroyed.

No wild beast can equal the sea in mangling its prey. The waves are full of talons. The wind bites, the billows devour, the waves are like ravening jaws. The ocean smites like a lion with its heavy paw, seizing and dismembering at one and the same moment.

The ruin conspicuous in the Durande presented the peculiarity of being detailed and minute. Much of it seemed done on purpose. The beholder was tempted to exclaim, 'What shameful mischief!' The ripping of the planking was edged here and there artistically. This peculiarity is common with the ravages of the cyclone. To chip and tear away is the caprice of the great devastator. Its ways are like those of the professional torturer. The disasters which it causes wear a look of ingenious punishments. One might fancy it actuated by the worst passions of man. It refines in cruelty like a savage. While it is exterminating it dissects bone by bone. It torments its victim, avenges itself, and takes delight in its work. It even appears to sink to petty acts of malice.

Cyclones are rare in our latitudes, and for that reason, are the more dangerous, being generally unexpected. A rock in the path of a heavy wind may become the pivot of a storm. It is probable that the squall had thus rotated upon the point of the Douvres, and had turned suddenly into a waterspout on meeting the shock of the rocks, a fact which explained the casting of the vessel so high among them. When the cyclone blows, a vessel is of no more weight in the wind than a stone in a sling. The damage received by the Durande was like the wound of a man cut in two. It was a severed trunk from which issued a mass of *débris* like the entrails of a body. Cordage hung floating and trembling, chains swung clattering; the fibres and nerves of the vessel were bare and exposed. What was not smashed was disjointed.

Fragments of the sheeting resembled currycombs bristling with nails; everything bore the appearance of ruin; a handspike had become nothing but a piece of iron; a sounding-lead, nothing but a lump of metal; a halliard, an end of rope; a strand of cord, a tangled skein; a bolt-rope, a thread in the hem of a sail. All around was the sad evidence of destruction. Nothing remained that was not destroyed: nothing hung together in the dreadful mass, but all was torn and dislocated. Everything was sinking, and falling away; a rolling mass of planks, iron-work, cables, and beams had been arrested just at the great fracture of the hull, whence the slightest additional shock must have hurled them into the waves. What was left of the powerful frame, formerly so triumphant, was split here and there, revealing through large openings the melancholy gloom of the interior.

The foam from below spat its flakes in contempt upon this shattered and deserted outcast of the sea.

CHAPTER III

THE CONDITION OF THE DURANDE

Gilliatt had not calculated on finding only a portion of the ship remaining. Nothing in the description of the captain of the *Shealtiel* had led him to expect the division of the vessel amid-ships. It was probable that the 'frightful crash' heard by the captain of the *Shealtiel* marked the moment when this had taken place under the shock of a tremendous sea. The captain had, doubtless, worn ship just before this last heavy squall; and what he had taken for a great sea was possibly a water-spout. Later, when he drew nearer to observe the wreck, he had only been able to see the stern – the remainder, that is to say, the large opening where the forepart had given way, having been hidden from him among the masses of rock.

With that exception, the information given by the captain of the Shealtiel was correct. The hull was useless, but the engine remained perfect.

The masts had fallen over the side; but the funnel was not even bent. The heavy iron plating which supported the machinery had kept it together, and in one piece. The planks of the paddle-boxes were disjointed, like the leaves of wooden sunblinds; but through their apertures the paddles could be seen in sound condition. A few floats only were missing. Besides the machinery, the stern capstan had resisted destruction. Its chain was there, and might still be of service. The planking of the deck bent at every point, and was tottering throughout. On the other hand, the trunk of the hull, fixed between the Douvres, held together, as already said, and appeared strong.

There was an appearance of derision in this preservation of the machinery: something which added to the irony of the misfortune. The gloomy malice of the invisible powers of mischief, displays itself at times in such bitter mockeries. The machinery was saved, but its preservation rendered it none the less lost. The ocean seemed to have saved it only to destroy it at leisure. It was like the playing of the cat with a mouse.

Its fate was to remain there and be dismembered day after day. It was to be the toy of the savage pleasures of the sea. It was slowly to dwindle, and, as it were, to melt away. For what could be done? That this vast block of mechanism, massive and delicate, condemned to fixity by its weight, delivered up in that lonely place to the elements, exposed in the grip of the rock to the fury of the wind and wave, could, in spite of the frown of that implacable spot, escape gradual destruction, seemed beyond the dreams of madness.

The Durande was the prisoner of the Douvres. How could she be extricated? How could she be freed from her bondage? The escape of a man is difficult; but what a problem was this – the escape of a huge and ponderous machine.

CHAPTER IV

MAKING A PRELIMINARY SURVEY

And on all sides Gilliatt was pressed by demands upon his labours. The most urgent, however, was to find a safe mooring for the sloop; then a shelter for himself.

The Durande having settled down more on the larboard than on the starboard side, the right paddle-box was higher than the left. Gilliatt climbed the paddle-box on the right. From that position, he was able to study the ground-plan of the group. This survey was the preliminary step of his labours.

The Douvres, as we have already described, were like two high-gable ends, forming the narrow entrance to a straggling alley of small cliffs with perpendicular faces. It is not rare to find in primitive submarine formations these curious kinds of passages, which seem hewn with a hatchet. This defile was tortuous, and was never without water even at low tide. A strong current traversed it at all times from end to end. The sharpness of its turnings was favourable or unfavourable, according to the nature of the prevailing wind; sometimes it broke the swell and caused it to fall; sometimes it exasperated it. The latter effect was the most frequent. An obstacle rouses the anger of the sea, and pushes it to excesses. The foam is the exaggeration of the waves.

The two chains of rocks, leaving between them this sort of street in the sea, formed stages at a lower level than the Douvres, gradually decreasing, until they sunk together at a certain distance beneath the waves.

The wild winds in these confined and tortuous passages between the rocks are subjected to a similar compression, and acquire the same malignant character. The tempest chafes in its sudden imprisonment. Its bulk is still immense, but sharpened and contracted; and it strikes with the massiveness of a huge club and the keenness of an arrow. It pierces even while it strikes down. It is a hurricane contracted, like the draught through the crevice of a door.

There was another such gullet of less height than the gullet of the Douvres, but narrower still, and which formed the eastern

entrance of the defile. It was evident that the double pro-
longation of the ridge of rocks continued the kind of street
under the water as far as the Man-Rock, which stood like a
square citadel at the extremity of the group. At low tide,
indeed, which was the time at which Gilliatt was observing
them, the two rows of sunken rock showed their tips, some
high and dry, and all visible and preserving their parallel
without interruption.

'The Man' formed the boundary, and buttressed on the
eastern side the entire mass of the group, which was protected
on the opposite side by the two Douvres. The whole, from a
bird's-eye view, appeared like a winding chaplet of rocks,
having the Douvres at one end and 'The Man' at the other.
The Douvres, taken together, were but two gigantic shafts of
granite protruding vertically and almost touching one
another, and forming the crest of one of the mountainous
ranges lying beneath the sea. Those immense ridges are not
only found rising out of the unfathomable deep. The surf and
the squall had broken them up and divided them like the teeth
of a saw. Only the tip of the ridge was visible; this was the
group of rocks. The remainder, which the waves concealed,
must have been enormous. The passage in which the storm
had planted the Durande was the way between these two
colossal shafts.

This passage, zigzag in form as the forked lightning, was of
about the same width in every part. The eternal movement of
the ocean had so fashioned it. From one extremity to the other
of the defile, the two parallel granite walls faced each other at a
distance which the midship frame of the Durande measured
exactly. Between the two Douvres, the widening of the Little
Douvre, curved and turned back as it was, had formed a space
for the paddles. In any other part they would have been
shattered to fragments.

The high double façade of rock within the passage was
hideous to the sight. When, in the exploration of the desert of
water which we call the ocean, we come upon the unknown
world of the sea, all is uncouth and shapeless. So much as
Gilliatt could see of the defile from the height of the wreck,
was appalling. In the rocky gorges of the ocean we may often
trace a strange permanent impersonation of shipwreck. The

defile of the Douvres was one of these gorges, and its effect
was exciting to the imagination. The oxydes of the rock
showed on the escarpment here and there in red places, like
marks of clotted blood; it resembled the splashes on the walls
of a slaughter house. The rough marine stones, diversely
tinted – here by the decomposition of metallic amalgams
mingling with the rock, there by the mould of dampness,
manifested in places by purple scales, hideous green blotches,
and ruddy splashes, roused ideas of violence and murder. It
was like the unwashed walls of a chamber which had seen the
scene of a tragedy; or it might have been imagined that men
had been crushed to death there, leaving traces of their fate.
The peaked rocks produced an indescribable impression of
accumulated agonies. Certain spots appeared to be still dripping with the carnage; here the wall was wet, and it looked
impossible to touch it without leaving the fingers bloody. The
blight of massacre seemed everywhere. At the base of the
double parallel escarpment, scattered along the water's edge,
or just below the waves, or in the worn hollows of the rocks,
were huge rounded masses of shingle, some scarlet, others
black or purple, which bore a strange resemblance to internal
organs of the body; they might have been taken for human
lungs, or heart, or liver, scattered and putrifying in that dismal
place. Giants might have been disembowelled there. From top
to bottom of the granite ran long red lines, which might have
been compared to oozings from a funeral bier.

Such aspects are not uncommon in caverns of the sea.

CHAPTER V

A CHAPTER UPON THE SECRET CO-OPERATIONS
OF THE ELEMENTS

Men who, by the unhappy chances of sea-voyages, happen to
be condemned to a temporary dwelling upon a rock in
mid-ocean, find that the form of their inhospitable refuge is by

no means a matter of indifference. There is the pyramidal-shaped rock, a single peak rising from the water; there is the circular rock somewhat resembling a round of great stones; and there is the corridor-rock. The latter is the most alarming of all. It is not only the never-ceasing agony of the waves between its walls, or the noise of the imprisoned sea; there are also certain obscure meteorological characteristics, which appear to belong to his parallelism of two marine rocks. The two straight sides seem a perfect electric battery.

The first result of the peculiar position of these corridor-rocks is an action upon the air and the water. The corridor-rock acts upon the waves and the wind mechanically by its form; galvanically, by the different magnetic action rendered possible by its vertical height, its masses in juxtaposition and contrary to each other. This form of rock attracts to itself all the forces scattered in the winds, and exercises over the tempest a curious power of concentration. Hence there is in the neighbourhood of these breakers a certain accentuation of storms.

It must be remembered that the wind is composite. The wind is believed to be simple; but it is by no means so. Its power is not merely dynamic, it is chemical as well; but this is not all, it is magnetic. Its effects are often inexplicable. The wind is as much electrical as aerial. Certain winds coincide with the *aurora borealis*. The wind blowing from the bank of the Aiguilles rolls the waves one hundred feet high; a fact noted with astonishment by Dumont-d'Urville. The corvette, he says, 'did not know what to obey.'

In the south seas the waters will sometimes become inflated like an outbreak of immense tumours; and at such times the ocean becomes so terrible, that the savages flee to escape the sight of it. The blasts in the north seas are different. They are mingled with sharp points of ice; and their gusts, unfit to breathe, will blow the sledges of the Esquimaux backwards on the snow. Other winds scorch. The simoon of Africa is the typhoon of China and the samiel of India. Simoon, typhoon, and samiel, are believed to be the names of demons. They descend from the heights of the mountains. A storm vitrified the volcano of Toluca. This hot wind, a whirlwind of inky colour, rushing upon red clouds, is alluded to in the Vedas:

'Behold the black god, who comes to steal the red cows.' In all these facts we trace the presence of the electric mystery.

The wind indeed is full of it; so are the waves. The sea, too, is composite in its nature. Under its waves of water which we see, it has its waves of force which are invisible. Its constituents are innumerable. Of all the elements the ocean is the most indivisible and the most profound.

Endeavour to conceive this chaos so enormous that it dwarfs all other things to one level. It is the universal recipient, reservoir of germs of life, and mould of transformations. It amasses and then disperses, it accumulates and then sows, it devours and then creates. It receives all the waste and refuse waters of the earth, and converts them into treasure. It is solid in the iceberg, liquid in the wave, fluid in the estuary. Regarded as matter, it is a mass; regarded as a force, it is an abstraction. It equalizes and unites all phenomena. It may be called the infinite in combination. By force and disturbance, it arrives at transparency. It dissolves all differences, and absorbs them into its own unity. Its elements are so numerous that it becomes identity. One of its drops is complete, and represents the whole. From the abundance of its tempests, it attains equilibrium. Plato beheld the mazy dances of the spheres. Strange fact, though not the less real, the ocean, in the vast terrestrial journey around the sun, becomes, with its flux and reflux, the balance of the globe.

In a phenomenon of the sea, all other phenomena are resumed. The sea is blown out of a waterspout as from a syphon; the storm observes the principle of the pump; the lightning issues from the sea as from the air. Aboard ships dull shocks are sometimes felt, and an odour of sulphur issues from the receptacles of chain cables. The ocean boils. 'The devil has put the sea in his cauldron.' said De Ruyter. In certain tempests, which characterize the equinoxes and the return to equilibrium of the prolific power of nature, vessels breasting the foam seem to give out a kind of fire, phosphoric lights chase each other along the rigging, so close sometimes to the sailors at their work that the latter stretch forth their hands and try to catch, as they fly, these birds of flame. After the great earthquake of Lisbon, a blast of hot air, as from a furnace, drove before it towards the city a wave of sixty feet high. The oscillation of the ocean is closely related to the convulsions of the earth.

These immeasurable forces occasionally produce extraordinary inundations. At the end of 1864, one of the Maldive Islands, a hundred leagues from the Malabar coast, actually foundered. It sunk like a shipwrecked vessel. The fishermen who had sailed from it in the morning, found nothing when they returned at night; scarcely could they distinguish their villages under the waves. On this occasion boats were the spectators of the wrecks of houses.

In Europe, where nature seems restrained by the presence of civilization, such events are rare and thought impossible. Nevertheless, Jersey and Guernsey at one time formed part of Gaul, and at the moment of writing these lines, an equinoctial gale has demolished a great portion of the cliff of the Firth of Forth in Scotland.

Nowhere do these terrific forces appear more formidably conjoined than in the surprising strait known as the Lyse-Fiord. The Lyse-Fiord is the most terrible of all the Gut Rocks of the ocean. Their terrors are there complete. It is in the northern sea, near the inhospitable Gulf of Stavanger. The water is dark and heavy, and subject to intermitting storms. In this sea, and in the midst of this solitude, rises a great sombre street − a street for no human footstep. None ever pass through there; no ship ever enters. It is a corridor ten leagues long, between two rocky walls of three thousand feet in height. Such is the passage which gives admission to the sea. The defile has its elbows and angles like all these streets of the sea − never straight, having been formed by the irregular action of the water. In the Lyse-Fiord, the sea is almost always still; the sky above is serene; the place awful. Where is the wind? Not above. Where is the thunder? Not in the sky. The wind is beneath the sea; the lightnings within the rock. Now and then there is a convulsion of the water. At certain moments, when it may be there is not a cloud in the sky, nearly half way up the perpendicular rock, at a thousand or fifteen hundred feet above the water, and rather on the southern than on the northern side, the rock suddenly thunders, lightnings shoot forth, and then retire like those toys which lengthen out and spring back again in the grasp of children. They contract and enlarge; strike the opposite cliff, re-enter the rock, issue forth again, recommence their play, multiply their tips of flame, strike wherever they can, and then are extinguished with sinister abruptness. Flocks of birds fly in terror. Nothing is more mysterious than that artillery issuing out of the invisible. One cliff attacks the other, raining lightning blows from side to side. Their war concerns not man. It signals the ancient enmity of two rocks in the impassable gulf. In the Lyse-Fiord, the wind whirls like the water in an estuary; the rock performs the function of the clouds; and the thunder breaks forth like volcanic fire. The strange defile is a voltaic pile; the plates of which are the double line of cliffs.

CHAPTER VI

A STABLE FOR THE STEED

Quite familiar with marine rocks, Gilliatt could grapple in earnest with the Douvres. First of all, as we have said, it was essential to find a safe shelter for the sloop.

The double row of reefs, which stretched behind the Douvres, connected itself here and there with other rocks, and suggested the existence of blind passages opening out into the straggling way, and joining again to the principal defile like branches to a trunk.

The tips of the further reefs, left out of the water by the ebbing tide, extended close under the escarpment of the Man to a sort of creek, enclosed nearly on all sides by rocks. Here was a possible harbourage. It had the shape of a horseshoe, and opened only on one side to the east wind, which is the least violent of all winds in that sea labyrinth. The water was shut in there, and almost without motion. The shelter seemed fairly safe. Gilliatt, moreover, had not much choice. If he wished to take advantage of the low water, it was important to hurry. The weather continued to be fine and calm, and the sea was for a while gentle.

Gilliatt descended, unmoored the sloop, re-embarked, and pushed out into the water. He used the oars, coasting the side of the rock, and having reached the Man-Rock, he examined the entrance to the little creek. A fixed, wavy line in the still water, a sort of wrinkle, invisible to any eye but that of a sailor, denoted the channel.

Gilliatt studied it for a moment; then he held off a little in order to steer well into the channel; and suddenly with a stroke of the oars he entered the little bay. The anchorage appeared to be excellent. The sloop would be protected there against almost any damages of wind or weather.

Gilliatt placed the sloop as near as he could to the Man, but still far enough to avoid grazing the rock; and he cast his two anchors. That being finished, he folded his arms, and considered his position.

The sloop was sheltered. One problem was solved. But another remained. Where could he now shelter himself?

He had the choice of two places: the sloop itself, with its little cabin, which was scarcely habitable, and the summit of the Man-Rock, which could be scaled without difficulty.

From one or other of these refuges it was possible at low water, by jumping from rock to rock, to gain the passage between the Douvres where the Durande was fixed, almost without wetting the feet.

But low water lasts but a short while, and all the rest of the time he would be cut off either from his shelter or from the wreck by more than two hundred fathoms. Swimming among breakers is always difficult; and if there is the least commotion in the sea it is impossible.

He was compelled to abandon the idea of shelter in the sloop or on the Man.

No resting-place was possible among the neighbouring rocks, for the summits of the lower ones vanished twice daily beneath the rising tide, and the summits of the higher ones were constantly swept by the foam, and promised nothing but an unwelcome drenching.

No choice remained but the wreck itself. On it Gilliatt hoped it might be possible to find a refuge.

CHAPTER VII

A SHELTER FOR THE WORKMAN

Half-an-hour afterwards, Gilliatt having returned to the wreck, climbed to the deck, descended to the hold, and completed the survey of his first visit.

By the capstan he had raised to the deck of the Durande the package which he had made of the lading of the sloop. The capstan worked well. Bars for turning it were not wanting. Gilliatt had only to choose among the heap of wreckage.

He found among the fragments a chisel, and this he added to his little stock of tools.

Besides this – for in such complete poverty of appliances everything counts for a little – he had his knife in his pocket.

Gilliatt worked during the whole day on the wreck, clearing away, propping, arranging.

At nightfall he observed the following facts.

The entire wreck quivered in the wind. The whole trembled at every step he took. There was nothing strong except the part of the hull jammed between the rocks which contained the engine. There the beams were powerfully supported by the granite walls.

To fix his home in the Durande would be imprudent. It would increase the weight; while instead of adding to her load, it was important to lessen it. To burden the wreck was the very contrary of what he desired.

It was unfortunate enough to be compelled to work on it. The disturbance which the wreck would have to withstand would necessarily distress it, possibly beyond its strength.

Besides, if any accident should happen in the night while he was asleep, he must perish. No assistance would be possible. In order to help the shattered vessel, it was absolutely essential that he should remain outside it.

How to be outside and yet near, was the problem, yet there remained nothing but the two Douvres. They seemed hopeless. From below, one could distinguish upon the upper plateau of the Great Douvre a kind of protuberance.

High rocks with flattened summits, like the Great Douvre

and 'The Man', are a sort of beheaded peaks. They abound among the mountains and in the ocean. Certain rocks, especially those met with in the open sea, bear marks like half-felled trees. They have the appearance of having received blows from an axe. They have been subjected, in fact, to the blows of the gale, that indefatigable ally of the sea. There are other still more profound causes of marine convulsions. Hence the innumerable bruises upon these primeval masses. Some of these sea giants have their heads struck off. In some cases these heads, from some unexplained cause, do not fall, but remain shattered on the summit of the mutilated trunk. This singularity is not rare. The Devil's Rock, at Guernsey, and the table, in the Valley of Anweiler illustrate some of the most surprising features of this strange geological riddle. Doubtless some such phenomena had shaped the summit of the Great Douvre.

If the protuberances which could be observed on the plateau were not a natural irregularity in the stone, it must necessarily be some remaining fragment of the shattered summit. Perhaps the fragment might contain some excavation – some hole into which a man could creep for shelter. Gilliatt asked for nothing more.

But how was he to reach the plateau? How could he scale that perpendicular wall, hard and polished as glass, half covered with the growth of seaweed, and having the slippery look of a soap covered surface?

The ridge of the plateau was at least thirty feet above the deck of the Durande. Gilliatt took out of his box of tools the knotted cord, hooked it to his belt by the grapnel, and set to work to scale the Little Douvre. The ascent became more difficult as he proceeded. He had forgotten to take off his shoes, and this increased his difficulty. With great labour and straining, however, he reached the point. Safely arrived there, he raised himself and stood erect. There was hardly room for his feet. To make it his lodging would be difficult. A Stylite might have been content there; Gilliatt, more luxurious, wanted something more comfortable.

The Little Douvre, leaning towards the great one, appeared from a distance to be saluting it, and the space between the Douvres, which was some score of feet at the foot, was but eight or ten at the highest point. From the spot to which he had ascended, Gilliatt saw more distinctly the rocky excrescence which in part covered the plateau of the Great Douvre.

This plateau rose three fathoms at least above his head. A precipice separated him from it. The curved escarpment of the Little Douvre sloped away out of sight beneath him.

He unfastened the knotted rope from his belt, took a hurried glance at the dimensions of the rock, and slung the grapnel up to the plateau.

The grapnel scratched the rock, and slipped. The knotted rope with the hooks at its end fell down beneath his feet, swinging against the side of the Little Douvre.

He tried again; slung the rope further, aiming at the granite protuberance, in which he could see crevices and scratches.

The cast was, on this occasion, so neat and skilful, that the hooks caught.

He pulled from below. A portion of the rock broke away, and the knotted rope with its heavy iron came down once more, striking the escarpment beneath his feet.

For the third time he slung the grapnel.

It did not fall.

He put a strain upon the rope; it resisted. The grapnel was firmly fixed.

The hooks had caught in some fracture of the plateau which he was not able to see.

It was necessary to trust his life to that unknown support, and he did not hesitate.

To descend once more to the deck of the Durande, in order to devise some other step, was out of the question. A slip was probable, and a fall almost certain. It was less difficult to climb than to descend.

Gilliatt's movements were decisive, as are those of all good sailors. He always proportioned his efforts to the work in hand. Hence the prodigies of strength which he executed with ordinary muscles. His biceps were no more powerful than that of ordinary men; but his heart was firmer. He added, in fact, to strength which is physical, energy which belongs to the moral faculties.

The feat to be accomplished was appalling, for he had to cross the space between the two Douvres, hanging only by this slender rope. Gilliatt tested the cord again; the grappling-iron still held firm.

Covering his left hand with his handkerchief, he grasped the knotted cord with his right, which he covered with his left; then stretching out one foot, and striking out sharply with the other against the rock, in order that the impetus should prevent the rope twisting, he jumped himself from the height of the Little Douvre on to the escarpment of the great one.

His clenched fists struck the rocks; the handkerchief had loosened, and they were scratched; indeed, they narrowly escaped being crushed.

Gilliatt remained hanging there a moment dizzy, but he was sufficiently master of himself to release his grasp of the cord.

A few moments passed in jerks and oscillations before he could catch the cord with his feet; but he succeeded at last. Recovering himself, and holding the cord between his bare feet as with two hands, he gazed into the depth below. He had no fear as to the length of the cord, which had often served him for great heights. The cord, in fact, trailed upon the deck of the Durande.

With the knowledge that he could descend again, he began to climb hand over hand, and still clinging with his feet, in a few moments he gained the summit.

Never before had any creature without wings found a footing there. The plateau was covered in parts with the dung of birds. It was an irregular trapezium, a mass struck off from the colossal granite prism of the Great Douvre. This block was hollowed in the centre like a basin – a work of the rain.

He found at the southern angle of the block a mass of superimposed rocks, probably fragments of the fallen summit. These rocks, looking like a heap of giant paving-stones, would have left room for a wild beast, if one could have found its way there, to hide himself between them. They supported themselves confusedly one against the other, leaving interstices like a heap of ruins. They formed neither grottos nor caves, but the pile was full of holes like a sponge. One of these holes was large enough to admit a man.

This recess had a flooring of moss and a few tufts of grass. Gilliatt could fit himself in it as in a kind of sheath. The recess at its entrance was about two feet high. It contracted towards the bottom. Stone coffins sometimes have this form. The mass of rocks behind lying towards the south-west, the recess was sheltered from the showers, but was open to the cold north wind.

He was satisfied, for the two problems were solved; the sloop had a harbour, and he had a shelter.

He was now in a position to work at leisure upon the Durande. The Great Douvre was his home; the Durande his workshop.

Nothing was more simple for him than going to and fro, ascending and descending.

He dropped down easily by the knotted cord on the deck.

The day's work was good, the undertaking had commenced well; he was content, and now began to feel hungry.

He untied his basket of provisions, opened his knife, cut a slice of beef, took a bite out of his loaf, drank from his can of fresh water, and supped admirably.

To do well and eat well are two satisfactions. A full stomach is like an easy conscience.

His supper being ended, there was still before him a little daylight. He took advantage of it to begin the lightening of the wreck – a matter of urgency.

He had spent part of the day in collecting the fragments. He put on one side, in the strong compartment which contained the machine, all that might be of use, such as wood, iron, cordage, and canvas. What was useless he flung into the sea.

The cargo of the sloop raised to the deck by the capstan, compact as he had made it, was an encumbrance. Gilliatt surveyed the species of niche within his reach, in the side of the Little Douvre. These natural closets, not enclosed, it is true, are often seen in rocks. It struck him that it might be possible to keep some stores in this place, and he accordingly placed in the back of the recess the boxes containing his tools and clothing, and his rye-meal and biscuit. In the front – a little too near the edge perhaps, but he had no other place – he placed his basket of provisions.

He had taken care to remove from the box of clothing his sheepskin, his loose coat with a hood, and his waterproof overalls.

To lessen the hold of the wind upon the knotted cord, he fastened the lower extremity to one of the riders of the Durande.

The Durande being much driven in, this rider was bent a good deal, and it held the end of the cord as firmly as a tight hand.

A difficulty with the upper end of the cord still remained. To control the lower part was well, but at the top of the escarpment at the spot where the knotted cord met the ridge of the plateau, he feared that it would be fretted and worn away by the sharp edge of the rock.

Gilliatt searched among the heap of waste in reserve, and took from it some sailcloth, and from a bunch of old cables he pulled some strands of rope-yarn with which he filled his pockets.

A sailor would have guessed that he meant to bind with these pieces of sail-cloth and ends of yarn, the part of the rope upon the edge of the rock, so as to save it from all friction.

Having provided himself with these things, he drew his overalls over his legs, put on his waterproof over his jacket, drew its hood over his red cap, hung the sheepskin round his neck by the two legs, and in this complete panoply, he grasped the cord, now firmly fixed to the side of the Great Douvre, and mounted to the assault of that gloomy citadel in the sea.

In spite of his scratched hands, Gilliatt regained the summit. The last faint tints of sunset were paling soon in the sky. Upon the sea beneath, it was already dark. A little light still lingered upon the height of the Douvre. Gilliatt took advantage of the dying daylight to bind the knotted rope. He wound it round again and again at the part which passed over the edge of the rock with a bandage of canvas strongly tied at every turn. The whole resembled in a measure the padding which actresses place upon their knees, to prepare them for the agonies and supplications of the fifth act. This accomplished, Gilliatt rose from his stooping position.

For some moments, while bruised in his work, he had had a dim sense of a strange fluttering in the air. It resembled, in the stillness of the evening, the noise which an immense bat might make with the flapping of its wings. He raised his eyes. A great black circle was revolving over his head in the dim twilight sky. In pictures round the heads of saints, such circles are seen. These, however, are on a dark ground, while the circle around Gilliatt was dark upon a lighter ground. The effect was strange. It extended round the Great Douvre like the aureole of night.

The circle drew nearer, then retired; grew narrower, and then spread wide again. It was an immense flight of gulls, seamews, and cormorants; a vast multitude of affrighted sea birds. The Great Douvre was their lodging, and they were coming to roost for the night. Gilliatt was occupying a chamber in their home. Evidently their unexpected fellow-lodger alarmed them. A man there, was an object they had never seen before.

Their wild hovering continued for some time: they appeared to be waiting for the stranger to leave the place.

The flying multitude seemed at last to abandon their design. The circle suddenly took a spiral form, and the cloud of sea birds alighted upon 'The Man' rock at the extremity of the group, where they seemed to confer and deliberate.

Gilliatt, after lying down in his nook of granite, and covering a stone for a pillow, could still hear the birds for a long time chattering one after the other, or croaking, as if in chorus.

Then all was silent, and they slept – Gilliatt upon his rock, the birds upon theirs.

CHAPTER VIII

IMPORTUNAEQUE VOLUCRES

He slept soundly; but he was cold, and this woke him now and then. He had naturally placed his feet at the bottom, and his head at the entrance to his cave. He had not troubled to remove from his bed a number of sharp stones, which did not by any means make him comfortable.

At intervals he heard noises. It was the rising tide entering the caves of the rocks with a sound like the discharge of cannon.

All the circumstances of his position conspired to produce the effect of a vision. Hallucinations seemed to surround him. The darkness of night increased this effect; and Gilliatt felt himself plunged into a region of unrealities. He asked himself 'Is not this all a dream?'

Then he slept once more; and this time, in a real dream, found himself at the Bû de la Rue, at the Bravées, at Saint Sampson. He heard Déruchette singing; he was among realities. While he slept he seemed to awake and live; when he awoke again, he appeared to be dreaming.

In truth, from henceforth he lived in a dream.

Towards the middle of the night a confused murmur filled the air. Gilliatt had a vague knowledge of it even in his slumber. It was a breeze rising.

Once, when awakened by a cold shiver, he opened his eyes wider than before. Clouds were moving in the zenith; the moon was hurrying across the sky, with one large star following closely behind her.

Gilliatt's mind was full of incidents of his dreams. The wild outlines of things in the darkness were exaggerated by this confusion with the impressions of his sleeping hours.

At daybreak he was half frozen: but he slept soundly.

The sudden daylight awoke him from a slumber which might have been dangerous. The alcove faced the rising sun.

Gilliatt yawned, stretched himself, and jumped out of his sleeping place.

His sleep had been so deep, that he could not at first remember the incident of the night before.

By degrees the feeling of reality returned, and he thought of breakfast.

The weather was calm; the sky cool and clear. The clouds were gone; the night had cleared the horizon, and the sun rose brightly. Another fine day was beginning, Gilliatt felt happy.

He threw off his overcoat and his leggings; rolled them up in the sheepskin with the wool inside, fastened the roll with a length of rope-yarn, and pushed it into the cavern that it might be sheltered in case of rain.

He proceeded to make his bed – a task which consisted in removing the stones which had troubled him.

This done, he descended by the cord to the deck of the Durande and approached the niche where he had placed his basket of provisions. He had placed it near the edge, and the wind in the night had blown it down, and rolled it into the sea.

Clearly it would not be easy to recover it. There was a spirit of mischief and malice in a wind which had sought out his basket in that place.

Hostilities had began. Gilliatt understood the warning.

To those who live in a state of rude familiarity with the sea, it is natural to regard the wind as an individual, and the rocks as living beings.

Nothing remained but the biscuit and rye-meal, except the shell-fish, and it was useless to think of subsisting by net or line fishing, for fish are averse to the neighbourhood of rocks.

He breakfasted on a few limpets which he found it difficult to pluck from the rocks; and, in doing so, he ran great risk of breaking his knife.

While making his scanty meal, he was sensible of a strange disturbance on the sea. He looked around.

A swarm of gulls and seamews had just alighted upon some low rocks, and were flapping their wings, tumbling over each other, screaming, and shrieking. All were swarming noisily over the same spot. This horde with beaks and talons were pillaging Gilliatt's basket.

Rolled down upon a sharp point by the wind, it had burst open. The birds had flocked round immediately. They were carrying off in their beaks all sorts of fragments of provisions. Gilliatt recognized from the distance his smoked beef and his salted fish.

The birds had taken their revenge. Gilliatt had robbed them of their lodging, and they stole his supper from him.

CHAPTER IX

HOW GILLIATT MADE USE OF THE ROCK

No rain fell for a week, although it was the rainy season, and for this Gilliatt felt thankful. But the work he had undertaken surpassed, in appearance at least, the power of human hand or skill. Success seemed so improbable that the effort seemed madness.

It is not until a task is fairly grappled with that its difficulties become fully manifest. There is nothing like making a commencement for making evident how difficult it will be to arrive at the end. Every beginning is a struggle against resistance. The first step is an exorable undeceiver. A difficulty which we come to touch pricks like a thorn.

Thus Gilliatt found himself immediately in the presence of obstacles.

In order to raise the engine from the wreck in which it was buried, with any chance of success – in order to accomplish a salvage in such a place and in such a season, it seemed necessary to be many men. Gilliatt was alone; a complete apparatus of carpenters' and engineers' tools and implements were requisite. Gilliat had a saw, a hatchet, a chisel, and a hammer. He wanted a good workshop and a good shed; but he had not a roof to shelter him. Provisions, too, were necessary, but he had not even bread.

Any one who could have seen Gilliatt working on the rock during the first week would have been puzzled to guess the nature of his operations. He seemed to be no longer thinking of the Durande. He was busy among the breakers, absorbed in saving the smaller parts of the wreck. He took advantage of every high tide to strip the reefs of everything which the shipwreck had scattered among them. He went from rock to rock, gathering up whatever the sea had dispensed – rags of sail-cloth, pieces of iron, splinters of panels, shattered planking, broken yards – a beam, a chain, a pulley, as the case might be.

At the same time he carefully surveyed all the recesses of the rocks. To his great disappointment none were habitable. He had suffered from the cold in the night, where he lodged between the stones on the summit of the rock, and he would gladly have found some better refuge.

Two of those recesses were somewhat large. Although the natural pavement of rock was almost everywhere oblique and uneven, one could stand upright, and even walk within them. The wind and the rain wandered there at will, but the highest tides did not reach them. They were near the Little Douvre, and could be approached at any time. Gilliatt settled that one should serve him as a store-house, the other as a forge.

With all the sail, rope-bands, and all the reef-earrings he could collect, he made bundles of the fragments of wreckage, tying the wood and iron together, and packing the canvas in parcels. He lashed all these together carefully. As the rising tide approached these packages, he began to drag them across the reefs to his storehouse. In a hollow of the rocks he had found a top rope, by means of which he had been able to haul the large pieces of timber. In the same way, he dragged from the sea many portions of chains which he found scattered among the breakers.

He worked at these tasks with wonderful activity and tenacity. He accomplished whatever he attempted – nothing could withstand his perseverance.

Before the end of the week he had gathered into his warehouse of marine stores, and ranged into order all this shapeless mass of salvage. Every portion had its place. The entire wreck was there classed and ticketed. It was a sort of chaos in a store-house.

He had succeeded in discovering the little anchor in the hollow of a reef, where the receding tide had left it uncovered.

It what had been Tangrouille's cabin he had found a piece of chalk, which he preserved, reflecting that he might have a use for it.

This salvage of débris was finished in a week; the rock was swept clean, and the Durande was lightened. Nothing remained to burden the hull but the machinery.

The portion of the fore-side bulwarks which hung to it did not distress the hull. The mass hung without dragging, being, in a measure, sustained by a ledge of rock. It was, however, large and broad, and heavy to drag, and would have encumbered his warehouse too much. This bulwarking looked something like a boat-builder's stocks. Gilliatt left it where it was.

He had been profoundly thoughtful during all this labour. He had sought in vain for the figurehead – the 'doll', as the Guernsey folks called it, of the Durande. It had been carried away by the waves. Gilliatt would have given his fingers to find it – if he had not had such great need of them at that time.

At the entrance to the storehouse and outside were two heaps – a heap of iron for forging, and a heap of wood for burning.

He was always at work at the break of day. Except his time of sleep, he did not take a moment for rest.

And the wild sea birds, flying to and fro, watched him as he worked.

CHAPTER X

GILLIATT'S FORGE

Having finished his warehouse, Gilliatt built his forge.

The other recess chosen had within it a kind of passage like a gallery in a mine of moderate depth. He at first had an idea of making this his abode, but the draught was so continuous in this passage, that he was compelled to abandon it. This current of air, never ceasing, first gave him the notion of the forge. Since it could not be his chamber, he was determined that it should be his smithy. To bend obstacles to our will is a great step towards success. The wind was his enemy, and he determined to make it his servant.

The proverb applied to some kinds of men – 'fit for everything, good for nothing' – may too be applied to the hollow of rocks. They give no advantages gratis. On one side we find a hollow fashioned in the shape of a bath; but it lets the water run away through a fissure. Here is a rocky chamber, but roofless; here a couch of moss, but oozy with wet; here a chair, but composed of stone.

The forge which Gilliatt planned was roughly designed by nature; but nothing could be more troublesome than to reduce this rough sketch to workable shape, to change this cavern into a smith's shop. With three or four large rocks, in shape like a funnel, and terminating in a narrow fissure, chance had made there a species of huge ill-shapen blower, of very different power to those old forge bellows of fourteen feet long, which poured out at every breath ninety-eight thousand inches of air. This was a very different sort of construction. The proportions of the hurricane do not admit of definite measurement.

This excess of force was an embarrassment. The never ceasing draught was difficult to regulate.

The cavern had two inconveniences; the wind went through it from one end to another; so did the water too. This was not the water of the sea, but a little trickling stream, more like a spring than a torrent. The foam, cast incessantly by the surf upon the rocks, had filled with sea water a natural cave placed among the lofty rocks which overlooked the excavation. The overflowing of this reservoir caused a fall of water of about an inch in breadth, and descending about thirty feet. The rains also helped to fill the reservoir. From time to time a passing cloud poured a shower into the rocky basin, always overflowing. The water was too brackish to drink, but bright and clear. This rill of water fell in graceful drops from the extremities of the long sea grasses, as from the ends of a tress of hair.

The idea of making this water serve to regulate the draught in the cave struck Gilliatt. By means of a funnel made of planks roughly put together to form two or three pipes, one of which was fitted with a valve, and of a large tub arranged as a lower reservoir, without checks or counterweight, and completed solely by air-tight stuffing above and air-holes below, Gilliatt, who, as we have already said, was clever at the forge and mechanic's bench, managed to construct, instead of the forge-bellows, which he did not possess, an apparatus less perfect than what is known now-a-days by the name of a 'cagniardelle', but less rude than what the people of the Pyrenees anciently called a 'trompe'.

He had some rye-meal, and he made with it some paste. He had also some white rope, which picked out into tow. With this paste and tow, and some plugs of wood, he stopped all the crevices of the rock, leaving only a little air passage made of a powder-flask which he had found aboard the Durande. This powder-flask was directed horizontally to a large stone, which Gilliatt made the hearth of the forge. A stopper of tow served to close it when necessary.

After this, he heaped up the wood and coal upon the hearth, struck his steel against the rock, caught a spark upon a handful of loose tow, and this having ignited, he lighted his forge fire.

He tried the blower: it worked well.

Gilliatt felt the pride of a Cyclops: he governed air, water, and fire. Master of the air; for he had given a kind of lungs to the wind, and changed the rude draught into a useful blower. Master of water, for he had converted the little cascade into a 'trompe'. Master of fire, for out of the damp rock he produced a flame.

The cave being almost entirely open to the sky, the smoke issued freely, blackening the curved escarpment. The rocks which seemed destined for ever to receive only white foam, became acquainted with black smoke.

He chose for an anvil a large smooth round stone, of the necessary shape and dimensions. It formed a base for the blows of his hammer; but one that might fly and was very dangerous. One of the extremities of this block, rounded and ending in a point, might for want of anything better, serve instead of a conoid bicorn; but the other kind of bicorn of the pyramidal form was wanting. It was the ancient stone anvil of the Troglodytes. The surface, polished by the waves, had almost the firmness of steel.

He regretted not having brought his anvil. As he did not know that the Durande had been broken in two by the tempests, he had hoped to find the carpenter's chest and all his tools generally kept in the fore hold. But it was, as it happened, the forepart of the vessel which had been carried away. These two excavations which he had found in the rock were contiguous. The warehouse and the forge communicated with each other. Every evening, when his work was finished, he ate a little biscuit soaked in water, a sea-urchin or a crab, or a few *châtaignes de mer*, the only food to be found among those rocks; and shivering like his knotted cord, climbed again to sleep in his cell upon the Great Douvre.

The very materialism of his daily occupation increased the kind of abstraction in which he lived. To be steeped too deeply in realities is in itself a cause of visionary moods. His bodily labours, with its variety of details, took nothing from the sensation of stupor which arose from the strangeness of his position and his work. Ordinary fatigue is a chain which binds man to the earth; but the very peculiarity of the enterprise he had undertaken kept him in a sort of ideal twilight region. There were times when he seemed to be striking blows with his hammer in the clouds. At other times his tools appeared to him like arms. He had a strange feeling, as if he were providing against some hidden danger of attack. Untwisting ropes, unravelling threads of yarn in a sail, or propping up a couple of beams, appeared to him at such times like fashioning engines of war. The thousand minute pains which he took about his salvage operations produced at last in him the effect of precautions against aggressions barely concealed, and easily anticipated. He did not know the words which express the ideas, but he perceived them. His instincts became less those of the worker; his habits more those of the savage.

His business there was to subdue and direct the powers of nature. He had a vague perception of this. A strange enlargement of his ideas!

All around, as far as the eye could reach was the immense prospect of endless labour wasted. Nothing disturbs the mind more than the contemplation of the diffusion of forces at work in the unfathomable and limitless space of the ocean. The wind tends naturally to enquire the object of these forces. The unceasing movement in space, the restless sea, the clouds ever hurrying somewhere, the vast mysterious lavishness of effort, all this is a problem. Whither does this perpetual movement tend? What do these winds construct? What do these herculean blows build up? These howlings, shocks, and sobbings of the storm, in what do they result? and what is the reason of this tumult? The ebb and flow of these questionings is eternal, as the flux and reflux of the sea itself. Gilliatt could speak for himself; his work he knew, but the agitation which surrounded him far and wide at all times perplexed him with its unceasing questionings. Unknown to himself, mechanically, by the mere pressure of eternal things, and without any other effect than a strange, unconscious bewilderment, Gilliatt, in his dreamy mood, blended his own toil somehow with the prodigious wasted labour of the waves. How, indeed, in that position, could he avoid the influence of that mystery of the dread, toiling ocean? how escape meditating, so far as meditation was possible, upon the movement of the waves, the perseverance of the foam, the imperceptible wearing away of rocks, the wild beatings of the blustering winds? How terrible that never ceasing recommencement, that ocean bed, those Danaïdes-like clouds, all that toil and weariness for no end!

'For no end? Say not so! But for what end? O Thou Infinite Unknown, that is known to none other but to Thee!'

CHAPTER XI

GILLIATT MAKES A DISCOVERY

Men sometimes visit a rock near the coast; but never one in mid-ocean. Why should any one go there? No food can be obtained there; no fruit-trees are there, no pasture, no beasts, no water suitable for man's wants. It towers aloft, with its steep sides and summits above water, its sharp points below. Nothing is to be found there but dreadful shipwreck.

These rocks are strange places. The sea is alone there; she works her own will. There is no token of terrestrial life to disturb her. Man is a terror to the sea; she is shy of his approach, and her deeds hide from him. But she is bolder among the solitary sea rocks. The everlasting soliloquy of the waves is not troubled there. She labours at the rocks, repairs its damage, sharpens its peaks, making them rugged or renewing them. She pierces the granite; she dismembers, perforates, and grooves; fills the rock with cells, and makes it sponge-like, hollows out the inside, or sculptures it without. In that secret mountain which is hers, she makes caves and palaces. She has her monstrous vegetation, floating plants which bite, and monsters which take root; and she conceals all this terrible magnificence in the twilight of her depths. Among the isolated rocks no eye watches over her; no spy embarrasses her actions. It is here that she develops at liberty her mysterious side, which is inaccessible to man. Here she stores all strange secretions of life. Here the unknown wonders of the sea are gathered together.

The geological changes of the earth are trifling compared with the vast operations of the ocean. These habitations in the sea, these pyramids, and spouts of the foam practise a mysterious art which the author has elsewhere called 'the Art of Nature'. Their style is known by its vastness. The effects of chance here appear design. Its works are of many kinds. They abound in the mazy entanglement of the rock-coral groves, the sublimity of the cathedral, the extravagance of the pagoda, the vastness of the mountain, the delicacy of the jeweller's work, the horror of the sepulchre. They are filled with cells like the wasps' nests, with dens like menageries, with subterranean passages like the haunts of moles, with dungeons like Bastiles, with ambuscades like a camp. They have their doors but they are barricaded; their columns, but they are shattered; their towers, but they are tottering; their bridges, but they are broken. Their compartments are unaccommodating; these are fitted only for birds, those only for fish. Their architectural style is variable and inconsistent; it regards or disregards at will the laws of equilibrium. Fearful overhanging blocks threaten, but do not fall; the human mind cannot guess what power supports their bewildering masses. Blind entrances, gaps, and ponderous suspensions multiply and vary in infinite variety. The mighty unknown architect plans nothing, but succeeds in everything. Rocks piled together in confusion from a monstrous monument, defy reason, yet maintain equilibrium. Here is something more than strength; it is eternity. But order is wanting. The wild tumult of the waves seems to have passed into the wilderness of stone. It is like a tempest petrified and fixed for ever. Nothing is more impressive than that wild architecture; always standing, yet always appearing to fall; in which everything appears to give support, and yet to lack it. A struggle between opposing lines has resulted in the construction of an edifice, filled with traces of the efforts of those old antagonists, the ocean and the tempest.

This architecture has its terrible masterpieces, and of such the Douvres was one. The sea had shaped and finished it with a sinister solicitude. The treacherous waters licked it into shape. It was hideous, dangerous, dark, and full of hollows. It had a complete system of submarine caverns branching out and losing themselves in unfathomable depths. Some of the orifices of this labyrinth of passages were left exposed by low tides. A man might enter, but not without danger.

Gilliatt determined to explore these grottoes, for the purpose of his salvage work. There were none which were not repulsive. Everywhere about the caverns that strange aspect of an abattoir, those singular traces of slaughter, appeared in all the exaggeration of the ocean. No one who has not seen in excavations of this kind, upon the walls of granite, these hideous frescoes of Nature, can form an idea of their strangeness.

These cruel caverns, too, were false and sly. Woe betide him who would loiter there. The rising tide filled them to their roofs. They were obstructed by heaps of shingle, piled up in their recesses. Some of their huge smooth stones weighed more than a ton. They were of every proportion, and of every hue; but the greater part were the colour of blood. Some, covered with a hairy and sticky seaweed, seemed like large green moles burrowing their way into the rock.

Several terminated abruptly, others, main arteries of a weird circulation, lengthened out in the rock in dark and winding fissures. They were the streets of the submarine city; but they gradually narrowed from their entrances, and at length left no room for a man to pass. Peering in by the help of a lighted torch, one could see nothing but black hollows dripping with moisture.

One day, Gilliatt, exploring, ventured into one of these fissures. The tide favoured the attempt. It was a bright day of calm and sunshine. There was no fear of any danger from the sea.

Two necessities compelled him to undertake these explorations. He had to gather fragments of wreckage to aid him in his labour, and to look for crabs and crayfish for food. Shell-fish had begun to fail him on the rocks.

The fissure was narrow, and the passage difficult. Gilliatt could see daylight beyond. He made an effort, contorted himself to the best of his ability, and penetrated into the cave as far as he could.

He had reached, without knowing it, the interior of the rock, upon the point of which Clubin had steered the Durande. Though abrupt and almost inaccessible without, it was hollow within. It was full of galleries, pits, and chambers, like the tomb of an Egyptian king. This network of caverns was one of the most intricate of all that labyrinth, fashioned by the water, undermined by the restless ocean. The branches of this subterranean maze probably communicated with the sea without by more than one issue, some gaping at the level of the waves, the others profound and hidden from view. It was near this spot, but Gilliatt of course did not know it, that Clubin had dived when intending to swim to the vessel.

In this cave Gilliatt wound about, clambered, struck his head at times, bent low and rose again, lost his footing and regained it, advancing with difficulty. Gradually the gallery widened; a glimmer of daylight appeared, and he found himself suddenly at the entrance to a strange and dreadful cavern.

CHAPTER XII

THE INTERIOR OF A PALACE UNDER THE WAVES

The glimmer of daylight was fortunate, for had he taken one step more, Gilliatt would have fallen into a pool, perhaps without bottom. The waters of these cavern pools are so cold and paralyzing that they often prove fatal to the strongest swimmers.

There is, besides, no means of climbing or of supporting oneself on any part of their steep walls.

He stopped. The crevice from which he had issued ended in a narrow and slippery projection, a sort of corbel in the peaked wall. He leaned against the side in order to survey it.

He was in a large cave. Above his head was a roofing similar to the interior of a huge skull, which might be imagined to be recently dissected. The dripping ribs of the striated indentations of the roof served to imitate the branching fibres and ragged sutures of the bony cranium. A ceiling of stone and a watery floor. The rippling waters between the walls of the cave were like waved paving tiles. The grotto was enclosed on every side. Not even an air-hole could be seen. No crack in the wall, no fissure in the roof. The light came from below and through the water, a strange, gloomy light.

Gilliatt, the pupils of whose eyes had contracted during his explorations of the dim corridor, could easily distinguish everything around him in the pale glimmer.

At his feet under the water he could discern a sort of drowned arch. This arch, a natural ogive, fashioned by the waves, was glittering between its two dark and profound supports. It was by this submerged porch that the daylight entered into the cavern from the open sea. A strange light shooting upward from a gulf.

The glimmer spread out beneath the waters like a large fan, and was reflected on the rocks. Its direct rays, divided into long, broad shafts, appeared in strong relief against the darkness below, and becoming brighter or duller, from one rock to another, looked as if seen here and there through sheets of glass. There was light in the cave; but it was an unearthly light. The beholder might have dreamed that he had descended in some other planet. The whole cave represented the interior of a gigantic death's-head, and of a strange splendour. The vault was the hollow of the brain, the arch the mouth; the sockets of the eyes were missing. The cavern, in turn, swallowing and rendering up the flux and reflux through its mouth wide opened to the full noonday without, seemed to drink the light and vomit forth bitterness; a type of some beings intelligent and evil. The light, in traversing this inlet through the vitreous medium of the sea-water, became green, like a ray of starlight from Aldebaran. The water, filled with the moist light, appeared like a liquid emerald. A tint of aqua-marina of beautiful delicacy spread a soft hue throughout the cavern. The roof, with its cerebral lobes, and its rampant ramifications, like the fibres of nerves, gave out a tender reflection of chrysoprase. The ripples reflected on the roof were falling in order and dissolving again incessantly, and enlarging and contracting their glittering scales in a mysterious and mazy dance. They gave the beholder an impression of something weird and spectral: one wondered what prey secured, or what expectation about to be realized, moved with a joyous thrill this wonderful network of living fire. From the projections of the vault, and the angles of the rock, hung lengths of tender fibrous plants, probably bathing their roots in the rock in some pool of water above, and distilling from their silky ends one after the other, a pearl like a drop of water. These drops fell into the water now and then with a musical splash. The effect of the scene was singular. Nothing more beautiful could be imagined; nothing more mournful could be found.

It was a palace of wonders, in which death for ever sat smiling yet sad.

CHAPTER XIII

WHAT COULD BE SEEN THERE CLEARLY; AND WHAT BUT DIMLY

Dazzling to the eyes, yet a place of shade – such was this wonderful cavern.

The movement of the sea made itself felt throughout the cavern. The oscillation without raised and lowered the level of the waters inside, with the regularity of respiration. A mysterious life seemed to permeate this great organism, as it silently rose and fell.

The water had a weird transparency, and Gilliatt distinguished at various depths submerged recesses, and surfaces of projecting rocks ever of a deeper and a darker green. Certain sombre hollows, too, could be seen, probably of unfathomable depth.

On all sides of the submarine porch, rude elliptical arches, filled with shadows, indicated the position of small lateral caves, low alcoves of the central cavern, accessible, perhaps, at certain tides. Little sandy beaches of a few feet wide, laid bare by the action of the water, stretched inward, and disappeared in these recesses.

Here and there sea-weeds of more than a fathom in length waved to and fro beneath the water, like long tresses waved in the wind, and the observer could catch glimpses of a forest of sea plants.

The wall of the cavern, from the roof down to the depth at which it became invisible – was tapestried with that prodigious efflorescence of the sea, seldom seen by human eyes, which the old Spanish navigators termed *praderias del mer*. A luxuriant moss, enlarged while concealing the protuberances of rock. From all the projecting points hung the thin fluted strips of varech, which sailors use as weather indicators. The light air which stirred in the cavern waved their shining bands to and fro.

Under these vegetations there showed themselves from time to time some of the rarest gems of the ocean's jewel box. Bell-shaped limpet shells, like tiny huts, were in all parts adhering to the rocks, distributed in settlements, in the alleys between which prowled oscabrions, the beetles of the sea. A few large pebbles found their way into the cavern; shell-fish took refuge there. The crustacea are the grandees of the sea, who, in their lacework and embroidery avoid the rude contact of the pebbly crowd. The glittering heap of their shells, in certain spots under the water, gave out strange irradiations, amidst which the eye caught glimpses of azure and gold, and mother-of-pearl, of every tint.

Upon the side of the cavern, a little above the water-line, a beautiful and strange plant, fastening itself, like a fringe, to the border of sea-weed, continued and completed it. Thick, fibrous, intertwined, and black, this plant exhibited large confused and dusky festoons, everywhere dotted with little flowers of the colour of lapis-lazuli. In the water they seemed to glow like tiny blue flames. Out of the water they were flowers; beneath it they appeared sapphires. The water rising and inundating the basement of the grotto, covered with these plants, seemed to sow the rock with precious stones.

One of the marvels of the cavern was the rock itself. Forming here a wall, there an arch, and here again a pillar, it was in some places rough and bare, and sometimes close beside, was covered by nature's hand with the most delicate carving. Strange traces of mind mingled with the massive solidity of the granite. It was the wonderful art-work of the ocean. Here a kind of panel, square, and covered with round embossments in various positions, simulated a bas-relief. Before this sculpture, with its indistinct designs, a man might have imagined Prometheus roughly sketching for Michelangelo. It seemed as if that great genius with a few touches could have finished the vague labours of the giant. In other places the rock was damasked like an eastern shield, or engraved like a Florentine vase. There were portions which appeared like Corinthian brass, then like arabesques, as on the door of a mosque; then like Runic stones with obscure and mystic prints of claws. Plants with twisted creepers and tendrils, crossing and recrossing upon the groundwork of golden lichens, covered it as it were with filigree. The grotto resembled in some wise a Moorish palace. It was a union of barbarism and of goldsmith's work, with the awe-inspiring and rugged architecture produced by the elements.

The magnificent stains of the sea covered, as with velvet, the angles of granite. The escarpments were festooned with large-flowered bindweed, sustaining itself with graceful ease, and ornamenting the walls as by intelligent design. The wondrous light which came from beneath the water, at once a submarine twilight and an Elysian radiance, toned down and blended all harsh outlines. Every wave was a prism. Fragments of rainbows seemed floating in the transparent dawn. In other corners there was seen a kind of moonlight in the water. Every kind of splendour seemed to mingle, forming a mystic twilight. Enchantment reigned over all.

Could it be daylight which entered by this casement beneath the sea? Was it really water which quivered in this dusky pool? Were not these arched roofs shaped from sunset clouds to imitate a cavern to men's eyes? Was not this solid shaft about to vanish and melt into thin air? What was that cunning jewellery of glittering shells, half concealed beneath the wave? Life, and the green earth, and human voices were so far away! What magic of enchantment haunted this mysterious light?

At the end of the cavern, which was oblong, rose a Cyclopean archivolte, singularly exact in form. It was a species of cave within a cave, and here, behind a sheet of bright verdure, out of the waves rose a stone with square sides, and bearing some resemblance to an altar. The water surrounded it. It seemed as if a goddess had just descended from it. One might have fancied there that some spiritual form beneath that crypt or upon that altar dwelt for ever pensive in naked beauty, but grew invisible at the approach of mortals. The day-dream of an intruder might evoke again the marvellous vision. A flood of pure light falling upon ivory shoulders; a forehead bathed with the light of dawn; an Olympian visage oval-shaped; a bust full of mysterious grace; arms modestly drooping; tresses unloosened in the aurora; a body delicately modelled of snowy whiteness, half-wrapped in a sacred cloud, with the glance of a virgin; a Venus rising from the sea, an Eve issuing from chaos; such was the dream which filled the mind of him who entered here.

The beauty of the recess seemed made for this celestial presence. It was for the sake of this fairy of the cavern, this queen born of the waves, it was for her – as the mind, at least, dreamed – that this subterranean dwelling had been thus carefully walled in, so that nothing might ever disturb the solemn shadows and the majestic silence around about that divine spirit.

Gilliatt, sensible of mixed emotions, stood there for a time, musing and filled with the beauty of the spot.

Suddenly, a few feet below him, in the lovely transparence of that water like liquid jewels, he became aware of the approach of something. A kind of long ragged band was moving amidst the oscillation of the waves. It did not float, but advanced of its own will. It had an object; and was moving rapidly. It had something of the form of a jester's bauble with points, which hung flabby and undulating. It seem covered with a dust which could not be washed away by the water. It was more than horrible; it was foul and loathsome. He felt that it was something monstrous. It was living; unless, indeed, it were only a delusion. It seemed to seek the obscurer portion of the cavern, where finally it vanished in the darkness. The deep shadows grew darker as its ill-omened form glided into them, and vanished from sight.

BOOK II

HARD WORK

CHAPTER I

WORKING WITH SCANTY RESOURCES

The entrance to the cavern had been difficult, and the exit was more so. Gilliatt, however, succeeded in reaching his starting-point, and felt no desire to return. He had not found in it what he sought, and he had no time to waste in curiosity. He put his forge into use; he wanted tools, and so set about making them. For fuel he had the wreck; water was his motive power, the wind was his bellows, a stone for an anvil; for art, he had instinct, and for power, will.

The elements seemed inclined to aid him, for March came in with fine weather. The bright blue sky, the calm of the ocean, and the peaceful serenity of the noontide, all seemed to exclude every idea of evil intentions on the part of the elements. The sea glittered in the bright rays of the sun. A kiss is often the prelude to an act of treachery, and with such caresses the sea is lavish. There was very little wind; the bellows worked all the better for this – too much wind would have been a hindrance. Gilliatt possessed a saw, and he made use of the iron hands of the blacksmith – the pincers and pliers. By degrees Gilliatt manufactured his tools, and constructed his weapons of warfare. He made a screen for his forge with a piece of tarpaulin.

One of his chief labours was the sorting and repairing of his pulleys. He mended the blocks and sheaves; he cut off the shattered ends of the joists, and re-shaped them. He had, for his carpentry, pieces of wood of every description stowed away, and sorted. This formed his reserve of supports and levers, of which he might at any moment stand in need.

Gilliatt repaired the cables, great and small. He frayed out the torn sails, and thus made excellent yarn, with which he made twine, and with this he spliced the ropes. When he had finished with the ropes, he set to work upon the chains. He was able, thanks to the anvil, to forge large rings. With these rings he joined the broken chain, and formed lengths. To work unaided at a forge is very trying; he managed, however, to do it. True, he had only to make small articles, and he could hold them in one hand with his pincers, whilst he hammered with the other. He cut into lengths the iron bars of the captain's bridge, and beat one end into a point and the other into a broad, flat head, in this way making large spike nails about a foot long.

He had often to put a fresh edge to his axe, and to file the teeth of his saw; for doing the latter work he had made for himself a three-sided file.

He sometimes used the capstan of the Durande; the hook of the chain broke, he made another. By aid of pincers and pliers, and using his chisel like a turnscrew, he commenced the removal of the paddle-wheels, and, with much trouble, he succeeded. He contrived to stow the wheels away in the paddle-boxes which protected them. With these, Gilliatt made two large boxes, in which he packed all the parts of the wheels, carefully numbering them with the chalk he had found.

He placed these two cases on the strongest part of the deck of the Durande.

When this work was done, Gilliatt found himself face to face with his great difficulty, which was how to dispose of the engines.

To take the paddle-wheels to pieces had been practicable, but to do the same to the engines was out of the question, for there Gilliatt knew very little about their mechanism.

Should he endeavour to take them to pieces piece by piece, he needed other tools than those which he possessed, or which he could make in a cave, with the wind for bellows and a stone for an anvil. In attempting to take the engines to pieces, there was a great danger of ruining them utterly.

Here he seemed face to face with something impossible.

What could he do?

CHAPTER II

A GIGANTIC UNDERTAKING

An idea struck Gilliatt.

The mason-carpenter of Salbris, in the sixteenth century, when science was still in its infancy – before the Amontons had found the first law of friction, Lakin, the second, or Colomb, the third – without guide or counsel, and with no other helper than his son – a child – with clumsy tools, solved, in the clock-tower of the church of Charité-sur-Loire, five or six problems in which statics and dynamics were inextricably mixed up. Since that wonderful operation, by which he found means, without breaking a single wire or throwing the cog of a single wheel out of gear, to lower, in one piece, by a wonderfully simple invention, from the second story to the first, the massive clock of iron and copper, as large as a watchman's box, with its movement, cylinders, barrels, drums, hooks, and weights – one of which weighed five hundred pounds – its bells, peals, its apparatus for striking the hours, and all its complicated machinery – since this man, whose name even has been forgotten, performed this miracle, no such bold attempt, such as Gilliatt meditated, had ever been undertaken.

Gilliatt's operation was more difficult, therefore his success would be more glorious.

The weight, the delicacy of the apparatus, the difficulties were as great in moving the engines of the Durande as in the case of the clock of Charité-sur-Loire.

The Gothic mechanic had an assistant in his son; Gilliatt was quite unaided. There was a crowd from Meung-sur-Loire, Nevers, and Orleans, which could have assisted the mason of Salbris, and who certainly encouraged him by sympathetic applause. Gilliatt had no one near him – no sound, save the roar of the wind, no crowd, save the tumultuous waves.

There is nothing equal to the timidity of rashness, unless it be its daring. Where ignorance becomes bold she has a sort of compass to work by, and that compass is an intuition of the truth, oftener more apparent to the mind of simplicity than to the brain of philosophy.

To be ignorant invites you to endeavour, for ignorance is a dream, and curiosity, which ever forms part of a dream, develops into a power.

Knowledge often prevents great attempts. Had Columbus been a good geographer, he would never had discovered America.

The second man to ascend to the summit of Mont Blanc was a learned man – Saussure; the first was a shepherd – Balmat.

But the cases which we cite are exceptions, and in no way detract from science, which will ever maintain its place. An ignorant man may hit upon a discovery by luck, but the man of science invents.

Gilliatt's boat was anchored in the little bay, where the sea left it in peace, and he had, as the reader will remember, arranged everything so as to keep up communication with it. He one day measured it carefully, paying especial attention to its breadth of beam; then he went back to the Durande and measured the floor of the engine room. He found that, without the wheels, it was quite two feet less than the breadth of his boat, so there was room for the engines in it. But the problem to be solved, was how and by what means he could get them into the sloop.

CHAPTER III

GILLIATT'S MASTERPIECE RESCUES LETHIERRY

Any person lingering about the scene of Gilliatt's labours would have seen a strange sight between the Douvres Rocks. Four powerful beams, at equal distances from each other, stretched from one Douvre to the other, jammed firmly between the rocks, thus rendering their hold very secure. On the Little Douvre their extremities rested on projections of the rock. On the Great Douvre their ends had been driven into the rock by blows of a hammer, wielded by the powerful hand of a workman standing upon the beam which he was driving in. These supports were longer than the space between the rocks, hence the firmness with which they were fixed, and the incline which they had. They formed an acute angle from the Great Douvre, and an obtuse one from the Little Douvre. Their inclination was slight, but it was not the same in all, which was a defect. But for this they might have been prepared for the laying of a ship's deck. To these beams were attached four sets of hoisting apparatus, each one of which had its pendent and tackle fall, with the peculiarity of having the blocks with two sheaves at one end of the beam, and a single pulley at the other. This distance, which was too great not to be dangerous, was, perhaps, necessitated by the operations to be effected. The blocks were strong, and the pulleys firm. Cables were attached to this tackle, which, from a distance, looked like mere threads; and beneath this aerial suspension of blocks and timber the huge wreck of the Durande seemed suspended in the air by slender cords.

But she was not yet suspended.

Under the cross-beams, eight perpendicular apertures had been cut in the deck – four on the starboard and four on the port side of the engines, and eight others underneath them, through the keel. Four cables, descending vertically from four blocks, entered through the holes in the deck, passed out again by the openings in the keel beneath the machinery, and re-entered the vessel at the other side, passing upward through the deck, returning to where they had started from, and secured round the beams. Here a tackle held them together, bound to a single cable, capable of being guided by one man. This single cable passed over a hook and through a dead-eye, which kept it in check. This combination enabled the four pulleys to work together, and acted as a check upon the suspending powers, forming a kind of dynamical rudder in the hands of the superintendent of the operation, and maintaining every portion in a proper balance. This ingenious mode of hoisting had some of the qualities of the Weston pulley of the present day, united with the ancient polyspasten of Vitruvius. Gilliatt had utilized the idea, though he had never heard of Vitruvius – who died many years back; or Weston – who is alive now. The length of the cables differed according to the unequal slope of the beams, and, by this means, corrected the inequality. The ropes were dangerous, for the twine with which they were spliced might break; chains would have been better, but chains would have slipped on the tackle.

The whole arrangement was full of faults, but, as the work of one unskilled man, it was miraculous. We have been forced to abridge the explanation of the apparatus. Many details have been omitted which would only prove a source of confusion.

The top of the funnel passed between the two middle beams.

Without being aware of what he was doing, Gilliatt had played the part of a plagiarist, and had, after the lapse of three centuries, reproduced the mechanism of the carpenter of Salbris – a mechanism full of errors, and dangerous to the person who directed its operations. Let us remark here, that even the greatest faults in construction do not prevent machinery from working in some sort of a manner or other. It may go clumsily, but it moves and works. The obelisk in the Square of Saint Peter's, at Rome, was raised in its position contrary to all the rules of statics. The carriage of the Czar, Peter the Great, was so built that it seemed ready to overturn at each turn of the wheels, but for all that, it went along fairly. What numerous faults there were in the machinery at Marly! Almost everything was wrongly put together. Yet, in spite of that, it gave Louis XIV a sufficiency of water.

Having confidence in his plan, Gilliatt was so certain of success that he had fixed on his boat two pairs of iron rings on each side, corresponding to the four rings on board the Durande, to which the chains of the funnel were fastened. He had evidently conceived a complete and definite plan. Having every chance against him, he felt that the best thing that he could do would be to take every precaution. He made several arrangements which seemed unnecessary – a sure sign that he had considered the matter thoroughly. His manner of working would have puzzled a looker-on, even though familiar with mechanical operations. Any spectator of his labours – who had seen him, at the risk of breaking his neck, driving in the great nails which he had made, into the bases of the two Douvres, at the entrance of the rocky passage, would never have guessed the use to which these nails were to be put, and would most probably have asked why he was taking such trouble. If, however, he had seen Gilliatt measuring the portion of the bulwarks which adhered to the wreck, then fastening a cable to the upper edge, then cutting it away with blows of his hatchet from the broken fastenings which held it in its place, and finally, with the assistance of the tide pulling it through the rugged channel, which moved it from below whilst Gilliatt dragged it from above, and, by dint of great labour, fasten with the cable this heavy mass of planks and beams – wider than the entrance of the passage itself – to the spikes driven into the base of the Little Douvre, the onlooker would have, perhaps, found it even more difficult to comprehend, why Gilliatt if he wished, for the purpose of carrying on his operations, to clear the channel between the two Douvres of all wreckage, had not allowed this mass to fall into the sea, so that it might be swept away as the tide receded.

But Gilliatt had reason for all he did. In order to fix the nails firmly in the base of the rocks he had taken advantage of every crack and crevice into which he had wedged pieces of wood, and had driven the nails into them. He had had the idea of doing similar work in the two rocks at the end of the passage on the eastern side, and fixed plugs of wood into all the crevices, as though he decided to prepare them for the reception of the higher spikes. But this appeared to be but a precaution on his part, and, for economy's sake, he could not afford to be wasteful of his material.

When the first difficulty was overcome, another presented itself. Unhesitatingly Gilliatt passed from one to the other, with the step and power of a Hercules.

CHAPTER IV

SUB RE

The man who had achieved all this, was in appearance terrible to behold.

In his arduous toil, he had exhausted nearly all his strength, and with difficulty regained it. Privations on the one hand, and weariness on the other, had emaciated him. His hair and beard had grown long and ragged. He had but one shirt left that was not in tatters. His feet were bare, for the wind had carried away one shoe, whilst the sea had taken the other. Splinters from his anvil had covered his hands and arms with cuts and scratches; which, if not deep, were rendered very painful by the salt water.

Hunger, cold, and thirst, were wearing him out. His fresh water was gone. His rye-meal had been eaten, and he had only a little biscuit remaining, which he had to break with his teeth – all the water, in which he used to soak it, having been used. Day by day his strength grew less.

The cruel rock was killing him. Where to obtain water was the first problem; how to procure food the second; where the sleep the third. He ate, when he caught a crayfish or a crab. He drank, when he saw a sea-bird alight on a rock; then he would clamber up to the spot and, sometimes, he rewarded by finding a little fresh water in some hollow in the rock. He drank after the bird, sometimes even with it; for the gulls and seamews had become used to his appearance, and no longer flew away from him. However hungry he felt, he never attempted to injure them. He had, as it will be remembered, a superstitious feeling regarding the feathered race. The birds, on their side – now that his hair was long and shaggy, and his beard unkempt – had no longer any fear of him. The change in his appearance had inspired them with confidence; they looked upon him no more as a man, but classed him with the wild goats.

Gilliatt and the birds were now very good friends. As friends in adversity, they mutually aided each other. So long as any meal remained, he would break up little portions of the cakes he had made, and scatter them about for their food, and they in their turn, guided him to the places where he could obtain fresh water. He ate the shell-fish that he collected raw, and eaten thus, in some measure his thirst was quenched. As for crabs, having no pot to boil them in, he roasted them between two stones brought to a red heat in his fire, after the fashion of savages. The equinoctial season had begun, and rain had commenced to fall heavily. Not showers or heavy falls, but in a regular deluge, which pierced through his clothes to the skin, and through the skin to the very bones. The rain yielded but little water for drinking purposes, but did not the less drench him thoroughly.

Niggardly in granting assistance, prodigal in heaping misery upon misery, such was this rain – an unkind blow from the sky. During a whole week Gilliatt endured the downpour, night and day. The rain was the greatest cruelty that the firmament could have inflicted on him. During the night, in his rocky lurking-place, his wearied frame could only enjoy a little slumber from its utter exhaustion. Large gnats which frequent the borders of the sea stung him, and he awoke covered with great blisters.

He fell a victim to a low fever, which gave him artificial strength; this fever, whilst acting as a help, ruins the constitution. Instinctively he chewed the moss, or sucked the leaves of the wild plants – a few of which grew in the crevices of the rocks. However, he paid little attention to his sufferings, and could give no time from his work to think of his own privations. He was getting on well with the work of rescuing the engines of the Durande, and he was satisfied. Frequently his work compelled him to plunge into the sea, and, after swimming a short distance, to land again. His clothes were soaked with salt water, which continually remains damp. Gilliatt lived constantly in a drenched condition. But use is second nature. Those poor families – old men, mothers, young girls, only half clad, and little children who pass the winter in the open air, exposed to the rain and snow, all huddled together in the street corners of London – live and die, not knowing what it is to be dry.

To suffer all this, to be drenched to the skin, and to endure all the agonies of thirst, was a strange species of torture which Gilliatt grew accustomed to. At times he sucked the rain-drops from his coat sleeve. The fires which he kindled were hardly sufficient to warm him. Fire in the open air does not impart much warmth; you are warm on one side and frozen on the other. Even when Gilliatt was perspiring he shivered. In the midst of a fearful silence, he felt all about him a strong spirit of opposition. He could detect the element of hostility closing around.

For him nature had a melancholy silence, and its non-activity was like a menace. A veil of unpleasantness surrounded him. He suffered from burns and shivering; the fire ate into his flesh; the water froze him; thirst threw him into a fever; the wind tore his clothes; hunger gnawed at his vitals. The combination of all these ills brought him down to the lowest depth of exhaustion. Obstacles, terrible in their nature, closed upon him in silence, apparently irresponsible for the ills they were inflicting, but full of a terrible unanimity, and he felt them weigh him down relentlessly. He had no means of escaping from them. It was as though he were persecuted by some living power. It was impressed upon Gilliatt's inner being that there was some hidden hatred working against him. He could avoid it by flight, but as he had elected to remain at his post, he must face it. He had against him an impenetrable hostility; could he not expel it, it would get the better of him. It! What? Who was it? The unknown. It clasped him tightly, pressed him almost to suffocation, and stopped his breath. He was being slowly murdered by the invisible; each day this mysterious vice gave an extra turn. The situation of Gilliatt, in the midst of all this, resembled an unfair duel, in which someone is playing the traitor.

This unity of unknown powers surrounded him. He felt that there was a plot on foot to get rid of him. It is thus that the iceberg chases the portion which has been detached from it. With the air of having scarcely touched him, this conspiracy had rent his clothes to tatters, had left him bleeding and in distress, and, so to speak, disabled him before the battle had commenced. He did not cease his toil for all that; but as the work itself progressed, the worker lost ground. It might be said that cruel nature, dreading the bold spirit that he exhibited, had adopted a plan of attacking his bodily strength, but Gilliatt maintained a bold front, and waited. The sea had commenced the attack, would the sea continue it?

The Douvres – those granite dragons lying in ambush in the open sea – had granted him shelter. They had permitted him to enter and do as he wished; but their hospitality was that of the wild beast who welcomes the traveller to his den with open jaws.

The trackless surface, the unfathomable space all around

him and over his head, so filled with opposition to the will of man.

The relentless and silent determination of phenomena following the course mapped out for them.

The mighty laws of nature, implacable and passive, with all their ebbs and flows; the rocks themselves, whose every point is a centre of the irradiation of currents; the wind, indescribable, plot to strangle with blighting contempt the rashness of a mortal. The blasts of winter, the clouds, the waves that besieged and slowly closed around and imprisoned him, separating him from all companionship, was like a dungeon built up stone by stone around a living man. Everything seemed hostile to him – nothing on his side – he felt himself abandoned in solitude, enfeebled, forgotten, and broken down. His stores gone, his tools broken and useless; he suffered the pangs of hunger and thirst by day, and the freezing cold by night. His sufferings had inflicted upon him wounds, tatters, and rags, under which were painful sores, mangled hands, eyes burning with the glance of fever, but in them, for all that, the fixed light of determination. Magnificent light! – the invisible light of will! The eye of man is so constructed that it shows the virtue latent within. Its pupil tells how much true courage lurks within us.

Gilliatt's task seemed to tend towards the impossible; success was doubtful, and much effort had to be spent to attain a slight result, and this it was that imbued the struggle with a nobility and pathos peculiarly its own. That so much toil, such nights of danger, and such days of hardship should have been necessary in order simply to fix four beams over a wreck, and to sort and place upon one side that portion of it that was worth saving, and to adjust four blocks, with their ropes, was but one of the things attendant upon his lonely task.

But Gilliatt had undertaken this; indeed, had chosen it of his own free will. Fearing to trust an associate who might prove a rival – he had undertaken to work alone. The crushing enterprise, the risk, the danger, the toil which daily increased, the possible destruction of the salvor with its own work of salvage – famine, fever, nakedness, and distress – he had chosen all these for himself! Such was his sublime egotism. He resembled a man confined in a room, from which the air is being gradually pumped out. Vitality was leaving him slowly but surely, and yet he scarcely perceived it. But though bodily strength may fail, the will still remains.

Hope is but a secondary power, subordinate to the superior one of will, and is as nothing beside the miracles which will can accomplish. All the ground that Gilliatt lost from weakness he regained by fixity of purpose. The wasting away of the physical man under the devouring influence of the wilderness of the elements only served to give power and vigour to the moral side of his nature. Gilliatt was sensible of no fatigue, or, to speak more correctly, he would not yield to it. The soul that refuses to yield to the weakness of the body is an immense power in itself. He was not conscious of anything but the graduated steps in the progress of his task. He was miserable without knowing it. His end, which he so nearly attained, deceived him with illusions, and he submitted to suffering with no other thought than that contained in the words, '*Nil desperandum!*' The intoxication of his work flew to his head – strength of will is a potent drug. Its effects are termed heroism.

Gilliatt had become a kind of ocean Job, but he was a Job wrestling with difficulties – a Job fighting and keeping a bold front to affliction and distress – a Job determined to conquer. A bold combination of Job and Prometheus, if such names are not too grand to be applied to the poor fisher of crayfish and crabs.

CHAPTER V

SUB UMBRA

During the night Gilliatt, who felt a strange and indescribable emotion, awoke and peered out into the darkness.

His eyes were opened out on to the black night; the situation was a dismal one, and filled his mind with anxiety.

Such a thing as darkness can be felt. A strange roofing of shadow, a deep obscurity which no diver can penetrate – a light mingled with a darkness which half deadens and shrouds it – a

light in infinitesimal atoms, like minute seeds or the fine dust
of ashes – myriads of tiny lamps possessed of no illuminating
power – a diffusion of glittering particles, like sparks of fire
driven before the wind, and stopped short in their career – the
tumult of the whirlwind mingled with the silence of the grave
– a problem the solution to which must be sought at the foot
of the precipice – an enigma, showing and concealing its face –
the infinite, with the mask of darkness hiding its lineaments –
such is the night. Its oppressive weight lies heavily upon the
soul of man.

This conjunction of all mysteries – the cosmic mystery, the
unexplained revelation of Fate – crushes down human intellect. The presence of darkness acts in a different way upon
human nature. In the presence of night, man recognizes his
own incompleteness. He sees the gloom and feels his own
weakness. The dark sky is a blind man. Face to face with the
night, man bends, kneels, prostrates himself, crouches down,
and crawls to some cavity in the earth in which to hide his
head, or else vainly seeks for wings. Almost always he tries to
fly from the presence of the Unknown. He asks himself what
it is; he trembles, he bends his head before it, and yet
sometimes he wishes to go to it.

Where?

Yonder!

Where is that? What is it?

Curiosity upon this point is certainly forbidden, for on this
road all bridges that span the gulf are invisible. The arch in the
road to the Infinite is gone. But the thirst for that knowledge
which is forbidden has a fascination peculiarly its own, like the
giddy depth of the precipice. Where the foot may not tread, the
eye may reach; where sight fails, intellect may attain. There is
no man, however feeble his intellectual power may be, who
does not make the effort. The seeker after this mystery either
pursues or recoils before it, according to the depth of his soul.
In some natures it enlarges; with others it reduces the intellect.
The outlook is gloomy, for with it the indefinite mingles.
Should the night be still and cloudless, it is a depth of shadow,
but should it be stormy, it is an ocean of cloud. Its immeasurable depths half reveal themselves and yet mock our eager gaze –
close themselves against our explanations, but yet leave

themselves open to conjecture. Myriads of points of light only make the darkness beyond yet more gloomy – carbuncles, sparks, stars, existences revealed in unknown worlds; angry defiances to those who venture to approach too near the light – boundaries in the illimitable – beacons, where all is boundless, where all measurements fail – unfathomable and beyond all human power of measurement. One shining microscopic point, then another and another, it is the imperceptible linked with the gigantic. The light over there is a focus, that focus is a star, that star is a sun, that sun is a universe, and that universe is nothing. In the realm of the infinite number is a cypher. And yet those worlds, which are nothings, exist, and through them we experience the difference between the now existent and the never-to-be.

The inaccessible adds to the inexplicable, and this is the heavens, from a contemplation of which arises the mystery of the sublime phenomenon of the growth of the soul from reverence.

Whilst a feeling of awe is characteristic of man, the beast does not possess it. Intellect discovers in this supreme terror its eclipse and its proof.

Darkness is one of these influences over man – it produces fear; at the same time it is complex, hence the dread. Its combination weighs upon the spirit, and takes away all desire to resist it. Its complexity compels us to look outside ourselves, as though we were dreading some unexpected assault. We are resigned, but, at the same time, are on our guard. We are in the presence of That, whence comes our submission? of the Whole, whence comes our defiance? the unity of darkness contains a multiple – mysterious but visible in matter, sentient to the thought. It causes silence; the more reason to be on our guard.

Night is one of the mysteries of Nature. Bowed down with ties of intense solitude, it weighed heavily upon Gilliatt's brain. He did not understand it, but he felt its all-powerful influence. He possessed a wealth of deep, though clouded, intellectual thought, and a wild, unfettered soul.

CHAPTER VI

GILLIATT PLACES HIS SLOOP IN READINESS

The salving of the machinery which Gilliatt was meditating resembled closely an attempt at an escape from prison; and we all know what fertility of brain power, what patience and perseverance has been displayed in such achievements, as well as the industry that has been shown in them – industry carried to an almost impossible pitch – patience to a point of veritable agony. The man Thomas, for example, imprisoned in Mount Saint Michael, found means to conceal a large portion of his dungeon wall in his mattress. Another prisoner at Tulle, in 1820, removed a quantity of lead from the prison roof upon which the prisoners took exercise. Where did he get the knife to remove it? No one could imagine. Melted the lead. With what fire? That remained a mystery. Cast it. In what mould? This question can be answered. In a mould made of bread-crumbs. With this lead and this mould he made a key, and with this key he opened a lock of which he had never seen more than the key-hole. Much of this strange ingenuity was possessed by Gilliatt. He had once scaled and descended the cliff of Boisrosé. He was the Trenck of the wreck, the Latude of the machinery.

The ocean, like a keeper, kept strict watch over him, and unpleasant and annoying as the rain was, it had been of some benefit to him. He had collected a small quantity of fresh water, but he had no sooner filled his can than he emptied it. His thirst was insatiable.

On the last day of April, or it may have been later – all his preparations were complete. The floor of the engine-room was, as it were, framed by the eight cables of his tackling – four on one side and four on the other. The openings in the deck and keel through which these cables passed had been made circular. The planking had been sawn through, the timber cut with an axe, the iron work with a file, and the sheating with a chisel. That part of the keel immediately under the engine was cut away square, and was ready to descend with it, at the same time supporting it. All this huge swinging mass was only held up by one chain, which was kept in its position by a notch that had been filed in it. At this portion of the operations, when the end was so nearly attained, haste becomes prudence.

It was ebb tide – a favourable moment at which to commence. Gilliatt had succeeded in removing the axle of the paddle-wheels, the ends of which might have caught and checked the descent, but he had managed to make this ponderous mass fast in the engine-room. It was time to finish now or never. Gilliatt was not worn out – his will kept *him* up – but his tools were useless. The forge was rapidly becoming worn out. The stone anvil was shattered, and the blower no longer worked. The small fall of sea-water had left saline deposits in the joints, which prevented its having free play. Gilliatt went to the bay at the foot of the Man-Rock and examined his boat, to see that all was in order; he paid great attention to the four rings placed on the port and starboard sides; then, weighing anchor, he took the oars and brought his craft right under the Durande. The passage between the rocks was just wide enough to admit his boat, and there was plenty of water. Gilliatt had ascertained this on the day of his arrival. The feat, however, was difficult, and required delicate precision. The operation was the more delicate that he had to back in stern foremost, so that the mast and rigging of his boat should remain outside the wreck of the Durande. These embarrassments rendered Gilliatt's work awkward. It was not like entering the bay of the Man-Rock, where a turn of the tiller was sufficient; here it was necessary to push, drag, row, and take soundings all at the same time, and this took him over a quarter of an hour; but at last he succeeded, and the boat was now in position underneath the Durande, and firmly fixed there by means of two anchors. The strongest of these was placed so as to hold against the most powerful wind – that of the south-west. Then, with the aid of a lever and the capstan, Gilliatt lowered the two boxes containing the paddle-wheels into his boat, which were all ready in the slings. These cases served as ballast. Having got rid of these two boxes, Gilliatt fastened to the hook of the capstan-chain the sling of the regulating tackle gear, which was intended to act as a check upon the pulleys. Owing to the peculiar class of work upon which he was engaged, the very defects of his boat were of service to him. She had no deck; there was therefore more space for her cargo, which he could place in her bottom. Her mast stood well forward – too forward, perhaps, for some uses – so that there was more facility for loading her; and as the mast was outside the wreck, it in no way hindered her exit. His boat was like a great wooden shoe; but on the sea nothing is safer or more trustworthy than a boat of this description.

Whilst thus engaged, Gilliatt perceived that the sea was rising.

CHAPTER VII

A SUDDEN PERIL

The wind blew very light, from the west – a disagreeable habit which winds have during the equinox. The rising sea differs in its effects upon the Douvres, according to the quarter from which the wind is blowing. According to this the waves pour into the passage either from the east or from the west. If the sea comes in at the eastern extremity, it is comparatively gentle, but if through the western, it is always a raging, angry wave. This is because the east wind, blowing across the land, has but little force, whilst that from the west brings with it all the accumulated powers of the vast Western Ocean. The slightest breeze from that direction is to be feared. It rolls in vast billows from illimitable space, and hurls an angry sea against the mouth of a channel too narrow to admit it all at once. A sea which rushes through an aperture is always dangerous. Water is like a crowd of people; when the quantity which enters is less than the quantity that desires to effect an entrance, there is a terrible crush in the crowd, and a fierce upheaving in the waves. As long as the west wind blows, however slight the breeze may be, the Douvres are, twice a day, the victims of its fury. The tide pours in through the narrow channel, the rocks offer resistance, the channel yields not, and the wave, thus curbed, roars and rebounds violently, and dashes with impatient fury against the rocky sides of the passage; so that, with a light breeze from the west, the Douvres offer a singular spectacle. Outside, all is calm and tranquil, whilst within, a violent tempest is lashing the rocks, sending up clouds of foam as they dash against the granite walls. This local agitation can hardly be termed a tempest: it is but a sudden rebellion of the waves, but it is terrible. As for the north and south winds, they take the rock on the other side, and cause but little surf in the channel. The eastern entrance, it must be borne in mind, was close to the Man-Rock, and the dangerous opening to the west is at the opposite extremity, exactly between the two Douvres. It was in this opening that Gilliatt had anchored his boat under the hull of the Durande.

With the wind blowing from a dangerous quarter, a catas-trophe seemed inevitable. To be sure there was certainly not much wind, but yet sufficient to do a great deal of harm. Scarcely many hours had elapsed, when the sea, which was rising fast, would pour itself through the channel of the Douvres. Its first waves were already breaking on the outer reefs. The swell, fed by the Atlantic Ocean, would come without storm or tempest, and in one vast, overwhelming wave, bringing with it all the forces collected by it in its course from the shores of America to the coasts of Europe – a distance of two thousand leagues. This wave – one of the ocean's gigantic barriers – would rush to the gap, and, being caught by the two Douvres, standing like watch-towers at the entrance, or like pillars at the commencement of a defile, swelled by the tide, augmented by resistance, repulsed by the rock, and impelled onwards by the wind, it would strike the granite barriers with a mighty shock, and, with a thousand tossings and tumblings, with all the fury of a confined sea, would rush between the rocks, and, striking the boat and the Durande, would most likely shiver them to pieces.

A protection must be prepared to ward off this possibility, and Gilliatt was equal to the emergency. In some way it was necessary to prevent the sea from entering in too great a volume, without shutting it out entirely – in a sense to resist it, and at the same time to yield to it – to hinder the compression of the water in the channel, and to turn the deluge into a simple flood – to break the violence of the waves, and to soothe them into partial gentleness; and therefore it was necessary to substitute for the barrier that lashed them into rage the barrier which would mitigate their fury. Gilliatt with all that ingenuity which he found so much more efficient than mere brute force, sprang from rock to rock, like a wild goat in its native mountains, or like a monkey in its forest retreat, using the slightest pinnacle or projection as a rest for his feet; leaping into the water; emerging from it again; swimming in the pools; clambering up the rocks with a rope in his mouth and a hammer in his hand, he detached the cable which held the forward bulwarks of the Durande suspended from and made fast to the base of the Little Douvre, fashioned out of the ends of hawsers some sort of hinges, and, making this huge panel fast to the large nails driven into the rock, caused this vast mass to revolve on its hinges, like the gate of a great sluice, and so fixed that it would form a rudder to the force of the waves; one end being against the Great Douvre, whilst the other was firmly secured to the smaller one. Then he managed, by the same means as he had used before – that is to say, the big nails – to fix it by the same fastenings against the larger rock as he had done against the smaller, and made this enormous mass of woodwork fast against the two entrance pillars; completed its security by a chain hung across it like a sword-belt over a breast-plate, and in less than an hour this barrier against the inroads of the sea was finished, and the channel between the rocks closed as by a folding door. This massive apparatus, composed of beams and planks, which, flat on the surface of the sea, would have been a raft, but which, standing up, resembled a wall, had been, the tide assisting him, handled by Gilliatt with all the dexterity of a conjuror.

He had stolen a march on the sea; it might almost be said that the barrier had been set up before the sea had had time to prevent it. It was one of these occasions upon which Jean Bart might have uttered the famous expression of which he made use every time that he escaped shipwreck – 'The Englishman has been check-mated.' It is a well-known fact that Jean Bart, whenever he wished to ridicule the sea, called it, 'The Englishman'.

Having now fixed the barrier securely, Gilliatt's thoughts turned to his boat. He slackened the cables sufficiently to permit her to rise with the tide – what old sailors called 'anchoring with bearings'. Gilliatt had not for a moment permitted himself to be taken by surprise; every need had been carefully foreseen. The eye of a sailor could have detected this at once in the two pulleys of the top ropes, cut into the shape of snatch blocks, and fixed in the stern of the boat, through which ran two ropes passing through the rings of the anchors.

The tide had now begun to flow; half-flood had arrived – a time when, even in calm weather, the force of the waves may be considerable. What Gilliatt expected, happened. The waves hurled themselves against the barrier, and broke as they met it; and then, with all that dangerous power taken from them, rolled underneath it. Outside was the swell; within was deadened by infiltration. Gilliatt as it were had designed a kind of forked gridiron, and the vanquishing sea rolled peacefully through and beneath it.

CHAPTER VIII

MOVEMENT, WITH SMALL PROGRESS

The climax had at last arrived, and the problem to be solved was how to place the engine on board the boat.

Deep in thought, Gilliatt remained some minutes holding the elbow of his left arm in his right hand, and his left hand pressed to his temple. Then he clambered on to the wreck, a portion of which (the engines) was to be removed, and the rest (the hull) was to remain. He severed the four slings which fastened the four chains of the funnel to the port and starboard sides. The slings were only of rope, so that he easily cut them with his knife. Thus set free, they hung down by the side of the funnel. From the wreck he climbed on to the apparatus that he had constructed, tested the beams with his foot, examined the blocks, looked at the pulleys, tried the cables, gave an eye to the splicings, and saw that his untarred twine was not soaked through; found that nothing was wanting and everything was ready; then, springing from his props on to the deck, he took his post near the capstan, in that part of the Durande which was to remain grasped in the clutch of the Douvres. This was the post from which he was to commence his labours.

Impressed with his deep responsibility, his bosom unaffected by any useless feelings of emotion, he took one last glance at his tackle; then, seizing his file, began to cut the chain which kept the whole mass suspended. The chain of the capstan, which regulated the gear, was within easy reach of his hand. All of a sudden there was a crash; the chain, half cut through by the file, snapped suddenly, and the whole apparatus began to oscillate. Gilliatt had only just time to spring to the regulating tackle, the chain of which beat wildly against the side of the rock, the eight cables stretched, and the whole mass, sawn and cut through, tore itself away from the wreck; the entire interior of the Durande opened, and the iron flooring of the engine-house appeared through the keel. Had not Gilliatt so promptly grasped the regulator the whole must have fallen, but his powerful hand was ready at the right moment, and it descended steadily.

When Pieter, the brother of Jean Bart – that powerful and talented drunkard, that poor fisherman of Dunkirk, who spoke so familiarly to the Grand Admiral of France – saved the sloop *Langeron* when in distress in Ambleteuse Bay, and, in order to draw the heavy floating mass through the breakers of the raging bay, he reefed the mainsail with marine reeds, trusting that they would break away at the right moment and give the sail to the winds. He trusted to this rupture, as Gilliatt had trusted to the chains breaking at the right moment, and the strange rashness was crowned with equal success on both occasions.

Gilliatt's manipulation of the regulator acted admirably. Its function, as it will be remembered, was to put a check upon the powers of the apparatus, thus reduced from many to one, and to bring them all into united operation. It had somewhat similar properties to the bridle of a bowline, except that, instead of being used to trim a sail, its duties were to balance with due equilibrium the somewhat complicated mechanism. Standing erect by the capstan, Gilliatt had, we may say, his hand on the safety-valve of the whole thing. This was certainly a remarkable result of his inventive genius, and a wonderful coincidence of forces was the result.

As the engine of the Durande descended in a solid mass towards the boat, the boat rose slowly to receive it – the wreck and the boat that came to its aid assisting each other by opposite movements, and meeting each other half way, spared themselves half the labour. The rising tide raised the boat, and brought it closer to the Durande. The sea was now more than conquered – it was tamed, and took its part in the work. The swell lifted the boat gently, taking as much care of it as if it had been made of porcelain. Gilliatt combined and proportioned the two labours – that of the water and that of the apparatus, and like some impressive statue holding sway over all around it, he regulated the speed of the descent by the rate of the ascension. There was no hitch in the arrangements, no jerk from the waves, no slip in the tackle – it was a strange confederacy of all kinds of forces united together and tamed. On one side was gravitation lowering the engine, on the other the sea raising the boat towards it. The attraction of the earth, which we call weight, seemed to unite and to serve Gilliatt as faithful slaves. Their submission knew neither stop or stay and, under the control of a commanding spirit, these passive powers became active auxiliaries. Every minute the work progressed, and the interval between the wreck and the boat perceptibly diminished. The conjunction was effected in silence and, as it were, in a sort of terror of the man who was standing there directing it all. The element had received an order, and was preparing to execute it.

As the tide stopped flowing, the cables ceased to unwind. Suddenly, but without commotion, the pulleys ceased to work and the block stopped. The engine, as though lowered by a powerful hand, had taken its place in the boat. It stood there, straight, upright, firm, and immovable. The iron flooring remained with its four corners resting evenly in the bottom of the boat.

It was all over! Gilliatt had succeeded at last.

The poor fellow gazing at it, wondered at his own success, which was not spoilt by joy. He was bowed by the weight of his intense happiness. He felt his limbs bend beneath him, and, in his hour of triumph, the man, whom no danger had been able to daunt, began to tremble.

He looked at the boat beneath the wreck, and at the engine in the boat. He could hardly believe his senses. He had never believed in ultimate success. A miracle had been performed by him, and he looked on the result with astonishment.

This state of mind did not last. Like a man who starts suddenly from a dream, he rushed to his saw and cut the eight cables; then, separated from the boat, owing to the rising tide, by only ten feet, he jumped into it, and, taking a bundle of thin rope, made four slings, which he passed through the rings prepared beforehand, and fastened on each side of his boat the four chains of the funnel, which an hour before had been firmly fixed on board the Durande. The funnel once secured, he disengaged the upper part of the machinery. A square portion of the planking of the Durande still adhered to it. Gilliatt took out the nails and released the boat from this encumbrance of planks and joists, throwing them upon the rocks on one side. This lightening of his boat was a sensible improvement. His boat remained steady under the weight of the engines, as he had expected that it would do; she only sank to a fair water-line. The Durande's engine, though weighty, was not so heavy as the rocks and the gun which he had brought from the Isle of Herm on the day of the regatta.

His task was over; nothing now remained for him but to return to Guernsey.

CHAPTER IX

A VICTORY GAINED BUT LOST IMMEDIATELY

But there is many a slip 'twixt cup and lip, and all was not yet finished. To reopen the channel closed by his improvised sluice-gate – to take his boat out of the rock – was clearly the first thing to be done. Every moment was precious. Hardly a breath of wind, scarcely a ripple on the waters – a lovely evening, which gave promise of a fine night. The sea perfectly calm, but the reflux beginning to be felt, it was indeed the very hour for leaving the reef. The falling tide would take him out of the Douvres, and he would have the benefit of the rising tide for his return to Guernsey. He ought to be at Saint Peter's Port early in the morning. But now an unexpected obstacle presented itself. Gilliatt had allowed one thing to escape his foresight. The engines were free, but the funnel was still held prisoner. The sea in lifting up the boat to the wreck, whilst it lessened the dangers of the descent, and assisted the removal of the engines, had left the top of the funnel in the square opening in the yawning hull of the Durande. It was imprisoned there as safely as between four walls. This complicated matters. It appeared as if the sea, forced to obey Gilliatt, had at the last moment changed its mind. What the ebb-tide had done, the flood would undo. The chimney, some eighteen feet in height, had nearly eight feet in the interior of the Durande, and the sea would fall nearly twelve feet, so that as the boat sank lower there would be plenty of room for the chimney to be easily disengaged from the wreck.

But how long would this take? In six hours it would be nearly midnight. How could he follow the channel through the breakers in the dark, when it was even difficult to do so by the light of day; and how dare he risk the open sea, so full of treacherous shoals, in the dark and gloom of the night? If he were forced to wait until the next day, those six lost hours would make him lose at least twelve. He could not even think of abridging his labours by reopening the mouth of the passage; the barrier would be necessary for the approaching tide.

Nothing was now left for Gilliatt to do, but to sit down and rest, and watch his opportunity, a thing that Gilliatt had not done since he had taken up his abode on the rock. This enforced idleness irritated and annoyed him almost as much as if it had been brought about by his own fault. He muttered to himself 'What would Déruchette say, if she saw me idling like this?' Perhaps after all, a little repose was necessary. His boat was now at his disposal, and he determined to pass the night in her. He ascended the Great Douvre and brought back his sheepskin, supped on a few shell-fish, and, feeling very thirsty, drank the last few mouthfuls of water that remained in the bottom of his can; wrapped himself up in his sheepskin, the wool of which gave him a pleasurable sensation, and, crouching down like a watchdog beside the engine, drew his cap over his brows and fell asleep. He slept soundly. After such labour men sleep well.

CHAPTER X

THE SEA'S WARNING

Towards morning he woke up suddenly, as if moved by some hidden power.

High above his head, the rocks were lighted up by a bright white light. On the dark face of the rock there was a reflection like that of a mighty glare.

From whence came this light?

From the sea.

It was a wondrous sight.

It appeared as though a mass of flame. As far as the eye could stretch – on the rock and beyond it – the sea was filled with fire. This blaze had nothing of the red glare of volcanoes or furnaces; no sparkling, no heat, no purple edging and no noise. Ghastly trails of a bluish tint looked like the folds of a winding sheet.

A dull pale light reflected on the wave. It was the spectre of a fire more than a fire itself. It resembled the hideous illumination of the inside of a sepulchre by the light of an unearthly dream.

It was as though darkness was struggling with fire that wished to consume it.

The night – the vast, wide-spreading night – appeared to form the fuel of this pale flame. It was a weird illumination, issuing out of darkness. Shadow was one of the component parts of the spectral light.

Sailors thoroughly understand all these phosphorescences, so full of warning to the mariner. These appearances are not at all extraordinary.

Looked at in this light things lose their individuality. A spectral glimmer renders them transparent; rocks become mere outlines; cables and anchors look like bars of iron brought to a white heat. The fisherman's net, seen beneath the wave, resembles welded links of fire. Half the oar is ebony; the other, as it dips into the water, resembles solid silver. As the drops of water fall from it they seem to sow the wave with silvery stars. The wake of each vessel looks like a comet. The sailors drenched with the spray, appear like men on fire. Plunge your hand beneath the surface, and you draw it forth with a glove of fire on it. But the flame is dead, and does not burn. Your arm becomes a firebrand. You see the strange creatures of the sea rolling about as though in liquid fire. The foam is a cloud of sparks. Fish are tongues of flame, or morsels of lightning darting through pallid depths.

This peculiar light had made its way through Gilliatt's eyelids; it was this that had aroused him from his sleep.

His waking was well-timed.

The ebb tide had exhausted itself, and the flow had begun to rise. The funnel of the engine, which had been released from its prison during Gilliatt's sleep, was about once more to be seized by the yawning cavity above it.

Slowly it rose; a foot more would have been sufficient to imprison it again. The tide rises a foot in half-an-hour: Gilliatt had therefore half-an-hour before him to effect its deliverance.

With a bound, he sprang up, yet, urgent as was the necessity for immediate action, he could not refrain from contemplating the phosphorescence of the ocean, and meditating upon it.

Gilliatt and the sea were old friends. Although he had often suffered from her, yet for many years she had been his companion. That mysterious creature called the ocean had nothing in her most secret depths which he could not divine. By dint of observation, and from the solitary life he led, Gilliatt had become skilled in all her changes; he was what is called weather-wise. He ran to the top-ropes and payed out some cable, and then, when she was no longer restrained by the anchors, he seized the boat-hook, and, pressing sharply against the walls of the passage, pushed the boat some fathoms from the wreck, and closer to his recently-formed barrier. In ten minutes the boat was withdrawn from beneath the shattered hull of the Durande; no more fear now of the funnel being caught again. The tide might rise as fast as it liked; but, for all that, Gilliatt made no preparations for leaving the rock. He glanced once more at the phosphorescent waters, then he weighed the anchors; but it was only to let them go again and moor the boat more securely than ever nearer to the entrance of the passage.

That light in the sea, which he had been observing so intently, was threatening, but it had done him good service. Had it not been for its appearance he would still have been asleep, and the dupe of the night. It had aroused him, and made objects round him visible. It shed an ill-omened light over the rock. But these gleams, threatening as they appeared to Gilliatt, had this much use in them; that they had rendered the coming change visible, and enabled him to take his precautions; and now, whenever he wished to set sail, his boat, upon which was the engine, was at liberty.

But Gilliatt now seemed less and less inclined to take his departure. His boat safely anchored, he sought for a chain, the strongest that he had in his storehouse, and fastened it to the nails driven into the Douvres; he strengthened it inside with a rampart of planks and joists, already protected by another double chain. Far from opening the exit, he barred it more securely. The phosphorescent light had enabled him to work, but it was dying away, and the dawn was drawing near, Gilliatt stood still and listened.

CHAPTER XI

WHISPERINGS IN THE AIR

Strange fancies rushed through his brain and he thought he heard a faint and indistinct murmur coming towards him across the wide expanse of ocean. These sounds issue at certain hours from the bosom of the mighty deep. He listened eagerly. The distant sound began once more. Gilliatt shook his head; he knew too well what it meant. In another moment he was at the eastern entrance, which, until then, had been left open, and, with powerful strokes of his hammer, he was hastily driving spike nails into the crevices of the granite, forming the sides of the passage leading to the Man-Rock as he had before done in the one between the Douvres. The fissures in these rocks had been already prepared and wedged with heart of oak. This side of the rock was much weather-beaten, and there were many cavities in it, and Gilliatt was able to fix more nails than he had been able to do in the base of the Douvres.

Suddenly, as though by signal, the phosphorescent light was extinguished, and the dawn, becoming every moment brighter, replaced it.

Gilliatt now dragged thither beams, ends, and chains, and, without for a moment relaxing his efforts, began to construct, across the channel leading to the Man-Rock, with beams placed horizontally and secured by cables, one of those barriers which the science of to-day had adopted and called a breakwater. Those who have witnessed, at Rocquaine, in Guernsey, or at Bourg-d'eau, in France, the effect produced by some stakes planted in the rocks, will readily comprehend the advantages of these simple preparations. Breakwaters are the fortifications against the tempest. It is useless to fight against the sea unless you take advantage of the divisibility of its power.

The sun had risen bright and pure, the heaven was clear, the sea calm, and Gilliatt hurried in his work; he was calm, too, but, in his haste, there was a tinge of anxiety. He jumped from rock to rock, from the breakwater to the store, and back again to the breakwater dragging with him sometimes a rider and sometimes a binding stake. The reason for his having stowed away all these timbers was now apparent. He had done so in anticipation of a danger which was now imminent. A strong iron bar served as a lever to move the heavy timbers with. The work was executed with such rapidity that it rather resembled a growth than a construction. He who has not witnessed the formation of a military pontoon can have no idea of the celerity with which such works can be effected.

The channel to the eastward is narrower than the western one, and had an entrance of less than six feet. The smallness of the aperture aided Gilliatt, as the space to close and fortify was so much less; the breakwater here would therefore be stronger and much more simple. Horizontal beams were therefore sufficient, the upright ones being useless.

The front timbers of the breakwater were now placed in position, and Gilliatt climbed upon it and listened.

The almost indistinct murmur had more meaning to it now. Gilliatt continued his work. He supported it with the Durande's cat-heads, bound to an outer line of beams by ropes passed through pulleys. He secured the whole with chains.

The whole apparatus was little more than a gigantic hurdle, having beams for stakes and chains instead of wattles, and was plaited together, not built.

He added to the fastenings, and put in additional nails where they were required; for, having secured a large quantity of bar-iron in the wreck, he had been enabled to manufacture a great store of nails.

He ate and worked at the same time. He was very thirsty, but he had drained his can of its last drop of water at supper the night before, but still he worked manfully on.

He inserted four or five pieces of timber, then, once more mounting the barricade, he listened. The sounds in the distant horizon had ceased and all was silent. The sea was calm and beautiful, meriting all those complimentary epithets which landsmen address to her when she behaves well to them – 'a mirror', 'a lake', 'smooth as oil', 'calm as a sheep', and many others. The deep blue of the heavens contrasted with the deep green of the sea; the sapphire of the one could envy the emerald of the other. Neither had the advantage. Not a cloud in the heavens, not a streak of foam on the sea, and above them shone the glorious sun of April. It was impossible to hope for a more lovely day.

A long dark line of birds of passage appeared in the distant horizon. Their flight appeared to be a hurried one, and they were making direct for the land, and Gilliatt hastened to his work on the breakwater. He raised it as high as he could – as high as the curved sides of the rock would permit. Towards noon the sun seemed hotter than it should have been for the time of year. Midday is the critical period of the twenty-four hours, and Gilliatt, standing upon the powerful framework which he had erected, looked long and fixedly at the ocean.

It was more than calm; it seemed absolutely stagnant. Not a sail was to be seen. The sky was still limpid, only it had changed from blue to white. This white had a strange look. On the western horizon there was a slight ominous patch of cloud. This remained in the same place, but seemed gradually to spread and to increase in size. Near the breakers the waves began to quiver, but very gently.

Gilliatt had done well to erect his breakwaters, for there was a storm approaching. The elements had decided not to surrender their prey without a struggle.

BOOK III

THE STRUGGLE

CHAPTER I

EXTREMES MEET

There is nothing more disastrous than a late equinox. A strange phenomenon then occurs in the sea, which is called the meeting of ocean winds.

At such seasons – particularly at the period of the full moon, at the moment when it is least to be expected – a sudden calmness manifests itself on the sea. Its vast eternal movement ceases. It seems to have grown weary and fallen into a kind of languor, and longs for rest. Every atom of bunting – from the humble steamer of the fisherman's boat to the ensign of the man-of-war – hang motionless from the masts. The Admiral's pennant and the Royal and Imperial banners all sleep. Suddenly they begin to flutter gently.

The moment has now come, if there be clouds in the sky, to watch their formation; if it is the hour of sunset, to look for redness in the west; if it is night, to examine the halo around the moon.

The storm glass is now useful to the mariner, if he is fortunate enough to possess one – to examine the instrument and to take his precautions against the south wind, if the mixture in the glass resembles crushed sugar; against the north wind, if it exfoliates in crystallizations like brakes, or brambles, or fircones. Then, too, the poor Irish or Breton fisherman, after having consulted some mysterious gnomon, with figures upon it, engraved by the Romans, or, perhaps, by the evil spirits – one of those straight enigmatical stones, called in Brittany a Menhir, and in Ireland a Cruach – hauls up his boat upon the shore.

The calmness both of sea and sky continue.

Meanwhile day breaks radiantly, and Nature smiles. It was this that filled the writers and prophets of ancient times with religious horror, for men then exclaimed against the falseness of the sun.

The imperfect vision of latent possibility is denied to man by the fatal obscurity of an existing state of things. Nothing is more to be dreaded and feared than the mask with which the ocean conceals her intending convulsions.

A storm beneath a calm.

Often hours, and sometimes days, pass in this way. Pilots direct their telescopes to all points of the compass. The features of old sailors harden into severity, arising from the secret rage that consumes them, as they look for fresh changes.

Suddenly and without warning, a loud, confused murmur is heard, like a mysterious conversation carried on in the air, but nothing is to be seen.

The wide expanse remains impassive.

Yet the sound increases, and grows louder and louder, whilst the dialogue becomes more distinct.

There is something hidden beyond the horizon.

A something terrible: it is force.

The wind, or rather that vortex which we call gales, is the outcome of this.

The Indians call them the Marouts; the Jews as the Kéroubims; the Greeks as the Aquilons. These are the invincible winged birds of prey of the Infinite; and these winds are rushing upon us.

CHAPTER II

THE WINDS OF THE SEA

Who will explain the true meaning of this mystery, and from whence do they come? Are they from the fathomless depths?

Their gigantic pinions require the breadth of the gulfs of ocean, their wide-spreading wings require the illimitable distances of the solitudes of the desert. Those wide-extending plains of blue – the Atlantic and the Pacific – are their favourite resorts. They collect there in troops. Commander Page once saw seven water-spouts at once in the open sea. They are there in all their native ferocity. They plot over the disasters that they will cause. Their business is to watch over the eternal ebb and flow of the tides. We are ignorant how far their powers go; we know not what are their wishes. They are the sphinxes of the abyss, and Vasco de Gama was their Oedipus. In the gloom of that wide and ever-moving expanse they appear with their features draped in clouds. He who catches a glimpse of their livid lineaments in that wide dispersion, feels himself in the presence of an invincible force. It might be said that human intelligence caused them uneasiness, and that they rebelled against it. The mind of man is not to be conquered, but the elements sometimes prove stronger. What can be done against this power, which cannot be grasped? The gentle breeze swells up until it smites, and then lulls down to gentleness once more. The winds begin the battle by violence and tumult, and defend themselves by dying away into space. Do we go to meet them, or do they come to us? Varied orders of battle and swiftly-repeated blows disconcert the most courageous. They are as often retreating as advancing. They are impalpably tenacious. Who can oppose them? Colombus, perceiving them approaching his vessel, mounted the poop of the *Pinta*, and addressed them in verses from the Bible. Surcouf insulted them: 'Here come the gang!' he would exclaim. Napier discharged his guns at them. Chaos is theirs entirely, and by means of its power they wreak their mysterious vengeance. The home of the winds is more terrible than the den of lions. How many corpses are lying in those deep abysses in space, by which the bitter, pitiless winds pass with angry howls? We hear them wherever they go, but they listen to no one. Every deed of theirs is a crime. None knew upon whom they have placed their angry hands, flecked with the foam of the surf. What impious ferocity do they exhibit in shipwrecks! What insults to Providence! They have, at times, the air of hurling their foam against the Creator. They are the tyrants of unknown regions.

Things impossible to be described go on there. A spectre on horseback rides through the gloom; the air is full of forest sounds; nothing can be seen, but the tramp of cavalry is heard. It is day; suddenly it changes to night; a hurricane comes, and night changes to day. The Polar Lights are shining. Whirlwinds pass in inverse ways, and interlaced in a sort of hideous dance, a kind of stamping of a plague on the water. An over-burdened cloud opens and falls on the sea. Other clouds, with red light, flash and roar, then frown again angrily. The cloud, once emptied of its lightnings, grows black, like an extinguished coal. Sheets of rain dissolve into mist. There is a furnace, upon which it rains; here are waves from which the flames issue. The white gleam of the sea beneath the falling rain is reflected far and wide. In the inaccessible darkness great sheaves of shadow quiver. Occasionally there is a convulsion. Rumour becomes tumult, as the wave becomes surf. The horizon oscillates continuously, and murmurs in a low tone. Strange outbursts disturb the monotony. You can almost imagine that you can hear the sneezing of hydras. Cold and hot blasts succeed each other. The shuddering of the sea announces a coming terror from the depths of the waters. Suddenly, the hurricane descends upon the ocean, like a wild and thirsty beast seeking water. A strange draught. The sea rises to the invisible mouth; a waterspout is formed. In the presence of the waterspout the thunder itself is silent.

Such are these terrible unknown regions.

Water is incompressible, and is therefore supple. It slips from your grasp without an effort of its own. Forced into a corner on one side, it escapes on the other. It is thus that the water becomes the wave, and the billows are a sign of its freedom.

CHAPTER III

THE EXPLANATION OF THE NOISES

The expansion of winds generally descend upon the earth at the time of the equinox. At this time, the equilibrium of the poles and tropics are in the balance, and the colossal atmospheric tides pour their flow upon one hemisphere, and their ebb upon another. There are two signs of the Zodiac which rule these matters – Libra and Aquarius.

The storms are now in season, and the sea hides their coming in silence.

Often the sky has an evil look – it is palid, and a thick dark veil obscures its face. Sailors look with uneasiness at this angry aspect of the clouds, though it is the air of its tranquillity that alarms them the most. A smiling sky in the equinox is a tempest in silk and velvet. It is skies like this that especially engage the attention of mothers, wives, and daughters, when eagerly examining the distant horizon.

When the autumnal storms delay their advent, it is because they are collecting their forces, and amassing their fury for destruction. Beware of the tempest that has been long in coming. 'The sea pays its old debts.' Though the delay may be a long one, the sea only exhibits her impatience by a more profound calm; only the magnetic influence is shown by the fiery appearance of the sea. Fire issues from the waves, electric air produces phosphoric water. The sailors experience a strange feeling of languor. These seasons are very dangerous for iron ships, as they are particularly liable to variations of the compass. And many are lost in this manner. To those who are acquainted with the sea, its aspect at this time is very strange and interesting. It seems to be longing for and yet afraid of the coming cyclone. Certain nuptials, though strongly urged by nature, are received in the same fashion. The lioness, in her moments of passion, flies before the lion. The sea also has its passions, hence its state of trembling expectancy. The gigantic union is in course of preparation. This marriage, like those of the Roman emperors, is celebrated by human sacrifices. The *fête* is accompanied with disasters.

From far-off depths, from unapproachable latitudes, from the gloomy region of solitude, and from the boundless realms of the free ocean, the winds pour in.

Be prepared then, for this is the equinox!

A storm is now in process of formation. In the old legends of heathen mythology, these entities were recognized indistinctly moving on the mighty stage of nature. Eolus conspired with Eoreas. In order to divide their tasks equally, element allies itself with element. One has to give power to the wave, the cloud, and the stream. The night, too, is a confederate, and must be employed. There are compasses to falsify, beacons to be extinguished, lighthouses to be obscured, and stars to be hidden. The sea must co-operate. A dull murmur precedes every storm. Far away, beyond the horizon, the hurricane whispers its last commands before it sets forth. This is the noise that is heard afar off in the darkness, amidst the startled silence of the sea.

It was this dreaded murmur which had reached the ears of Gilliatt. The phosphorescence of the sea had been his first warning, the low, dull whisper the second.

The wind is complex, but the air is one; and so it follows that all storms are compounds – a principle that results from the unity of the air. Both heaven and the sea, in all their entirety, take part in the storm. All these powers are mustered for the battle. A wave is a gust below; a gust is a wave on high. To be caught in a whirlwind is to be in the hands of both sea and sky. Menier, who is a great marine authority, the pensive astronomer of the little cottage of Cluny, said: 'The wind of everywhere is everywhere.' He did not believe in winds being confined, even in narrow seas. In his idea there were no such things as midstream winds. He declared that he could recognize a wind as it wandered about the house.

The wind is ubiquity itself. If the demon Legion exists, he can be no other than the wind.

Winds are certainly more prevalent in certain regions than in others. Nothing is more sure than that continuous air-currents do exist, and that one day aerial navigation will be carried out by aerial vessels, thus utilizing the currents of the winds.

The fraternity of the air and the wind cannot for a moment be denied. There are rivers of wind, streams of wind, and brooks of wind, only their branches are the reverse of the branches of water; it is brooks that arise from streams, and streams from rivers, instead of falling into them as they do on land; and instead of concentrating, they disperse. This dispersion composes the solidarity of the winds and the unity of the atmosphere. The displacement of one particle of matter results in the displacement of another. All winds move together. To these profound causes of amalgamation must be added the irregular surface of the globe, whose lofty mountains pierce the firmament, causing the winds to twist and turn and deviate from their course, and determining the course of counter-currents and unbanded radiation.

This phenomena of the wind is caused by the oscillation of two oceans one upon the other – the ocean of air upon the ocean of water, resting on these currents, and thus acquiring a sort of trembling motion.

The indivisible is not divided into compartments. No partition separates wave from wave. The Channel Islands feel the blast from the Cape. Universal navigation contends everywhere with the same monster. The sea is a hydra. Under that unity reposes infinite variety.

CHAPTER IV

TURBA TURMA

There are thirty two points of the compass, consequently this tells us that there are thirty-two winds – that is to say, thirty-two points; but these points may be divided. Classed by its direction, the wind is incalculable; classed by its kinds, it is infinite. Homer himself would have shrunk from the task of enumerating them.

The Polar current encounters the tropical current – cold and heat are thus combined. The waves of the wind issue forth, and are swollen up, dispersed, shattered in all directions in fierce streams. The dispersion of the winds to the four corners of the horizon causes a terrible disturbance.

Every wind which blows is forced there. The wind of the Gulf Stream, which disgorges the fogs of Newfoundland; the wind of Peru – that silent land, where thunder is never heard; the wind of Nova Scotia; the whirlwinds of Fer, in the China seas; the wind of Mozambique, which destroys canoes and junks; the electric wind of Japan, whose coming is announced by strokes on a gong; the wind of Africa, which dwells between Table Mountain and the Mountain of the Devil; the wind of the equator, which passes over the trade winds, describing a parabola, whose point is always to the west; the Plutonion wind which issues from craters; the singular fiery blast, which bursts from the volcano Awa, and occasions a perpetual olive-tinted cloud in the north; the monsoon of Java, against whose ravages the inhabitants built fortifications, which they call hurricane houses; the wind that the English call the Bush Wind. The Pampero in Chili, and the Rebojo at Buenos Ayres, which bears away the gigantic condor to the sea, and saves him from the lurking-place, where the Indian, bow and arrow in hand, is waiting for him; the chemical wind, which, according to Lemery, produces thunderbolts from the clouds; the Harmattan of the Kaffirs; the Polar snow-driver, which attaches itself to the icebergs; the wind of the Gulf of Bengal, which reaches to Nijini-Novogorod, in which is held the great Asian fair; the wind of the Cordilleras, which makes the woods and forests quiver; the wind of the Australian Archipelago, where the hunters take the honey of the wild bees, hidden under the forked branches of the giant eucalyptus, the sirocca, the minstral, the hurricane, the dry winds, the inundating, the diluvian, and the torrid winds, which scatter dust on the plains of Brazil and over the streets of Genoa; which both obey and revolt against diurnal rotation. Those winds which work together, conspiring to do mischief – one undoing the work of the other – those old winds which attacked Columbus, and nearly prevented Magellan's approach to the Pacific; and those which dismasted Philip II's Armada. Then there are the winds that bring frogs, locusts, and living things across the sea, and a thousand other different varieties, whose names and qualities it would be impossible to enumerate. The Douvres, as Gilliatt was building his break-waters, heard their distant gallop.

The combined army was coming.

On one side there was a legion in battle array.

Upon the other there was only Gilliatt.

CHAPTER V

GILLIATT AND HIS ALTERNATIVES

The powers had chosen their time well.

Still chance, if it exerts itself, is skilful.

So long as the boat had been moored in the little bay, near the Man-Rock, and so long as the machinery had been secure in the wreck, the position of Gilliatt was safe.

The boat was secure, and the machinery beyond the reach of danger. The Douvres, which held the engine in its grasp, had certainly condemned it to a lingering destruction, but protected it against sudden accidents. In any case, had the engine been destroyed, Gilliatt would have escaped uninjured, for he had still his boat as a means of retreat.

To wait until his boat had been removed from its anchorage where she could not have been harmed, and to allow her to be moored in the passage of the Douvres; to watch until she was entangled amongst the rocks, and to allow Gilliatt to carry out all his operations for the rescue of the engine, and to put it safely on board his sloop, and even to lend a helping hand to his success, was but a trap that the elements had laid for him. Now, for the first time, he began to see, in all its sinister nature, the trick that the ocean had been for so long a time preparing to play him. The engine, the boat, and her owner, were now all three in the passage between the rocks.

It was easy for the hurricane to direct its attack upon one point; and to shatter the boat, sink the engine, and drown Gilliatt, this could all be done at once and at the same moment. No situation could have been more critical than that of Gilliatt.

Dreamers believe the sphynx to be concealed behind a cloud, and if this belief is correct, it certainly seemed to have placed him on the horns of a dilemma.

What was he to do?

To remain was terrible; to go was the act of a madman!

CHAPTER VI

THE COMBAT

To the summit of the Great Douvres Gilliatt climbed. From thence he could cast his eye over the wide ocean. The appearance on the western side was appalling. A vast wall seemed to have been erected – a wall of cloud, barring the mighty expanse from side to side, and arising from the horizon to the zenith. This wall, ascending with a perfectly straight surface, without a crack or a crevice in it, seemed to have been built with the aid of the square and the plumb-line. It looked more like a granite cliff than a cloud. The precipitous face of the cloud was perfectly straight at the southern extremity, but, towards the north, curved a little, like a bent sheet of iron, and showed the slippery face of an inclined plane. This dark bank of cloud grew and increased, but its entablature was always on a level with the line of the horizon, which was becoming indistinct in the approaching darkness. Silently, and foot by foot, this airy fabric ascended. Not an adulation, not a wrinkle, not a projection broke its uniform appearance. This immovability in motion presented a curious and weird appearance. The pallid scene, in the midst of a sickly transparency, illumined this feature of the *Apocalypse*. The cloud had now invaded the greater portion of the open space, shelving like the fearful slope of the abyss.

It seemed as though some huge, shadowy mountain was rising between earth and sky. It was nightfall at mid-day. There was a suffocating heat, like that coming from an open furnace – a fiery blast, that seemed to issue from that strange chaotic mass. The sky changed from blue to white, the white became like a gigantic slate. No breath of air in the sky, no wave in the sea, no sound. The sea was dull and leaden-hued, and far as the eye could see was deserted. The birds had all disappeared. The growth of the monstrous mass increased perceptibly. The enormous bank of cloud, advancing upon the Douvres, may be termed a battle-cloud. An ominous mass of vapour, through whose openings stealthy glances seemed to be cast on the spectator.

This slow and regular advance was terrifying. Gilliatt fixed his eyes on the cloud and thought: 'I was thirsty, but you will supply me with enough to drink.' He remained for a time, his eyes fixed on the cloud; it appeared as if he were studying the coming storm. His cap was in the pocket of his jacket; he took it out, and placed it on his head. From the cavity of the rock, in which they had lain so long unused, he took out and put on his oilskin-coat and his overalls, as a knight buckles on his armour. We have said that he had lost his shoes, but his feet from custom no longer suffered from the rocks.

Prepared in this way, he took a glance at his breakwaters, grasped the knotted cord, descended quickly from the summit of the rock, and hastened to his storehouse. In another moment he was hard at work. With the nails, rope, and beams that remained he was building a second framework, which he placed twelve feet behind the first one, at the eastern entrance to the channel. Deep silence reigned all around; not even the tufts of grass in the crevices of the rock moved in the air.

Then all at once the sun disappeared, and Gilliatt raising his eyes, saw that the cloud had covered it. There was an immediate extinction of the day.

The wall of cloud had altered its aspect; it no longer maintained its unity. It had bent over on attaining the zenith, from whence it spread over the remainder of the sky. The formation of the tempest was visible, like strata of the earth in a cutting, and the layers of rain could be distinguished from the beds of hail. There was no lightning, but a horrible diffused glare. The smothered respiration of the storm could be heard. Gilliatt, too, was silent, and watched the masses of vapour above his head shaping themselves into pent-up heaps. A long ashen-hued band laid heavily, every now and then lengthening out on the horizon, and on the zenith was a similar band, but lead-coloured. Livid, ragged atoms of cloud hung down from the sky to the mist below. A thin, white cloud, divided the high, dark wall obliquely from north to south.

One of its extremities hung down into the sea. At the spot where it touched the waves a dense red vapour was discernible through the darkness. Below this long, pale cloud were many smaller ones, very dark, and hanging low in the heavens, flying aimlessly about, as if they knew not in what direction to turn. The enormous cloud at the back increased rapidly, and continued to eclipse the sun, enfolding it in its gloomy embrace. In the east, behind Gilliatt, there was only one small, clear space, and that was closing up rapidly. Though there was no wind, a strange flight of grey, downy atoms flew by, as if some gigantic bird was pluming itself behind the bank of cloud. A close, dark ceiling had formed, which touched the sea at the horizon, and melted away into the darkness. There was a feeling as if some unknown presence was approaching. It was vast, towering, and sinister. Suddenly the heavens were rent by a deafening peal of thunder, like the upsetting of some huge article of furniture in a giant's chamber. No flash preceded the deafening crash. There was one clap only, and then silence reigned supreme. There was a pause, as when hostile forces are taking up their ground. Then, at intervals, were seen, huge, shapeless flashes, unaccompanied by thunder. Not a sound, but all showed bright and distinct in every flash. The wall of cloud had changed to a cavern, full of arches and vaulted halls. Outlines of figures could be descried; monstrous heads were discernible; necks seemed to be stretched forth, and were seen for a moment and then vanished. A cylinder of vapour, straight, round, and dark, capped by a white mist, simulated the funnel of a huge steamboat engulfed by the waves, yet still smoking. Sheets of cloud imitated the folds of enormous flags. In the midst, under a dark, red canopy, a thick mass of fog sunk motionless and inert, impenetrable to the electric fires – a sort of hideous conception in the bosom of the tempest.

Gilliatt suddenly felt a breath of wind. Two or three large drops of rain plashed on the rock beside him. Then again came a peal of thunder. The wind was rising; the terror of the darkness had reached its foundations; a wide gap was visible in it; the deluge, hitherto restrained, rushed towards it, and the gap became a vast gulf, filled with rain. The outburst of the storm had commenced. It was a moment inspiring awe and terror.

Rain, wind, lightning, thunder, waves dashing upwards to the clouds, foam, hoarse roarings and shriekings, all come mingled as though a horde of monstrous creatures had suddenly broken loose. The wind roared as loudly as the thunder; the rain fell in torrents from the sky. For a lonely man like Gilliatt, shut up in a lonely rock of the ocean, with an overloaded boat, there could not be a more terrible position. The danger of the sea, which he had overcome, was nothing to that of the storm by which he was now surrounded.

Encompassed on all sides by danger, Gilliatt had, at the last moment, displayed a wonderful amount of ingenious strategy. He had secured the enemy's territory as the seat of his operations; he had made use of the rocks, so that the Douvres, formerly his enemy, were now aiding him in his gigantic struggle. Gilliatt had built a fortress from the sepulchre. He was ensconced firmly in this wonderful stronghold of ocean. The place was besieged, but well defended. He had, as it were, placed his back to the wall, and boldly faced the hurricane. He had barricaded the narrow entrance – the road of the billow. This was the best thing that he could have done. Ocean, like other tyrants, can only be brought to reason by barricades. His sloop might be considered secure on three sides. She was firmly wedged in between the two walls of the channel, and made fast by three anchors; she was protected on the north by the Little Douvre, on the south by the Great one, though these terrible rocks more often wrecked vessels than saved them. On the western side, a frame of timbers, made fast to the rock, sheltered her – a well-tried obstacle, that had withstood the force of the flood-tide; a veritable gate of a fortress, having for its door-posts the Douvres themselves. There was no danger from that side. It was from the east that danger was to be anticipated. On that side there was no protection, save that of the breakwater. A breakwater is an apparatus for dividing and distributing the force of the waves, and requires, at least, two frames, but Gilliatt had only had time to construct one; he was compelled to build the second when the tempest was almost upon him. Fortunately, the wind blew from the north-west. Now north-west wind made little impression on the Douvres. It attacked the rock on one side, and did not drive the waves into either of the channels, but drove them harmlessly against the rocks. The first attack of the storm had been badly arranged. But the wind now attacked in a curve, and it was likely that some sudden change would take place. If it should veer round to the east before the second framework could be finished the peril would be great. The sea would gain free access to the channel, and all would be destroyed.

The tempest increased. A storm heaps blow upon blow, and in this lies its strength as well as its weakness. Its fury enables human intellect to triumph over it, and to defend itself. All the vastness of the ocean in its fury precipitated itself upon the Douvres. Voices without number were heard. Who was it shouting? The sea was singing its battle-song, a song as old as Time. At one moment it seemed as though the word of command was being given; then came clamours, the blare of trumpets, strange trepidations, and then that loud, majestic roar which we term the *voice of the deep*. The indefinite and fleeting eddies of the wind whistled as they tore up the waves. The billows, transformed into giant quoits, were hurled against the rocks by unseen athletes. Enormous masses of surf flowed over the rocks. Torrents above, foam below, and the din was still increasing. The artillery of the clouds thundered, the hail discharged itself in volleys, and the waves rushed to the assault. As far as the eye could reach, the sea was all in foam. Doors of flame were opened, clouds seemed to consume one another. Floating configurations rushed against each other and united, each taking the other's shape. There was a roar in the sky as of musketry.

Gilliatt took no heed, but bent his head over his work. The second framework was nearly finished. The blows of his hammer replied to the thunder, and could be heard above the roar of the elements. His head was bare, for the wind had carried away his cap. His thirst was excessive; he was parched with fever. Small pools had formed in fissures of the rock, and from time to time he took some water in the hollow of his hand, and drank. Then, not deigning to glance at the storm, he continued his labours. A moment might cause the gain or loss of all. He knew what would happen if the breakwater was not completed in time. Of what use to lose time in watching for the face of Death, which came nearer every second.

The turmoil around him was like that of a vast bubbling cauldron. There was noise and strife on every side. There were moments when the lightnings descended as if they were coming down the rungs of a ladder. They struck continually upon the same points of the rock, where they were, probably, metallic veins. Hailstones fell as large as his fist. The storm now veered round to the west, and was lashing the barricades between the two Douvres; but he had confidence in his breakwater. These barricades were formed of the fore-part of the Durande, and yielded to the shock of the waves. Elasticity is a resistance. Against the force of the waves, a collection of wood, chained and fastened, will oppose the rush of the waters more effectually than a stone breakwater. The barriers of the Douvres fulfilled these conditons. They were, beside, so ingeniously made fast that the wave, striking them underneath, pressed and consolidated the work against the rocks. The wind was only able to cast flakes of foam over the barriers upon Gilliatt's boat. On that side all that the storm could do was to cast its foam at its enemy, who was securely sheltered from its impotent fury.

The foam, pouring in on all sides, was like flakes of wool. The angry ocean poured over the rocks, and filled every crevice with water, and retired again from the chinks in the granite, forming a number of small fountains, which fell in threads of silver into the sea. The second framework of the eastern barrier was nearly completed. A little more labour, and this new outwork could take part in the contest.

Suddenly there was a brilliant brightness – the rain ceased, the clouds rolled back, the wind had just shifted, a kind of dark, lofty window opened in the zenith, and the lightnings were extinguished. It seemed like the end, but it was but the beginning.

The change of wind was from the south-west to the north-east, and the storm was preparing to attack again with a new army of hurricanes. The north was about to rush to the assault.

The attack now coming from the east was directed against the weaker point of the position. Gilliatt stopped his work, and looked around him. He took his stand upon a curved projection of the rock behind the second barrier. If the first hurdle had been carried away it would have destroyed the second – which was not yet firmly fixed, and must certainly have crushed him. In the position which he had chosen he would have been dead before he could have seen the sloop and the engine beaten to fragments, and swallowed up in the boiling turmoil of waters. Such was his risk. He accepted it boldly. When all his hopes were wrecked, what could he hope for save death – to die the first; for, in his mind, the engines represented a living being? Thrusting aside from his eyes his wet hair, he grasped his hammer and waited. And not for long. A flash of lightning gave him the signal.

The livid opening in the zenith closed, and a deluge of rain fell. All again grew dark, and there was no light, save the intermittent flashes of lightning. The attack had recommenced in earnest. A heavy swell, visible in the glare of the lightning, was rolling on the eastern side, beyond the Man-Rock. It resembled a huge cylinder of glass; it was green, without a fleck of foam, and stretched right across the sea. It was rushing upon the breakwater, increasing in volume as it drew near. It was a kind of gigantic pillar, rolling on its side upon the surface of the ocean.

The great wave struck the Man-Rock, broke in two, and passed on. The two broken portions rejoined, and, forming a mountain of water, fell perpendicularly on the breakwater. This wave was in the shape of a huge beam. This battering-ram crushed against the breakwater with a terrible shock. For some moments nothing was to be seen but sea, for the spot was completely covered with foam. Nothing was visible but a seething mass of raging waters, the whiteness of a winding-sheet, blown about by the wind from the tomb.

Nothing could be heard but the roar of the storm, carrying destruction with it. When the foam had disappeared, Gilliatt was still at his post. The barrier had held firm. Pliant as a hurdle and firm as a wall, the breakwater had stood the strain. The great wave was vanquished.

A rivulet of foam, running down the slope of the rock, died away as it reached the sloop. The man who had thus muzzled the ocean allowed himself no moment for repose. The storm, fortunately, turned aside its rage for a time. The fury of the waves spent themselves upon the faces of the rock. There was a lull, and Gilliatt took advantage of it to complete the inner barrier. Thus occupied he spent the day. The hurricane continued its violence upon the flank of the rocks. The receptacles of fire and water in the heavens poured out their contents unceasingly. When the night came it was hardly noticed, so profound was the darkness; and yet it was not utter darkness. The storms, alternately illuminating and blinding by their lightnings were intervals of the visible and invisible. All was weird light, then black darkness.

A phosphoric zone, tinged with the purple hues of the Aurora Borealis, floated like a ghastly flame behind the dense clouds, giving to everything a spectral appearance, and making the rain-drifts luminous. This light proved serviceable to Gilliatt, and aided him in his work. By its aid he was able to repair the forward barrier. The breakwater was almost complete. As he was making fast the last beam with a strong cable, the wind blew directly in his face, He raised his eyes; it had shifted to the north-east, and the attack upon the channel had recommenced. Gilliatt glanced at the breakwater. An enormous wave rolling in broke on it with a heavy shock; a second followed, then another, and another – five or six in a tumultous rush – and, lastly, one larger than all. This last had a strange resemblance to something living. It would have been easy to imagine, in that heaving mass of water, the shape of fins. It fell with enormous violence, and broke on the barriers in a storm of foam. Torn to atoms in a series of fits and gushes, it resembled some monster being crushed to death upon the rocks. The waters rushed through, subsiding but devastating as they did so. A shiver shook the rock to its roots. The foam, tossed on high, resembled the spouting of a whale. As it subsided it showed what damage it had inflicted; the last had been successful. This time the breakwater had not escaped uninjured. A long, ponderous beam, wrenched from the first barrier, had been carried over the second, and hurled violently upon the projecting rock, where Gilliatt had been standing just before. Fortunately he had not returned to his former position; had he done so, he would have been killed upon the spot. There was something remarkable in the fall of this beam, which, by preventing the framework from rebounding, saved Gilliatt. Between the projecting rock and the interior of the channel there was a cavity, resembling a place cut out by a hatchet.

One end of the beam, as it was cast into the air, had caught in this notch, which had thus been enlarged. The idea seized

Gilliatt of leaning heavily upon the other end of this beam. The beam, caught firmly by one end in the notch, which it had widened, projected like an outstretched arm. This projected parallel with the anterior wall, and the disengaged end stretched from its resting-place some twenty inches. Gilliatt raised himself, by means of hands, feet, and knees, to the rock, and placed his back against the giant lever. The beam was long, and its raising power was thus increased. The rock was already loosened, but he had to strain again, and the sweat poured from his forehead. There was a loud cracking noise; the gap, spreading into a fissure, opened, and the heavy mass fell into the passage beneath, with a noise of thunder. The mass of stone fell unbroken, and rested in its bed like a cromlech. The beam, which had acted as a lever, fell with the rock, and Gilliatt, slipping forward, narrowly escaped being precipitated with it into the gulf below. The passage was full of huge round stones, and the monolith stretched right across the two parallel rocks, and formed a kind of wall between the two sides, touching the rocks at both ends. This fall formed a species of *cul-de-sac*, still to be seen, and the water behind this barrier is generally calm and still. This was an obstacle more strong than the forward timbers of the Durande fixed between the two Douvres, and it was but just in time.

The buffets of the waves had continued. When it meets with an obstacle the sea becomes more obstinate. The first breakwater was beginning to break up. One breach in a breakwater is serious, for it spreads and repairs are impossible, for the waves would overwhelm the workmen.

A flash of lightning showed Gilliatt the damage done: beams thrown here and there, and a huge rent in the middle. The second breakwater was uninjured. The block of stone which Gilliatt had thrown down had one defect, in spite of its strength – it was too low; the sea could not get through it, but would burst over it. It was useless to think of building it higher. Nothing but masses of rock could be placed on a barrier of stone; but how could he detach them and drag them into position? And how could they be raised or fixed? Timber he might add, but rocks, impossible!

The lack of height in this granite isthmus perturbed him considerably, and it was not long before the effects of this fault were felt. The attacks upon the breakwater were unceasing; the heavy seas seemed to have determined to destroy it. A kind of trampling sound was heard upon the shaken fabric. All of a sudden a binding stake, rent from the shattered frame, was swept over the second barrier and across the transverse rock and carried through the windings of the channel until it was lost to view. He feared that it would destroy the boat. Luckily, the water in the interior, enclosed on all sides, was but little affected by the turmoil without. The waves there were comparatively small, and the shock would not be heavy. But had had no time to dwell upon a possible mishap, for every danger was uniting at one moment; the tempest had concentrated its attacks upon his vulnerable side, and the peril was imminent. For a moment the darkness was intense – the lightning ceased to flash; it was a sinister alliance – the cloud and the ocean; then came a sombre, heavy clap of thunder.

This was followed by a violent outburst. The breakwater, in front of the barrier, had been wrenched away; and the beams were whirling about in the foaming billows. The sea was employing the first breakwater as a battering-ram with which to destroy the other.

Gilliatt felt what a general must experience when he sees his advanced guard driven in. The second row of beams resisted the shock, for they were firmly fastened. But the shattered frame was very heavy, and at the mercy of the waves, which hurled it to and fro; the ropes and chains, which still held together, prevented it from going entirely to pieces, but its qualities as a means of defence rendered it a terrible engine of destruction. Instead of a buckler it was a battering-ram, for ends of beams and timbers projected on all sides. The tempest could not have found a more suitable weapon.

This was the projectile; the sea, the catapult. Blow followed blow with mournful regularity, and Gilliatt, behind the barricade which he had erected, listened to the efforts that Death was making to force an entrance. He thought sadly how, had it not been for the funnel of the Durande having been caught by the wreck, he would have been in Guernsey with his sloop in safety, and the engines rescued.

But now the work of destruction was accomplished. The whole of the breakwater, with its double apparatus crushed

and heaped together, came back in a torrent of foam, and
rushed on to the stone barricade where it stopped. All the
fragments lay heaped together – a mass of beams, through
which the waves still rushed, breaking and destroying as they
did this. Though conquered, the breakwater still struggled
bravely. The sea had broken it, and in turn was broken by its
conquered foe, which though shattered, was still effective. The
rock which checked its progress still held firmly. The channel,
as we have said, was very narrow at this point, and the
conquering wind had heaped together all the fragments of the
breakwater, and driving the shattered ends into the mass, had
rendered it a strong and solid file. Though broken, it was still
impregnable. Only some portions were carried away by the
waves. One was hurled through the air near Gilliatt; he felt the
wind as it passed by him. Some huge waves, however, which,
as in all storms, returned with great regularity, continued to
sweep over the ruins of the breakwater. They fell into the
channel, and, in spite of its turns and angles, rendered the water
within rough. The waves began to rush ominously through it.
The wild kisses given to the rocks by the waves were plainly
audible.

How could he prevent this agitation of the waters from
reaching his sloop? It would not take long for the wind to make
a storm in the interior of the rock, and then his boat would
founder, and the engines sink to the bottom of the ocean.
Gilliatt shuddered as this thought struck him, but he was not
discouraged; his was a soul that never thought of surrender.

The hurricane had now discovered a way of attack, and
rushed madly between the two Douvres. Suddenly, from
behind Gilliatt, was audible a fearful crash, echoing and
reverberating through the passage louder and more terrible
than he had yet heard. It came from the direction of the boat,
and a blaze of lightning at once revealed the situation. A wave,
rushing through the eastern entrance, had been met by a gust of
wind from the other side. A disaster was at hand. As yet, the
sloop appeared to have sustained no damage; moored as she
was, she afforded but little hold to the storm, but the wreck of
the Durande was in sad distress.

It presented considerable surface to the storm, being entirely
out of the water, and suspended in the air. The hole which

Gilliatt had cut to release the machinery had weakened the hull – the deck-planking was bent like the leaves of a book; the breaking-up had begun. It was the crash of this that Gilliatt had heard, and when he drew near, the sight presented to him seemed to be beyond repair.

The opening had become a gaping wound, and the wind, acting on this, had rent away the planking. This fracture cut the wreck into two pieces; the back part nearest to the boat had remained firm, clasped in the hold of the rocks; the other portion, nearest to Gilliatt, was hanging down. A fracture, as long as it will hold, is a sort of hinge. This mass was swinging on its fractures, as if upon joints, moving backwards and forwards with a sad and grinding noise.

Fortunately, the boat was no longer beneath it; but this swinging motion shook the other half of the hull still fastened firmly in the rocks. From shaking to falling is a short step. Under the persistent assaults of the wind, the swinging portion could easily carry the other, which almost touched the boat, and then boat, engine, and all would be swallowed up.

Gilliatt had this in his mind.

Here was the catastrophe he had dreaded – how was he to avert it? He was one of those to whom danger is a power. He pulled himself together in a moment. He ran to his storehouse and provided himself with an axe. The hammer had done its work well: now it was the turn of the hatchet. Then he mounted on the wreck, and took his stand upon that portion of the deck that had not yet given at all, and, bending over the precipice between the two rocks, began to cut away the broken beams, and to sever whatever retained them fixed to the hull. To complete the separation of the two portions of the wreck, to lighten that part which still remained firm, and to throw into the sea the portion that had become the prey of the winds, was the operation that he was about to commence. This was perilous. The portion of the wreck that was hanging down, acted on by the wind and its own weight, was only held up at certain points. The whole resembled a folding screen, one leaf of which, hanging down, beat against the other. Five or six pieces, bent and twisted, but not started, hung together: The fractures groaned and creaked at each gust of the wind, and the axe, so to speak, had but to help the wind to complete its work. The smallness of the portion that hung together, whilst it rendered Gilliatt's work easy, increased the danger. At any moment it might give way beneath his feet. The tempest had reached its height. The storm up to this time had been terrible. The convulsion of the sea had reached the heavens. Up to that time the clouds had had the mastery; they had seemed to work their own imperious will, and to afford that impulse which lashed the winds to fury, whilst they still preserved a kind of ominous lucidity. Below was madness, above was anger. The heavens are the breath, the sea but the foam; hence the superiority of the wind. But it had become intoxicated with its own power. It was nothing but a whirlwind. It was blindness giving birth to the night. Tempests, at times, grow mad – when all the firmament is filled with a species of delirium – when heaven knows not what it does, and hurls its lightnings blindly. It was the hour of terror; the quivering of the rock was at its height. Every storm has its climax, but this time it had deviated from its appointed course. It was the storm's evil hour. At that moment 'the wind', as Fuller says, 'is a furious madman'. It is at this time that the tempest gives forth all that electric fluid, which Piddington calls the 'waterfall lightning'. It is at that moment that in the blackest clouds appears – no one can guess why, unless it be to gaze upon the universal terror – a bluish circle of light, which old Spanish sailors call the 'eye of the tempest'.

This gloomy eye was fixed upon Gilliatt, whose gaze, however, was fixed on the heavens. He raised his head. After every stroke of his axe, he looked upwards almost proudly. He was, or seemed to be, too near to the brink of destruction not to feel haughty. He took care only to place his feet on solid resting-places of the wreck. He risked his life, but yet he was careful of it. He also was worked up to a pitch. He seemed to have gained in lucidity what the tempest had lost. His strength seemed to be doubled. He was full of courage; the strokes of his hatchet seemed like notes of defiance. A pathetic struggle: on the one side was an unconquerable will; on the other, unlimited power. It was a question who should prove the conqueror.

In the wide expanse of the heavens, the clouds took the shape of vast hideous masts. Terror, in its worst forms, appeared. The rain came from the sea, the surf from the clouds; the phantoms of the winds bent down towards him; meteoric faces grew purple as they gazed upon him, and then died away, leaving the darkness more hideous than ever; there was nothing to be seen but torrents pouring in on all sides – raging sea, clouds heavy with rain, of ashen hue, ragged and torn, executing wild gyrations in the firmament.

Contending with this delirium of power, which combined to struggle against him, skill was the only weapon that Gilliatt had to wield. He wished to hurl down all the shattered portions of the wreck, and so he weakened the fractures that acted as hinges, without breaking them altogether, leaving a few fibres that held together the whole. Suddenly he paused, with his axe raised high in the air – the work was over, the entire mass fell between the Douvres just beneath Gilliatt, who stood above it, bending over it and looking down upon it. It plunged perpendicularly into the sea, and splashed the foam high upon the rocks; but was caught by the narrow walls before it reached the bottom, and remained stationary, showing, some twelve feet above the wave, the vertical mass of planking forming a wall between the Douvres, like the rock thrown into the passage a little higher up, and allowing only a small stream of water to filter through it at each end – and this was the fifth barricade utilized by Gilliatt in that narrow ocean street. The storm, in its blindness, had aided him in this last work. And now, however severe the wind and the storm, the boat and the engine were safe, for the waves could no longer menace them. Between the barricade which closed the passage on the west, and the new one which protected them on the east, no disturbance, either of wind or sea, could reach them.

From all this Gilliatt had drawn safety. The storm had acted as his ally. He stooped, and from a rain-pool in the rock, he filled the hollow of his hand, drank, and turning to the storm, exclaimed, 'Fool!' Human intelligence, combating with brute force, experiences a feeling of ironical joy in demonstrating the stupidity of its enemy. Gilliatt felt the necessity of insulting his conquered adversary, a feeling which is as old as the heroes sung in Homer's lays.

He descended to his boat and examined it by the gleam of the lightning. It was time that someone should have come to her assistance, for it had been roughly treated for the last few hours, and had begun to give way; but as the sea around her grew calm, and as her anchors all held, she was in no very evil plight. As for the engine, the four chains had kept it perfectly steady.

After Gilliatt finished his inspection, a white object dashed past him, and was lost in the gloom. It was a seagull.

It was a pleasing apparition: for when the birds return, the storm is abating.

Another good sign was that the thunder redoubled its peals. The rain stopped all of a sudden. There was only a surly growl in the heavens. The storm ceased with a suddenness of a plank falling to the ground. It had lasted for twenty hours. The wind which had brought the storm, bore it away. A dark pile of cloud was scattered over the horizon. The mist broke up and dispersed. From one end to the other of the hostile line, there were signs of defeat. There was a hoarse, gradually-decreasing murmur, a few last drops of rain fell, and all the cloud that had been charged with rain and thunder, like some terrible war chariot, broke up and fled.

The blue sky began to make its appearance.

For the first time, Gilliatt felt that he was weary. Sleep pounces on fatigue like a bird on its prey. Gilliatt felt his limbs bend beneath him, and casting himself into his boat, without stopping to choose a place, was soon buried in slumber. He remained thus for some hours, stretched at full length and motionless, hardly to be distinguished from the joists and beams amidst which he lay.

BOOK IV

OBSTACLES IN THE PATH

CHAPTER I

GILLIATT IS NOT ALONE IN HIS FEELING OF HUNGER

He awoke feeling very hungry.

It was now calmer and the sea subsiding, but it was still too much agitated to allow him to leave the rock at once. Besides, the day was too far advanced. With the heavy freight that she had on board, in order to reach Guernsey before midnight, he would have to set off in the early morning. Although he was suffering from the pangs of hunger, Gilliatt commenced by stripping himself, the best way of getting warm. His clothes had been soaked through by the storm, but the rainwater had washed out the salt from the sea, so that all he had to do was to dry them.

He was only partially clothed, and had nothing on but his trousers, which he turned up to his knees; he spread out and secured with large stones, in different portions of the rock, his shirt, his jersey, his overcoat, his leggings and his sheepskin.

The thought now occurred to him of getting something to eat.

He had recourse to his knife, which he always kept sharp and fit for use, and with it he detached from the rock a few limpets, similar to the *clonisses* of the Mediterranean. These are, as it is well known, eaten raw, but after so many various and severe labours such a meal was rather a scanty one. He had no more biscuit, but of water there was now no scarcity – he was inundated with it. He took advantage of the tide being out to wander about the rocks in search of crayfish. Sufficient rock was uncovered to give him hopes of a successful search. Only he did not remember that he could no longer cook anything. Had he taken the pains to go to his storeroom, he would have found it deluged with rain; his wood and coal were under water, and of his tow, which served instead of tinder, every atom was wet through. He had no means of lighting a fire.

As for the other things, his blower was completely out of order, the screen of the hearth of his forge was entirely broken down. The storm had pillaged his workshop. With such tools as had escaped damage Gilliatt would, at a pinch, have done carpenter's, but not blacksmith's work. But just now his thoughts were not on his workshop. His appetite led him in another direction, and, without much reflection, he had set out in pursuit of food. He wandered about, not in the channel between the rocks, but outside at the back of the breakers. It was on that side that the Durande, ten weeks before, had struck upon the reef, the outside portion of which was more favourable for his search than the interior. At low water crabs have a custom of leaving their holes, and warming themselves. These misshapen creatures love the midday sun. It is a strange sight to see them emerge from the water in the full light of day. When you look at them, with their awkward, sidelong walk, clambering heavily from crevice to crevice in the lower stages of the rocks, like the steps of a staircase, you are compelled to confess that there are strange things in the sea.

Gilliatt had almost lived upon crabs for over two months. On this day, however, both crabs and crayfish were wanting. The storm had caused them to take refuge in their hiding-places, and they had not yet ventured out. Gilliatt held his open knife in his hand, and every now and then, scraped up a shell-fish from under the seaweed, which he ate as he pursued his search. He was nearing the spot where Sieur Clubin had perished. As Gilliatt had made up his mind that for his meal he must be contented with the sea-urchins, or the *châtaignes de mer*, a clattering sound at his feet attracted his attention. A large crab, terrified at his approach, had dropped into a pool of water. The water was not deep enough to conceal it from Gilliatt's sight. He chased the crab along the base of the rock; the crab fled.

Suddenly, it vanished.

Had it taken refuge in some crevice under the rock?

Wishing to effect its capture Gilliatt clutched some of the projections of the cliff, and bent over to see where it had gone.

As he suspected, there was an opening in which the crab had sought refuge.

It was more than an opening; it was a kind of a porch. The sea flowed under it, but it was not deep. He could see that the bottom was covered with large pebbles, which were clothed with marine vegetation, showing that they were never dry. They looked like a number of infants' heads covered with green hair.

With his knife between his teeth, and, with the assistance of his hands and feet, he descended the face of the rock, and leaped into the water, which reached up to his armpits. He entered the porch, and found himself in a rough kind of passage, with a rudely vaulted ceiling overhead. The walls were polished and slippery. He had lost sight of the crab. He was within his depth, but, as he advanced down the passage, he began to leave the light of day behind him, and his eyes were hardly yet accustomed to the darkness. After advancing some fifteen paces the vaulted roof above his head ceased – he had got to the end of the passage; the space was more open, and, consequently, there was more light; besides, his eyes were growing more used to the semi-twilight, as he could distinguish objects better. A surprise was in store for him. It was the same strange cavern into which he had penetrated more than a month before. Only, this time he had entered from the sea. He had just come through the sunken arch which he had noticed before; for at certain times of the tide it evidently afforded a practicable entrance. Now that his eyes were accustomed to the light, he saw better and better. He was filled with wonder. He was once more in that strange palace of shadow – that vaulted roof, those pillars, those ruddy blood-coloured stains on the walls, that marine vegetation which seemed studded with brilliant gems, and, at the end, that chamber resembling a sanctuary, and that stone which was so like an altar.

Opposite him, high up in the rock, he saw the cavity by which he had entered, and which, from the point where he stood, was quite inaccessible. He noticed near the arch those dark and gloomy cavities which he had before contemplated from a distance. Those caves within a cave were now close to him; they were quite dry and easy of entrance. Nearer yet than this recess he perceived, just above the level of the water, a horizontal crevice in the granite. He thought it likely that the crab had taken refuge there, and, plunging his hand in, begun to grope about in the darkness.

Suddenly his arm was grasped, and a feeling of indescribable horror crept over him.

Something living – thin, rough, flat, icy, and slimy – from the dark depth of the cavity had entwined itself round his arm, and was crawling up towards his breast. Its pressure was like that of a strap being drawn tight, and its steady persistence like that of a drill. In less than a second, a something, he knew not what, but felt that it was of a spiral form, had closed round his wrist and elbow and reached his shoulder, and a pang went through his body below his armpit.

Hastily he drew back, but the power of motion had almost left him. He was rooted to the spot. With his left hand, which still remained free, he grasped the knife which was between his teeth, and, setting his back to the rock, made a super-human effort to withdraw his arm. He only succeeded in loosening the deadly embrace for a moment, which again immediately tightened.

It was supple as leather, strong as iron, and cold as steel. A second object, long and pointed, emerged from the cavity, like a tongue issuing from a pair of monstrous jaws. It seemed for a moment to lick Gilliatt's naked chest, then, stretching itself out until it became longer and thinner, it crept over his flesh and wound itself round him. At the same time a terrible and indescribable sense of pain compelled every nerve and muscle of his body to quiver. He felt hundreds of blunt points penetrating his flesh – it seemed as if innumerable minute mouths had fastened upon his body and were seeking to drain his very blood.

Still a third undulating, whip-like shape issued from the rock and lashed his body with a quivering movement; suddenly, it fixed itself upon him as firmly as the others had done.

Again his agony was wrought up to a terrible pitch, but Gilliatt uttered no cry. There was sufficient light for him to see the repulsive shapes that had wound around him. A fourth ligature – but this time with the swiftness of an arrow – darted towards his stomach, and clasped it in its foul embrace.

Escape now seemed impossible, he could not sever or tear away the slimy bands which held his body so tightly, and which adhered to it by a number of suckers. Each of these was the focus of strange and agonising pains. He felt that numberless minute mouths were devouring him at once.

A fifth long, slimy object glided from the cavity. It passed by the others, and wound itself round Gilliatt's chest so tightly that he could hardly draw his breath. These whip-like ribbons were pointed at the end, but grew broader, like the blade of a sword towards the hilt, and all five evidently sprang from a common centre. They crept and glided all over him. He felt those strange pressures, which seemed to proceed from the suction of miniature mouths, shift their position from time to time.

Finally, a huge slimy mass, round and flattened, issued from below the cavity. It was the centre to which these five limbs were attached, like the spokes of a wheel. On the opposite side of this loathsome monster could be seen the commencement of three other tentacles, the ends of which were concealed beneath the rock.

Two eyes were in the centre of this slimy mass.

These were fixed upon Gilliatt.

Now he knew that he was in the clutches of a devil-fish, and gave himself up for lost.

CHAPTER II

THE DEVIL-FISH

To know what a devil-fish is like, you must have seen one, and to compare it to the hydras of ancient lore would only raise a smile of ridicule.

We are prone to believe that the intangible which floats through our dreams may be realized in the Realm of the Possible. Attractive forces, which have the power to take form and to give shape to the creation, form dreams. The unknown performs these miracles for us, and uses its power to create monsters, but it was left for heaven to create the devil-fish.

Orpheus and Homer could do no more than imagine all this.

When Providence thinks fit, it excels in the production of monsters. The meaning of this is a constant source of doubt to the deep thinker.

Such a monster as the whale has bulk, whilst the devil-fish is comparatively small; the hippopotamus is covered with a coat impenetrable to weapons, the devil-fish is bare; the jaraca utters a hissing sound, the devil-fish is mute; the rhinoceros has a horn, the devil-fish has none; the scorpion has a sting, not so the devil-fish; the shark has pointed fins, the devil-fish has none; the lion has claws, the devil-fish has none; the crocodile has a terrible jaw, the devil-fish has no teeth; but for all that, it has more terrible arms than all these fearful creatures put together.

What is this devil-fish? Is it a vampire in the ocean or what?

Any bold swimmer, who may be attracted by the beauty of those spots amongst the breakers, where the sea exhibits all its charms; where the deep, still waters hide all the magnificence of the ocean; where are the homes of many a scaly denizen of the deep, runs the risk of meeting it, should he venture into those waters. Should you do so, cast aside curiosity and avoid it. You may enter his den filled with wonder, you may leave it paralysed with fear. A meeting like this is quite possible amidst the rocks in the open sea.

A grey-coloured form undulates partly in the water; it is as thick as a man's arm, and about a foot and a-half in length. It looks like a bundle of rags, and resembles in shape a closed umbrella without a handle. This awkward mass advances towards you slowly; suddenly it expands; eight long tentacles extend from around a face with two dull glassy eyes. Their slow undulations are like lambent flames. They resemble the spokes of a wheel, and are four or five feet in diameter. It darts upon its prey and harpoons its victim.

It curls itself round its victim, covering him and enveloping him in its slimy folds. Below it is yellow, above it is ashen coloured. No comparison could fitly describe this strange hue. It looks like a beast made of ashes inhabiting the sea. It is a spider in its shape; a chameleon in its rapid changes of hue. When disturbed it becomes purple. Its most disgusting characteristic is its impalpability. Its slimy folds strangle; its very touch paralyzes. It looks like a mass of scorbutic gangrened flesh; it is a hideous picture of loathsome disease. Once fixed there is no release. It clings closely to its prey. How does it do so? By creating a vacuum. The eight long antennae are large at the root and tapering to a sharp point. On the lower side of each of these are two rows of pustules, decreasing in size, the larger ones towards the root and the smaller towards the point. There are twenty-five in each row – that is, fifty upon each antenna. Altogether there are four hundred. Each of these pustules is a perfect cupping-glass. They are cartilaginous substances, cylindrical and horny. On the larger species they decrease from the size of a five-franc piece to that of a pea. They can penetrate to the depth of an inch. This apparatus for suction has all the delicacy of a keyboard. It comes forward and then disappears; it obeys the slightest impulse of the creature to which it belongs. The most exquisite sensibilities cannot equal the power of contraction that these suckers possess, proportioned, as they always are, to the interior movements of the creature, and to the exterior incidents. It is like a sensitive plant. This monster is termed by sailors a 'poulp', the scientific name which is cephaloptera, whilst in legendary lore they are known as krakens. In the Channel Islands they are spoken of as pieuvre.

It is seldom found in Guernsey; of small size in Jersey; but is very common and of great magnitude in Sark. One which was killed there was found to measure four feet across, and its four hundred suckers could be easily discerned as the monster thrust them out convulsively in the agonies of death.

According to Denis Montford – one of those careful observers, whose marvellous intuition rises or falls to the level of a wizard – the poulp has human passions, and can hate. In fact, in the absolute, to be hideous is to hate. When swimming it remains, as it were, in a scabbard. It moves with all its parts drawn up under it. It resembles a sleeve with the closed fist in it, sewn up at the cuff. This fist, which is the head, cleaves the water, and advances with a vague undulating movement. It has two large but indistinct eyes, resembling the colour of the sea. When the pieuvre is in pursuit of prey, or lying in wait, it grows smaller, and draws itself together; it reduces itself, as it were, and is scarcely discernible in the half-light beneath the sea. It looks like a portion of the waves, and has no appearance of being a living creature. The pieuvre is a hypocrite; you pay no attention to it, when suddenly it opens itself and darts upon you. A lump of slime that has an instinct – can anything be more horrible? A glutinous substance, with a leaven of hatred in it. This terrible and voracious creature delights in the most limpid depths of the sea. Its approach is heralded by no sound, which makes it the more dangerous. No sooner do you perceive it than you are in its clutches. At night – and more especially in the warm summer evenings – it becomes phosphorescent. This frightful creature has its passions and its submarine unions. It makes itself beautiful; it shines; it illuminates itself and, from the summit of some rock, it can be perceived gleaming through the gloom of the waves – a pallid irradiation – a spectral sun.

The pieuvre swims, but it can walk as well; it is half fish and half reptile. It crawls along the bottom of the sea. In walking it uses its eight antennae, and crawls along like a caterpillar. It has neither bones, flesh, nor blood: it is flabby. There is nothing inside it. It is a mere skin; you can turn it inside-out, like the fingers of a glove. There is one orifice in the centre of its tentacles. What is this orifice? Is it a mouth or a vent? The same opening serves both purposes: it is the entrance and the exit. Its body is of icy coldness.

All jelly-fish are repulsive. The swimmer who comes in contact with that gelatinous mass, which envelops the limbs, which the hands can grasp and the nails tear without its destroying life – a species of sticky, slimy, living creature – may inspire disgust, but not the terror caused by the appearance of the pieuvre – a head of Medusa, surounded by eight serpents.

No grasp is equal in strength to the sudden clutch of the cephaloptera.

It is an infernal machine that attacks you. You are struggling with a void which possesses eight antennae, no scratches, no bites, but an indescribable suffocation. A bite is to be feared far less than a wound caused by suction. A wound from a claw is simply the beast entering your flesh, but in an attack by suckers, it is your body that is drawn into that of the beast. Your muscles swell, your sinews are twisted, your blood boils, and is horribly mingled with the slime of the creature. The terrible wretch grows upon you by a thousand foul mouths. The hydra incorporates itself with the man, and the man with the hydra; you become one and the same. The hideous dream is in your bosom. The tiger can but devour you; the poulp, horrible to relate, draws you into its system. He drags you to him and into him; bound helplessly; glued where you stand, utterly powerless, you are gradually emptied into a loathsome receptacle, which is the monster itself.

To be eaten alive is terrible: how much more so to be dissolved, as it were, while still living! It is worse than being buried alive.

Science has rejected the existence of these strange creatures, and even rejects established facts; but all the same it has decided to study them, to dissect them, to class and catalogue them, and to write their names on a label, preserve specimens, and put them under glass-cases in the museums. They entered them into the question of their nomenclature, classed them as mollusks, invertebrates, radiata, determined their position in the animal kingdom, place them above the calmarus, and below the cuttle-fish, divide them into large and small kinds, allow the existence of the smaller species sooner than the large ones – a habit of scientific men in all parts of the world, who are always more microscopic than telescopic. They examine into their construction, and call them cephaloptera: they count their antennae and call them octopodes. This done, let them alone. What science relinquishes, philosophy takes up.

Philosophy, in her turn, studies these creatures; she does not go so far, but yet further than science. She does not dissect them, but she ponders over them. Where the scalpel has been at work, she plunges into the hypothesis. She seeks for the final cause – that terrible torture of the thinker. These creatures disturb his ideas of the Creator. They are a series of hideous surprises; they are pleasure-spoilers of the spectator. He gazes at them in terror. They are forms devoted to evil. What can be said of these treasons of creation against itself? Who can solve this mystery?

All is conjecture, and we fall back on the theory of what is possible. Monsters are impious in the concrete. Atoms of shadow issue from the mass; something incases itself, rolls, floats, condenses, borrows elements from the darkness of the ambient air; submits itself to unknown polarizations, gains life, and, moulding itself into some unknown form of obscurity, and, with some strange spirit of the miasma as its companion, wanders away, spectral-like, amongst living and breathing things.

For what purpose are they created? But we are falling back again on the eternal question.

These monsters are spectres as well as creatures; they exist, yet their existence is improbable. They are dwellers in the waters of death. Their very improbability complicates their existence. They touch upon the frontier of humanity, and are yet denizens of the realms of imagination.

Their existence is a certainty which disconcerts our certainty. Optimism, which is, perhaps, the truth, loses its countenance in their presence. They form the visible outer ring of a black circle. They mark the transition of one reality into another. They seem to belong to that commencement of terrible creatures which the dreamer sees confusedly through the loophole of the night.

The generating of monsters, first in the invisible and then in the possible, has been guessed at – perhaps, even perceived – by the magi and philosophers in their severe ecstasies. From this comes the conjecture of the existence of a hell. The demon is the tiger of the invisible. The wild beast devouring souls has been denounced to mankind by two visionaries, one called John and the other Dante.

Were the circles of shade prolonged indefinitely – if within one ring there were another, and this were to go on to an illimitable extent; if that chain – which, for our own part, we are resolved to doubt – really exists, it is certain that the pieuvre at one end proves that there is a Satan at the other, for a criminal at one extremity proves the existence of a crime at the other. Every evil, like every perverted intellect, is a sphinx, and a terrible one, propounding for solution a fearful problem – the enigma of evil.

Is it this perfection of evil which has sometimes caused mighty intellects to incline to the belief of a double god, towards the redoubtable dual heresy of the Manichaeans?

The Chinese, in the palace of the Emperor of China, have a representation of a shark eating a crocodile, which is devouring a sea-serpent, which is eating an eagle, which is preying on a swallow, which, in its turn, is devouring a caterpillar.

Thus all nature seems in process of evolution, that before our eyes is either eating or being eaten. Those devoured, devour each other.

Scientific men, however, who are also philosophers, and consequently benevolent towards creation, find, or believe they find, an explanation of this. Bonnet, of Geneva – that curiously accurate reasoner, who was opposed to Buffon, as, in later times, Geoffrey Saint Hilaire was to Cuvier. The explanation they give is this: Universal death requires universal burial. The devourer's mission is to entomb. All things enter into others. Decay is nourishment – a terrible sweeping away of matter. Man, the carnivorous, is also a burier. Our life is made up of death. Such is the terrible jaw – we are, practically speaking, mere tombs.

In our twilight world this fatality of order produces monsters. You say, For what purpose?

This is the reason.

But is this the solution? Is this the answer to our questions? And, if this is so, why is there not some different order of things? And so the question springs up again.

Let us live; quite so.

But let us also strive that death be progress. Let us aspire to a world in which matters are not so obscure. Let the conscience that leads us thither be our pride; for let us never forget that the best is only attained through the better.

CHAPTER III

HOW THE COMBAT ENDED

This then was the terrible thing that held Gilliatt enfolded in its loathsome embrace.

Such was the monster – the dweller in the grotto – the hideous genius of the place – the gloomy demon of the water.

The foul creature lived in the midst of all this splendour. On the day of the previous month in which Gilliatt had entered the cave, the dark outline seen by him in the water was the frightful monster in its home, and when he visited the cavern, for the second time, in pursuit of the crab, and had thrust his hand into the cavity in which he supposed that it had taken refuge, the pieuvre was there lying in ambush, and waiting for its prey.

Gilliatt did not expect to find such a tenant in this secret lurking-place. He had thrust his hand into the hole to feel for a crab, and the pieuvre had seized him.

It grasped him like a vice.

He was the fly in this terrible spider-web. He was up to his waist in the water, his feet planted on the slippery pebbles at the bottom, his right arm paralysed by the flat coils of the tentacles of the pieuvre, and his chest almost hidden beneath the interlaced crossings of the terrible bandage.

Of the eight arms of the devil-fish, three were clasped around Gilliatt in this fashion; clinging to the granite on one side and to the man on the other, the monster bound its victim to the rock. Two hundred and fifty suckers were at work upon Gilliatt at once.

To be grasped by an enormous hand, the elastic fingers of which, measuring more than a yard in length, were, on the inside, covered with living blisters, eating into the very flesh. What a terrible complication of agony and loathing!

As we have before said, it is impossible to tear away the folds of the devil-fish. The more you endeavour to do so, the tighter it clings. It only makes it hold the closer. Its clutch increases with your efforts. The more the victim struggles, the tighter grow the folds.

Gilliatt's only hope was in his knife. He had only his left hand free, but, as we know, he could use that well. It might have been said of him that he had two right hands.

He held the open knife in his hand.

The tentacles of the pieuvre cannot be severed – it is a leathery substance, impossible to cut with a knife: it slips away from the blade; besides, from its mode of attack, cutting these coils would lacerate the victim's flesh. It is likewise a dangerous adversary, but there is a way of resisting it. The fishermen of Sark know this, as does everyone who has seen them make certain abrupt movements in the sea. The purpoises, too, know it, and have a way of snapping at the cuttle-fish, poulps, and calmar floating on the sea without heads. In fact, the only vulnerable part of the poulp is the head. Gilliatt knew this but he had never seen a pieuvre so large a size before. At his first encounter he found himself face to face with one of the most enormous dimensions. Many a man would have been rendered powerless from terror alone.

A struggle with a pieuvre resembles, in a way, a fight with a bull; there is a certain moment of which it is necessary to take advantage. With the bull it is when he lowers his neck; with the devil-fish, when it thrusts forward its head. It is a momentary movement, and he who fails to take advantage of it is lost. All that we have related had not taken many minutes, but Gilliatt felt the two hundred and fifty suckers working with increased power.

This fearful creature is full of cunning; it endeavours to stupefy its prey, and therefore seizes it and waits.

Gilliatt now grasped his knife firmly, but the suction became stronger and more painful.

He gazed at the pieuvre, which returned his gaze.

In a moment the monster detached its sixth tentacle from the rock, and, darting it at Gilliatt, endeavoured to seize his left arm. At the same time it thrust its head sharply forward. One second more, and that hideous mouth would have been fastened on his chest. Bleeding from his sides, and with both his arms bound, he would have been a dead man. Now was Gilliatt's opportunity. He avoided the threatening movement, and, at the instant that the creature made a bite at his chest, he struck a decisive blow with his knife. There were two convulsions in reverse directions – that of Gilliatt and that of the pieuvre. It was like the meeting of two flashes of lightning. Gilliatt had plunged the point of his knife into the flat, slimy substance, and with a rapid circular movement, like the flourish of a whip, he tore off the head as a man draws a tooth. It was all over in an instant. The creature dropped at once; the terrible folds relaxed; it fell like a mass of wet linen; the suckers ceased their work of destruction, and relaxed their hold on rock and man. The body sank into the water. Panting with his efforts, Gilliatt could see, on the pebbles at his feet, two shapeless masses of slimy matter, the head on one side and the remainder on the other. Fearing that it might seize him again in a last convulsive movement of agony, he hastily withdrew beyond the reach of its tentacles. The pieuvre, however, was dead, and Gilliatt closed his knife.

CHAPTER IV

NOTHING REMAINS CONCEALED, NOTHING IS LOST

In slaying this hideous monster, he was only just in time – he was almost stifled; his right arm and his chest were purple with the pressure. There were numberless little swellings upon them, and here and there the blood was flowing. The best cure for such wounds is salt water, and Gilliatt plunged his arm into the sea, and, taking some water up in his hand, rubbed his chest. Under the friction the swellings subsided. When he drew back farther into the water he had, without perceiving it, approached a kind of cave which he had remarked before, not far from the cavity from which the pieuvre had darted upon him. This cave slanted inwards, and was dry. The pebbles which were heaped up there had raised the bottom beyond the height of ordinary tides. This cavity had a low arched entrance, through which it was possible to penetrate by stooping. The strange green light that has been before referred to penetrated within it and lighted it up feebly.

Whilst engaged in rubbing his swellings, Gilliatt chanced to cast his eyes mechanically in this direction, and caught sight of the interior of the cave.

He started back, rooted to the spot, for at the end he seemed to see a face which grinned at him through the shadow.

The word 'hallucination' was new to Gilliatt, but he knew what it was well enough. Those mysterious combats with the invisible, which, for want of a better term, we call 'hallucinations', are portions of our nature. Be they illusions or be they realities, visions are a fact.

Those who have these gifts will ever be dreamers. Gilliatt, as we have said before, was one.

His depth of soul sometimes produced the gift of prophecy. A solitary life, in solitary places, often produces this result. He believed that he was the dupe of one of those illusions, which he had more than once imagined he had seen in his nocturnal wanderings. The cavity was something in the shape of a lime-kiln. It was a low-roofed niche, with projections like basket-handles. The abrupt arch contracted gradually at the other end, where the rocky wall joined it and closed it up. He entered it and, bending his head, advanced towards the end.

There was a something grinning.

It was a skull, and not only the skull, but an entire skeleton, which was lying in the dark recesses of the cave.

A sight like this simply prompted a courageous man as Gilliatt to continue his researches.

He looked all round him.

He found himself surrounded by a legion of crabs; they made no movement: all were dead, and there was nothing left but empty shells. They lay here and there in heaps upon the pebbles which formed the floor of the cave.

With his eyes fixed upon the other object, Gilliatt had walked through them without perceiving them.

At the extremity of the little chamber there was a greater heap – a motionless bristling-up of claws, antennae, and mandibles. Open claws sticking up, and holding nothing. The long cases did not move under their coating of prickles, and, turned upside down, exhibited their livid hollows; these heaps resembled a breach, in the attack upon which the stormers had fallen in masses.

The skeleton which Gilliatt had seen was under this heap – the skull, the vertebrae, the thighs, the tibias, and the long, knotty fingers, with the nails still remaining on them. The frame of the ribs was full of crabs, and yet a living heart had once beat there. A green mould filled up the bony sockets of the eyes. Shellfish had left their slime upon the orifice where the nose had been. In the cave, hidden in the heart of the rock, there was neither seaweed nor marine plants, or a breath of air. All was still, and the teeth were clenched in a ghastly smile.

This strange palace of the deep, with its encrustment of gems of the ocean, had finished at last by revealing its secret. It was the den of the devil-fish; it was the tomb of the man whose bones lay there.

The skeleton of the man and the remains of the crabs waved weirdly in the reflections of the subterranean waters which trembled on the walls and roof. The horrible multitude of crabs seemed as though they were completing their repast. Nothing could have a more strange appearance than the dead devourers of carrion grouped around their dead prey.

Gilliatt had penetrated into the pantry of the pieuvre. It was a dismal sight, and filled the spectator with horror; the crabs had eaten the man, and the pieuvre had, in his turn, devoured the crabs. There was not a sign of clothing on the skeleton. The man must have been seized naked. Gilliatt stopped, and removed the crabs from the bones. Who could this man have been? The skeleton was admirably articulated; it looked as though it had been prepared for a museum of anatomy. Every morsel of flesh had gone, not a muscle remained, and every bone was perfect. Had Gilliatt ever studied anatomy he could have borne evidence to this fact. The skeleton was buried beneath the crabs, and Gilliatt disinterred it. All of a sudden he bent over it more eagerly. He had perceived a kind of ligature round the spinal column.

He eagerly examined it.

It was a leather belt, that had evidently been buckled round the waist of the man during his lifetime.

The buckle was rusty, and the leather was mouldy. Gilliatt drew the belt towards him; the vertebrae resisted his efforts, and he was forced to break through the obstruction in order to remove the belt. It was in a fairly good state of preservation, but a crust of small shells had begun to form on it.

He felt the belt, and discovered a hard, square object in it. It was useless to try and unbuckle it, and he cut the leather with his knife. In it was a little iron box and a few pieces of gold. Gilliatt counted them – there were twenty guineas. The iron box was an old sailor's tobacco-box, opening with a spring. It was much rusted, and tightly closed. The spring would no longer act, owing to the effects of the water. Once more his knife served Gilliatt well, a pressure with its point caused the lid to fly open.

Some papers were inside.

Small slips of paper, very thin, folded in four; they were damp, but not injured. The close-fitting lid had preserved them. Gilliatt unfolded them.

They were bank-notes, of a thousand pounds sterling each, making altogether twenty-five thousand francs.

Gilliatt folded them up and put them back into the box, and, profiting by the small space which remained, put the twenty guineas on the top of them, and closed the box in the best way he could.

Then he examined the belt.

The leather had been enamelled on the outside, but was rough in the interior. On this yellow surface were some letters, traced in a thick kind of ink. Gilliatt deciphered them, and read the words, 'Sieur Clubin'.

CHAPTER V

SHOWS HOW DEATH MAY LIE IN THE DIFFERENCE BETWEEN SIX INCHES AND TWO FEET

Having replaced the box in the belt, and the belt in the pocket of his trousers, Gilliatt left the skeleton to the crabs, with the dead pieuvre by his side. Whilst he had been with the skeleton and the pieuvre, the tide had risen, and he could only effect his exit by diving through the arch, but he was a past-master in all these sea-gymnastics, and managed to do this without trouble. It is easy to understand the drama that had taken place here ten weeks before – one monster seized upon another. The pieuvre had seized Clubin.

In this terrible spot two hypocrites had met. There had been in the depths an encounter between two existences of watchfulness and darkness, and the monster had executed the sentence on the man – a sinister act of justice. The crabs feed on carrion, the devil-fish on crabs. The devil-fish seizes on any object which swims near him – an otter, a dog, a man, if it is strong enough – drinks its blood, and lets its body sink to the bottom of the sea; the crabs are the burying-beetles of the sea. The scent of putrifying flesh attracts them; they eat the body, and the pieuvre eats them. Dead things disappear in the crab, and the crab disappears in the pieuvre. We have already touched upon this law of supply and demand.

Clubin had become the victim of the pieuvre.

It had held him down, and so drowned him, whilst the crabs had devoured him. A passing wave had washed him into the cavity of the rock, where Gilliatt had found his bones.

Gilliatt retraced his footsteps, hunting in the holes of the reef for the sea-urchins and limpets; he did not want any more crabs; it was too much like eating human flesh, and he only thought of supping as well as he could before leaving. There were no more obstacles now. Great storms are always followed by days of calm, so that there was nothing more to be dreaded from the sea. Gilliatt had made up his mind to leave the next day. It was necessary to keep up, for that night, the barrier, on account of the tide, but at daybreak he would remove it, and, getting his boat out of the channel between the Douvres, to set sail and steer for Saint Sampson. There was a gentle breeze from the south-east, exactly the kind of wind to suit him. It was the first quarter of the May moon, and the days were long. Gilliatt returned from his search amongst the rocks with the sharp edge of his appetite taken off; the twilight was immersed by the pale light that came from the rising moon, and the tide, having reached its height, was beginning to fall. The funnel of the engine towering above his boat, which had been spattered with the foam of the tempest, was covered with a deposit of salt, which gleamed like silver in the moonbeams.

This was a reminder to Gilliatt that the storm had thrown a good deal of sea and rain into the boat, and that there was, no doubt, six inches of water in the hold. The scoop that he had for the purpose would, he thought, be sufficient to throw this out.

Having examined her, he started back in amazement. There was nearly two feet of water in her.

This was a terrible catastrophe – his boat was leaking! She had been gradually filling during his absence, and twenty inches' increase was a very dangerous thing. A little more, and she would have foundered. Had he returned an hour later he would very likely have found the mast and the funnel above water.

Not a moment was to be lost. It was necessary to find out the hole at once, and stop it; then to bale out the boat, or, at any rate, to lighten her in some manner. The Durande's pump had been lost, so that he was reduced to his scoop to empty out the water. To seek for the leak was the most urgent. He set to work at once, without giving himself time to dress; in his anxiety he felt neither cold nor hunger. The boat continued to fill. Happily, there was no wind; the boat's motion would have caused her to sink.

It was dark. The moon had set.

Crouching on his hands and knees, half-buried in the water; he poked about for a long time, and at last discovered where the mischief lay. During the storm, at one of the most critical moments, the boat had been thrown violently against the rocks, and one of the sharp points of the Little Douvre had made a hole in her hull. This leak, unfortunately – it might be almost said maliciously – had been made at the juncture of the two sides – a fact which, joined to the fury of the gale, had prevented him from seeing it at once.

The bad feature about the hole was that it was a large one; but, fortunately, though the vessel was sunk lower than usual by the weight of the water, she was still much above the customary water-line. At the time when the accident had happened the waves had rushed violently into the passage, and the boat had sunk a little under the weight of the sea, so that, even after the subsidence of the water, the weight, having raised the water-line, had kept the hole under the surface of the sea. Hence the extreme danger. But if he could succeed in stopping the hole he could afterwards empty the boat, which would then rise to her proper water-line, and the fracture would be above the water, so that the repairs could be easily effected; and Gilliatt, as we have said, had all his carpenter's tools in fair order.

What a cloud of uncertainty had now invaded the whole matter, and what fresh dangers, what unlucky chances? He could hear the water trickling in remorselessly. The least shock would make her founder. What a misfortune! Perhaps even now it was too late. Gilliatt bitterly reproached himself. He ought to have looked at once to see if she had sustained any damage. He had been a fool to attribute those six inches of water to the foam and the rain. How angry he was with himself for having wasted his time in sleeping and eating. He almost brought himself to think that the storm and the dark night was his own fault.

He heaped these reproaches upon himself during the intervals of his toil, but they did not prevent him from paying every attention to the work upon which he was engaged. The leak had been found; this was the first step; the second was to stop it. That was all that it was possible to do for the time, for a carpenter's work cannot be carried on under water. One favourable circumstance was that the leak was in the space between the two chains which held the funnel fast on the starboard side. The oakum, with which it was necessary to stop it, could be fixed to these chains.

The water was gaining; it was now between two and three feet deep, and reached to his knees.

CHAPTER VI

DE PROFUNDIS AD ALTUM

Having at his disposal, amongst the other stores belonging to his boat, a fair-sized tarpaulin, with lanyards at the four corners,

Gilliatt took it, and fastening the lanyards at the corners to the two rings which supported the chains of the funnel on the side of the leak, threw it overboard. The tarpaulin fell like a sheet between the Little Douvre and the boat, and sank. The pressure of the water, endeavouring to enter the fracture in the hull, fixed it tightly against the timbers of the boat, and caused it to adhere to the spot where the leak was, which it closed effectually. The tarred canvas thus interposed between the interior of the hold and the water outside, not a single drop of which could enter. The leak was mastered, but not yet closed; it was a respite only.

Gilliatt took the scoop and began to bale out the boat. It was high time to lighten her. The work warmed him a little, but he was fearfully fatigued. He was compelled to confess to himself that he could not continue the work and make the hold water-tight. He had scarcely eaten anything, and had the humiliation of feeling himself exhausted.

He calculated the progress of his work by the sinking of the water from his knees downwards, but the fall was very slow. Besides, the influx of the sea was only checked; the evil was alleviated, but not cured entirely. The tarpaulin, thrust into the hole by the force of the sea, began to swell out, looking like a closed fist endeavouring to thrust its way through. The canvas, strong and thickly-coated with tar, resisted, but the tension and swelling continued, and it was far from certain that the canvas would not yield, and at any moment the swollen portion might burst and the leakage re-commence.

Masters of vessels in distress know very well that there is no other resource but an application of stuffing under such circumstances. They collect together all the rags of canvas, pieces of blanket and other things, and thrust them into the bulging canvas in the leak, but Gilliatt did not now possess the necessary stuffing. Everything of the kind that he had collected in his storehouse had been either used up in the course of his work or blown away by the storm. As a last chance, he might have been able to find some pieces by searching the rocks. The boat was sufficiently lightened to permit him to leave her for a quarter-of-an-hour, but how could he conduct the search without any light, for he was in utter darkness? There was no moon, nothing but the sombre sky, studded with stars. He had no dry tow to make a match with; no tallow for a candle, no fire to light it, and no lantern to shelter it in. All was confused and indistinct, both in the boat and on the rock. He could hear the water lapping against the wounded side, but he could not see the fracture, and it was by feeling that he satisfied himself of the increasing swelling of the tarpaulin. It was impossible for him in the darkness to search for those shreds of canvas and fragments of tow scattered about on the rocks. How could he find them when he could not see a foot before him? Gilliatt gazed sadly on the obscurity of the night. So many stars and not one candle. The liquid load in the boat had lessened, but the outer pressure increased. The bulging of the tarpaulin was getting larger; it was like an abscess ready to burst. The situation, which a little while before had looked better, now assumed a more menacing aspect. A stuffing of some kind was urgently required, and he had no materials left but his clothes. He had, it may be remembered, laid them out to dry on some of the projecting rocks of the Little Douvre. He gathered them together, and placed them in the boat. He took his oilskin coat and, kneeling down in the water, forced it into the hole, pushing out the tarpaulin and consequently emptying it. To the coat he added his woollen shirt, and his jersey – everything available. He had only one article of clothing left – his trousers. He took them off, and increased and made firmer the plug. It was finished at last, and seemed as if it would answer. The plug went right through the side of the boat, with the tarpaulin outside to protect it. The water, in its efforts to enter, pressed against the barrier, and spread it out over the hole, blocking it at the same time. It was a species of outside compress. Inside the boat – the centre only of the bulging having been driven out – there remained, all round the hole, a sort of circular pad, formed of tarpaulin, which the very inequalities of the fracture rendered firm. The leak was stopped, but the position was most precarious. The sharp points of the fracture, which held the tarpaulin tight, might at any time pierce it and make holes by which the water might enter. In the darkness, Gilliatt could not see this. It was very doubtful if the plug would hold until daylight. He returned to his work of emptying out the water, but he was so exhausted that he could hardly raise the scoop; he was naked, and shivered with the cold. He felt that the end was terribly near.

One hope of safety flashed across his brain. A sail might pass in sight. Some fishermen, who might by accident be in the neighbourhood of the Douvres, would come to his aid. The moment had arrived when a helper had become a necessity. With a man and a lantern all might yet be saved. Two could easily bale out the boat, and when she was once empty she would rise to her proper water-line. The fracture would be above the water, and he would be able to place a piece of planking over the hole, and so make a thoroughly good job of it. If not, it would be necessary to wait for daylight – to wait through the whole dreary night – a delay which might prove ruinous. The force of impatience seized on him. Suppose that the lights of some vessel were even now in sight, he might trace the summit of the Great Douvre and make signals of distress. The weather was fine; there was no wind, and a man making signals on the top of a rock beneath a starry heaven might very likely be noticed. A captain of a vessel, or even the skipper of a fishing-boat, would not be in these waters without, as a matter of precaution, keeping a good look-out on the Douvres with his telescope. He hoped some one might observe him. He climbed on to the wreck, seized the knotted cord, and ascended to the top of the rock. No sail, no light – the sea was one vast solitude. No assistance was at hand, and how could he continue the struggle? A feeling of depression, such as he had never experienced before, crept over him; he felt utterly helpless.

A fatality had now assumed the mastery over him. After all his toil – after all his success, after all the resolution that he had displayed – he and his boat, with the engines of the Durande on board, were about to become the prey of the ocean. He had no more means of continuing the combat. He must remain perfectly passive. How could he prevent the tide from flowing, the water from coming in, and the weary night from enduring? The frail plug was what all his hopes were centred in. He had, in constructing it, exhausted and stripped himself and he could do no more to make it stronger or more secure; as it was, so must it remain, and nothing further could be done. The sea could do what it liked with this hastily-constructed apparatus; and how could he hope that it would resist the pressure of the waves? He had left it to continue the fight, for he had retired baffled and disheartened. The swelling of a wave would tear open the fracture. It was merely a question of more or less pressure.

The fertility of his brain was now to be put to the test. The whole affair was going to be fought out between the mechanical quantities. Gilliatt would no longer assist his ally or repulse his enemy. He could only remain the spectator of a combat, upon which his life or death depended. Gilliatt, who up to this time had been the directing intelligence, was now reduced to act the part of mere passive resistance. None of the trials or terrors which he had gone through had in any way approached the last crowning glory.

From the day that he had taken up his abode upon the Douvres he had found himself surrounded by solitude. This solitude did more than surround him – it wrapped him in its embraces. A thousand threats had been daily held out to him. The blast was then ready to blow, and the sea to roar. It was as impossible to gag the one as to muzzle the other. And yet he had fought bravely; mere man as he was, he had struggled hard with the ocean and wrestled with the storm.

He had made head against other anxieties and other necessities. He had become familiar with every shape of distress. He had had to work without tools, raise weights without aid, solve problems without scientific knowledge; to live without food, drink, bed, or shelter. On that terrible rock, as upon a rack, he had been tortured by all the cruel torments of Nature – Nature who can be either a monster or an executioner, as the fit seizes her.

He had conquered solitude, hunger, and thirst; he had vanquished cold and fever, triumphed over work and defeated sleep. He had triumphed over all the obstacles that had banded themselves together to bar his way. After his privations there were the elements, then the storm, then the devil-fish, and, lastly, the spectre of coming death.

But a melancholy ending was to be the finish of all. On the very rock which Gilliatt had counted on leaving as a conqueror, Clubin's skull grinned upon him sardonically. Winter, famine, fatigue, the wreck to pull to pieces, the engines to tranship, the equinoctial storms, the wind, the thunder, the devil-fish, all these were as nothing compared to the leak. Gilliatt had had fire to enable him to endure the cold, the limpets of the rock to allay his hunger; rain to slake his burning thirst; industry and energy to enable him to contend against the difficulties of his task; the breakwaters against the waves of the ocean, and his knife to save him from the deadly embrace of the devil-fish. But for that little task he could find no remedy.

This had been the sinister farewell of the storm, the coward's blow, the treacherous stroke given by the vanquished to the victor. The tempest, as it fled, launched this Parthian shaft. The enemy had rallied for a moment and dealt one last deadly blow. The storm he had been able to baffle, but how resist the stealthy progress of the leak? If the plug gave – if the fracture opened, the boat must inevitably founder. It was like the ligature that ties the artery becoming undone; and, when once the boat had sunk, with all that heavy weight of machinery, there was no means of raising her again. The tremendous efforts of two months' Titanic labours would end in nothing. To begin again was hopeless; he had no longer a forge or materials. Perhaps, at daybreak, he should see the results of his labours sink surely and slowly into the abyss. How terrible to feel the cruel power beneath you, and the sea snatching from you the reward of your toils!

When the boat had sunk, nothing was left for him but death from hunger or cold, like the hapless mariner on the Man-Rock.

For two months the intelligences which hover over the earth had witnessed these things. Ranged on one side were the mighty ocean, the winds, the lightnings, and the meteors; on the other, a man. On one side the sea; on the other, a human intellect; on one, the Infinite; on the other, an atom. The contest had been long and doubtful, and now all his gallant efforts had resulted in defeat. He had no longer any clothes. He was naked in the presence of the vast, and overwhelmed by the sensation of that immense unknown, no longer knowing what was required of him; confronted with the shadow in the presence of that irreductible obscurity, amidst the hoarse roar of the waves, the surf, the foam, and the breeze; under the clouds, under the vast scattered forces, under that unknown firmament of wings, stars, and of sepulchres; under the possible, mingled with the unfathomable, having around and beneath him, the ocean, and above him the constellations – he gave up the struggle, and, casting himself down on the rock, with his face to the heavens, he raised his hands humbly, and cried aloud, 'Have mercy!' Crushed by the immensity, he prayed. He was there alone on a rock in the midst of the sea, surrounded by all the black obscurity of night; stricken down, utterly prostrated, crushed as though with a thunderbolt, nude as a gladiator in the arena – only in the place of the arena there was the ocean, and, in place of ferocious beasts, the terrible darkness; in place of the thousand fixed eyes of the audience, the glance of the Unknown, in place of the vestal virgins, the stars; in the place of Caesar – GOD! He felt his whole being melted away in cold, weariness, powerlessness, prayer and gloom, and his eyes closed.

CHAPTER VII

ALL IS SAVED

Some hours had passed, and the sun rose in all its brilliancy. Its first beam fell upon a motionless form, stretched on the summit of the Great Douvre; it was Gilliatt. He was still prostrate on the rock. His bare form, though pinched with the cold, did not even quiver. His closed eyelids had a pallid hue. It would have been hard for a spectator to have said whether it was a living man or a corpse that was spread out before him. And still the sun beamed upon him. If there was yet life in the prostrate form, one single, chill blast would have sufficed to extinguish it; but the wind began to blow warm, soft, and life-giving; it was the breath of May ushering in the coming spring; and still the sun ascending in the bright-blue sky, its beams falling more and more directly upon the prostrate form, and, little by little, enveloping Gilliatt. He never moved. If he breathed, it was with that faint respiration which would hardly tarnish a mirror.

The sun rose higher, its rays falling more fully upon Gilliatt. The wind, which up to this time had been merely warm, was now growing almost scorching.

The bare form, with all its limbs stiff and rigid, still remained motionless, but the skin seemed to be recovering its natural hue.

The sun, which had now reached its altitude, shone almost perpendicularly on the summit of the Douvre. An immense flood of light fell from on high. The gigantic reflection from the sea, so calm and limpid, joined itself to it. The sun's rays warmed the rock, which threw some of its acquired heat upon the prostrate form. The breast of Gilliat heaved. He lived.

The sun still continued fondly to caress him. The wind, which was the wind of noon and spring, breathed on him gently as it neared him.

Gilliatt made a slight movement.

The sea was quite calm. Its murmur was like the lullaby of a nurse beside the cradle of a sleeping infant. The waves seemed to shine to soothe the rock with their caresses. The sea-birds, who knew Gilliatt's form so well, fluttered above him in vague disquietude, uttering plaintive cries. They appeared to be calling to him. A seamew, who, no doubt, knew him better than the rest, was tame enough to perch near him; it began to speak to him in its own tongue, but Gilliatt paid no attention to it. The bird hopped upon his shoulder and gently pecked at his lips.

Gilliatt opened his eyes. He rose from the rock, stretched himself like a lion aroused from sleep, and, running to the edge of the platform, gazed down into the passage between the Douvres.

The boat was still there, unharmed. The plug had maintained its position well; the waves had evidently had but little effect on it.

All was saved.

He no longer felt any fatigue. Gilliatt was himself once again. His swoon had resulted in a profound slumber. He descended and baled out the boat, saw that the hold was perfectly dry, and that the fracture had risen above the under tier; then he dressed, ate, and drank, and felt once again happy.

When he was able to examine the hole in the boat in broad daylight, he found that it required more work than he had imagined at first.

The injury was a grave one, and would take a whole day to repair.

However, on the morrow, with the break of day, after having removed the barrier, and so opened the entrance to the passage, clothed in the rags with which he had stopped the leak, having round his waist Clubin's belt, and seventy-five thousand francs, standing upright in the newly-repaired boat, by the side of the rescued engine, with a favourable breeze and a tranquil sea, Gilliatt pushed off from the Douvres.

He directed his course for Guernsey. As he left the rocks, anyone who had witnessed his departure might have heard him hum, in a low voice, a familiar air.

THIRD PART

BOOK I

NIGHT AND THE MOON

CHAPTER I

THE BELL AT THE HARBOUR

Forty years ago, Saint Sampson was little more than a village. The Saint Sampson of to-day, is a town of some importance in the Channel Islands.

After the winter was over, and spring-time had come, the people were not long out of bed after sunset. Saint Sampson was an ancient parish which had long been accustomed to the sound of the curfew-bell, and which had a traditional habit of blowing out the candle at an early hour. Those old Norman villages are famous for early roosting and the villages are great rearers of poultry.

The inhabitants of Saint Sampson, except some rich families among the townsfolk are, generally speaking, a population of quarriers and carpenters, the latter being mostly engaged in ship repairing. The quarrying of stone and the fashioning of timber goes on all day long; here the labourer with the pickaxe, there the workman with the mallet. At night they sink with fatigue, and sleep soundly.

On a certain evening, in the commencement of the month of May, after watching the crescent moon for some instants through the trees, and listening to the step of Déruchette, walking alone in the cool air in the garden of the Bravées, Mess Lethierry had returned to his room looking on the harbour, and had retired to rest; Douce and Grace were already in bed. Except Déruchette, the whole household were sleeping. Door and shutters were everywhere closed. Footsteps were silent in the streets. Some few lights, like winking eyes about to close in rest, showed here and there in windows in the roof, indicating the hour of domestics going to bed. Nine had already struck in the old Romanesque belfry, surrounded by ivy, which shares with the church of Saint Brélade at Jersey the peculiarity of having for its date four ones (IIII), which are used to signify eleven hundred and eleven.

The success of Mess Lethierry at Saint Sampson brought him great popularity. The success at an end, there had come a void. It might be imagined that ill-fortune is contagious, and that the unsuccessful have a plague, so rapidly are they put in quarantine. The young men of well-to-do families avoided Déruchette. The isolation around the Bravées was so complete, that its inmates had not even yet heard the news of the great local event which had that day set all Saint Sampson in a ferment. The rector of the parish, the Revd Ebenezer Caudray, had become rich. His uncle the magnificent Dean of Saint Asaph, had just died in London. The news had been brought by the mail sloop, the Cashmere, arrived from England that very morning, and the mast of which could be perceived in the anchorage of Saint Peter's Port. The Cashmere was to depart for Southampton at noon on the morrow, and, so the rumour ran, to convey the reverend gentleman, who had been suddenly summoned to England, to be present at the official opening of the will, not to speak of other urgent matters connected with an important inheritance. All day long Saint Sampson had been conversing on this subject. The Cashmere, the Revd Ebenezer, his deceased uncle, his riches, his departure, his possible preferment in the future, had formed the foundations of that perpetual buzzing. A solitary house, still uninformed on these matters, had remained at peace. This was the Bravées.

Mess Lethierry was reposing in his hammock, but only partially undressed.

Ever since the wreck of the Durande, to get into his hammock had been his habit when feeling weary. Every captive has recourse to stretching himself upon his pallet, and Mess Lethierry was the captive of his grief. To go to bed was a truce, a gain in breathing time, a suspension of ideas. He neither slept nor watched. Strictly speaking, for two months and a half – for so long was it since his misfortune – Mess Lethierry had been in a sort of somnambulism. He had not yet regained possession of his faculties. He was in that cloudy and confused condition of intellect with which those are familiar who have undergone overwhelming afflictions. His reflections were not thought, his sleep was no repose. By day he was not awake, by night not asleep. He was up, and then gone to rest, that was all. When he was in his hammock forgetfulness came to him a little. He called that sleep. Chimeras floated about him, and within him. The nocturnal cloud, full of confused faces, traversed his brain. Sometimes it was the Emperor Napoleon dictating to him the story of his life; sometimes there were several Déruchettes; strange birds were in the trees; the streets of Lons-le-Saulnier became serpents. Nightmares were the brief respites of despair. He passed nights in dreaming, and his days in reverie.

Often he would remain all the after part of the day at the window of his room, which looked out upon the port, with his head drooping, his elbows upon the stone, his ears resting on his fists, his back turned to the whole world, his eye fixed on the old massive iron ring fastened in the wall of the house, at only a few feet from his window, where in the old days he used to moor the Durande. He was intently gazing at the rust which gathered on the ring.

His life had now become a void and he was reduced to the mere mechanical habit of living.

It is generally accepted as a fact, that when brave men are deprived of their most cherished aim, they will come in this pass. Life is a voyage; the idea is itinerary. The plan of their course gone, Fate has a secret discretionary power. It is able to touch with its rod even our moral being. Despair is almost the destitution of the soul. Only the greatest minds resist, and for what?

Mess Lethierry's grief did not seek relief in prayer, he was always meditating, if absorption can be called meditation, in the depth of a sort of cloudy abyss. Broken words sometimes escaped him like these, 'There is nothing left for me now, but to ask yonder for leave to go.' There was a certain contradiction in the nature, complex as the sea, of which Mess Lethierry was, so to speak, the product. To be powerless is a certain strength. In the presence of our two great expressions of this blindness – destiny and nature – it is in his powerlessness that man has found his chief support in prayer. Man seeks succour from his terror; his anxiety bids him kneel.

At times, when he was in a happy state of mind, God existed for him almost in visible contact. Lethierry addressed Him, pledged his word to Him, seemed at times to hold familiar intercourse with Him. But in the hour of his misfortune, a phenomenon not unfrequent – the idea of God had become eclipsed in his mind. This happens when the mind has created for itself a deity clothed with human qualities. In the state of mind in which he existed, there was for Lethierry only one clear vision – the smile of Déruchette. Beyond this all was dark.

Evidently, on account of the loss of the Durande, and of the blow which it had been to them both, this pleasant smile had been rare. Déruchette seemed always thoughtful. Her playfulness and childlike ways, were gone. She was never seen now in the morning, at the sound of the cannon which announced daybreak. Her expression at times was very sad, a serious thing for that sweet nature. She made an effort, however, sometimes to laugh before Mess Lethierry and to divert him; but her cheerfulness grew tarnished from day to day – gathered dust like the wing of a butterfly with a pin through its body. Whether through sorrow for her uncle's sorrow – for there are griefs which are the reflections of other griefs – or whether for any other reasons, she appeared at this time to be much inclined towards religion. In the time of the old rector, M. Jaquemin Hérode, she scarcely went to church, as has been already said, four times a year. Now she was, on the contrary, assiduous in her attendance. She missed no service, neither of Sunday or of Thursday. Pious souls in the parish remarked with satisfaction that amendment. For it is a great blessing when a girl who runs so many dangers in the world turns her thoughts towards God. That enables the poor parents at least to be easy on the subject of love-making and what not.

She walked for an hour or two in the evening, in the garden of the Bravées, whenever the weather permitted. She was almost as silent there as Mess Lethierry, and almost always alone. Déruchette was the last to retire for the night. This, however, did not prevent Douce and Grace watching her a little; spying is such a relaxation after household work. As to Mess Lethierry, in his abstracted state of mind, these little changes in Déruchette's habits were not noticed by him. Moreover, his nature had little in common with the Duenna. He had not even remarked her regularity at her devotions. Tenacious of his prejudices against the clergy and their sermons, he would have seen with little pleasure these frequent attendances at the parish church. It was not because his own moral condition was not undergoing change. Sorrow is a cloud which changes form.

As we have said, strong and healthy minds are sometimes almost overthrown by great misfortune; but it is not always thus. Manly characters such as that of Mess Lethierry, experience a reaction in a given time. Despair has its backward stages. From overwhelment we rise to dejection; from dejection to affliction; from affliction to melancholy. Melancholy is a twilight state; suffering melts into it and becomes a sombre joy. Melancholy is the pleasure of being sad.

These plaintive moods were not for Lethierry. Neither the nature of his temperament nor the character of his misfortune suited those delicate shades. But at the moment at which we have returned to him, the reverie of his first despair had for more than a week been tending to disperse; without, however, leaving him less sad. He was more inactive, was always dull; but he was no longer overwhelmed. A certain perception of events and circumstances was returning to him, and he began to experience something of that phenomenon which may be called the return to reality.

In this way he listened to the conversation of those about him. Grace came one morning quite triumphant, to tell Déruchette that he had taken up a newspaper. This half acceptance of realities is in itself a good symptom, a token of convalescence. Great afflictions produce a stupor; it is by such little acts that men return to themselves. This improvement, however, is at first only an aggravation of the evil. The dreamy condition of mind in which the sufferer has lived, had served, while it lasted, to blunt his grief. His sight before was thick. He felt little. Now his view is clear, nothing escapes him; and his wounds re-open. Each detail that he perceives serves to remind him of his sorrow. He sees everything again in memory, every remembrance is a regret. All kinds of bitter aftertastes lurk in that return to life. He is better, and yet worse. Such was the condition of Lethierry. In returning to full consciousness, his sufferings had become more distinct.

It was a sudden shock which recalled him to his proper senses.

On the 20th of April, a double-knock at the door of the lower room of the Bravées announced the arrival of the afternoon postman. Douce had opened the door; there was a letter.

The letter bore the postmark 'Lisbon', and was addressed to Mess Lethierry.

Douce conveyed the letter to Mess Lethierry, who was in his room. The latter placed it mechanically upon the table, where it remained an entire week without being opened.

However, one morning Douce said to Mess Lethierry: 'Shall I brush the dust off your letter, sir?'

This question seemed to rouse him from his lethargy.

'Yes, yes! The letter,' he said; and he opened it, reading as follows:

On board the *Tamaulipas*, 10th March.
To Mess Lethierry.

You will no doubt be glad to receive some news respecting me. I am on board the above vessel, bound for the port of Guam. Among our crew is an A.B. named Tostevin, a native of Guernsey, who is returning in the ship, and will have some facts to communicate to you. We have spoken the barque *Herman Cortes*, bound for Lisbon, and I have put this letter on board of her. You will be astonished to learn that I am going to turn over a new leaf, and intend to be as honest as Sieur Clubin. I am bound to believe that you know of certain recent occurrences; nevertheless, it is, perhaps, not altogether superfluous to send you a full account of them. I have returned you your money. Some years ago, I borrowed from you, under somewhat unusual circumstances, the sum of fifty thousand francs. Before leaving Saint Malo lately, I placed in the hands of your confidential man of business, Sieur Clubin, on your account, three bank-notes of one thousand pounds each; making together seventy-five thousand francs. You will no doubt find this reimbursement sufficient. Sieur Clubin acted for you, and received your money, including interest, in a very remarkable manner. He appeared to me, indeed, singularly zealous. This is, in fact, my reason for apprising you of the facts.

Once your confidential man of business, now,
RANTAINE.

Memo: Clubin was armed with a revolver, which will explain the circumstance of my having no receipt.

He who has never touched a torpedo, can have no notion of the effect produced on Mess Lethierry by the reading of this letter. He recognized both the writing and the signature. As to the facts which the missive contained, at first he understood nothing.

The excitement, however, soon gave movement to his faculties. The effective part of the shock he had received lay in the phenomenon of the seventy-five thousand francs entrusted by Rantaine to Clubin; this was a riddle which set Lethierry's brain to work. Conjecture is a healthy occupation for the mind. Reason is awakened, and logic is called into play.

Public opinion in Guernsey had been undergoing a reaction on the subject of Clubin: that man of such high reputation for honour during many years; that man so unanimously regarded with esteem. People had began to question and to doubt; there were wagers pro and con. Some light had been thrown on the question in singular ways. The figure of Clubin began to become clearer, that is to say, he began to be blacker in the eyes of the world.

A majesterial inquiry had taken place at Saint Malo, for the purpose of ascertaining what had become of the coastguardman, No. 619. The authorities had got upon a false scent, a thing which happens not unfrequently. It had started with the supposition that the man had been decoyed by Zuela, and shipped aboard the *Tamaulipas* for Chili. This ingenious supposition had led to a considerable amount of wasted conjecture. The short-sightedness of justice had got on a wrong scent, and had failed to take note of Rantaine; but in the progress of inquiry the authorities had come under other clues. The affair, so obscure, became complicated. Clubin had now become mixed up with it. A coincidence, perhaps a direct connection, had been found between the departure of the *Tamaulipas* and the loss of the Durande. At the wine-shop near the Dinan Gate, where Clubin thought himself entirely unknown, he had been recognized. The wine-shop keeper had talked; Clubin had bought a bottle of brandy that night. For whom? The gunsmith of Saint Vincent Street, too, had talked. Clubin had purchased a revolver. For what object? The landlord of the 'Jean Auberge' had talked. Clubin had absented himself in an inexplicable manner. Captain Gertrais-Gaboureau had talked; Clubin had determined to start, although warned, and knowing that he might expect a great fog. The crew of the Durande had talked. In fact, the collection of the freight had been neglected, and the cargo badly stowed, a negligence easy to comprehend, if the captain had determined to wreck the ship. The Guernsey passenger, too, had spoken. Clubin had evidently imagined that he had run upon the Hanways. The Torteval people had spoken. Clubin had visited that neighbourhood a few days before the loss of the Durande, and had been seen walking in the direction of Pleinmont, near the Hanways. He had with him a travelling-bag. 'He had set out with it, and come back without it.' The birds'-nesters had spoken: their story seemed to be possibly connected with Clubin's disappearance, if instead of ghosts they supposed smugglers. Finally, the haunted house of Pleinmont itself had spoken. Persons bent on obtaining information, had climbed and entered the windows, and had found inside – what? The very travelling-bag which had been seen in Sieur Clubin's possession. The authorities at Torteval had taken possession of the bag and had it opened. It was found to contain provisions, a telescope, a chronometer, a man's clothing, and linen marked with Clubin's initials. All this in the gossip of Saint Malo and Guernsey became more and more like a case of fraud. Obscure hints were brought together; there seemed to have been a singular disregard of advice; a desire to encounter the dangers of the fog; a suspicious negligence in the stowage of the cargo. Then there was the mysterious bottle of brandy; a drunken helmsman; a substitution of the captain for the helmsman; a manipulation of the rudder, to say the least, unskilful. The heroism of remaining behind upon the wreck began to be looked upon with suspicion. Besides, Clubin had evidently been deceived as to the rock he was on. Granted an intention to wreck the vessel, it was easy to understand the choice of the Hanways, the shore easily reached by swimming, and the intended concealment in the haunted house awaiting the opportunity for flight. The travelling-bag, that suspicious preparative, completed the demonstration. By what link this affair connected itself with the other affair of the disappearance of the coastguardsman nobody knew. People imagined some connection, and that was all. They had a glimpse in their minds of the look-out-man, No. 619, alongside of the mysterious Clubin – quite a tragic drama. Clubin possibly was not an actor in it, but his presence was visible in the side scenes.

However, the supposition of a wilful destruction of the Durande did not explain everything. Certainly there was a revolver in the story, but no part had yet been assigned to it. The revolver, probably, belonged to the other affair.

Public opinion is to certain extent, keen and true. Its instinct excels in those discoveries of truth by pieces and fragments. Still, amidst these facts, which seemed to point very clearly to a case of barratry, there were serious difficulties.

There was a consistency in everything appertaining to the affair; but a basis to work on was wanting. People do not wreck vessels for the pleasure of wrecking them. Men do not run all those risks of fog, rocks, swimming, concealment, and flight without an interest. What could have been Clubin's interest? The act seemed plain, but the motive was puzzling. Hence a doubt in many minds. Where there is no motive, it is natural to infer that there was no act.

The missing link was what was wanting, and the letter from Rantaine seemed to supply it. This letter furnished a motive for Clubin's supposed crime.

Rantaine was the prime mover. He had descended from above with a lantern in his hand. His letter was the light on the affair. It explained everything, and even promised a witness in the person of Tostevin. The part which it at once suggested for the revolver was decisive. Rantaine was undoubtedly well informed. His letter pointed clearly the explanation of the mystery.

There could be no excuse for Clubin's crime. He had premeditated the loss of the Durande; the proofs were the preparations discovered in the haunted house. Even supposing him innocent, and admitting the wreck to have been accidental, would he not, at the last moment, when he had determined to sacrifice himself with the vessel, have entrusted the seventy-five thousand francs to the men who escaped in the long-boat. The evidence was striking. What had become of Clubin? He had probably been the victim of his crime. He doubtless perished upon the Douvres.

These surmises, which were not far from the reality, had for several days occupied the mind of Mess Lethierry. The letter from Rantaine had done him the service of setting him to think. He was at first shaken by his surprise; then he made an effort to reflect. He made another effort more difficult still, that of inquiry. He was induced to listen, and even seek conversation. At the end of a week, he had become, to a certain degree, in the world again; his thoughts had regained their coherence, and he was almost restored. He had emerged from his confused and troubled state.

Even admitting that Mess Lethierry could ever have entertained any hope of the reimbursement of his money, Rantaine's letter destroyed that last chance. It added to the catastrophe of the Durande this new wreck of seventy-five thousand francs. It put him in possession of that amount just so far as to make him sensible of its loss. The letter revealed to him the extreme point in his ruin.

This will account for the new and very painful sensation, which we have already spoken of. He began to take an interest in his household – what it was to be in the future – how he was to set things in order; matters of which he had taken no heed for two months past. These trifling cares wounded him with a thousand tiny points, worse in their aggregate than the old despair. A sorrow is doubly burdensome which has to be endured in each item, and while disputing the ground, inch by inch with fate for that already lost. Ruin is endurable in the concrete, but not in the dust and fragments of the fallen edifice. The great fact may overwhelm, but the details torture.

The catastrophe which lately fell like a thunderbolt, becomes now a cruel persecution. Humiliation comes to aggravate the blow. A second desolation succeeds the first, with features more repulsive. You descend one degree nearer to annihilation.

No remembrance is more bitter than that of one's own gradual fall from a social position. Ruin is very simple. A violent reverse; a cruel turn of fate; a catastrophe once for all. Be it so. We submit, and all is over. You are ruined: it is well; you are dead? No; you are still living. On the morrow you know it well. By what? By the pricking of a pin. Yonder passer-by omits to recognize you; the tradesmen's bills rain down upon you; and yonder is one of your enemies, who is smiling. Perhaps he is thinking of Arnal's last joke; but it is all the same. The joke would not have appeared to him so inimitable but for your ruin. You read your own sudden insignificance even in looks of indifference. Friends who use to dine at your table become of opinion that three courses were an extravagance. Your faults are now patent to everybody; ingratitude having nothing more to expect, proclaims itself openly; every idiot has foreseen your misfortunes. The malignant pull you to pieces; the more malignant profess to pity. And then come a hundred paltry details. Nausea succeeds to grief. You have been wont to indulge in wine; you must now drink cider. Two servants, too! Why, one will be too many. It will be necessary to discharge this one. Flowers in your garden are out of place; you will plant it with cabbages. You used to make presents of your fruits to friends; you will send them henceforth to market. As to the poor, it will be absurd to think of giving anything to them. Are you not poor yourself? And then there is the painful question of dress. To have to refuse a wife a new bonnet, what a torture! To have to refuse one who has made you a gift of her beauty a trifling article; to haggle over such matters, like a miser! Perhaps she will say to you, 'What! rob my garden of its flowers, and now refuse one for my bonnet!' Ah me! to have to condemn her to shabby dresses. The family table is silent. You fancy those around think you unkind. Beloved faces have become clouded. This is what is meant by falling in the social scale. It is simply to die day by day. To be struck down is like the blast of the furnace; to decay like this is positive torture. An overwhelming blow is a sort of Waterloo, a slow decay, a Saint Helena. Destiny, incarnate in the form of the first named, has still some dignity; but how sordid is that of the latter. Fate becomes then a paltry huckster. Reduced to humbler proportions, every ruined man has traversed those two phases.

On the day we have mentioned, and which was one of the first evenings of May, Lethierry, leaving Déruchette to walk by moonlight in the garden by herself, had retired to bed more depressed than ever.

Obnoxious but necessary and repulsive details, peculiar to worldly misfortune; all these trifling cares, which are at first insipid, and afterwards harassing, were revolving in his mind. A sullen load of miseries! Mess Lethierry felt that his fall was irremediable. What could he do? What would become of them? What sacrifices should he be compelled to impose on Déruchette? Whom should he discharge – Douce or Grace? Would they have to leave the Bravées? Would they not be compelled to leave the island? To be nothing where he had been everything; it was terrible.

And to think that the old times had gone never to return. To recall those journeys to and fro, uniting France with those numberless islands; the Tuesday's departure, the Friday's return, the crowd on the quay, those great cargoes, that industry, that prosperity, that proud direct navigation, that machinery embodying the will of man, that all-powerful boiler, that smoke, all that reality! The steamboat had been the final crown of the compass; the needle indicating the direct track, the steam-vessel following it. One proposing, the other executing. Where was she now, his Durande, that mistress of the seas, that queen who had made him a king? To have been so long the man of ideas in his own country, the man of success, the man who revolutionized navigation; and then to have to give up all, to abdicate! To cease to exist, to become a bye-word, an empty bag which was once full. To belong to the past, after having so long represented the future. To come down to be an object of pity to fools, to witness the triumph of routine, obstinacy, selfishness, ignorance. To see the old barbarous sailing cutters crawling to and fro upon the sea: the old ideas young again; to have wasted a lifetime; to have been a light, and to suffer this eclipse. Ah! what a sight it was upon the waves, that noble funnel, that prodigious cylinder, that pillar with its volume of smoke, that column grander than any in the Place Vendôme, for on that, there was only a man, whilst on this progress was surmounted. The ocean was subdued; it was certainty upon the open sea. And had all this been witnessed in that little island, in that little harbour, in that little town of Saint Sampson? Yes, it had been witnessed. And could it be, that having seen it, all had vanished to be seen no more.

All this was torture to Lethierry. There is such a thing as mental anguish. Never, perhaps, had he felt his misfortune more bitterly. A certain numbness follows this acute suffering. Under the weight of his sorrow he gradually dozed. He remained in this condition for some hours, feverish, sleeping a little, meditating much. Such torpors are accompanied by an obscure labour of the brain, which is inexpressibly wearying. Towards the middle of the night, a little before or a little after, he shook off his lethargy. He aroused, and opened his eyes. His window was directly in front of his hammock. He saw something extraordinary. A form was before the window; a marvellous form. It was the funnel of a steam-vessel.

Lethierry stared, and sat bolt upright in bed. The hammock oscillated like a swing in a tempest. Lethierry stared. A vision filled the window frame. There was the harbour flooded with the light of the moon, and against that glitter, quite close to his house, stood forth, tall, round, and black, a magnificent object.

Lethierry sprang from his hammock to the window, lifted it, and leaned out.

The funnel of the Durande was before him.

He recognized it.

The usual chains supported it, made fast to something, which, beneath the funnel, he could not properly distinguish.

Lethierry staggered, turned his back to the window, and dropped in a sitting posture into his hammock again.

Then he advanced again to the window, and once more saw the same vision.

In a moment, and like a flash of lightning, he was out upon the quay, carrying a lantern.

A sloop carrying a deckload from which issued the straight funnel before the window of the Bravées, was made fast to the old mooring-ring of the Durande. The bows of the sloop stretched beyond the corner of the wall of the house, and were level with the quay.

There did not appear to be anyone on board.

The vessel was of a strange shape, but all Guernsey would have recognized it. It was the old Dutch sloop.

Lethierry was very soon on board; and ran forward to the deckload.

There it was, entire, complete, intact, standing square and firm upon its cast-iron flooring; the boiler had all its rivets, the axle of the paddle-wheels was raised erect, and made fast near the boiler; the brine-pump was in its place; nothing was wanting.

Lethierry examined the engine. The lantern and the moon helped him in his examination. He went over every part.

He noticed the two cases at the sides. He examined the axle of the wheels. He went into the little cabin; it was empty. He returned to the engine, and felt it, looked into the boiler, and knelt down to examine it inside.

He placed his lantern in a position, where the light, illuminating the machinery, produced almost the illusion of an engine-room with its fire. Then he burst into a mad laugh, sprang to his feet, and with his eye fixed on the engine, and his arms outstretched towards the funnel, he cried aloud, 'Help!'

The alarm-bell was upon the quay, at a few paces distant. He ran to it, and began to pull the chain violently.

CHAPTER II

MORE OF THE HARBOUR BELL

Without accident of hitch of any kind, though his rate of progress was somewhat slow on account of the heavy burden of the sloop, Gilliatt had arrived at Saint Sampson after dark, and nearer ten than nine o'clock. He had calculated the time. The half-flood had arrived. There was plenty of water, and the moon was shining; so that he was able to enter the port. The little harbour was silent. A few vessels were moored there, with their sails stowed, their tops over, and without lights. At the far end a few others were visible, high and dry, where they were undergoing repairs; large hulls dismasted and stripped with their planking open at various parts, lifting high the ends of their timbers, and looking like huge dead beetles lying on their backs with their legs in the air.

Gilliatt, as soon as he had cleared the harbour mouth, examined the port and the quay. There was no light to be seen either at the Bravées or elsewhere. The place was deserted, save, perhaps, by some one going to or returning from the parsonage-house; nor was it possible to be sure even of this; for the night blurred every outline, and the light of the moon, always gives to some objects an imaginary appearance. The distance added to the indistinctness. The parsonage-house at that period was situated on the other side of the harbour, where there stands at the present day an open mast-house.

Gilliatt had silently approached the Bravées, and had made the sloop fast to the ring of the Durande, under Lethierry's window, and leaped ashore.

On leaving the sloop behind him by the quay, he turned sharply round the angle of the house, passed along a narrow street, then along another, did not even notice the pathway which branched off leading to the Bû de la Rue, and in a few minutes found himself at that corner of the wall where there was a quantity of wild flowers growing. Many a time concealed behind the bushes, seated on a stone, in the summer days, he had watched here through long hours, even for whole months, often tempted to climb the wall, over which he contemplated the garden of the Bravées and the two windows of a little room seen through the branches of the trees. The stone was there still; the bushes, the low wall, the angle, as quiet and dark as ever. Like an animal returning to its retreat, gliding rather than walking, he made his way in. Once seated there, he made no movement. He looked around; saw again the garden, the pathways, the beds of flowers, the house, the two windows of the chamber. The moonlight fell upon his dream.

He seemed to be looking on some glorious vision, and was fearful that all would vanish. It was almost impossible that all these things could be really before his eyes; and if they were, it could only be with that imminent danger of melting into air which belongs to things divine. A breath, and all must be dissipated. He trembled at the thought. Not far off, at the side of one of the walks in the garden, was a wooden seat painted green.

Gilliatt gazed at the two windows. He thought of the slumber of some one possibly in that room. Behind that wall she was no doubt sleeping. He wished himself elsewhere, yet would sooner have died than go away. It was she, that vision, that purity in the clouds, that form haunting him by day and night. She was there! He thought of her so far, and yet so near as to be almost within his reach; he thought of that impossible ideal drooping in slumber, and like himself, too, visited by visions; of that being so long desired, so distant, so impalpable – her closed eyelids, her face reclining on her hand; of the mystery of sleep in its relations with that pure spirit, of what dreams might come to one who was herself a dream. He dared not think beyond, and yet he did. His fancy indulged him with those familiarities; the notion of how much that was feminine disturbed his thoughts. The darkness of night emboldens timid imaginations to take these furtive glances. He was vexed within himself, feeling on reflection as though it were pro-fanity to think of her so boldly; yet still constrained, in spite of himself, he tremblingly gazed into the invisible. He shuddered almost with a sense of pain as he pictured her room, a petticoat on a chair, a mantle fallen on the carpet, a band unbuckled, a handkerchief. He imagined all this, and his Soul was for a time in contemplation among the stars.

The contemplation of the stars is for the human heart of a poor man like Gilliatt not less than that of the very rich and great. There is a certain degree of passion by which every man becomes wrapped in a celestial light. With a rough and primitive nature, this truth is even more applicable. An uncultivated mind is easily touched with dreams. Delight is a fulness which overflows like any other. To see those windows was almost too much happiness for Gilliatt.

Suddenly he looked and fancied he saw her.

Through the branches of some bushes, already thickened by the spring, there issued with a spectral slowness a celestial figure, a dress, a divine face, almost a shining light beneath the moon.

Gilliatt felt his senses leaving him; it was Déruchette.

She approached, and suddenly stopped. She walked back a few paces, stopped again: then returned and sat upon the wooden bench. The moon shone through the trees, a few clouds floated among the pale stars; the sea murmured to the shadows in an under-tone, the town slumbered, a thin haze was rising from the horizon, the melancholy was profound. Déruchette inclined her head, with those thoughtful eyes which look attentive yet see nothing. She was seated sideways, and her head was uncovered. Her delicate neck and her hair could be plainly seen. She toyed mechanically with a ribbon, twisting it round one of her fingers; the half light showed the outline of her hands like those of a statue; her dress was one of those shades which by night looked white: the trees stirred as if they felt the enchantment which she shed around her. The tip of one of her feet was visible. Her lowered eyelids had that vague contraction which suggests a tear checked in its course, or a thought suppressed. There was a charming indecision in the movements of her arms, which had no support to lean on; a sort of floating mingled with her every posture. It was rather a gleam than a light – rather a grace than a goddess; the folds of her dress were exquisite; her face, which might inspire adoration, seemed meditative, like portraits of the Virgin. It was terrible to think how near she was; Gilliatt could hear her breathe.

The rustling of the branches set in motion by the stirring breeze portrayed the inexpressible silence of the night. Déruchette, beautiful, divine, appeared in the twilight like a creation from those rays and from the perfumes in the air. That wide-spread enchantment seemed to concentrate and embody itself mysteriously in her; she became its living manifestation. She seemed the out-blossoming of all that shadow and silence.

But all this weighed heavily on Gilliatt. He was dumb-founded; what he experienced is not to be told in words.

Emotion is always new, and the word is always enough. Hence the difficulty of expressing it. Joy is often over-whelming. To see Déruchette, to see her herself, to see her dress, her ribbon, which she twined around her finger, was it possible to imagine it! Was it possible to be thus near her; to hear her breathe? She breathed! then the stars might breathe also. Gilliatt felt a thrill through him. He was the most miserable and yet the happiest of men. He knew not what to do. His delirious joy at seeing her prostrated him. Was it indeed Déruchette, and he so near? His thoughts, bewildered and yet fixed, were intoxicated by that figure as by a dazzling jewel. He gazed upon her neck – her hair. He did not even say to himself that all that would now belong to him, that before long – to-morrow, perhaps – he would have the right to unknot that ribbon. He would not have conceived for a moment the audacity of thinking even so far. Love was with Gilliatt like honey to the bear. He knew not what possessed him. The nightingale sang. He felt as though life was leaving him.

The thought of rising, of leaping over the wall, of speaking to Déruchette, never entered his mind. If it had, he would have turned and fled. If anything resembling a thought had begun to dawn in his mind, it was this; that Déruchette was there, that he wanted nothing more. Suddenly, a noise aroused them both – her from her reverie – him from his ecstasy. Some one was walking in the garden. It was not possible to see who was approaching on account of the trees. It was the footstep of a man.

Déruchette raised her eyes. The steps drew nearer, then ceased. The person walking had stopped. He must have been quite near. The path beside which was the bench wound between two clumps of trees. The stranger was there in the alley between the trees, at a few paces from the seat. The branches were so formed that Déruchette could see the new comer while Gilliatt could not. The moon cast a shadow on the ground beyond the trees which reached to the garden seat.

Gilliatt could see this shadow, and he could also see Déruchette. She was very pale, and her lips were partly open, as with a suppressed cry of surprise. She had just half risen from the bench, and sunk again upon it. There was in her attitude a mixture of fascination with a desire to fly. Her surprise was enchantment mingled with timidity. She had upon her lips almost the light of a smile, with the fulness of tears in her eyes. She seemed as if transfigured by that presence; as if the being whom she saw before her belonged not to this earth. The reflection of an angel was in her look.

The stranger now spoke, and Gilliatt heard these words:

'I see you, mademoiselle, every Sunday and every Thursday. They tell me that once you used not to come so often. It is a remark that has been made. I ask your pardon. I have never spoken to you; it was my duty; but I come to speak to you to-day, for it is still my duty. It is right that I speak to you first. The *Cashmere* sails to-morrow. This is why I have come. You walk every evening in your garden. It would be wrong of me to know your habits so well, if I had not the thought that I have. Mademoiselle, you are poor; since this morning I am rich. Will you be mine?'

Déruchette clasped her two hands in a suppliant attitude, and looked at the speaker, silent, with fixed eyes, and trembling from head to foot.

The stranger resumed:

'I adore you. God made not the heart of man to be silent. He has promised him eternity with the intention that he should not be alone. There is for me but one woman upon earth. It is you. I love you. My faith is in God, and my hope in you. What wings I have you bear. You are my life, and already my supreme happiness.'

'Oh, sir,' said Déruchette 'there is no one to answer in the house!'

The stranger again spoke:

'Yes, I have had a dream. Heaven has not forbidden us to dream. You are like a glory in my eyes. I love you deeply, mademoiselle. To me you are holy innocence. I know it is the hour at which your household have retired to rest, but I had no choice of any other moment. Do you remember that passage of the Bible which some one read before us; it was the twenty-fifth chapter of Genesis. I have thought of it ever since. M. Hérode said to me, you must have a rich wife. I replied no, I must have a poor wife. I speak to you, mademoiselle, without venturing to approach you; I would step even further back if it was your wish that my shadow should not touch your feet. You alone are supreme. You will come to me if such is your will. I love and wait. You are the living form of a benediction.'

'I was not aware, sir,' stammered Déruchette, 'that any one remarked me on Sundays and Thursdays.'

The stranger continued:

'We are powerless against things celestial. Law is love. Marriage is Canaan; for me you are the promised beauty.'

Déruchette replied, 'I was not conscious that I did wrong any more than other persons who are strict.'

The voice continued:

'The Almighty manifests his will in the flowers, in the light of dawn, in the spring; and love is of his ordaining. You are beautiful in this holy shadow of night. This garden has been tended by you; in its perfumes there is something of your breath. The affinities of our souls do not depend on us. They cannot be counted with our sins. You were there, that was all. I was there, that was all. I did nothing but feel that I loved. Sometimes my eyes rested upon you. I was wrong, but what could I do. It was through looking at you that all happened. I could not restrain my gaze. There are mysterious impulses which are above our search. The heart is the chief of all temples. To have your spirit in my house – this is the terrestrial paradise for which I hope. Say, will you be mine? As long as I was poor, I spoke not. I know your age. You are twenty-one; I am twenty-six. I go to-morrow; if you refuse me I return no more. Oh, be my betrothed; will you not? More than once have my eyes, in spite of myself, addressed to you that question. I love you; answer me. I will speak to your uncle as soon as he is able to receive me; but I turn first to you. To Rebecca I plead for Rebecca; unless you love me not.'

Déruchette drooped her head, and murmured:

'Oh! I do worship him.'

The words were spoken in a trembling and low voice, but Gilliatt heard them.

Her head was still lowered as if by shading her face she hoped to conceal her thoughts. No leaf among the trees was stirred. It was that solemn and peaceful moment when the slumber of external things mingles with the sleep of living creatures; and night seems to listen to the beating of Nature's heart. In the midst of that retirement, like a harmony making the silence more complete, rose the wide murmur of the sea.

The voice was heard again.

'Mademoiselle!'

Déruchette started.

Once more the voice spoke.

'You are silent.'

'What would you?'

'I await your reply.'

'God has heard me,' replied Déruchette.

Then the voice, almost sonorous, but softer than before, said:

'My betrothed. Come. Let the stars be witness of our first embrace.'

Déruchette arose, but remained an instant motionless, looking straight before her, doubtless in another's eyes. Then, with slow steps, her head erect, her arms drooping, but with the fingers of her hands wide apart, like one who leans on some unseen support, she advanced towards the trees, and a moment afterwards, instead of the one shadow upon the gravelled walk, there were two. They mingled together. Gilliatt saw at his feet the reflected embrace of those two shadows.

There are certain moments when time flows from us as the sands from the hour-glass, and we are not conscious of its flight. That pair on the one hand, who were ignorant of the presence of a witness, and saw him not; on the other, that witness of their joy who could not see them, but who knew of their presence – how many minutes did they remain thus in that mysterious suspension of themselves? It would be impossible to say. Suddenly a noise burst forth at a distance. A voice was heard crying 'Help!' and the harbour bell began to sound. It is probable that in those celestial transports of delight they heard no echo of that tumult. Any one who had sought Gilliatt then in the angle of the wall would not have found him.

BOOK II

GRATITUDE AND DESPOTISM

CHAPTER I

JOY AND PAIN

Mess Lethierry tugged at the bell vigorously, then stopped all of a sudden. A man had just turned the corner of the quay. It was Gilliatt.

Lethierry made towards him, or rather flung himself upon him; seized his hand between his own, and looked him in the face for a moment, silent. It was the silence of an explosion struggling to find an issue.

Embracing and shaking him with violence, and squeezing him in his arms, he compelled him to enter the lower room of the Bravées, pushed back with his boot the door which had remained half opened, sat down, or sank into a chair beside a great table lighted by the moon, the reflection of which gave a vague pallor to Gilliatt's face, and with a voice of intermingled laughter and tears, cried:

'My son! I knew it was you. The sloop, good heaven! Tell me the story. You went there, then. Why, they would have burnt you a hundred years ago! It is like a fairy tale! There isn't a screw missing. I have looked at everything already, recognized everything, handled everything. I guessed that the paddles were in the two cases. And here you are once more! I have been looking for you in the little cabin. I rang the bell. I was seeking for you. I said to myself, "Where is he, that I may devour him?" You must admit that wonderful things do come to pass. He has brought back life to me. You are an angel! Yes, yes; it is my engine. Nobody will believe it; people will see it, and say, "It can't be true." Not a tap, not a pin missing. The

293

feed-pipe has never budged an inch. It is incredible that there should have been no more damage. We have only to put a little oil. But how did you accomplish it? To think that the Durande will be moving again. The axle of the wheels must have been taken to pieces by some engineer. Give me your word that I am not crazy.'

He rose to his feet, breathed a moment, and continued:

'Assure me that I am not dreaming. What a revolution! You are my child, you are my son, you are my Providence. Brave lad! To go and fetch my good old engine. In the open sea, among those treacherous rocks. I have seen some strange things in my life; nothing like that. I have known Parisians, who were veritable demons, but I'll defy them to have done that. It beats the Bastile. I have seen the natives labouring in the *Pampas*, with a crooked branch of a tree for a plough and a bundle of thorn-bushes for a harrow, dragged by a leathern strap; they get harvests of wheat that way, with grains as big as hedgenuts. But that is a trifle compared with your feats. You have performed a wonder – a real one; let me hug you. How they will gossip in Saint Sampson. I will set to work at once to build the boat. It is astonishing that the crank is all right. Gentlemen, he has been to the Douvres: I say to the Douvres. He went by himself. The Douvres! It is impossible to find a worse spot. Do you know, have they told you, that it's proved that Clubin sent the Durande to the bottom for the purpose of swindling me out of money which he had to bring me? He made Tangrouille drunk. It's a long story. I'll tell you another day of his piratical tricks. Foolish man that I was to have had confidence in Clubin. But he trapped himself, the villain, for he couldn't have got away. We will begin at once to rebuild the Durande. We'll lengthen her by twenty feet. They build them longer now than they did. I'll order the wood from Norway. Now I have got the machinery they will have confidence in me again.'

Mess Lethierry lifted his eyes to heaven, and muttered, 'Yes, there is a power above!'

Then he placed his right hand to his head, and tapped his forehead, an action which indicates a project passing through the mind, and he continued:

'But, to begin again at once, on a large scale, a little ready money will be necessary. Oh! if I only had my seventy-five thousand francs that the thief Rantaine returned, and which that villain Clubin stole.'

Gilliatt slowly felt in his pocket, and drew out something which he placed before him. It was the leather belt. He opened it out upon the table; in the inside the word 'Clubin' could be seen by the light of the moon. He then took out of the receptacle of the belt a box, and out of the box three pieces of paper which he unfolded and handed to Lethierry.

Lethierry looked at them. It was light enough to read the figures which were perfectly visible. Mess Lethierry took the three notes, placed them on the table one beside the other, stood for a moment dumb; and then began again:

'These! You are a marvel. My bank-notes! all three. A thousand pounds each. My seventy-five thousand francs. Why, you must have gone down to the infernal regions. It is Clubin's belt. Good heavens! I can read his cursed name. Gilliatt has brought back engine and money too. There will be something to put in the papers. I will buy some timber of the finest quality. I guess how it was; you found his carcase; Clubin mouldering away in some corner. We'll have some pine and oak; we'll have a first-rate planking – oak within and pine without. In old times they didn't build so well, but their work lasted longer; much. We'll build the hull perhaps of elm. Elm is good for the parts in the water. To be dry sometimes, and sometimes wet, rots the timbers; the elm requires to be always wet; it's a wood that feeds upon water. What a splendid new Durande we'll build. The lawyers will not trouble me again. I shall want no more credit. I have some money of my own. Did ever any one see a man like Gilliatt. I was struck down to the ground, I was a dead man. He comes and sets me up again as firm as ever. And all the while I was never thinking about him. He had gone clean out of my mind; but I remember everything now. Ah! by the way, you know you are to marry Déruchette.'

Gilliatt with his back to the wall, like one who staggers, said in a low, but distinct voice:

'No.'

This reply startled Mess Lethierry.

'How, no!'

Gilliatt responded:

'I no longer love her.'

Mess Lethierry walked to the window, opened and reclosed it, took the three bank-notes, folded them, placed the iron box on top, scratched his head, seized Clubin's belt, and flinging it violently against the wall, exclaimed:

'You must be mad.'

He then thrust his hands into his pockets, and said:

'You do not love Déruchette? What! was it at me, then, that you used to play the pipes?'

Gilliatt, still leaning against the wall, turned pale. As he became pale, Lethierry coloured.

'What an idiot you are! Not love Déruchette. Very well; make up your mind to love her, for she shall never marry any one else. A nice thing certainly; and you think that I believe you. If there is anything really the matter with you, send for a doctor; but don't talk nonsense. You can't have had time to quarrel, or get out of temper with her. It is true that lovers are great fools sometimes. Come now, what are your reasons? If you have any, say. People as a rule don't make fools of themselves without good cause. But, I have wax in my ears; perhaps I didn't understand. Repeat what you have just now said.'

Gilliatt repeated the words:

'I said, No!'

'You did say, No. I know all about that, but you must be a lunatic to repeat it. You must be mad. You said, No. Here's a stupidity beyond description. What! you don't even like Déruchette? Oh, then, we will put it down to affection for the old man that you did all these things? It was for the sake of the old one that you went to the Douvres, that you endured hunger and thirst, and ate the limpets off the rocks, and had fog, the rain, and the wind for your bedroom, and brought me back my Durande, just as you might bring a pretty girl her canary that had escaped from its cage. And the tempest we had three days ago. Do you think I don't remember it? You must have had a rough time of it! It was in the midst of all this misery alongside of my old craft, that you shaped, and cut, and turned, and twisted, and dragged about, and filed, and sawed, and carpentered, and schemed, and performed more miracles there by yourself than all the saints in paradise. Ah!

you annoyed me enough once with your bagpipe. They do not think much of such harmony in Brittany. Always the same monotonous tune too, foolish fellow. And now you say you don't love Déruchette? I don't know what can be the matter with you. I recollect it all now. I was there in the corner; Déruchette said, "He shall be my husband;" and so you shall. You don't love her! Either you must be mad, or else I am mad. And you stand there as though you were dumb. I tell you you are not at liberty to do all the things you have done, and then say, after all, "I don't love Déruchette." People don't do others services in order to put them in a passion. Well; if you don't marry her, she shall remain single all her life. In the first place, I shall want you. You must be the pilot of the Durande. Do you imagine I mean to part with you? No, no, my brave boy; I don't intend to let you go. I have got you now; I'll not even listen to you. Where will they find a sailor like you? You are the man I want. But why don't you say something?'

Meantime the harbour bell had aroused the neighbourhood. Douce and Grace had risen, and had just entered the lower room, silent and astonished. Grace had a candle in her hand. A group of neighbours, composed of townspeople, sailors, and peasants, who had rushed out of their houses, were outside on the quay, gazing in wonderment at the funnel of the Durande in the sloop. Some, hearing Lethierry's voice in the lower room, began to glide in by the half-opened door. Between the faces of two worthy old women appeared that of Sieur Landoys, who had the good fortune always to find himself where he would have regretted to have been absent.

Some men feel a satisfaction in having witnesses of their good fortune. This kind of support which a crowd presents pleases them at such times; their delight draws a new life from it. Mess Lethierry suddenly perceived that there were persons about him; and he welcomed the audience at once.

'Ah! my friends, you are here? I am delighted to see you. You have heard the news? That man has been there, and brought it back. How d'ye do, Landoys? When I woke up just now, the first thing I saw was the funnel. It was under my window. They make pictures of Napoleon's deeds; but I think more of that than of the battle of Austerlitz. You have just left

your beds, my good friends. The Durande has found you
sleeping. While you are putting on your night-caps and
blowing out your candles there are others working like
heroes. We are a set of cowards and do-nothings; we sit at
home eaten up with rheumatism; but happily that does not
prevent there being some of another stamp. The man of the
Bû de la Rue has arrived from the Douvres rock. He has
rescued the Durande from the bottom of the sea; and fished up
my money out of Clubin's pocket, from a greater depth still.
But how did he do it? The Durande is back again. The
tempests may rage now; that cuts the ground from under
them. My friends, I can inform you that there was no
shipwreck after all. I have examined all the machinery. It is
perfect. The valves work easily. You would think them made
yesterday. You know that the waste water is carried away by a
tube inside another tube, through which come the waters
from the boilers; this was to economize the heat. Well; the two
tubes are there as good as ever; in fact everything is complete.
She is all there, wheels and all. Ah! you shall marry her.'

'Marry the engine?' asked Sieur Landoys.

'No; Déruchette; yes; the engine. Both. He shall be my
double son-in-law. He shall be captain of both. Good day,
Captain Gilliatt; for there will soon be a captain of the
Durande. We are going to start in business once again. There
will be a gigantic trade, cargoes of oxen and sheep. I would
not exchange Saint Sampson for London now. And there
stands the prime mover of all this. It was a strange adventure, I
can tell you. You will read all about it in *Mitchell's Maritime
Register.*'

'These are for the poor, Sieur Landoys. Give those sover-
eigns from me to the constable of Saint Sampson. You
recollect Rantaine's letter. I showed it to you. Very well; I've
got the bank-notes. Now we can buy some oak and fir, and set
to work. Look you! Do you remember the weather of three
days ago? What a hurricane of wind and rain! Gilliatt endured
all that upon the Douvres. That didn't prevent his taking the
wreck to pieces, as I might take my watch. Thanks to him, I
am on my legs again. Old "Lethierry's Galley" is going to run
again, ladies and gentlemen. A large nut with two wheels and
a funnel. I always had that idea. I used to say to myself, one

day I will do it. That was a good long time back. It was an idea that came in my head at Paris, at the coffee-house at the corner of the Rue Christine and the Rue Dauphine, when I was reading a paper which had an account of it. Do you know that Gilliatt would think nothing of putting the machine at Marly in his pocket, and walking about with it? He is wrought-iron, that man; tempered steel, a mariner of invaluable qualities, an excellent smith, an extraordinary fellow, more astonishing than the Prince of Hohenlohe. That is what I call a man with brains. We are children by the side of him. Sea-wolves we may think ourselves; but the sea-lion is there. Hurrah for Gilliatt! I do not know how he has done it: but certainly he must have been the devil. And how can I do other than give him Déruchette.'

For some time Déruchette had been in the room. She had glided in like a shadow, had sat down almost unperceived behind Mess Lethierry, who stood before her, loquacious, stormy, joyful, abounding in gestures, and talking in a loud voice. A little while after her another silent apparition had appeared. A man attired in black, with a white cravat, holding his hat in his hand, stood in the doorway. There were now several candles among the group, which had gradually increased in number. These lights were near the man attired in black. His profile showed itself against the dark background with the clearness of an engraving on a medal. He leaned with his shoulder against the framework of the door, and held his left hand pressed to his forehead. There was an expression of utter anguish in his face and contracted lips, as he looked on and listened with profound attention. The standers-by having recognized M. Caudray, the rector of the parish, had fallen back to allow him to pass; but he remained upon the threshold. There was hesitation in his posture, but decision in his looks, which now and then met those of Déruchette. Mess Lethierry did not observe the rector, but he saw Déruchette. He kissed her fervently upon the forehead; stretching forth his hand at the same time towards the corner where Gilliatt was standing. 'Déruchette,' he said, 'we are rich again; and there is your future husband.' Déruchette raised her head, and look bewildered.

Mess Lethierry continued:

'The marriage must take place immediately, the formalities here are not very strict; the dean can do what he pleases; people are married before they have time to turn round. It is not as in France, where you must have bans, and publications, and delays, and all that. You will be able to boast of being the wife of a brave man. No one can say he is not. I thought so from the day when I saw him come back from the Herm with the little cannon. But now he comes back from the Douvres with his fortune and mine, and the fortune of this country. A man of whom the world will talk a great deal more of one day. You said once, "I will marry him;" and you shall keep your word; you will have children, and I shall be grandpapa; and you will have the good fortune to be the wife of a noble fellow. At all events, you will not have married, like so many other silly girls about here. But where are you, Gilliatt? Nobody can see you. Everybody! Shew a light. I betroth you to each other, my children: here stands your husband, here my son, Gilliatt of the Bû de la Rue, that noble fellow, that great seaman; I will have no other son-in-law, and you no other husband. I pledge my word to that once more in God's name. Ah! you are there, Monsieur Caudray. You will marry these young people for us.'

Lethierry's eyes had just fallen upon the rector.

Douce and Grace brought two candles and placed them upon the table.

Gilliatt's face was pallid. He was in the condition in which he had that morning set sail from the rocks; in rags, his bare elbows showing through his sleeves; his beard long, his hair rough and wild; his eyes bloodshot, his skin peeling, his hands covered with wounds; his feet naked. Some of the blisters left by the devil-fish were still visible upon his arms.

Lethierry gazed at him.

Déruchette had fainted.

CHAPTER II

THE LEATHER TRUNK

At early dawn Saint Sampson was all astir, and the people from Saint Peter's Port began to flock there. The story of the Durande had caused a commotion in the island. There was a crowd on the quay staring at the funnel standing erect in the sloop. Many were anxious to on board; but Lethierry, after making a survey of the whole by daylight, had placed two sailors on watch, with instructions to prevent any one approaching it. The funnel, however, furnished food enough for contemplation. The crowd gazed with astonishment. They talked of nothing but Gilliatt.

Mess Lethierry could be seen from outside the house, seated at a table before the window, writing, with one eye on the paper and another on the sloop. He was so completely absorbed that he had only once stopped to call Douce and ask after Déruchette. Douce replied, 'Mademoiselle has gone out.' Mess Lethierry replied, 'She is right to take the air. She was a little unwell last night, owing to the heat. This and her surprise and joy, and the windows being all closed, overcame her. She will have a husband to be proud of.' And he had gone on with his writing. He had already finished and sealed two letters, addressed to two important shipbuilders at Hamburg. He now finished a third.

The noise of a vehicle upon the quay caused him to look up. He leaned out of the window, and observed coming from the path which led to the Bû de la Rue a boy pushing a wheelbarrow. The boy was going towards Saint Peter's Port. In the barrow was a portmanteau of brown leather.

Mess Lethierry called out to the lad:

'Where are you going, my boy?'

The boy replied.

'To the sloop *Cashmere*.'

'What for?'

'To put this trunk on board.'

'Good; you shall take some letters for me.'

Mess Lethierry tied up the three letters which he had just written, and handed the packet to the boy.

'Say to the skipper of the *Cashmere* they are my letters, and take care of them. They are for Germany – via London.'

'I can't tell that to the captain, Mess Lethierry.'

'Why?'

'The sloop is not at the quay.'

'Oh!'

'She is at anchor in the roads.'

'True.'

'I can only speak to the waterman who takes things off.'

'Well tell him, then, to look to the letters.'

'All right, Mess Lethierry.'

'When does the *Cashmere* sail?'

'At noon.'

'It will be high-water then.'

'But she will have the wind against her,' answered the lad.

'My boy,' said Mess Lethierry, pointing with his forefinger at the engine in the sloop, 'do you see that? There is something which does not wait for winds and tides.'

The boy put the letters in his pouch, took up the handles of the barrow again, and went on his way towards the town. Mess Lethierry called, 'Douce! Grace!'

Grace opened the door.

'What is it, Sir?'

'Come in and wait.'

Mess Lethierry took a sheet of paper, and began writing again. If Grace, standing behind him, had been curious, and had leaned forward while he was writing, she might have read as follows:

'I have written to Hamburg for timber. I have appointments all the morning with carpenters for the estimate. The rebuilding will go on fast. You must go yourself to the Deanery for a licence. It is my wish that the marriage should take place as soon as possible; immediately would be better. I am busy about the Durande. Do you interest yourself in Déruchette.'

He signed it 'Lethierry'. He placed it in an envelope, but did not take the trouble to seal it and simply handed it to Grace, saying:

'Deliver that to Gilliatt.'

'To the Bû de la Rue?'

'Yes.'

BOOK III

THE SAILING OF THE

CASHMERE

CHAPTER I

THE HAVEN

When there is a crowd of people at Saint Sampson, Saint Peter's Port seems deserted. A point of curiosity at a given place is like an air-pump. News travels fast in small places. Going to see the funnel of the Durande under Mess Lethierry's window had been, since sunrise, the business of the Guernsey folks. Every other event was eclipsed by this. The death of the Dean of Saint Asaph was forgotten, together with the question of the Revd Mr Caudray, his sudden riches, and the departure of the *Cashmere*. The machinery of the Durande brought back from the Douvres rocks was the talk of the day. People could not believe it. The shipwreck had appeared so extraordinary, the work of salvage seemed impossible. Everybody hastened to assure himself of the truth by the help of his own eyes. Business of every kind was suspended. Long strings of townsfolk with their families, from the 'Vesin' up to the 'Mess', men and women, gentlemen, mothers with children, infants with dolls, were coming by every road or pathway to see 'the thing of life' at the Bravées, turning their backs upon Saint Peter's Port. Many shops at Saint Peter's Port were closed. In the Commercial Arcade there was absolute stagnation in buying and selling. The Durande alone claimed attention. Not a single shopkeeper had done any business worth speaking of that morning, except a jeweller, who was

303

surprised at having sold a wedding-ring to 'a sort of man who appeared in a great hurry, and who asked for the house of the Dean'. The shops which remained open were centres of gossip, where loiterers discussed the miraculous salvage. The Esplanade was deserted. One might have imagined it to have been Sunday. A visit from a Royal personage to review the militia at the Ancresse could not have emptied the town more completely. All this hubbub about 'a nobody' like Gilliatt, caused a good deal of shrugging of the shoulders among persons of grave and correct habits.

The church at Saint Peter's Port with its three gable-ends placed side by side, its transept and its steeple, stands at the water's side at the end of the harbour, and nearly on the landing-place itself, where it welcomes those who arrive, and gives the departing 'God speed'. It represents the capital letter at the beginning of that long line which forms the front of the town towards the sea. It is both the parish church of Saint Peter's Port and the chief place of the Deanery of the whole island. Its officiating minister is the surrogate of the bishop, a clergyman in full orders.

The harbour of St Peter's Port is one of some importance at the present day. Years ago it was enclosed by two enormous thick walls, beginning at the water's edge on both sides, and curving till they almost joined again at the extremities, where there stood a diminutive lighthouse painted white. Under this lighthouse, a narrow gullet, bearing still two rings of the chain with which it was the custom to bar the passage in ancient times, formed the entrance for vessels. The harbour of St Peter's Port might be well compared to the claws of a huge lobster opened a little way. This kind of pincer took from the ocean a portion of the sea, which it compelled to remain calm. But during the easterly winds the waves rolled heavily against the narrow entrance, the port was agitated, and it was better not to enter. This is what had happened with the Cashmere that day, and the reason why she had anchored in the roads.

Vessels, during the easterly winds, preferred this course, which besides saved them the harbour dues. On these occasions the boatmen of the town came in their boats to fetch passengers at the landing-place or at stations on the shore, and carried them with their luggage, often in heavy seas, but always without accident, to the vessels about to sail. The east wind blows off the shore, and is very favourable for the passage across: the vessel at such times rolls, but does not pitch.

When a vessel happened to be in port, embarkation was from the quay. When she was in the roads they took their choice, and embarked from any point of the coast near the moorings. The 'Havelet' was one of these creeks. This little harbour (which is the signification of the word) was near the town, but was so solitary that it seemed far off. This solitude was owing to the shelter of the high cliffs of Fort Saint George, which overlooked this retired inlet. The Havelet was accessible by several paths. The most direct was by the water's side. It had the advantage of leading to the town and to the church in five minutes' walk, and the disadvantage of being covered by the sea twice a day. The other paths were more or less abrupt, and led down to the creek through gaps in the steep rocks. Even in broad daylight, it was dusk in the Havelet. Huge blocks overhanging it on all sides, and thick bushes and brambles cast a sort of soft twilight upon the rocks and waves below. Nothing could be more peaceful than this spot in calm weather; nothing more tumultuous during heavy seas. Thanks to recent improvements, this wild nook no longer exists. Fine, straight lines have taken the place of these wild features; masonry, quays, and little gardens have made their appearance; earthwork has been the rage, and taste has finally subdued the eccentricities of the cliff, and the irregularities of the rocks below.

CHAPTER II

DESPAIR CONFRONTED BY DESPAIR

Just before ten o'clock in the morning, the crowd at Saint Sampson, by all appearance, was increasing. Feverish with curiosity, the multitude was moving towards the north; and the Havelet, which is in the south, was more deserted than ever.

However, there was a boatman. In his boat was a travelling bag. The boatman seemed to be waiting for some one.

The sloop Cashmere was still at anchor in the roads, and there was as yet no sign of her getting under weigh.

Anyone, who had listened from one of the ladder-paths overhead, could have heard a murmur of words in the Havelet, and if he had leaned over the overhanging cliff might have seen, at some distance from the boat, in a corner among the rocks and branches, a man and a woman. It was Caudray and Déruchette, they stood face to face, looking into each other's eyes, and holding each other by the hand. Déruchette was speaking. Caudray was silent. A tear that had gathered upon his eye-lash hung there and did not fall. Grief and strong passion were imprinted in his calm countenance. A painful resignation was there too – a resignation hostile to faith, though springing from it. Upon that face, simply devout until then, there was the commencement of a fatal expression. He who had hitherto meditated only a doctrine, had begun to meditate on Fate, an unhealthy meditation for a priest. Faith dissolves under its action. Nothing disturbs the religious mind more than that bending under the weight of the unknown. Life seems a perpetual succession of events, to which man submits. We never know from which direction the sudden blow will come. Misery and happiness enter or make their exit, like unexpected guests. Their laws, their orbit, their principle of gravitation, are beyond man's grasp. Virtue conducts not to happiness, nor crime to retribution: conscience has one logic, fate another, and neither coincide. The future cannot be foreseen. We live in a confused state, and from hand to mouth. Conscience is the straight line, life is the whirlwind, which creates above man's head either black chaos or the blue sky. Fate does not practise the art of gradations. Her wheel turns sometimes so fast that we can scarcely keep pace with it. Caudray was a believer whose faith did not exclude reason, and whose priestly training did not shut him out from passion. Those religious systems which impose celibacy have reasons for so doing. Nothing really destroys the individuality of the priest more than love. All sorts of clouds seemed to darken Caudray's soul. He looked too long into Déruchette's eyes. These two beings worshipped each other.

There was in Caudray's eye the silent adoration of despair.

'Do not leave me,' said Déruchette. 'I shall not have strength to endure the parting. I thought I could bid you farewell. I cannot. Why did you come yesterday? You should not have come. I loved you; but knew it not. Only that day when M. Hérode read to us the story of Rebecca, and when your eyes met mine, my cheeks were like fire, and I thought only of how Rebecca's face must have burnt like mine; and yet, if any one had told me yesterday that I loved you, I might have ridiculed the idea. This is what is so terrible. It has been like a treason. I did not take heed. I went to the church, I saw you, I thought everybody there was like myself. I do not reproach you; you did nothing to make me love you; you did nothing but look at me; it is not your fault if you look at people; and yet that made me love you so much. I did not even suspect it. When you took up the book it was a flood of light; when others took it, it was but a book. You raised your eyes sometimes; you spoke of archangels; oh! you were my archangel. What you said penetrated my thoughts at once. Before then, I know not even whether I believed in God. Since I have known you, I have learnt to pray. I used to say to Douce, dress me quickly, lest I should be late at the service; and I hastened to the church. Such it was with me to love someone. I knew not the cause. I said to myself, how devout I am becoming. It is from you that I have learnt that I do not go to church for God's service. It is true; I went for your sake. You spoke so well, and when you raised your arms to heaven, you seemed to hold my heart within your two white hands. I was foolish; but I did not know it. Shall I tell you your fault? It was your coming to me in the garden; it was your speaking to me. If you had said nothing, I should have known nothing. If you had gone, I should, perhaps, have been sad, but now I should die. Since I know that I love you, you cannot leave me. Of what are you thinking? You do not seem to listen to me.'

Caudray answered:

'You know what was said last night?'

'Yes.'

'What can I do in opposition to that?'

They were silent for a time. Caudray continued:

'There is but one course left to me. It is to leave you.'

'And mine. Oh! how I wish there was no sea, but only sky. It seems to me as if that would settle all, and that our departure would be the same. It was wrong to speak to me; why did you speak to me? What will become of me? I shall die. You will be far off when I shall be in my grave. Oh! my heart will break. I am wretched; yet my uncle is not unkind.'

For the first time in her life Déruchette said 'my uncle'. Previous to this she had always said 'my father'.

Caudray made a sign to the boatman. Déruchette heard the sound of the boat-hook among the shingle, and the step of the man of the gunwale of the boat.

'Stay!' cried Déruchette.

'I must go, Déruchette,' replied Caudray.

No! You cannot abandon me thus. You are wise; you can find a means. It is impossible that you bade me come here this morning with the idea of leaving me. I have never done anything to deserve this; you can have no reproach to make me. Is it by that vessel that you intended to sail? I will not let you go. You shall not leave me. Heaven does not open thus to close so soon. I know you will remain. Besides, it is not time. Oh! how I love you.'

And pressing close to him, she clasped his neck, as if partly to make a bond of her two arms for detaining him, and partly with her joined hands to pray. He unfastened this gentle restraint, and Déruchette sank upon a projection of the rock covered with ivy, lifting by an unconscious movement the sleeve of her dress up to the elbow, and exhibiting her graceful arm. A pale suffused light was in her eyes. The boat was approaching.

Caudray fixed his eyes upon her for some moments, then kissed her on the forehead fervently, and in an accent trembling with anguish, and in which might have been traced the uprooting of his soul, he uttered the word which has so often resounded in the depths of the human heart, 'Farewell!'

Déruchette sobbed loudly.

Just at this moment they heard a voice near them, which said solemnly and deliberately:

'Why should you not marry?'

Caudray and Déruchette both looked up.

Gilliatt, who had approached by a bye-path, now stood before them. He was no longer the same man that he had appeared on the previous night. He had arranged his hair, shaved his beard, put on shoes, and a white shirt, with a large collar turned over, sailor fashion. He wore a sailor's costume, but all was new. A gold ring was on his little finger. He seemed profoundly calm. His sunburnt skin had become pale; a hue of sickly bronze overspread it.

They looked at him in wonder. Though so changed, Déruchette recognized him. But the words which he had spoken were so far from what was passing in their minds at that moment, that they had left no distinct impression.

Gilliat again spoke:

'Why should you say good-bye? Be man and wife, and go together.'

Déruchette trembled.

Gilliatt continued:

'Miss Lethierry is of age. It rests with herself. Her uncle is only her uncle. You love each other.'

Déruchette interrupted, but in a gentle voice, and asked, 'How came you here?'

'You wish to marry,' repeated Gilliatt.

Déruchette began to have a sense of the true meaning of his words. She stammered out:

'My poor uncle, what will he say!'

'If the marriage was yet to be,' said Gilliatt, 'he would refuse. When it is over all will be well. Besides, you are going to leave here. When you return he will forgive.'

Gilliatt added, with a touch of bitterness, 'And then he is thinking of nothing just now but the rebuilding of his boat. This will occupy his mind during your absence.'

'I cannot leave him unhappy,' said Déruchette, in a state of stupor which was not without its gleam of joy.

'It will only be for a short time,' answered Gilliatt.

Caudray and Déruchette had been, as it were, bewildered. They recovered themselves. The meaning of Gilliatt's words became plainer as their surprise diminished. There was a slight cloud still before them; but their part was not to resist. We yield easily to those who come to save. Objections to a return into Paradise are weak. There was something in the attitude of Déruchette, as she leaned imperceptibly upon her lover, which seemed to make common cause with Gilliatt's words. The enigma of the presence of this man, and of his utterances, which, in the mind of Déruchette in particular, produced various kinds of astonishment, was a thing apart. He said to them, 'Be man and wife!' This was clear; if there was responsibility, it was his. Déruchette had a confused feeling that, for many reasons, he had the right to decide upon her fate. Caudray murmured, as if plunged in thought, 'An uncle is not a father.' The probable scruples of the clergyman melted, and dissolved in his heart's love for Déruchette.

Gilliatt's tone became harsh, and like the pulsations of fever.

'You must not delay,' he said. 'You have time, and that is all. Come.'

Caudray observing him attentively; suddenly exclaimed:

'I remember you. It was you who saved my life.'

Gilliatt replied:

'I have no remembrance of it.'

'Yes,' said Caudray, 'at the extremity of the Banques.'

'I do not even know the place,' said Gilliatt.

'It was on the day when I arrived here.'

'Lose no time,' interrupted Gilliatt.

'And if I am not deceived, you are he whom we met last night.'

'Possibly.'

'Your name?'

Gilliatt now raised his voice.

'Boatman, wait there! We shall return. You asked me, Miss Lethierry, how I came to be here. The answer is very simple. I walked behind you. You are twenty-one. In this country, when persons are of age, and depend only on themselves, they may be married immediately. Let us take the path along the water-side. It is passable; the tide will not rise here till noon. But lose no time. Come with me.'

Déruchette and Caudray seemed to consult each other's eyes. They were standing close together. They were intoxicated with joy. They understood, as it were, without speaking.

'His name is Gilliatt,' said Déruchette.

Gilliatt interrupted them with a sort of tone of authority.

'Why do you linger?' he asked. 'I tell you to follow me.'

'Where?' asked Caudray.

'Over there!'

And Gilliatt pointed towards the church.

Gilliatt walked on before, and they followed. His step was firm.

As they approached the church, an expression dawned upon those two pure and beautiful countenances, which was soon to become a smile. The approach of the church lighted them up.

Caudray and Déruchette were scarcely conscious of what was happening. The interposition of this man was like the branch clutched at by the drowning. They followed their guide with the docility of despair, leaning on the first comer. Those who find themselves near death easily accept the accident which seems to save. Déruchette, ignorant of life, was confident. Caudray was more thoughtful. Déruchette it was true, was of age. The English formalities of marriage are simple, especially in primitive parts, where the clergyman has almost a discretionary power; but would the Dean consent to celebrate the marriage without inquiring whether the relations consented? This was a query. Nevertheless, they would soon find out. In any event there would be but a delay.

But what was this manner of man? and if it was really he whom Lethierry the night before had declared should be his son-in-law, what could be his meaning? The very obstacle itself had become a providence. Caudray yielded; but his yielding was only the rapid and tacit assent of a man who feels himself saved from despair. The path was uneven, and often wet and difficult to pass. Caudray, absorbed in thought, did not observe the occasional pools of water or the heaps of shingle. But from time to time Gilliatt turned and said to him, 'Mind those stones. Give her your assistance.'

CHAPTER III

THE FORETHOUGHT OF SELF-SACRIFICE

The clock struck ten as they entered the church.

On account of the early hour, and also by reason of the desertion of the town that day, few people were in the church.

However, near the altar, there were three persons. These were the Dean, his curate, and the registrar. The Dean, who was the Reverend Jacquemin Hérode, was seated; the curate and the registrar stood beside him.

Close by, upon a table, was a book. It was the parish register, and an attentive eye might have remarked a page on which was some writing, of which the ink was hardly dry. By the side of the registrar were writing materials.

The Dean rose on perceiving Caudray.

'I have been waiting for you,' he said. 'All is now ready.'

The Revd Jacquemin Hérode, in fact, wore his officiating robes.

Caudray looked at Gilliatt.

The Reverend Dean added, 'I am at your service, brother;' and bowed.

It was a bow which turned neither to right or left. It was evident from the direction of the Dean's gaze that he did not recognize the existence of anyone but Caudray, for Caudray was a clergyman and a gentleman. Neither Déruchette or Gilliatt, who was in the rear, were included in the salutation. His look seemed only for Caudray. The observance of these little attentions constitutes an important feature in the preservation of society.

The Dean continued, gracefully and with dignity:

'I offer you my congratulations, my colleague, from a double point of view. You have lost your uncle, and are about to take a wife; you are blessed with riches on the one hand, and happiness on the other, and, thanks to the boat which they are about to rebuild, Mess Lethierry will also be rich; which is as it should be. Miss Lethierry was born in this parish; I find the date of her birth in the register. She is of age, and is free to act for herself. Her uncle, too, who is her only relative, consents.

You are anxious to be united immediately on account of your approaching departure. This I can understand; but this being the marriage of the rector of the parish, I should like to have seen it performed in a proper sort of manner. I will not detain you longer than is absolutely necessary. The essentials will be soon complied with. The form is already drawn up in the register, and it requires only the names to be filled in. By the terms of the law and custom, the marriage may be celebrated immediately after the inscription. The proper declaration for the licence has been duly made. I take upon myself a slight irregularity; for the application for the licence ought to have been registered seven days in advance; but I yield to necessity and the urgency of your departure. Be it so, then. I will proceed with the ceremony. My curate will be witness for the bridegroom; as regards the witness for the bride ——'

The Dean turned round, Gilliatt made a movement of his head.

'Very good,' said the Dean.

Caudray stood like a statue; Déruchette was happy, but seemed powerless to move.

'Notwithstanding,' continued the Dean, 'there is still a hitch.'

Déruchette looked up.

The Dean continued:

'Mess Lethierry, through his representative here present applies for the licence for you, and has signed the declaration on the register.' And the Dean pointed to Gilliatt, which prevented the necessity of his mentioning his name. 'The messenger from Mess Lethierry,' he said, 'has informed me this morning that Mess Lethierry who was unable to come himself, desired that the marriage should take place immediately. This verbal message, is not sufficient. In consequence of having to grant the licence, and of the irregularity which I take upon myself, I cannot proceed so rapidly without seeing Mess Lethierry personally, unless some one can produce his signature. Whatever might be my desire to serve you, I cannot be satisfied with a mere message. I must have some written document.'

'There need not be any delay,' said Gilliatt, handing a paper to the Dean. The latter took it, pursued it at a glance, seemed to pass over some part as unimportant, and read aloud: 'Go to the Dean for the licence. I wish the marriage to take place immediately.'

He then laid the paper on the table, and proceeded:

'It is signed, Lethierry. It would have been more business-like to have addressed it to me. But since I am called on to serve a colleague, I am ready.'

Caudray looked again at Gilliatt. There are moments when mind and mind comprehend each other. Caudray felt that there was some deception; he had not the strength of purpose, perhaps he had not the idea of revealing it. Whether in obedience to a latent heroism, of which he had begun to obtain a glimpse; or whether from a deadening of the conscience, arising from a suddenness of the happiness placed within his reach, he uttered no word. The Dean took up his pen, and aided by the curate, filled up the spaces in the page of the register; then he rose, and by a gesture invited Caudray and Déruchette to approach the table.

The ceremony now commenced. It was a peculiar moment. Caudray and Déruchette stood close to each other in front of the minister. He who has ever dreamed of a marriage in which he himself was chief actor, may know the feeling which they experienced.

Gilliatt stood back in the shadow of the pillars.

Déruchette, who on rising in the morning, thinking only of death, had arranged herself in white. Her dress, which had been associated in her mind with mourning, was suited to her nuptials. A white dress is necessary for the bride.

Never had she appeared more beautiful. A ray of happiness was visible upon her face. Her features were remarkable. Their fault, if fault it be, lay in a certain excess of grace. Déruchette in repose, that is, neither disturbed by passion or grief, was graceful above all. The ideal virgin is the transfiguration of a face like this. Déruchette, betwixt sorrow and love, seemed to have caught that higher and more holy expression. It was the difference between the daisy and the lily.

Her tears had scarcely dried upon her cheeks; the traces of which formed a pleasing but sombre accompaniment of joy.

Standing near the table, the Dean placed his finger upon the open book, and asked in a distinct voice whether any present knew of any impediment to the union.

There was silence.

'Amen!' exclaimed the Dean.

Caudray and Déruchette advanced towards the table.

'Joseph Caudray, wilt thou have this woman to be thy wedded wife?'

Caudray replied, 'I will.'

The Dean continued:

'Déruchette Lethierry, wilt thou have this man to be thy wedded husband?'

Déruchette, with an access of joy, whispered, rather than spoke, 'I will.'

Then followed the usual form of the Anglican service. The Dean looked around, and asked in solemn words:

'Who giveth this woman to be married to this man?'

Gilliatt responded, 'I do!'

Caudray and Déruchette felt a sense of oppression in spite of their joy.

The Dean next placed Déruchette's right hand in Caudray's; and the latter repeated after him:

'I take thee, Déruchette to be my wedded wife for better for worse, for richer for poorer, in sickness and in health, to love and to cherish till death do us part; and thereto I plight thee my troth.'

The Dean then placed Caudray's right hand in that of Déruchette, and the latter said after him:

'I take thee to be my wedded husband for better for worse, for richer for poorer, in sickness or in health, to love and to cherish till death do us part; and thereto I plight thee my troth.'

The Dean then asked for the ring. This request took them both by surprise. Caudray had no ring; but Gilliatt took off the gold ring which he wore upon his little finger. It was probably a wedding-ring which had been sold that morning by the jeweller in the Arcade.

The Dean first placed the ring upon the book, and then handed it to Caudray, who took Déruchette's left hand, placed the ring over her fourth finger, and said:

'With this ring I thee wed!'

'In the name of the Father, and of the Son, and of the Holy Ghost,' continued the Dean.

'Amen,' said the curate.

Then the Dean said, 'Let us pray.'

Caudray and Déruchette knelt down.

Gilliatt inclined his head.

So the two knelt before their God; while he seemed to bend under the burden of his anguish.

CHAPTER IV

'FOR YOUR WIFE WHEN YOU SHALL MARRY'

After the newly-married couple had left the church, they could see the sloop *Cashmere* making preparations for her departure, by hauling up the anchor.

'You are in time,' said Gilliatt, 'the sloop has not yet sailed.'

They chose again the same path leading to the Havelet.

Caudray and Déruchette walked in front, Gilliatt this time being behind. They were as two somnambulists. Their bewilderment had not passed away, but only changed in form. They took no heed whatever, of what was going on, or of what they did. They hurried on mechanically, scarcely remembering the existence of anything, feeling that they were united for ever, but scarcely able to connect two ideas in their minds. In ecstasy like theirs it is as impossible to think as it is to swim in a torrent. In the midst of their trouble and darkness they had been plunged in a whirlpool of delight; they bore a paradise within themselves. They did not speak, but conversed with each other by the mysterious sympathy of their souls. Déruchette hung on Caudray's arm.

Gilliatt's footsteps reminded them now and then that he was there. They were deeply moved, but could find no words. The excess of emotion results in stupor. Theirs was delightful, but overwhelming. They were man and wife: every other idea was postponed to that. What Gilliatt had done was well; that was all that they could grasp. Towards their guide they felt a deep but vague gratitude. Déruchette felt that there was some mystery to be explained, but not now. Meanwhile they accepted their unexpected happiness. They felt themselves controlled by the abruptness and decision of this man who conferred on them so much happiness with a kind of authority. To question him, to talk with him seemed impossible. Too many impressions rushed into their minds at once for that. Their absorption was complete.

Events succeed each other quickly. Their effect is overpowering; they deaden the senses. Falling upon existences habitually calm, they render incidents rapidly intelligible even to those whom they chiefly concern; we become scarcely conscious of our own adventures; we are overwhelmed without guessing the cause, or crowned with happiness without comprehending it. For some time Déruchette had been subjected to every kind of emotion: at first, surprise and delight at meeting Caudray in the garden; then horror at the monster whom her uncle had presented as her husband; and now her joy, a joy such as she had never known before, founded on a complicated enigma; the being of last night himself restoring her lover; marriage arising out of her anguish; this Gilliatt, the evil destiny of last night, become to-day her saviour! She could explain nothing to her own mind. It was evident that all the morning Gilliatt had been preparing the way for their marriage: he had done all: he had answered for Mess Lethierry, seen the Dean, obtained the licence, signed the necessary form; and thus the marriage had been brought about. But Déruchette understood it not. If she had, she could not have comprehended the reasons. They did nothing but close their eyes to the world, and – grateful in their hearts – yield themselves up to the guidance of this good demon. There was no time for explanations, and expressions of gratitude seemed out of place. They were silent in their trance of love. What little power of thought they retained was scarcely sufficient to guide them on their way – to enable them to distinguish the sea from the land, and the *Cashmere* from other vessels.

In a short time they were at the little creek.

Caudray got into the boat first. Just as Déruchette was about to follow, she felt her sleeve held gently. It was Gilliatt, who had placed his finger upon a fold of her dress.

'Madame,' he said, 'you are going on a journey quite unexpectedly. It has occurred to me that you would have need of a trousseau. You will find a trunk aboard the *Cashmere*, containing lady's clothing. It came to me from my mother. It was intended for my wife if I should marry. Permit me to ask your acceptance of it.'

Déruchette, partially aroused from her dream, turned towards him. Gilliatt continued, in a voice which was scarcely audible:

'I do not wish to detain you, madame, but I feel that I ought to give you some explanation. On the day of your misfortune, you were sitting in the lower room; you uttered certain words; it is easy to understand that you have forgotten them. We are not always compelled to remember every word we speak. Mess Lethierry was in great sorrow. It was certainly a noble vessel, and one that served his interests well. The catastrophe was recent; there was a great commotion. Those are things which one forgets in the ordinary way. It was simply a vessel wrecked on the rocks; one cannot always be dwelling on accidents. But what I wished to remind you of was, that as no one else offered to go, I went. They said the thing was impossible; but it was not. I thank you for listening to me. You can well understand, madame, that if I went there, it was not with the idea of displeasing you. This is a thing, besides, of old date. I know that you are in haste. If there was time, if we could talk about this, you might perhaps remember. But this is all useless now. The history of it goes back to a day when there was snow upon the ground. And then on one occasion that I passed you, I thought that you looked kindly on me. This is how it was. With regard to last night, I had not time to go to my home. I came from my labour; I was all torn and ragged; I startled you, and you fainted. I was to blame; people should not come like that to stranger's houses; I ask you to forgive me. I have nearly finished. You are about to depart. You will have a fine passage across; the wind is in the east. You will not blame me for troubling you with these things. Farewell. This is the last minute.'

'I am thinking of the trunk,' replied Déruchette. 'Why do you not keep it for your wife, when you marry?'

'I shall never marry,' replied Gilliatt.

'Do not say so,' said Déruchette; 'you are so good and kind.'

And Déruchette smiled. Gilliatt returned her smile, and assisted her to step into the boat.

In less than half an hour Caudray and Déruchette were on board the *Cashmere*.

CHAPTER V

THE GREAT TOMB

Gilliatt walked by the side of the water, passed rapidly through Saint Peter's Port, and then turned towards Saint Sampson. In his anxiety to avoid meeting anyone whom he knew, he avoided the highways now filled with pedestrians by his great achievement. He knew the bye-paths, and favoured solitary and winding routes; he had the shy habits of a wild beast who knows that he is disliked, and keeps at a distance. When quite a child, he had been quick to feel how little welcome men showed in their faces at his approach, and he had gradually contracted that habit of being alone which had since become an instinct. Now and then he turned and looked at the *Cashmere* in the roads, which was beginning to set sail. He walked with downcast eyes among the lower rocks at the water's edge. The tide was beginning to flow. He stopped suddenly, and, turning his back, looked for some minutes at a group of oaks beyond the rocks which concealed the road to Vale. They were the oaks at the spot called the Basses Maisons. It was there that Déruchette once wrote with her finger the name of Gilliatt in the snow. Many a day had passed since that snow had melted away, and so meditating, he pursued his way.

It was a lovely day; lovelier than any that had yet been seen that year. It was one of those days when May suddenly pours forth all its beauty, and when nature seems to have no thought but to rejoice and be happy. Amidst the many murmurs from forest and village, from the sea and the air, a sound of cooing could be distinguished. The first butterflies of the year were

resting on the early roses. Everything in nature seemed fresh –
the grass, the mosses, the leaves, the perfumes, the rays of
light. The sun shone as if it had never shone before. The
pebbles seemed bathed in coolness. Birds but lately fledged
sang out their deep notes from the trees, or fluttered among
the boughs in their attempts to use their new-found wings.
There was a chirping all together of goldfinches, chaffinches,
pewits, tomtits, woodpeckers, bullfinches, and thrushes. The
blossoms of lilacs, May lilies, daphnes, and melilots mingled
their various hues in the thickets. A beautiful kind of water-
weed peculiar to Guernsey covered the pools with an emerald
green; where the kingfishers and the water-fowl, which make
such graceful nests, came down to bathe their wings. Through
every opening in the branches appeared the deep blue sky. A
few lazy clouds followed each other in the azure depths. The
ear seemed to catch the sound of kisses sent from invisible lips.
Every old wall had its tufts of wallflowers. The plum-trees
and laburnums were in blossom; their white and yellow
masses gleamed through the interlacing boughs. The spring
showered all her gold and silver on the woods. The new
shoots and leaves were looking green and fresh. Calls of
welcome were in the air; the approaching summer opened her
hospitable doors for birds coming from afar. It was the time of
the arrival of the swallows. The clusters of furze-bushes
bordered the steep sides of hollow roads in anticipation of the
clusters of the hawthorn. The pretty and the beautiful reigned
side by side; the magnificent and the graceful, the great and the
little, each had their place. No note in the great concert of
nature was lost. Green microscopic beauties took their place in
the vast universal plan in which all seemed distinguishable as
in limpid water. Everywhere a divine fullness, a mysterious
sense of expansion, suggested the unseen effort of the sap in
movement. Glittering things glittered more than ever; loving
natures became more tender. The wide diffused harmony of
nature burst forth all around. The flower shadowed forth the
fruit; young maidens dreamed of their sweethearts. It was
nature's universal bridal. It was fine, bright, and warm;
through the hedges in the meadows children were seen
laughing and playing their games. The fruit-trees filled the
orchards with their heaps of white and pink blossom. In the

fields were primroses, cowslips, milfoil, daffodils, daisies, speedwell, jacinths, and violets. Women were plaiting hives in the open air; and the bees were abroad, mingling their humming with the murmurs of the sea.

The water had not yet risen at the further end of the harbour, when Gilliatt arrived at Saint Sampson, and he was able to cross it dry-footed unperceived behind the hulls of vessels being repaired.

The crowd was at the other end of the port, near the narrow entrance, by the Bravées. There his name was in every mouth.

From afar he saw the sloop in the place where he had moored it, with the funnel standing between its four chains; observed some carpenters at work, and confused outlines of figures passing to and fro; and he could distinguish the loud and cheery voice of Mess Lethierry, giving instructions.

He passed along the alleys behind the Bravées. There was no one beside him. All curiosity was concentrated on the front of the house. He chose the footpath alongside the low wall of the garden, but stopped at an angle. He saw once more the wooden garden seat where Déruchette was accustomed to sit, and glanced again at the pathway of the alley where he had seen the embrace of two shadows which had vanished.

He continued on his way, climbed the hill of Vale Castle, descended again, and directed his steps towards the Bû de la Rue.

The house was in the same state in which he had left it in the morning, one window was open, through which his bagpipe might have been seen, and lying on the table was the little Bible given to him in token of gratitude by the stranger whom he now knew as Caudray.

He unlocked the door, placed his hand upon it; turned it twice in the lock, put the key in his pocket and departed.

This time he walked not in the direction of the town, but towards the sea shore, crossing the parapet wall, he let himself down upon the rocks, and going straight on, he began to follow the long ridge of rocks which connected the Bû de la Rue with the great natural obelisk of granite rising erect from the sea, which was known as the Beast's Horn. This was the place of the Gild-Holm-'Ur seat. He strode on from block to block like a giant among mountains. To make long strides upon a row of breakers is like walking upon the ridge of a roof.

An old fisherwoman, who had been walking naked-footed among the pools of sea-water at some distance, and had just regained the shore, called to him, 'Take care; the tide is coming.' But he took no heed of her.

Arrived at the great rock of the point, the Horn, which rises abruptly from the sea, he stopped. It was the extremity of the promontory.

He looked anxiously around.

At sea a few boats were at anchor fishing. Now and then rivulets of silver glittered among them in the sun: it was the water running from the nets. The *Cashmere*, with her main-topsail set, was between Herm and Jethou.

Gilliatt rounded the rock, and came under the Gild-Holm-'Ur seat, at the foot of that kind of abrupt stairs where, less than three months before, he had assisted Caudray to come down. He ascended.

Many of the steps were already underwater. Two or three only were still dry, by which he climbed.

These steps led up to the Gild-Holm-'Ur seat. He reached the niche, contemplated it for a moment, pressed his hand upon his eyes, and let it glide gently from one eyelid to the other – a gesture by which he seemed to obliterate the memory of the past – then sat down in the hollow, with the perpendicular wall behind him, and the ocean at his feet.

At this moment the *Cashmere* was passing the half-submerged tower, which marks half way in the roads between Herm and Saint Peter's Port.

The sea was blue as far as the eye could reach. The wind flew from the east; there was a little surf in the direction of the island of Sark, of which only the western side is visible from Guernsey. In the distance appeared the coast of France like a mist, with the long yellow strips of sand about Carteret. Now and then a white butterfly fluttered by.

The wind was light. The blue expanse, both above and below, was tranquil.

The *Cashmere*, almost becalmed, had set her topsail and studding sails to catch the breeze. All her canvas was spread, but the light wind compelled her to hug the Guernsey coast more closely. She had passed the beacon of Saint Sampson, and was off the hill of Vale Castle. The moment was approaching when she would double the point of the Bû de la Rue.

Gilliatt intently watched her approach.

Everything was still. The tide seemed to rise in an imperceptible swell. The level of the water crept upward without a palpitation. The subdued murmur from the open sea was soft as the breathing of a child.

Towards the harbour of Saint Sampson, faint echoes could be heard of carpenters' hammers. The sounds, however, scarcely reached Gilliatt by reason of the mass of granite at his back.

The *Cashmere* approached, but with the slowness of a phantom ship.

Gilliatt watched her still.

Suddenly a sensation of cold caused him to look down. The sea had reached his feet.

He again looked out to sea.

The Cashmere was now quite near.

The rock in which the rains had hollowed out the Gild-Holm-'Ur seat was so completely vertical, and there was so much water at its base, that in calm weather vessels were able to pass without danger within a few cables' lengths.

The *Cashmere* was abreast of the rock, and her deck was distinctly visible. The rigging showed black against the heavens and in the magnificent expanse of the sea. The long sails, passing for a moment over the sun, became lighted up with a singular glory and transparence. The water murmured indistinctly; but no other noise marked the majestic gliding of that outline.

A man was at the helm; a cabin-boy was climbing the rigging; a few passengers were leaning over the bulwarks. The captain was smoking a cigar.

There was one spot on the deck on which the broad sunlight fell. It was on this corner that his eyes were fixed. In this sunlight were Déruchette and Caudray. They were sitting together side by side, like two birds, warming themselves in the noonday sun, upon one of these covered seats with a little awning which well-ordered packet-boats provided for passengers. Déruchette's head was leaning upon Caudray's shoulder; his arm was around her waist; they held each other's hands with their fingers interwoven. A celestial light was discernible in those two faces formed by innocence. Their embrace was expressive of their earthly union and their purity of soul. The seat was a sort of alcove, almost a nest; it was at the same time a glory round them; the tender aureola of love passing into a cloud.

The silence was like the calm of heaven.

Caudray's gaze was fixed in contemplation. Déruchette's lips moved; and, amidst that perfect silence, as the wind carried the vessel near shore, and it glided within a few fathoms of the Gild-Holm-'Ur seat, Gilliatt heard the tender and musical voice of Déruchette exclaiming:

'Look! It seems as though there were a man upon the rock.'

Leaving the point of the Bû de la Rue behind, the *Cashmere* glided on upon the waters, gradually decreasing in size against the horizon. The sea had now reached Gilliatt's knees.

He contemplated the vessel speeding on her way.

The breeze freshened. He observed the sloop run out her studding-sails and her stay-sails, to take advantage of the rising wind. She was already clear of the waters of Guernsey. Gilliatt followed the vessel with his eyes.

The tide was fast rising: time was fleeting.

The sea-gulls and cormorants flew about him restlessly, as if anxious to warn him of his danger. It seemed as if some of his old companions of the Douvres rocks flying there had recognized him. They hovered over his head in the same way as they would a drowning man at sea.

And thus an hour had passed.

The wind could be scarcely felt in the roads; but the form of the sloop was rapidly growing less. The sloop, according to all appearance, was sailing fast. It was already nearly off the Caskets.

There was no surf around the Gild-Holm-'Ur; no wave beat against its granite sides. The water rose gently. It was nearly level with Gilliatt's shoulders.

So another hour had passed.

The sloop was now veering to the north, and appeared a speck upon the open sea.

The gulls still hovered about Gilliatt, uttering sharp cries. Only his head was now visible. The tide was nearly at the full. Evening was approaching.

Gilliatt's eyes continued fixed upon the speck in the horizon. Their expression was unearthly. A strange lustre shone in their calm and tragic depths. There was in them the peace of vanished hopes, the calm but sorrowful acceptance of an end far different from his dreams. By degrees the dusk of heaven began to darken in them, though gazing still upon the point in space. At the same moment the wide waters round the Gild-Holm-'Ur and the vast gathering twilight closed upon them.

The sloop, now scarcely perceptible, had become a mere spot in the thin haze.

Gradually that spot grew paler.

Then it disappeared.

At that moment the head of Gilliatt disappeared. Nothing was now visible but the open sea.